A MIRAC
THE BABY

BY
MEREDITH WEBBER

STOLEN KISSES
WITH HER BOSS

BY
SUSAN CARLISLE

MILLS &
BOON

Meredith Webber lives on the sunny Gold Coast in Queensland, Australia, but takes regular trips west into the Outback, fossicking for gold or opal. These breaks in the beautiful and sometimes cruel red earth country provide her with an escape from the writing desk and a chance for her mind to roam free—not to mention getting some much needed exercise. They also supply the kernels of so many stories it's hard for her to stop writing!

Susan Carlisle's love affair with books began in the sixth grade, when she made a bad grade in mathematics. Not allowed to watch TV until she'd brought the grade up, Susan filled her time with books. She turned her love of reading into a passion for writing, and now has over ten Medical Romances published through Mills & Boon. She writes about hot, sexy docs and the strong women who captivate them. Visit SusanCarlisle.com.

A MIRACLE FOR
THE BABY DOCTOR

BY
MEREDITH WEBBER

MILLS & BOON

Published in Great Britain 2017
By Mills & Boon, an imprint of HarperCollins*Publishers*
1 London Bridge Street, London, SE1 9GF

© 2017 Meredith Webber

ISBN: 978-0-263-92660-6

Our policy is to use papers that are natural, renewable and recyclable
products and made from wood grown in sustainable forests. The logging
and manufacturing processes conform to the legal environmental
regulations of the country of origin.

Printed and bound in Spain
by CPI, Barcelona

Dear Reader,

Those of you who have been following the stories of the children brought up in foster care by the wonderful Hallie and Pop will have heard of Stephen—or *Sir* Stephen, as the boys called him when they teased. Well, he was tired of being teased and he wanted a story of his own.

I have touched on IVF in other stories, but as Stephen is a specialist this had to be a book about it. Embryologists, who take care of the eggs and sperm, are as important as the doctors—more so, according to some of them, like Francesca, especially now there is increasing use of IVM—In-Vitro Maturation. IVM saves women having to undergo a long series of injections in order to produce ripe eggs at the right time.

With IVM immature eggs are taken from the woman and matured in an incubator, and as Fran is proficient at this procedure she has ended up working with Steve on the lovely island of Vanuatu, in the South Pacific. The pure white sand beaches, the swaying palms and the heady scent of tropical flowers do the rest…

Meredith Webber

PS Marty, the playboy, gets his turn to tell his story in the next book!

PROLOGUE

FRANCESCA LOUISE HAWTHORNE put down the phone with a sigh.

A deep sigh!

Why had she stayed in Sydney?

Why hadn't she fled to the far ends of the earth after the divorce?

Sheer stubborn pride, probably!

She shrugged her shoulders and sighed again.

'Trouble?'

She turned at the sound of her boss's voice and smiled at the man who was part of the reason she *hadn't* fled. Dr Andrew Flint was one of the foremost IVF specialists in Australia—the best in Sydney as far as Fran was concerned—and his, admittedly early, work into IVM could revolutionise the way couples who had difficulty conceiving could have babies.

Could bring hope…

And she knew a lot about hope…

Andy had been the first specialist in Australia to work on in vitro maturation, where immature eggs were taken from women and grown to maturity in an incubator, and this work had excited Fran so much she hadn't considered leaving.

'Andy?' she said, when he'd been standing just inside the door of her office for a few moments.

This prompt was obviously not enough so she added, 'You wanted something?'

He smiled and shook his head.

'I did, but now I'm realising just how much I'll miss you if you say yes to what I've come to ask.'

Fran shook her head. Used as she was to deciphering her rather absent-minded boss's pronouncements, this one had her stumped.

'Which was?' she tried.

He was still smiling as he came closer to her.

'I've been asked to lend you to someone. Have you ever run across Steve Ransome? He runs an IVF clinic in the Alexandria area. He offers couples on limited incomes from some of the inner-city areas a reduced rate but his clinic has a high success rate so he has plenty of regular fee-paying clients.'

Fran shook her head.

'Doesn't ring a bell,' she said, refusing to think about high success rates and concentrating instead on where on earth this conversation might be going.

And why had he mentioned missing her?

At least trying to make sense out of Andy's rambling was distracting her from the mother's phone call—from the image of a smugly pregnant Clarissa that had lodged in her head...

'Well, no matter, he's a good bloke, and he's asked me to lend you to him.'

'Lend me to him?'

This was bizarre, even for Andy!

'For his clinic in Vanuatu.'

Andy made this pronouncement as if it cleared up the whole conversation, and beamed at her as if he'd managed something wonderful.

Fran rose to her feet and walked around her desk, pulling up a chair and turning to her boss.

'Please sit, Andy, then tell me this story from the beginning. I gather this doctor contacted you. Let's start there.'

Looking mildly put out, Andy sat.

'But I told you,' he protested. 'Vanuatu! Only for a few weeks—four, I think Steve said. I thought it would be great for you—tropical island, balmy breezes, getting out of Sydney when the weather's so lousy. It's work, of course, and he particularly asked if I had someone on staff who'd done some IVM work. I thought of you straight off. You've been looking a little peaky lately. The change will do you good. Hard to manage here without you, of course, but you've got all the staff trained so well, I'm sure they'll cope.'

Sufficiently intrigued to swallow yet another sigh, Fran pieced the random bits of information together.

'This man has a clinic in Vanuatu?'

Andy smiled again, practically applauding her grip on the situation.

'It's a giving-back thing, you see, or maybe paying forward—that's what he might have said,' he said, and although Fran didn't see or follow the paying forward part, she pressed on.

'And he needs an embryologist for four weeks?'

'I think it was four, or maybe six,' Andy said, his forehead crumpling as he tried to remember. Then he obviously gave up on that bit of irrelevant information and added, 'I said I was pretty sure you'd go. Friend in need—doing good work—that kind of thing. Right up your alley, I thought, and a lovely holiday thrown in.'

Realising she wasn't going to get much more from her boss, Fran changed tack.

'Perhaps I should speak to him, find out exactly what the job entails.'

Andy shook his head.

'Afraid not,' he said. 'He left yesterday. Asked me last week but I forgot and he phoned from the airport. Gave me the name of his practice manager and said she'd sort you out with flights and stuff. I've got the number here.'

Andy fished in his pocket, producing several screwed-up scraps of paper, uncrumpling them and glancing at each for a moment before stuffing them back into their hiding place.

'Ah, here we go! Name's Helen and the phone number's there.'

He handed the scrap of paper to Fran, who surveyed it dubiously. It certainly said Helen and there *was* a phone number but…

'I think he wants you soon—like yesterday,' Andy added, standing up and heading for the door. 'You'll still get your pay from here, of course, and he said something about having accommodation for you. Do keep in touch.'

On which note he disappeared out the door.

Having worked with Andy since graduating ten years earlier, Fran knew that was all she'd get out of him. In fact, if she asked him anything about it later in the day, he would probably stare blankly at her, the entire conversation lost in whatever was currently holding his attention.

So Fran leaned back in her chair and wondered about serendipity.

Ten minutes earlier she'd been pondering her stupidity in letting pride keep her in Sydney after her divorce from Nigel and his subsequent marriage to Clarissa.

Well, pride, and her attachment to Andy and his work!

Now here was an invitation to escape—if only for four weeks—plumped right into her lap in the most unlikely manner.

Piecing together what little she'd gleaned from Andy, she assumed this man he'd spoken of—Steve Ransome—was running some kind of IVF programme on the island of Vanuatu and needed a embryologist—in particular one with experience in the very new field of IVM.

She knew of Vanuatu, of course. An island nation in the South Pacific, originally under French rule, if she remembered rightly.

Sun, sand, crystal-clear water, palm-tree fronds waving languidly over brilliantly coloured flowers…

She looked at the rain lashing against her window and shivered because September, which should be bringing a little warmth, and a promise of spring, had so far provided nothing but rain and more rain, with temperatures more like winter.

And Clarissa was pregnant…

Her ex-husband's wife, Clarissa.

Her ex-husband, who'd hated every visit to the IVF clinic when Fran had been trying to get pregnant, who'd found the whole idea of IVF somehow humiliating—a slight on his manhood—and who now had a naturally pregnant wife…

And as Fran's mother's best friend, Joan, was Nigel's

mother, there'd no doubt be regular progress reports on the pregnancy of the wonderfully fertile Clarissa.

Doubt stabbed at her, making Fran wonder if the whole thing subtly underlined her mother's disappointment in Fran's failure to produce a child. Fran shook her head again.

No, her mother had been upset over the divorce, but more because of the two families' friendship.

But the friendship had survived between her mother and Joan and although her mother was nearly always travelling these days, they were obviously still in close contact. Blame mobile phones and the internet!

Which meant Fran would doubtless get updates on the pregnancy at regular intervals, each one probing all the still sore spots in Fran's heart and mind.

Getting away, if only for a month, was exactly what she needed.

Although…

She looked around the lab, seeing her workmates busy at their jobs.

After all the treatment she'd had, plus three unsuccessful IVF cycles, people had been surprised that she'd come back to work.

To work that was such an integral part of IVF programmes.

But here, in the big lab that dealt with so many specimens and eggs and tiny embryos to care for, she didn't ever know which couple had success, and who had failed. She was shut off from their success or their pain.

And her own remembered pain…

Fran smoothed out the piece of paper, checked the number and phoned a stranger called Helen.

CHAPTER ONE

STEVE PARKED THE battered four-wheel drive in the short-stay area of the car park and hurried towards the arrivals hall.

When he realised he hadn't a clue what the woman he was to meet looked like, he hurried back to the car, tore the top off a carton and hurriedly scrawled 'Dr Hawthorne' on it.

Okay, so the name on a card made him look like a limo driver, except that in flip-flops, shorts and a vivid print shirt he didn't even come close to their tailored elegance.

And the limo drivers, he noticed, now he was back in the crowd outside the customs area, were holding professionally printed signs.

He should have done better. After all, this woman was doing him a huge favour, coming out here on a moment's notice to cover for his usual embryologist.

He could at least have worn a quieter shirt.

It was the pelican's fault!

He'd been heading for the shower when two young boys had appeared with an injured pelican—hauling it behind them in a homemade go-cart. The bird had appeared to have an injured wing but its docility had made Steve suspect it had other injuries as well.

He'd explained to the boys that they needed a vet, then realised they could hardly drag it all the way to the north of the island where the vet had his practice. Packing all three of them—and the cart—into his car and driving them out there had seemed the only solution, which had left him too late to shower and change.

So now he was late, and probably smelling of fish.

It couldn't be helped. He was sure the woman would understand...

Passengers began to emerge, and he studied each one. The holidaymakers were obvious, already in party mode, smiling and laughing as they came through the doors, looking around eagerly for their first glimpse of the tropical paradise. Returning locals he could also pick out quite easily. Men in business suits or harassed mothers herding troops of children.

Then came a tall woman, light brown hair slicked back into some kind of neat arrangement at the back of her head, loose slacks and a blue shirt, a hard-case silver suitcase wheeling along behind her.

Elegant. Sophisticated.

Not Dr Hawthorne, he decided, as the embryologists he knew were more the absent-minded professor type, usually clad in distressed jeans and band name T-shirts beneath their lab coats.

The elegant woman paused, scanning the names held up in the crowd, passed by his and started towards someone else.

It was stupid to feel disappointed, there were plenty more passengers to come. Apart from which, she'd be a work colleague—work being the operative word.

'Dr Ransome?'

He turned, and there was the woman, strange green eyes studying him quite intensely.

Green?

He checked—maybe blue, not green, or blue-green, hard to tell.

'You *are* Dr Ransome?' she said with an edge of impatience. 'Helen told me you would meet me.'

'Sorry, yes,' Steve said, and held out his hand, realising too late that it was still holding his makeshift sign.

'Oops,' he said, tucking the sign under his arm.

He reached out to take the handle of her suitcase.

'The car's out this way,' he said, heading for the door. 'It was so good of you to come—so good of Andy to spare you. My usual embryologist had a skiing accident in New Zealand last month and is still in traction.'

Was he talking too much?

He usually did when he was rattled, and the cool, sophisticated woman walking beside him had rattled every bone in his body.

But why, for heaven's sake? It wasn't that there weren't—or hadn't been—other such women in his life.

He slid a sidelong glance towards her.

Composed, that's what she was, which put him at a disadvantage as, right now, he was…well, badly dressed and almost certainly in need of a shower. The boys had been trying to feed the bird small fish.

'Sorry about the rough sign, not to mention the clothes. There was this pelican, you see…'

She obviously didn't see, probably wasn't even listening.

He changed tack.

'Do you know Vanuatu? It's a great place—not only

the islands themselves but the people. Originally settled by the French, so many people still speak that language, although they speak English as well—tourism
has made sure of that.'

He reached the battered vehicle and immediately
wished it was more impressive—a limo perhaps.

Because she looked like a woman who'd drive in
limos rather than battered four-wheel drives?

But some demon of uncertainty had set up home in
his mind, and he heard himself apologising.

'Sorry it's not a limo, but the budget is always tight
and I'd rather spend money on the clinic.'

'Sounds reasonable to me,' she said coolly.

He lifted the silver case into the rear, and came
around to open the door for her, but she was already
climbing in. Elegantly.

He held the door while she settled herself, then held
out his hand.

'I'm sorry, I don't even know what to call you. It's
been a strange morning.'

She offered a cool smile but did take his hand in a
firm clasp.

'Francesca,' she said. 'But just call me Fran.'

He forcibly withdrew his hand, which had wanted
to linger in hers, and closed the door.

But not before noticing that her hair was coming just
slightly loose from its restraints, a golden-brown strand
curling around to touch her chin.

The sun would streak it paler still. And suddenly
he pictured this woman on one of the island's deserted
beaches, a sarong wrapped around her bikini, sun
streaks in the hair blowing back from her face as she
walked beside him.

His body stirred and he shook his head at the fantasy. For a start she was a colleague, and just looking at her he could see she was hardly the 'strolling on the beach in a sarong' type, not that that stopped the stirring.

'Have you been to the islands before?' he asked, as he settled behind the wheel, coaxed a muted grumble from the engine, and drove towards the exit gates.

'No, although I know many Australians holiday here.'

'I hope you'll like it. The climate's great, although it can get a trifle hot at times, and the people are wonderful.'

She turned towards him, the blue-green eyes taking in his bright shirt and, no doubt, the stubble on his unshaven chin.

The pelican again...

'Did you holiday here? Is that why you've come back here to work?'

He smiled, remembering his co-workers' disbelief when he'd told them of his plans to start the clinic.

'No, but we had a couple—Vanuatuans—who came to my clinic in Sydney. They were so desperate to have a child they had sold everything they had, including the fishing boat that was their livelihood, to fund their trip.'

The words pierced the armour Fran had built around her heart and she felt again the pain of not conceiving. Of not having the child she'd so wanted.

You're over this, she reminded herself, and concentrated on Steve's explanation.

'But to sell their boat—their livelihood?'

He turned more fully to her now, and the compassion she read in his face warmed her to the man with whom she would work—a scruffy, unshaven, slightly smelly, yet still a darkly attractive man.

Attractive?

What was she thinking?

But he was speaking, explaining.

'Why not sell the boat if they had no child to inherit it?' he said softly, and she felt the barb go deeper into her heart.

She nodded, thinking of the couple.

'Few people consider the side-effects of infertility,' she said softly, remembering. 'The loss of self-esteem, the feelings of pointlessness, the loss of libido that failure can cause, which must be devastating for any man, but would, I imagine, be even worse for people of proud warrior races like the islanders.'

He glanced her way, questions in his eyes, and she realised she'd spoken too passionately—come too close to giving herself away.

Talk work—that was the answer.

'So you came here? But not permanently? How does that work?'

He smiled.

'You'll see, but for now you should be looking about you, not talking work. This is Vila, capital of the island nation. You can still see a lot of the old buildings that have survived from the days the French ran the country.'

Fran looked around obediently and was soon charmed by the riot of colour in the gardens around all the buildings, from small huts to old colonial buildings, no longer white but grey with age, some in a state of disrepair, but all boasting trailing bougainvillea in rich red or purple, and white lilies running riot in unkempt garden beds. Ferns and big-leafed plants provided lush greenery, so altogether Fran's immediate impression was one of colour.

They drove up a hill, the buildings becoming smaller and more suburban, and right at the top sat what could only be a mansion with another large building further along the ridge.

They turned that way and an ambulance streaking towards it told her it was the hospital.

'Is the clinic at the hospital?' she asked.

'Not quite—but we're around the back here. A kind of adjunct to it,' her chauffeur told her. 'Our building used to be nurses' quarters but the hospital doesn't have live-in nurses any more.'

He pulled up in a driveway beside an enormous red bougainvillea that had wound its way up a tall tree.

Colour everywhere!

And warmth, she realised as she stepped out of the vehicle.

A warmth that wrapped, blanket-like, around her.

They had stopped beside a run-down building that seemed to ramble down the hill behind the hospital. It had cracks in the once white walls, and dark, damp-looking patches where plaster had fallen off. Vines seemed to be growing out of the top of it, and the over-all impression was of desertion and decay.

A tall local man came out to greet the car, holding out his hand to Fran.

'I am Akila. I am the caretaker here and will also take care of you,' he said, pride deepening an already deep voice. 'We are very pleased to have you come and work with us.'

He waved his hand towards the building.

'Outside this must look bad to you, but wait until you

see inside,' Akila told her, obviously aware of strangers' first impressions.

And he was right.

The foyer was painted bright yellow, making it seem as if the sunshine from outside had penetrated the gloomy walls. A huge urn of flowers—long stems of something sweet-scented and vividly red—stood against the far wall, grabbing Fran's attention the moment she came through the door.

A cheerful young woman appeared in a brightly flowered long flowing dress Fran recognised as a muu-muu. Zoe hugged Fran as Steve introduced her.

'This is where we live when we're here. Zoe will show you our quarters. Both she and Akila live locally and work at the hospital, but come down to help out when we are working on the island,' Steve said. 'Zoe keeps the place tidy for us and makes sure there is always food in the cupboards and refrigerator so we don't starve to death, while Akila is on call for any emergencies—of which we get plenty—power outages, et cetera. But don't worry we have generators which kick in to keep your incubator warm.'

Fran felt a niggle of apprehension, and for a moment longed to be back in her nice, safe, *big*, anonymous lab. These people were all too friendly. They were a team, but clearly friends as well. Why hadn't she considered that it would be a small and intimate staff in this island clinic?

Friendly!

A queasy feeling in her stomach reminded her just how long it had been since she'd done friendly! At first, the pain of the IVF failures had made her curl into herself, erecting a cool polite barrier that outsiders saw.

Then the divorce and the humiliating knowledge that Nigel and Clarissa had been involved for months had made her draw away from the few friends she hadn't shut out earlier. The only good thing that had come out of the whole mess was a better understanding of her mother, who had also built a protective shell around herself when *her* husband had departed. At last she now understood her mother's detached behaviour during her childhood years.

Hurt prevention...

Fran had drifted across the hall to touch the leaves and flowers in the big display while these thoughts tumbled through her head.

'I will show you your room,' Zoe said, bringing Fran abruptly back to the present.

'And I've got to check on something but I'll be over later and will take you through the whole facility then,' Steve added.

Fran felt a new wave of...not panic perhaps but definite uncertainty. Did she really need to see the whole facility? Of course she wanted to see the laboratory—it was where she would be working—and seeing how the place was set up would be interesting, but...

Something about the warm friendliness of the people was beginning to unsettle her—the realisation that they were all one big happy family, with Steve at the centre of it. It was threatening to cause cracks in barriers she had carefully erected between herself and others.

And all because they were *welcoming* her, were *friendly*? She could hardly resent that...

It had to be the heat, she decided, following Zoe across a courtyard filled with rioting plants, most with broad leaves and drooping fronds of flowers, and the same sweet, indefinable perfume.

'Ginger,' Zoe explained when Fran asked, and she looked more closely at the plants, not exactly surprised but trying to relate the small, bulbous roots she bought at the greengrocer to these exuberant, leafy plants.

The living quarters were adequate, freshly painted and clean, two bedrooms, a shared bathroom—she could live with that—and a combined living, dining, kitchen area.

'Steve, he barbecues,' Zoe told her, leading Fran out the back door onto a beautiful, shaded deck area, with a barbecue bigger and more complex than the kitchen back at her flat. 'He brought the barbecue here but it is for everyone who stays. Patients bring fish and chicken and he says they are best on barbecue.'

Fran smiled. It was obvious the giant barbecue was the subject of much conversation among the staff at the clinic.

Zoe then indicated which bedroom would be hers and left her to unpack. It was a spacious room, with two beds—king singles or small doubles, she couldn't tell—two wooden dressers with drawers, and a built-in cupboard. A vase filled with wide leaves and bright flowers stood on one of the dressers, welcoming her.

Uncertain of what lay ahead, Fran opted not to shower but simply to freshen up. She unclipped her hair, then made her way to the bathroom. She'd washed her face and was brushing out her hair when Steve arrived, calling hello from the front door.

She came out of her room, hairbrush still in her hand, anxious to tell him she'd only be a moment.

Steve stood in the doorway. Okay, so he'd assumed

she'd be a very attractive woman with her hair waving softly around her face, but *this* attractive? She was smiling, saying something, but all he could do was stand and gawp.

Fortunately for his peace of mind she disappeared back into her room, returning seconds later with her hair neatly restrained, though this time more casually in a low ponytail at the base of her skull, one tail of the scarf that held it dangling forward over her white shirt, drawing his attention to—

No, his attention wasn't going there.

'I'll show you our set-up,' he said, aware his voice sounded rough. And why wouldn't it because his mouth, for surely the first time in his life, had gone dry.

But his pride in the little clinic diverted his mind away from Fran as a very attractive woman—or almost diverted it—while he showed her around the rooms.

'It's very well set out, and far more complex than I'd imagined. You spoke about the couple who came to you in Sydney for IVF, and wanting to have something here, but this is impressive—it's got everything you need, just on a smaller scale.'

'I wanted to set up a place where couples can come and have their infertility investigated right from the start,' he explained. 'I can't help feeling people are sometimes prey to exploitation. As you know, the most common cause of women not ovulating is PCO, and polycystic ovary syndrome can be treated with drugs. I believe, before IVF is even mentioned, ethical specialists must determine the underlying cause of the problem, and if possible treat it.'

Fran gave a little shake of her head. These were thoughts she'd had herself. Not that any of the specialists she'd seen had been unethical, but it had often seemed to her that they rushed towards IVF as an answer without considering alternatives.

'I imagine drugs like clomiphene are a case in point,' she said, seeing the way his mind worked. 'With very little in the way of side-effects they can encourage the production of follicle-stimulating hormone, so the ovaries are better able to produce follicles. That in itself can lead to a previously infertile couple conceiving.'

'Or, unfortunately, it could sometimes lead to cysts in the ovaries, which means the patient needs to be checked regularly. That's why we employ a full-time O and G specialist who works at the hospital as well as here at the clinic. We want to be able to take a patient right through any treatment available, even Fallopian tube repairs, before resorting to IVF.'

'So you need a specialist on the ground, so to speak?' Fran said, following the conversation with increasing interest.

'Exactly! He does regular obstetric and gynae work at the hospital but he's also available for all the preliminary IVF checks and organises the counselling all couples need, as well as supervising the weeks of injections for any woman who will be using IVF.'

'Wow!' Fran muttered, unable to believe so much was happening from this small, run-down-looking building.

She looked again at the scruffily dressed man, and shook her head.

'Did you achieve all of this on your own?' she asked, and he smiled at her.

The smile surprised her. She'd seen versions of it before and thought it a nice smile, but this one set his whole face alight, shining in his dark eyes and wrinkling his cheeks with the width of his grin.

'Not quite,' he admitted. 'The partners back at my clinic in Sydney have given a lot in that they cover for me two or three times a year when I'm over here, and various patients I've had have talked to me about what they'd like in a clinic.'

She nodded, knowing exactly what she'd have liked in the places she'd seen so much of, but Steve was still talking.

'Then there are the people here. They are laid-back, casual and very family-oriented so something like an inability to have a child can cause them tremendous pain. I knew I had to set things up to make it as relaxed as possible for them. After all, they are the prime concern.'

'And you fund it all yourself?'

The question was out before she realised how rude it was.

Not that it appeared to bother him—he just ignored it.

'And here's the laboratory, such as it is,' Steve announced,

He'd left it until last, hoping she'd want to stay on and have a look around, check out where things were kept and see from the case notes, both written and on the computer, how things were done. Then he could go back to their quarters and, no, he refused to consider the cliché of a cold shower, but he could get away from her for a while and regroup.

Work out why this unlikely attraction was happening.

Attraction should be something that grew as you got to know someone—grew out of liking and respect...

Forget attraction, getting rid of the fish smell and doing something about the stubble on his chin were far more important issues right now.

Oh, *and* catching up with Alex to find out whether their new equipment had arrived…

But still he looked at Fran, bent over the boxes of coloured tags she'd pulled from one of the cupboards. She poked around in the contents for a while, then glanced up at him and smiled.

So much for his thoughts on attraction…

'You'll probably laugh at me,' she was saying, 'but I brought a whole heap of these things with me in my luggage, thinking maybe you wouldn't have the ones I've always used, but someone whose mind runs along the same lines as mine does has set up a basic identification system.'

'That someone was me.'

She looked surprised, and, probably because he was already off balance with the attraction business, he spoke more sharply than he need have.

'Lab staff aren't the only ones afraid of making a mistake, of giving a woman someone else's embryo. It's always in the back of my mind, even in the clinic back home where everything is computerised to the nth degree and ID is made with bar codes.'

Now she was taken aback, frowning at him.

'Of course you must worry, it's everyone's biggest concern, but usually it's left to the lab staff to make sure mistakes don't happen.' She grinned at him, defusing his mild annoyance but aggravating the attraction. 'It's certainly the lab staff who get blamed when things go wrong.'

She lifted a red wristband, a red marking pen, a roll of red plastic tape and a card of small red spots.

'How many patients are you expecting? I know you said earlier, but I can't recall the number,' she said. 'I'll make up packs of what we need for each of them—that way I won't be fishing in boxes later and will be less likely to make a mistake.'

She was here to work and she was making that abundantly clear, which was good as he could forget all the weirdness he'd been experiencing and get on with *his* job.

'Five, or maybe six,' he told her. 'I've just heard that there's one couple we're not sure about. Apparently it took longer than expected to shut down her ovaries and then to begin the stimulation so she may not be ovulating yet.'

'But surely she would be before we leave?' Francesca asked, the slight frown he was beginning to recognise as one of concern puckering her forehead.

'Yes, and although I do have other volunteers come out here to work, we like to have the same team on hand for the whole cycle of taking the eggs through to implantation, then confirmation of pregnancy.'

'Or confirmation that it didn't work that time,' Fran said, remembering her three thwarted attempts.

'That too,' Steve said, his voice sombre. 'It's the main reason I like the team to stay until we know, one way or another. At least then we can talk to the couple about what they would like to do next. Whether they want to try again later—explain the options, talk it all through with them.'

He'd really thought about it, Fran thought, studying the man who seemed to understand just how devastating a failed IVF treatment could be. But couldn't they still work with the sixth couple? Hadn't Andy said…?

'But rather than have them miss out, couldn't we stay a little longer?' she asked. 'I'm sure Andy said that it could be longer—six weeks he might have mentioned. Wouldn't that give us time?'

Fran realised she was probably pushing too hard—especially as a newcomer. But it seemed inconceivable to her that a woman would get this far into treatment then be told they couldn't go ahead until Steve could return or someone else could come over.

Steve shook his head, but it wasn't the headshake that bothered her, it was the look on his face—discouragement?

'And if six weeks isn't long enough?' he said quietly.

'Then we'd just have to stay on,' Fran declared. 'I know you must feel guilty about leaving your own practice longer than necessary, but a few days? Surely we can't just ignore this couple as if they're nothing more than names on a list.'

She waited for a reply, but all Steve did was look at her, studying her as if she was a stranger.

Had she let emotion seep into her words? She knew, better than anyone, that she had to separate her emotion from her work—that she had to be one hundred per cent focussed on whatever job she was doing—no room for emotion at all. But hadn't her argument been rational?

'Let's wait and see,' he finally replied, but he was still watching her warily.

Assessing her in some way…

Wondering if he'd made a serious mistake in asking for her…

He turned and walked away, leaving her with all the

red markers in her hands, no doubt remembering she'd said she wanted to sort the separate colours into packs. Well, she did intend to do that. Keeping track of everything in the laboratory was of prime importance, and as far as she was concerned, the laboratory's responsibility stretched across every sample taken. So she settled on a stool, marking syringes, specimen jars, test tubes, specimen dishes—everything—with coloured stickers or tape or even paint for things that wouldn't hold the coloured tape.

But her fingers stilled, and she looked towards the door through which Steve Ransome had disappeared.

Was it because he thought as she did about fertility treatments, or because he obviously cared so much about his patients that she found him attractive?

She considered the word. Certainly he was tall and well built, with dark hair, and eyes set deep beneath thick black brows. Nice enough nose, good chin...

But carelessly dressed, unshaven—scruffy!

Scruffily attractive?

Work, she reminded herself.

Five couples, five colours—no, she'd do six. Mr and Mrs Number Six were going to get just as good treatment as the others. Red, green, blue, purple, yellow and brown—she never used black as somewhere along the chain someone might use a black pen to write a note on a sample and confuse things. From this point on she usually thought of the couples in colours—Mr and Mrs Yellow's egg might be dividing beautifully, Mr Green's sperm was very healthy.

It made sense, especially in a foreign country where the names might be difficult to pronounce, and it kept things clear in her mind. A psychologist would tell her she did it to prevent herself bonding too closely with the couples and that was probably true as well, but her main function was to run the lab efficiently so every couple had the best chance of success. She packaged up what would be needed for each coloured couple, turning her mind now to all the questions she hadn't asked Steve.

Normal questions, like did they add a little serum from the mother's blood to the media in which they'd place the egg, and was serum extracted from the blood on site or at the hospital? It was a job she could do and she had a feeling adaptability was an essential attribute when working here, but was this lab purely for the fertilisation and maturation process or was it multi-purpose?

She finished her packages, two for each colour, one for use by the nurses and doctor interacting with the couples, and one for lab use, and went in search of Steve, wandering around the little clinic first, checking the procedure room, the ultrasound machine Steve would use to measure the size of the women's follicles to see if an egg was ready for collection, then use again to guide him when collecting them.

He'd lamented not having a laparoscope and perhaps when she returned home she could find an organisation willing to donate one.

'Were you looking for me?'

He was so close behind her that when she spun around she all but fell against him, needing to put her hand on his chest to steady herself.

Something sparked in Steve's eyes but she was too concerned with her own reactions to be thinking of his. The long-dormant embers of desire that an earlier smile had brought back to life flared yet again.

With nothing more than an accidental touch?

He mustn't guess!

That was her first thought.

So cover up!

That was her second.

Although it was far too late. They'd stood, her hand against his chest, for far too long, the tension she could feel in her body matched by what she felt in his—something arcing through the air between them—pulsing, electric.

She stepped back, sure she must be losing her mind that such fantasy could flash through it.

Talk work!

'I was thinking I could probably find an organisation or service club back home that could donate a laparoscope,' she said, backing off as far as the doorjamb would allow.

'It would come in handy, especially as a diagnostic tool,' he said, ice cool for all she'd seen something flicker in his eyes, and felt the tension—sure she'd felt an accelerated pulse. 'But since I started coming here, I've become adept at removing eggs with the ultrasound to guide me.'

'Imagine going back to the days when women needed an operation to remove them, sometimes in the middle of the night, because ovulation wasn't timed as well as it is today.'

This was good, carrying on a normal conversation with him for all the sudden heat and awareness flaring inside her.

'There are some funny stories of those days,' he said, smiling at her, although he seemed slightly surprised that she knew the history of IVF.

But, then, he didn't know *her* history.

He didn't know anything about her, which made her feel just a little sad as she walked with him across the courtyard towards their quarters.

'So, if you've seen enough, how about I take you for a quick drive around the town and we grab something to eat down on the foreshore? There's a great French restaurant on the front that most of the visiting staff use as a home away from home.'

'But Zoe said that monster barbecue is yours—that you cook?'

He grinned at her, alerting all the bits she'd just damped down.

'You make it sound somehow shameful,' he protested. 'I enjoy cooking—well, barbecuing—and patients bring us food so I feel obliged to cook it. Some of them have so little, yet they give whatever they can. But tonight there's no free gift so we might as well eat out.'

He hesitated for a moment, then said, 'You probably want to shower and change before we go. We'll leave in an hour? Is that okay with you?'

'I won't need an hour to shower and change,' she said. 'Embryologists still get called out at night from time to time, so I've retained my get up and go skills.'

He smiled again, something she was beginning to wish he wouldn't do because being attracted to a man she'd only just met was ridiculous. Just as ridiculous as reacting to something as simple as a smile.

'Ah, but in our case, remember, we share the bathroom, and after a morning wrestling with a pelican I, too, need to use it.'

'A pelican?'

'I'll tell you later,' he said, and for some obscure reason it sounded like a special promise.

'So the shower? You'll use it first?' he prompted, before adding with a teasing grin, 'Unless, of course, we shower together.'

She didn't blush—she hadn't, even when she was young—but she knew if she was a blushing type she'd have been ruby red. Not that she could let him guess *that* reaction.

'And wouldn't the other staff view that as unprofessional behaviour?' she asked, hoping she sounded far cooler than she felt.

'Maybe they wouldn't know,' he replied, the teasing note lingering in his voice. 'They don't live in, you know.'

He wasn't serious, she was one hundred per cent sure of that, yet there'd been an undertone in his voice that unsettled her even more than she was already unsettled.

An undertone she didn't want to think about.

Except the conversation did suggest that he *had* felt whatever it was that had arced between them...

'I just want to check something back at the lab,' she said, turning on the spot and hurrying away, calling over her shoulder, 'so you can have first shower.'

She was being ridiculous.

As if he'd be interested in her.

It was his way. Teasing and maybe a bit flirtatious—laid-back like the islanders—he was that kind of man.

Could she flirt back?

The idea excited her but deep down she knew she couldn't play that game. She'd never been able to flirt.

Oh, for Pete's sake, what was she doing, standing in this makeshift lab having a mental conversation with herself about flirting!

CHAPTER TWO

SHE STALKED BACK to the little apartment and shut herself in the bedroom where she stared at her 'casual' clothes and realised just how different the concept of 'casual' was here in the islands. Thinking of photographs she'd seen of Pacific islands, she'd thrown in one long, silky shift, not as voluminous as the muumuus all the women seemed to wear, but at least it would look more relaxed than slacks. It was pretty, too, a mix of blue and green in colour, a gift from a friend who'd claimed she'd bought it for herself before she realised the colours didn't suit her.

It was still unworn because it was then that Fran had found out about Nigel and Clarissa—such a cliché that had been! Coming home from work early because she wasn't feeling well! Desperately hoping it was a sign that she was pregnant—the test kit in her handbag—and Clarissa in her bed!

To make it a thousand times worse, the test strip had been, like all the others, negative...

So the lovely new shift had been inevitably tied to that devastating day and had been consigned to the back of her wardrobe.

At least now she could laugh about it—almost!

'Bathroom's free!'

Damnation! Even the man's voice was unnerving her. But as long as he didn't realise the effect he was having on her, it wouldn't matter, would it?

She had a shower and pulled on the dress, brushed her hair and turned to the mirror so she could twist it into a neat knot on the top of her head, but upswept hair didn't go with the neckline of the dress and she let her hair fall so it brushed her shoulders and hung softly about her face.

Yes, it went with the dress this way, but was the woman in the mirror really her? And if not, was she being someone else because she was going out to dinner with an attractive man?

An attractive *stranger*, she reminded herself.

The questions racing through her mind left her as nervous and uncertain as a teenager on her first date, and it was *that* thought which brought a return to sanity.

It was *not* a date, she was *not* a teenager. Steve was a colleague, nothing more. She swept the brush through her hair again, hauling it back, but the restraining rubber band she'd been going to use to hold it while she twisted it into a knot had slipped from her fingers and as she bent forward, searching the floor for it, she heard a knock on the far bathroom door and heard Steve's voice.

'Hour's up,' he said, and although she was fairly certain he was teasing and not desperate to get going, she opened the door, her hair still held up in her hands.

'Lost the band,' she explained, 'but I've more in my luggage. Won't be a minute.'

'Leave your hair down—you're in the islands,' he said. 'The expression "hang loose" belongs in Hawaii rather than Vanuatu, but it's just as pertinent here. Everything's fluid—time in particular—and once you get used to the fact that a ten o'clock appointment might arrive at eleven-thirty you'll be surprised how relaxed you become.'

The idea of an appointment being more than an hour late horrified her, but maybe she *could* get used to it.

Maybe.

She'd think about that later. In the meantime...

'And this has what to do with my hair?'

'Let it hang loose,' he suggested, producing the gentle smile that melted her bones. 'Let it hang loose and we'll find a flower to put behind your ear.'

There was a longish pause, during which she actually let go of her hair, running her fingers through it so it fell without tangles, wanting to tell him she wasn't a flower behind the ear kind of person, but before she could say anything he spoke again.

'Of course it will be up to you to decide which ear,' he said, leaving Fran so bemused she fled to her bedroom, muttering something about fetching her handbag while her mind searched for the source of the little ping it had given when he'd spoken of flowers and ears.

It *did* mean something, but in her befuddled state she had no idea what. She'd just have to hope they didn't find a flower so she wouldn't have to make a fool of herself doing the wrong thing.

She was stunning.

Steve watched her beat a hasty retreat into her bedroom, the long, silky dress clinging to the curves of her body, her hair, darkish but shot with light, bouncing on her shoulders.

This was the second time he'd seen her in the bathroom doorway with a brush in her hand, yet this time...

Maybe it was the dress. This time, with her arms raised to hold her hair, she'd reminded him of a painting he'd once seen, or a statue, something of spectacular beauty that had stuck in his mind, yet she seemed totally unaware of her allure.

Which made her all the more attractive...

There had to be at least a dozen reasons why he shouldn't get involved with this woman. At the top of the list was the probability that she wasn't interested in him, then the fact that they worked together, and he wasn't in the market for a serious relationship just yet, and he was fairly certain she was a serious relationship kind of person.

Although...

Experience told him that it was rare to be drawn to a woman who wasn't interested in him—attraction as strong as he was feeling was almost always mutual and although Francesca Hawthorne had given no hint of interest in him, he could put that down to the fact that women were more reluctant to reveal how they felt, as if being physically attracted to a man was somehow shameful.

Particularly, he guessed, women like Francesca.

Or was he kidding himself?

There was only one way to find out. He headed into the garden in search of a flower...

'Which ear?' he asked when he returned, brandishing the bright red hibiscus in front of Francesca.

'What do you mean, which ear?' she demanded, causing him to wonder if she would be bossy in bed?

The thought was so irrelevant—so irrational—he

shocked even himself, yet he couldn't help a surge of anticipation as well.

'Availability,' he explained, coming closer to her, breathing in the scent of woman beneath a light, flowery fragrance that might be nothing more than hair shampoo. 'It's an age-old custom—right ear for available women, left ear if you're taken. Left because it's closer to the heart, and in truth it's probably a tourist legend, not a local custom at all.'

He was too close. Fran's nerves were skirmishing with her brain, urging her to move closer, while her brain yelled for restraint.

Restraint!

It was practically a byword in her life, preached by her mother, confirmed by her husband, restraint in everything.

Not that her ex-husband had shown any restraint when it came to Clarissa...

Did that explain this sudden urge to fling it all away? To move out of the confining bounds of the life she'd always led? To forget the stupid guilt she'd felt when her father had left her and her mother, and the restraint she'd imposed on herself since that day.

Don't rock the boat had become her motto.

Foolishly?

'Definitely not taken,' she muttered, disturbed as much by the memories and the fight within her as the closeness of the attractive man.

'Good,' he said quietly as he slid the flower's delicate stem behind her right ear, letting his fingers brush against her jaw as he withdrew his hand, his eyes holding hers, sending messages she didn't want to understand.

Or didn't want to acknowledge?

'Now, should we drive or walk? It's up to you. The walk down is beautiful because you look out over the town and the sea, but coming back up the hill isn't fun if you're tired after your flight.'

Fran took his words as a challenge. Tired after her flight indeed!

'I hope I'm not so feeble I can't manage a flight *and* a walk up a hill all in one day,' she retorted, trying in vain to remember just how high the hill they'd driven up earlier might be.

Ha! So she's got some spirit, this sophisticated beauty, Steve thought, though all he said was, 'That's great.'

They set off, up past the hospital, along the ridge that looked out over a peaceful lagoon with small islands dotted about it.

'I love this view,' he said. 'You're looking down at the centre of Port Vila, and out over a few of the smaller islands. Some of the other islands in the group are much larger than this one, but Vila, or Port Vila, the proper name, is the capital.'

He continued his tourist guide talk as they walked, pointing out the smart parliament building, telling her of the cyclone that had hit just east of the town a few years back, and the earthquakes the island group had suffered recently.

'Yet people still live here—they rebuild and life goes on?'

She turned towards him as she spoke, obviously intrigued.

'It is their home,' he reminded her, and she nodded. 'Of course it is.'

'And your home? Has it always been in Sydney?'

Normal, getting to know you talk, yet it felt more than that. Something inside him wanted to know more of this woman who'd come into his life.

'Always Sydney,' she replied.

They were heading downhill now, traffic thickening on the road as they came closer to the waterfront.

'And you?' she asked, moving closer to him as they passed a group of riotous holiday makers.

'Sydney, then a little town on the coast, Wetherby, then Sydney again. It's complicated.'

She smiled at him.

'Like the pelican?' she teased. 'Seems you'll have a lot to tell me over dinner.'

Was she interested or just being polite?

Not that it mattered. He might be attracted to this woman but everything about her told him she wasn't a candidate for a mutually enjoyable affair and anything more than that was still a little way down his 'to-do' list.

Not far down but still…

He returned to tour guide mode, pointing out various buildings, and soon they were down at the waterfront, and she stopped, looking out over the shining water.

'It's a beautiful setting for a town, isn't it?'

'It is indeed,' he agreed. 'It's one of the reasons I never mind coming back here.'

'The people being another?' she said, and he turned towards her and smiled.

'Of course!'

He led the way along the boardwalk built out over the water's edge towards the restaurant in a quieter part of the harbour. But a cry made them both turn. A group of Japanese tourists was talking excitedly and pointing down into the water, crowding so closely to the edge they were in danger of falling in.

Steve ran back, Fran following more slowly, arriving in time to catch Steve's shirt as he threw it off and stepped out of his sandals, before diving into the inky depths beneath them.

'Ambulance!' he yelled when he resurfaced, before diving back down out of sight.

Fran turned to one of the locals who'd joined the group, and said, 'Ambulance?'

He nodded, holding up his cell phone to show he was already on it.

Which left Fran free to push back the excited onlookers and beckon the burly local who'd phoned the ambulance to come and join her.

Steve's head reappeared, a very dark head beside it.

'If you can lean over, I think I can pass him up.'

The breathless words weren't quite as clear as they might have been, but Fran understood and she and the local man lay down so they could lean forward towards the water.

With what seemed like superhuman strength, Steve thrust the slight form of a young man upwards, to be grabbed by the stranger next to Fran, then Fran herself.

Together they hauled him up, with a couple from the tourist party helping to lift him clear. Fran waved the crowd away again and rested their patient in the recovery position, while Steve swam towards some steps fifty yards away.

Fran cleared the young man's airway and felt for a pulse. Not even a faint one!

Rolling him onto his back, she pinched his nose and

gave five quick breaths, then changed position to begin chest compressions.

Steve arrived as she reached the count of thirty, so she let him take over the compressions while she counted and did the breaths. The ambulance siren was growing louder and louder as it neared them but they kept pumping and breathing until, finally, the young man gave a convulsive jerk, and Steve rolled him back into the recovery position before he brought up what seemed like a gallon of sea water.

He was breathing on his own, though still coughing and spluttering, when the ambos arrived to take over.

Fran and Steve stood together as the lad was strapped onto a gurney and loaded into the ambulance, and it was only when his shorts brushed against her that she realised he was still wet.

And somewhere in the chaos she'd lost his shirt.

Fortunately a backpacker appeared, holding the shirt and Steve's sandals.

'You two made a good team,' he said. 'No panic and straight into action. Done it before?'

Steve shook his head.

'Instinct,' he explained.

'And a bit of medical knowledge,' Fran added, feeling unaccountably pleased by the young man's words.

After handing over the shirt and sandals, the backpacker offered Steve a pair of board shorts.

'Might not be your style, mate, but better dry than wet,' he said cheerfully. 'You can keep them. I'm heading home and I could use a bit more space in my backpack.'

Obviously pleased by the offer, Steve stripped off his wet shorts, revealing a pair of lurid boxer shorts.

'Staff joke,' he explained as he pulled the dry shorts over them, then finished dressing with his shirt and sandals.

He turned to Fran, his arms out held.

'So, teammate, I might not be quite the picture of sartorial excellence you expected to be dining with, but will I do?'

'Definitely!' she said, then wondered why she felt there'd been a double meaning in her answer.

They finished the walk to the restaurant in companionable silence as if their brief response to the young man's drowning had somehow drawn them together.

'This is wonderful,' she said, as the waiter seated them at an outside table. 'And across there?'

She pointed to a small island with a row of thatched huts along the water's edge.

What she'd really wanted to know was how the young man might be faring, but common sense told her to leave that little interlude alone and not to make too much of it.

'One of many resorts,' he explained. 'Vanuatu's a tourist destination now. But that island over there, tiny as it is, has been settled for a long time. One of the colonial governors had a house there, and bits of it remain.'

'And it's only accessed by boat?'

Steve nodded. 'Look, the little boat is crossing now. It's about a five-minute trip but it does make that resort seem a bit special.'

A waiter interrupted them with menus and offers of drinks.

'Light beer for me,' Steve said. 'Fran?'

'I'd like a white wine, just a glass,' she told the waiter, who then rattled off a list of choices.

'Pinot Gris,' she said, getting lost after that in the list. And by the time their drinks arrived, they'd settled on their meals—steak for Steve and swordfish for Fran.

'Cheers,' he said, lifting his glass. 'And here's to a pleasant stay for you in Vanuatu. Hopefully you won't be called upon to save any more lives, although I must say you handled the situation enormously well.'

'Anyone would have done the same,' she said, ever so casually, although the compliment pleased her.

She touched her glass to his bottle, and echoed his 'Cheers' then took a sip of the wine, and nodded appreciation.

It was all Fran could do not to gulp at the wine.

Somehow, it seemed, the simple act of working together to save the young man had formed a bond between them.

Or maybe that was just her imagination! Running riot because the walk to the restaurant had set her nerves on fire?

The walk had certainly been fascinating, Steve pointing out special places, telling stories of the early European settlement, but it had been his presence—the nearness of him as they'd walked side by side—that had unsettled nerves she'd forgotten she had.

Oh, she'd been out with other men since her divorce, but none of them had made something—excitement—thrum along her nerves.

Maybe there was something in the richly perfumed tropical air—a drug of some kind—that heightened all the senses.

Or maybe seeing his broad, tanned chest, water nestling among the sparse hairs on his sternum, had stirred long-forgotten lust!

Or maybe she was just tired.

That was the most logical explanation for all these weird fancies...

But she didn't feel tired! She felt...alive.

'So, tell me about the pelican,' she said, to take her mind off nerves and feelings.

Steve grinned at her and she realised her question hadn't entirely worked because her nerves twitched in response to that grin.

'Local people know we're a clinic, but because we're not part of the hospital, they're not entirely sure what we do. Consequently, stories get around. We've had people calling in for physiotherapy and even marital counselling, but the pelican was a first.'

A real smile this time lit up his dark eyes, and pressed little smile lines into the corners of them.

'These two boys, about ten, I'd say, arrived dragging their go-cart behind them.'

He paused.

'You know go-carts—little boxy things on wheels that kids build themselves? They're great here because of the hills, though how some of them haven't been killed I don't know.'

'If they're going down a hill like the one we walked down, with the traffic, it would be suicidal. But anyway I know go-carts or at least the theory of them.'

'So the kids had this pelican in their go-cart. They'd found it near their home not far from the waterfront, and it appeared to have been hit by something—maybe a car. It had an injured leg and wing on one side and obviously couldn't fly and possibly couldn't walk as it sat quite contentedly in the cart.'

'And you don't do pelicans at the clinic?' Fran teased,

drawn into the story by Steve's obvious involvement with the boys and the bird.

He smiled again, and she refused to acknowledge her physical reaction.

Perhaps she *was* tired.

'The problem was that the vet's place is halfway round the island and although it's only a small island, it was too far for the boys to drag their cart.'

'So you offered them a lift?'

He nodded.

'Put them, the cart and the bird in the old vehicle and probably broke any number of road rules getting them there so I could get back to the airport to meet you.'

Their meals arrived and their conversation paused, pleasing Fran as it gave her the opportunity to study the man across the table from her.

Surreptitiously, of course...

He was good-looking, though not in a plastic film-star kind of way—more manly, somehow, with good facial bones and strong features.

Tanned, but of course working here for several months of the year would ensure a year-round tan, with a few flecks of grey appearing in his dark hair. Just strands, here and there, though they obviously didn't bother him.

But it was his smile, even his half-smile, quirking up at one corner of his mouth that sent the tingles down her spine.

Oh, for heaven's sake, you've just met the man, and you don't believe in love at first sight.

Not that it was love, only attraction.

But she didn't believe in that either...

'So, growing up?' she said, deciding talking was far

better than mulling over her reactions to the man. 'Sydney, and you mentioned…?'

'Wetherby!'

He said it as if the place was special to him, so she pursued it, wanting to keep a conversation going, but also wanting to know more about this man who had set up a clinic in this place and drove small boys and pelicans to vets.

'Wetherby?' she said.

Steve knew what she was asking, but did she really want to know?

And did he really want to talk about his childhood?

Usually not, but with *this* woman?

Maybe.

'Wetherby is a very small coastal town where, as one of my foster sisters always said, nothing ever happens.'

'Foster sisters?'

'My parents died when I was eight.'

Memories of that time flicked across his mind like images on a screen. The sheer disbelief that suddenly he didn't have his beloved mother, his laughing, boisterous father…

'How terrible for you.'

He looked at Fran across the table and knew she'd meant it. She'd known pain herself, he'd read it in her eyes earlier today, when they'd been discussing the IVM…

'It was hard. I'd been left with my nanny while they flew to America, to get me, they'd said, a brother or sister. At that age America is the place where movies come from so it seemed perfectly reasonable that you could pick up a child there as well. It was only later, with Hallie's help, that I pieced it all together.'

'Hallie?'

They'd finished their meals and pushed their plates to the side, and Fran was watching him over her glass as she sipped at the last of the wine.

'There was a foster home in Wetherby, and I honestly believe I won the jackpot, being sent there. Hallie was the housemother—Hallie and her husband Pop ran the place and somehow melded a mob of very divergent types into a family.'

Fran was frowning at him now, but no less lovely when she frowned.

'Had you no relation who would take you?' she asked, and he pulled his mind from his companion to go on, feeling a need to explain.

'I was the only child of only children, and it was because they'd both hated being only children that my parents were going to the US. IVF was fairly well established here but whatever problem my mother had, had prevented it working for her. My father flew so it must have seemed the natural thing for them to do— head off in search of someone who might help.'

'Such desperation,' Fran said quietly, 'but at least they both wanted the child they were seeking.'

He studied her for a moment, sure there was something behind the words, but before he could ask, she'd prompted him again.

'Go on.'

The gentleness in her tone led him back to the past.

'To answer your first question, I did have relations— I had a grandmother, my father's mother, and a grandfather on my mother's side—but neither of them were really capable of looking after me, even with the nanny. The obvious answer, to them, was boarding school.'

'At eight?' Fran queried, and Steve's answering nod told her it had not been good.

'I hated it,' he said simply. 'Fortunately, a close friend of my mother's saw the state I was in, and arranged for me to go into foster care, with the proviso I spend my Christmas holidays with my grandparents. They lived in adjacent houses, my parents having grown up together, and both of them had housekeepers who could look after me for the short time I was with them.

'But Wetherby was where you spent most of your time?'

'I lived there until I left to go to university, by which time my grandfather had died and my grandmother had gone into a nursing home. I sold my grandfather's house and bought an apartment in Sydney.'

'But kept the other house?'

He grinned at her.

'Well, the house was still my grandmother's, but it was also the house where I'd lived with my parents. It is a house made for a family, and I knew that's what I eventually wanted, so even after my grandmother died I kept it, and leased it out until I needed it.'

'And you need it now? You live there? With your family?'

'No family yet,' he told her, 'but, yes, I live there.'

'So you've come home,' she said, smiling at him, making all the attraction he'd felt from the moment he'd first seen her come rushing back to life within his body.

Really, this was just too much.

It was madness.

They were both here to work.

Holiday romance?

Even as the words whispered in his head he knew that wouldn't work.

Not with this woman.

She was, as Hallie would have said, a keeper. Although the first woman he'd thought had been a keeper had thrown his engagement ring at him and disappeared from his life.

Then and there, he'd decided to work through his list and wait until he'd achieved it all before he settled down with marriage and children. He smiled as he thought of that list, the original now so tattered he'd had to paste it into a book to prevent its total disintegration.

'Happy thoughts?' Fran asked, and he realised she'd caught the smile.

'More nostalgia,' he said. 'I was thinking about a list I wrote a long time ago.'

'A list?'

'Hallie knew just how lost I was when I arrived in Wetherby. One day she sat me down and said that what I'd been through was terrible, but that I couldn't live in the past. I needed to think about what I wanted for the future and to live for that.'

'Big job for, what—an eight-year-old?'

'I was ten by then, but it did make me think seriously about what I wanted. Unfortunately, all I could come up with was a family and that wasn't exactly possible right then. I talked to Hallie and she told me that anything was possible, that I just had to work out how to make it happen. She asked me, "Where would you start?"'

He could hear Hallie's voice in his head as clear as if the conversation had been yesterday.

'"With growing up?" I suggested, and I can see her smiling now. She found a piece of paper and told me to write it down, all the steps I'd need to take to get to growing up, so I wrote, "Finish school," and next I put, "Go to university, then get to be an IVF doctor—"'

'Ambition to be an IVF doctor at ten?' Fran asked, and he had to smile at the disbelief in her voice. 'Oh, because of your parents. Of course!'

She reached out and touched his hand where it was resting on the table, a touch that offered sympathy and understanding. It was all he could do not to turn it up and wrap this fingers around hers, but knew that would only confuse matters.

'So, at ten you decided to specialise in IVF without any idea of what that might entail.'

He grinned at her.

'Hallie helped out there, so I wrote down to study medicine, specialise in O and G *then* be an IVF doctor.'

'And was that the end of your list?'

'Of course not,' he said, enjoying this confession now. 'I was the only child of only children so it was natural that the last thing on the list—the ultimate goal—was to get married and have a heap of children. Hallie helped there too, explaining that children cost money, and getting established in a profession would take time and also cost money, so there were incidentals in the list before it got to the marriage and children.'

So forget all about attraction to this man, Fran told herself. With his list-driven ambitions he would already have the wife picked out.

'You must be nearly there,' she said, shaking her head at the dessert menu the waiter was offering her. 'Did your list specify a particular woman?'

He laughed.

'No, I didn't get that specific, although at ten I was madly in love with one of my stepsisters, Liane.'

'And are you looking for someone like Liane?'

Fran knew she shouldn't be pursuing this. Steve's future marriage—his whole life—was nothing to do with her. *Nothing!* It had to be the inexplicable attraction going on inside her that had her probing like this.

'There is no one like Liane,' he said, and the look of sorrow on his face told her more firmly than the words that the conversation was finished.

They left the restaurant, Steve explaining that, although they never took advantage of it, the restaurant refused to charge the clinic workers for their meals.

'It's their contribution to what we do,' he explained, as he took her elbow to walk back to the path along the harbour.

They paused near the little jetty where the boat crossed to the island resort and she looked around, appreciating this magical place through all her senses—the sight of the moon on the water, the competing aromas of flowers and sea and suntan lotion, the sound of the waves lapping against the beach, and the feel of the slightly damp tropical air brushing against her skin.

'It's beautiful.'

The words came out on a sigh, as she realised how constrained her life had been—how ordinary she'd made it—hurting after the divorce and retreating into the humdrum of everyday existence when she could have been here—or anywhere—helping others as Steve was doing, or simply enjoying carefree holidays.

Steve could have echoed the words, but he would have meant her—standing there, looking out to sea, the breeze blowing the fine material of her dress against her body, silhouetting her against the sky.

Her hair lifted softly around her face, and her skin seemed luminous in the moonlight.

Was it her beauty that had prompted him to pour out his life story to her over dinner?

He'd probably bored her rigid.

Yet somehow he felt she'd understood—that she'd suffered pain herself...

He wanted to ask her—about her life, about herself—but dinner had gone on longer than he'd expected and by the time they climbed the hill it would be late.

He hailed a cab.

'I could have walked,' she protested, as he held the door for her.

'And arrived back all hot and sweaty. Not tonight, when you've just arrived and haven't acclimatised. Besides, my wet boxers are chaffing,' he added with a laugh.

'Next time I'll walk,' she said firmly, and he hoped there would be a next time.

Now, why on earth had she said that? Fran wondered, as she rode back up the hill beside Steve.

As if the physical attraction between them wasn't enough, listening to him, hearing the pain he must have suffered lying behind his careful words, seeing the orphaned boy in her mind, she'd felt emotional attraction, which, she rather thought, would be far more dangerous than the physical stuff.

Harder to fight...

The ride was short, and she had to smile when, as they walked down to their accommodation, Steve said, 'Well, you've only yourself to blame for me pouring out my life story to you. You did ask. But mind, it will be your turn tomorrow—fair's fair!'

'My life story?' she said. 'Compared to yours it is as bland and predictable as milk—it could be summed up in about two lines. Was born, grew up, became an embryologist, got married, got divorced, still working as an embryologist.'

'Aha,' he said, as they reached her door, 'that's a very teasing summation. Tomorrow night we'll start with the "became an embryologist". Most people don't head off to university with that as an aim.'

'No, I studied science but liked the little bit of embryology I did in my set course, so pursued it.'

She looked at him, aware of his body close to hers, but hyper-aware that he was studying her face.

Searching for more information behind her words?

Or something else?

'Thank you for everything,' she said, because the longer they stood there the more she wanted to touch him. She stepped back, putting more space between them. 'Not only for dinner, but for bringing me here.'

She wanted to tell him that even after less than twenty-four hours in this magical place she felt her life had changed. But he'd think she was mad or, worse, wonder about her life back home that such a short time here could mean so much.

So she said goodnight and slipped inside her door, poking her head back out to say, 'Okay if I use the bathroom first?'

He was still standing where she'd left him, and he nodded but didn't move, his face puzzled as if he, too, felt something had happened between them.

* * *

Fran lay in bed the following morning, remembering all she'd learned about the man with whom she was working. She'd seen a little of the island, magical in the moonlight as well, but it had been the scrap of Steve's history—heavily edited, she guessed—that had caught and held her imagination.

She could even picture him as a young child, chewing at his pencil, as he made up his list.

And realising just how dedicated he had been, and no doubt still was, to that list, then she should forget about all the physical attraction she'd been feeling towards him.

Well aware that brief affairs or holiday romances weren't for her, she'd just have to steer clear of any opportunity for closeness between them.

Sure, she had to work with him, but that was work and if she gave it her full concentration, surely she wouldn't feel all the tingling awareness his presence was already causing her.

Thinking work, which had kept her going through all the trials and tribulations of the divorce, would surely get her back to normal!

Unable to sleep, Steve left for his run earlier than usual. The streetlights were still on, although dawn was breaking, the orange blaze in the eastern sky already heralding the rising sun.

Why, in the name of fortune, had he poured out his heart to Fran last night?

Well, not his heart but his life story—more or less.

Telling her about Wetherby, Hallie and Pop, Liane even. He never talked to anyone about Liane…

His feet pounded faster, and he could feel sweat breaking out all over his body.

If he cut short his run, he could be back in time to have breakfast with Fran.

Really, he should go back.

Nonsense, he rarely had breakfast with other visiting staff, just grabbed whatever was to hand when he came back from his run, or breakfasted at the hospital to catch up with the news there.

But she was new…

Or was it because he was attracted to her that he suddenly wanted to see her?

See her over breakfast…

That was worse because surely seeing someone over breakfast was—what—intimate?

Give me a break!

But without consciously realising it, he'd turned back towards the clinic.

Why shouldn't he have breakfast with her?

CHAPTER THREE

THANKFULLY SHE WAS out of the bathroom when he got back, so he showered and shaved, slipped into some respectable 'work' clothes—which here meant shirt and shorts—and found the woman who'd broken his running schedule sitting at the table, where, as usual, Zoe had laid out a variety of cereals, fruit, yoghurt and freshly baked pastries.

'The pastries are delicious,' Fran said as he joined her.

She looked cool and together in the same uniform as him—shirt and shorts, sandals, he suspected, on her feet.

Was he considering her clothes so that he didn't have to think about his physical reactions to the sight of her? Physical reactions he had never felt towards a virtual stranger.

Although, why shouldn't he be attracted to her? She had told him last night that she was divorced.

Though surely someone so lovely would already have another significant other...

'Good morning,' he said, settling opposite her, serving himself some cereal and fruit while his mind put his body firmly into place.

They were here to work!

'I like the couples to meet the whole team,' Steve began. 'It's easier to have the embryologist there in case they have questions. Our first couple is due at ten but island time is fairly flexible.'

She glanced up at him and he noticed a tiny flake of pastry on the corner of her lip.

He clutched his spoon tightly to stop himself from reaching out to brush it away, and prayed his colleague wasn't reading his body language.

'If you think it's important I'll be there,' Fran assured him, speaking coolly, formally, as if determined to steer away from the easy camaraderie they'd shared the previous evening.

After which she pushed her chair back, excused herself, and left, no doubt to remove the crumb of pastry herself.

Which was a good thing, wasn't it?

Well?

On one side, keeping things cool and professional between them was certainly the way he worked with colleagues at home, especially after the hash he'd made of his relationship with Sally. Their break-up had lost him friends and had forced him into setting up his own clinic sooner than he'd intended.

Here, with the small team, they were naturally close, becoming friends as well as colleagues, but no more than friends.

On the other hand...

He didn't really want to think about the other hand. About the fact that this might be the very woman with whom he could have his family.

He half smiled at the thought of Liane hearing him say this.

Forget the bloody family and choose a woman because you love her, she would have said.

But physical attraction wasn't love...

Mr and Mrs Red were the first of the couples they saw, coming in concerned, anxiety throbbing from them both as Steve ran through the procedures.

He did his best to help them relax, talking with Mr Red about the sperm sample they would need, explaining how they liked to take that first so he could be with Mrs Red when they extracted any eggs she might have.

The two tall, well-built islanders clung to each other like children, their handsome faces drawn with stress. And for all that she hadn't wanted to be there, it was the client's stress that prompted Fran to intrude in what should be Steve's part of the procedure, inserting herself into the conversation.

'Nothing makes it easier,' she told them in a gentle voice, 'so you just have to think of something you really hate, like going to the dentist, and realise that soon it will all be over.'

Mr and Mrs Red seemed to take that in, and they were soon reassuring her that they didn't mind at all, and the stiffness in the atmosphere melted away. Mr Red kissed his wife goodbye before being led off to a little room, after which Fran followed Steve as he took Mrs Red into the procedure room where he introduced her to Alex, the permanent doctor at the clinic.

'Alex tells us you have some lovely eggs ready for collection,' Steve said to Mrs Red. 'I want to have a look at them, then we'll give you a light sedative so you won't feel any pain and when your husband comes back we can collect them. Francesca is here to take care of them from the moment we get them.'

'Kind of like an egg midwife or perhaps a clucky hen,' she put in, because Mrs Red was looking distressed again. 'Believe me, no one will take better care of them than me.'

She took the woman's hand and gave the fingers a reassuring squeeze. Okay, she'd crossed the boundaries between doctor and embryologist and probably stepped on Steve's toes. But suddenly none of her need for restraint and remaining distant from the patient mattered as long as Mrs Red was as comfortable as she could be while they messed around with her body.

The ultrasound, operated by Alex, showed a number of follicles beautifully swollen, indicating that several eggs might be ready for collection. Mr Red came into the procedure room, smiling with relief that he'd done his part in the procedure. He took Fran's place by his wife's side as Alex sedated the woman and Steve used the ultrasound to guide him to her ovaries and draw up fluid from the ripe follicles.

Fran had her red-marked dish ready for the fluid Steve would collect and held it for him as he released it from the fine syringe. She carried it down to the laboratory, peering at it under the microscope, separating out four fine eggs and transferring them carefully into separate red-marked dishes, these with the special culture in them—fluid that would nurture the eggs while they were outside Mrs Red's body.

It was science, nothing more, she tried to tell herself, but somehow, in this magical place, it had become more personal.

Because she'd been shocked back into feeling by her attraction to Steve? Not that that was going anywhere...

But in spite of that, this day was unlike any other she'd ever spent in a lab; all her senses on full alert, excitement stirring within her.

She put the eggs in the incubator and turned her attention to Mr Red's sample, which had to be washed and examined for any problems or impurities.

'Well, you're feisty little buggers,' she was saying happily to the sperm when Steve walked into the lab.

'Do you always talk to your specimens?' he asked, and she tried to feel embarrassed but found she couldn't.

'Not usually,' she admitted 'but today I'm just happy that they look good and the eggs are good, too,' she added, refusing to have her positive mood dampened by this man. He might have tipped her world off course by making her feel again, but she quite liked the new direction it had taken and she was going to go with it.

'Actually,' she added, 'I do so little practical work these days, mainly supervising the younger embryologists, that I'm excited about this.'

There was no understanding smile.

Nothing!

Oh, well...

'I'm sorry if I intruded when I shouldn't have earlier but they both seemed so stressed.'

'Don't apologise. You managed to get them relaxed, which was wonderful. And we're a team, we work together for the best outcomes we can for the patients. Now, ready to go again? Mr and Mrs Utai are here.'

'Yellow.' Fran responded. 'I'll make them yellow.' She didn't add that she'd call them that, he'd think she was even more peculiar than he'd thought when he heard her talking to her specimen.

Steve watched as she put into the incubator the red dish she'd been examining when he'd come in, then break open the yellow pack. He liked that she was so organised—not that he'd doubted she would be. Right from their first meeting she'd given the impression of smooth efficiency.

Yet he'd glimpsed something of the woman underneath that polished exterior as she'd talked to the previous patients, empathising with them in a way he couldn't, winning their confidence with a few light-hearted comments.

He was intrigued, which wasn't good. Attraction was all very well, and *it* had reached a stage of undeniability, given the way his body was behaving in her presence, but to be interested in her as a person, that was different.

Patients awaited. He'd concentrate on them and think about his colleague later.

Or not think about her later—that would be a better idea.

'Done, done, done!'

It was late afternoon as Fran did a little dance in front of the incubator after she'd checked both the red and the yellow dishes, now with the sperm added to them, and tucked them back into the warm atmosphere they needed to meet and match.

She had no idea why she was feeling so positive about both couples but she was, although now her work was done for the day, she knew let-down could sneak in if she let it. Her own experiences had been so negative it was hard to stay positive, but in this magical place with the gentle, beautiful people, surely nothing could go wrong.

Steve came in as she was tidying the benches and setting out the coloured packs for the patients they'd see the next day.

'All done?' he asked, and she nodded, pleased she still felt positive enough to smile.

'You really like this work?' he queried, picking up on the smile.

'Don't you?' she challenged.

He frowned at her, then finally replied, 'Most of the time.'

'The failures?' she guessed, coming closer and reaching out to touch his hand, wanting to reassure him as she'd reassured the Reds earlier. 'They are not your fault. Everyone accepts that the medical team does the best they can. Everyone going into IVF understands the facts and figures, the chances of success and the even bigger chances of failure. They go because it *is* a chance and it's the doctors and their teams who are giving them that chance.'

He was still frowning, but she sensed it was a different kind of frown, so when he said, 'You're not really who you portray yourself as, are you?' she kind of understood and smiled at him.

'I think I was, but something's changed,' she told him, then she reached up and let her hair out of its restraining band, shaking her head to let her hair fly free. 'Must be the hang-loose thing,' she added, although inside the old her was quivering with shock at this behaviour. She'd not only stripped off her outer shell but she was admitting it to a man she barely knew.

'Good,' Steve said, although the loose hair and

bright smile had made him forget the cool and professional thing. 'Because now we're done for the day and I thought I'd take you for a drive to see something of the island. While Vila is the main town there are small settlements on the other side with farmland and beautiful beaches.

'I'd love that!' she said, her smile even brighter. 'Can you give me a few minutes for a quick shower?' She was peeling off her lab coat as she spoke, dumping it in the laundry bin, which Akila would collect later.

'We've plenty of time,' he assured her, and walked with her down to their quarters.

But his mind was playing with the words. Plenty of time—for what?

She was here for a month—a lifetime in a lot of affairs...

Not that he was thinking of an affair.

Was he?

She was true to her word, reappearing five minutes later, looking fresh and trim in clean shorts and a blue-green shirt that matched her eyes.

They climbed into the trusty four-wheel drive and Steve headed down through the town then turned south, pointing out resort after resort, until they turned off the main highway onto a road that wound through rainforest with patches of cleared farmland.

It was pleasant doing a sightseeing tour of the island, Fran thought, except that it put her in very close proximity to the man who was causing her body so many problems.

Then the view opened up before her, dark blue ocean stretching away to the horizon.

'Oh, that is so beautiful,' she murmured, forgetting

the discomfort of his proximity as she took in the small waves breaking against the white sand of the beach. 'And so quiet after the bustle of Vila.'

They dropped down onto the flat where the ocean was now only visible through a fringe of palm trees.

'Look, there are pigs.'

Steve was smiling, no doubt at her startled remark.

'Don't see many pigs where you live?' he teased, and she smiled too.

'Not poking around in the sandy dirt right beside the road,' she retorted, and the thread of tension she'd felt when she'd first joined him in the vehicle disappeared completely.

He stopped in a small, deserted car park.

'We're on the eastern side of the island now—or maybe south-eastern—and this is Eton, the water called Banana Bay. This place would be jumping if the surf was up, but the winds are wrong for surfing here at this time of the year.'

He turned to look at her, wanting to look at her.

Wanting more?

'Care to walk along the beach?'

'Care to walk along a deserted beach, fringed by palm trees, with crystal-clear water to paddle in? Who wouldn't?'

She was out of the car in an instant, bending to take off her sandals then throw them back into the footwell.

'Race you to the water!'

He let her win.

Of course he let her win—he was too busy watching the joy he could read in her movements to do more than follow slowly.

She kicked one foot into the tide, sending a rainbow

of droplets into the air as the setting sun caught them with its rays, and, watching her, Steve wondered if what he felt was love.

Couldn't possibly be, his sensible self assured him. Heartburn was a far more likely explanation for the tightness in his chest.

He joined her in the shallow water, splashing beside her as they strolled aimlessly along, until she stopped and turned to him, taking one of his hands in both of hers.

'I want to thank you,' she said, her eyes as serious as the tone of her voice, 'for bringing me here. I know I've only begun the work I'm doing with you, but already I know this is the best thing I've ever done.'

She paused and he wondered if she was searching for the words she needed, or if she was considering whether or not to say them.

Possibly the latter, he realised, as she added, 'I feel alive again.'

Trusting blue-green eyes looked into his.

'Truly alive. Hanging loose!'

There had to be something behind such an admission, something bad that had happened in her past, but right now it didn't matter what it was.

He reached out and put his hand on her neck, just beneath her hair.

'And just how loose are you hanging?' he asked quietly.

Fran studied him, suddenly all out of words. She'd gone too far—way too far. In fact, she was so far out of her comfort zone she had no idea how to proceed.

'I'm not entirely sure,' she admitted, but as the hand he'd tucked under her hair drew her closer, she suspected she was about to find out.

It was just a kiss, nothing more, or so she told herself as his lips met hers, but whatever rebellion against restraint that had already begun in her head was infecting her body as well, and she found herself responding, kissing him back, giving all the excited nerves free rein.

Just when she began to tremble she wasn't sure, but Steve must have felt it for he lifted his head and held her shoulders, looking down into her face.

'Okay?' he asked, dark eyes she could drown in looking deep into hers, an emotion she couldn't read making them appear even darker.

Beyond words, she nodded, wondering just where the conversation would go next, realising how little experience she'd had with men. It had always been Nigel, right from high school, and as far as she could remember, Nigel's kisses hadn't made her tremble.

Maybe they had at the beginning…

And after they'd separated, there'd been the odd date, usually set up by well-meaning friends, but although all the men she'd met were fine, there'd been no magic, and definitely no tremble-inducing kisses.

No deep connection that might have led to love.

Love?

When had love come into it?

But Steve was kissing her again and it was all she could do to keep upright, let alone answer questions!

This next kiss seared her skin, heat building within her as well. She clung to Steve, had to for support, and as his tongue probed her lips her mouth opened on a sigh, and she tasted him, teased his teasing tongue with her own, her hands around his neck now, holding his head to hers, while his arms held her close enough for her to know exactly how he felt.

A barking dog broke them apart, and they turned to see a black 'bitsa' lolloping down the beach towards them, an elderly islander well behind him.

Steve bent to scratch the dog behind its ears, talking quietly to it, while Fran stared at the man who seemed, with a kiss—well, two kisses—to have changed the direction of her life.

She'd always been a 'good' girl, and her husband had been her only lover. But Nigel's kisses had never made her want to strip off on a beach and make love on the sand.

Wild passionate love, given the heat of the kiss—kisses…

The islander was closer now, calling out a greeting.

Fran waved to him, then wandered back into the shallow water, splashing again, letting her body cool, while her mind churned with memories of heat and a dozen 'what-ifs'.

Steve spoke to the man, the language almost English but not quite. She recognised a little French and some native tongue mixed in.

'Bislama, the language spoken here,' Steve explained as the man and dog continued along the beach. 'It's a kind of hybrid pidgin English.'

'And you speak it?' Fran asked, studying this man who was full of surprises.

'A little,' he admitted. Then, with a smile that made her toes curl, he added, 'I couldn't have explained what we were doing on the beach but I suppose he guessed that!'

Fran could only stare at him, more unsure of herself than she'd ever been.

Steve read the shadows in her eyes—uncertainty, vulnerability, and perhaps a hint of fear as well.

Not that he wasn't totally thrown by the situation himself...

He took her hand so they could walk together.

'I don't normally kiss my embryologists,' he said, running his thumb across the soft skin on her hand.

She glanced up at him, looking worried now, so he smiled and added, 'And that's not because they've nearly always been men.'

Her low throaty chuckle made his body squirm with desire, but he'd chased away the shadows in her eyes.

'I'm not much of a casual kisser myself,' she said, and it was his turn to laugh.

Certain there was nothing more to say, not now anyway, he slipped an arm around her waist and was pleased when she did the same to him, so they could walk arm in arm along the beach, the setting sun turning the water into a sheet of pink that deepened to purple as the sun sank over the hill behind them.

'Best get back to the car before it's dark. Night comes quickly here,' he said, turning her around and wandering up across the dry sand towards the coconut palms.

'Tell me about yourself,' he said, when they were on the road back to the clinic again.

'I told you yesterday,' she replied. 'I've led a very dull, predictable life. But what of you—your real family— what were they like?'

Steve hesitated, then realised just how little he'd ever told anyone about his family. Maybe talking to Fran would help him sort out his muddled thoughts about his early childhood.

'I never knew my parents well—perhaps no child

does at eight. Maybe it's only later we put the bits and pieces together and see them as real people, but I didn't get that chance.'

He paused, searching for words to explain.

'They were fun, I know that. They had parties and I'd watch from the top of the stairs, see them laughing, sometimes dancing, always crowds of people around them.'

He tried to think back.

'They loved me, I'm sure of that, although they travelled a lot, something to do with family businesses, both my father's and my mother's family businesses. And I had a nanny who mostly looked after me. But when they were home, they always read my bedtime story, and tucked me in, and kissed me goodnight.'

Fran heard the words with a little ache in her heart. She didn't consider herself as having had a storybook childhood, even after her father had left them when she was five. But she had loads more memories of her parents than simply ones of people who kissed her goodnight.

And she'd had grandparents and cousins and memories of Christmas with the whole family gathered, twenty or thirty adults and children all eating roast turkey on a broiling hot summer's day.

She slid her hand across to rest on Steve's knee, giving it a little squeeze of encouragement.

'Go on,' she prompted.

'I think I told you they were both only children. They'd grown up next door to each other, in big houses overlooking the harbour.'

'Plenty of money.' It was a statement, not a question, and Steve nodded his agreement.

'It's how I've been able to start this clinic, and some other ventures back at home.'

But money can't buy love, or so they say, Fran thought, understanding now Steve's strong desire for a family of his own—something he'd never actually had.

Relations, yes, but a family?

'You were lucky with your foster home,' she said, realising where his knowledge of what a family could be like came from.

'I was,' he said. 'Luckier than anyone would believe.'

He turned towards her and smiled.

'Why else would I have family at the top of my to-do list? Well, literally, it's at the bottom but it's the ultimate goal.'

Fran pasted a smile on her face, although inside she could feel the pain of what could never be.

Stupid really, to have connected to this man on the basis of two kisses, but connect she had.

Closely!

And, no, it couldn't possibly be love—love had to be nurtured, grown from small beginnings.

Didn't it?

Whatever! This man was not for her.

Except?

Just for here?

An affair?

Could she handle that?

The trembling began again, although her mind was more steadfast.

Good grief, of course she could. She was a mature woman, already married and divorced, and if she'd managed a father who'd deserted her, and a mother who never seemed to have recovered from the desertion, plus three failed cycles of IVF, *and* the advent of Clarissa into Nigel's life, without completely cracking up, she could handle anything!

They were on the road up to the clinic now, quiet at this time of the evening, and Steve had lifted one hand off the steering wheel to cover hers where it lay on his knee.

'That was great,' he said. 'We'll have to do it again.'

The kissing?

Perhaps she could handle anything but uncertainty.

'The drive part or the beach part?' she asked as they pulled up by the huge bougainvillea.

His frown told her she'd lost him, but as his eyes searched her face, the frown was replaced by a smile.

'Both,' he said firmly. 'But definitely the beach part.'

He used the hand that still held hers to draw her closer, and brushed his lips across hers, sending tremors of need through her body.

But before she could respond he'd drawn back, getting out of the car and coming around to help her out, smiling at her as if something had been settled, though what, she had no idea.

'I've got to see Alex about something but will see you for dinner,' he said, squeezing her fingers before releasing them.

How she got back to their lodging with her knees shaking so much, Fran didn't know, but she *did* make it.

She pressed her hands to her cheeks, feeling the heat in them for all she didn't blush, then sank onto the bed, wondering what came next.

Should she say something? Indicate she'd be happy to have an affair with him?

Surely not, that would sound far too clinical!

Besides, it might not be what he wanted…

Perhaps, she decided as she stood up and gathered her toiletries, she'd leave it all to Steve. Undoubtedly he knew a whole lot more about flings, affairs and holiday romances than she did.

Probably about sex too!

The thought snuck into her head and she felt her cheeks grow hot again. Maybe she did know how to blush.

Unfortunately, checking out her wardrobe for something to put on after her shower brought her down to earth with a thud. Last night in the long blue dress she'd looked attractive enough to interest Steve, but as far as the rest of her clothes were concerned, that was it for soft and pretty. Everything else was strictly practical, tailored linen shorts and sensible shirts, not a flower or a floating panel in sight.

Disappointment rocketed through her body and although she told herself it was utterly stupid to want to look pretty for Steve and that at her age she should know better, the disappointment remained like a solid lump of ice in the middle of her chest.

Although…

What had Zoe said when she'd shown Fran around?

Something about muumuus in a bottom drawer of the dresser? People coming from different climates and often not having anything cool to wear?

Fran examined the dresser. She hadn't needed the bottom drawer so hadn't opened it, but now she did and gazed in wonder at the brightly flowered muumuus folded neatly in it. All new with tags—presumably people who used them took them home and paid to replace them, which is what she'd do, she decided, pulling out the least vibrant of them, a dusky blue with purple flowers—truly the least vibrant!

Could she wear it?

Wouldn't she look foolish?

She folded the garment and returned it to the drawer, her fear of looking foolish overcoming any stupid desire to look pretty for Steve, but even as his name sounded in her head, his voice came through the door.

'If you need something cool to put on after your shower, there is always a collection of muumuus in a bottom drawer.'

The spurt of what had to be jealousy that shot through her shocked her so much she knew she wouldn't wear any of the pretty garments. Although he *had* said he didn't usually kiss his embryologists so maybe he just knew about the garments rather than having any specific experience with them—or the women in them!

She headed for the bathroom only to find it in use, Steve obviously having decided she'd finished in there.

Totally lost now, ill at ease, and wondering what on earth she was getting herself into, she wandered out the back door, clutching her toiletries bag, clean undies, shirt and shorts, and blinked at the sight before her eyes.

Someone—surely not Steve—had spread flowers across the centre of the outdoor table, the barbecue lid was up and the coals beneath the grill plate were heating, while along the benches on both sides of the grill, banana leaves were spread with food—sliced vegetables, a whole fish, fruits she didn't recognise, the lot covered with a fine net to protect them from insects.

Could she really wear her shirt and shorts to such a feast?

If she was actually considering a fling with Steve, couldn't she go the whole way—wear the pretty muu-muu?

But uncertainty still dogged her, the restraint she'd developed throughout her childhood brought on by the fear of losing her remaining parent, and then continuing in her marriage. *My colleagues, clients and friends expect the best of everything*, Nigel had always said, but nothing showy or obtrusive.

Until she felt arms circle her from behind, and Steve press a kiss on her shoulder.

'You're fretting about the kisses, aren't you? They don't have to lead anywhere, you know. We can be all grown-up and pretend to each other—denying the attraction that seems to have sprung up between us. Although I doubt it will go away. As far as you're concerned, I find you a very sexy woman, but the last thing I'd want, Francesca, is to push you into something you don't want.'

She turned in his arms and pressed her body against his, wanting him yet still uncertain, although as he kissed her again, this time just beneath her ear, the desire for him grew strong enough to chase away uncertainty.

'My friends call me Fran,' she said, giving in to the delight of his kisses which, now, were trailing down her neck.

'Fran or Francesca, you are delectably kissable,' he said, then he lifted his head, dropped a light kiss on her lips, turned her towards the house and patted her on the backside. 'Go shower while I cook or we'll never eat,' he said, making things sound so normal she trotted off to do as she was told, although when she dressed after the shower she did leave the top buttons of her shirt undone.

CHAPTER FOUR

'No muumuu?' Steve teased, then he shook his head.' 'Actually, I think you're more of a sarong type.'

He disappeared into his room and returned with a rolled-up piece of material in dark blue with unlikely green hibiscus flowers on it.

'These are left for the men—they wear them tied around their waist, but it would fit you as a sarong, wrapped around and tied above the breasts. You could try it now, or for dinner tomorrow.'

The slight smile curling his lips suggested he was already imagining her in it, and though she was sure she never blushed, she was also sure her cheeks were heating.

'Thank you,' she managed. 'Maybe tomorrow.'

But just imagining the sarong, led to images of Steve untying it, unwrapping her, and heat swamped her body.

She plonked down on a chair beside the table—one where she could watch him as he worked—wondering why this man, of all the men she'd met and worked with, could affect her as he did, sending her spinning right off her stable axis into the unknown.

Her mind whirled as she sought for answers, while her fingers idly picked up flowers from the central display, poking them randomly into her hair for something to do.

She looked at the sarong, and excitement skittered inside her, churning her stomach so badly she was sure she wouldn't be able to eat, when even her normally sensible brain was remembering beach kisses and wondering where they would lead.

Or perhaps that was her body talking…

She lifted a frangipani flower, creamy white with a vivid yellow centre, and breathed in the heady perfume. Tucked it in between her breasts, where the undone buttons showed just a hint of a deep cleavage.

Would Steve like her breasts?

The thought was foreign to her yet it brought warmth sweeping downward between her legs, and a heaviness that made the restraints of her bra uncomfortable.

The idea that she, sensible, practical Francesca Hawthorne, could be sitting lusting over an almost stranger was unfathomable, but that's certainly what was happening. She could feel the moisture gathering, her nipples pebbling, just thinking about what lay ahead…

Sensible, practical Francesca, however, did recover sufficiently to ask if there was anything she could do to help, but Steve only half turned and smiled at her, a warm, delighted kind of smile.

'Relax, that's what you can do. In fact, there might be something here to help with that.'

He reached into a cupboard under one of the side benches and held up a small bottle of beer.

'Beer, wine, something soft? The French influence spreads to alcohol here in Vanuatu so the wines are usually French and very good. A light, dry white perhaps?'

She nodded agreement then realised she could at

least get it for herself and stood up, moving towards him, flowers falling from her hair as she did so.

Totally embarrassed, she raised her hands to pull them out, but he caught her hands.

'Hanging loose,' he reminded her, touching the frangipani nestled between her breasts. 'Remember?'

All right, so she *could* blush! She'd obviously not had any need for blushes before.

She bent and found the wine, together with some glasses, frosted with cold, but as Steve had already knocked the top off the beer, she pulled out only one, unscrewing the top off the wine—pleased screw-tops had become commonplace so she didn't have to fight a cork—and poured herself a glass of the pale liquid.

It was deliciously cold, and so refreshing she'd finished her glass before she realised it, and though tempted to pour another one, she waited, deciding to have one with her meal, determined not to look as if she needed the Dutch courage of alcohol to get her through whatever might lie ahead.

But thinking of what might lie ahead set her body on fire once again, so she poured another glass of wine, and a glass of cold water as well.

Was he always so aware of women he'd been kissing? Steve wondered. Or was it because Francesca—Fran—was so different from his usual women that he was hyper-aware of her? It was obvious she was feeling awkward and uncertain after what had happened at the beach and this knowledge made him feel very protective of her. Made him want to hug and reassure her, but touching her was dangerous.

So cooking for her, eating with her, became a kind of foreplay, unusual for him but no less tantalising for that.

The meal done, they sat at the table and talked of work, of experiences they'd had, Fran—yes, he liked the shortened version—proving a humorous conversationalist as well as an intelligent one.

She could joke about her lab work, which obviously fascinated her, and told stories of the things that had happened there, but she steered away from personal questions and he guessed for all her talk of happy family Christmases there'd been pain and disillusion in her life.

He'd have liked to ask but she was talking about work again.

'About the IVM?' Fran asked, although what she really wanted to know was more about this man. 'Andy mentioned you wanted someone with experience in taking immature eggs and maturing them in the incubator. Is there some reason you'd consider doing that here?'

He grinned at her, no doubt guessing she was deliberately introducing work into the conversation to keep away from anything personal, but the hint of mischief in his expression did something weird deep inside her.

More than physical attraction?

Surely not!

She concentrated on his answer.

'I know the idea is still very new,' he was saying, a smile still lurking around his lips, 'and it's probably presumptuous of me to want to try it here, but there's a couple who have been through two cycles of IVF and each time the drugs have made the woman quite ill.'

He paused, looking around the deck before he looked back at her.

'I wouldn't have given her the second lot of treatment if she hadn't been insistent.'

'Desperate for a baby?'

Steve nodded.

'So I thought,' he began, breaking into Fran's thoughts of the couple she didn't know, and what they must have suffered, 'that instead of giving her the drugs we take a few immature eggs and raise them in the incubator, then fertilise them when they're ready.'

'That's a fabulous idea,' Fran told him, secretly thrilled at the idea of having total responsibility for nursing the immature eggs to maturity. 'Andy has had a good deal of success with IVM, and I've been involved with the immature eggs. Me and a couple dozen lab assistants and other embryologists.'

But here they'd be *her* babies, those little eggs, and the thought of having sole responsibility for them made her smile at the man who had brought her to this place.

Unfortunately he smiled back and she felt again that tug of something deep inside.

Don't think about it!

'You cooked so I'll clear up,' she said, standing up and collecting the scattered dishes and cutlery from the table, walking to the kitchen, so aware of Steve the nerves in her spine were prickling from his presence behind her.

She rinsed off the plates and tucked them in the dishwasher, wiped down benches, dithering.

Two kisses on the beach didn't mean a thing, really, so why the dithering?

Because she wanted them to mean something—to at least lead somewhere…

She went into the bathroom to wash her hands and freshen up, splashed water on her face and returned to the table outside, where Steve had moved their chairs together so they could look out through the wilderness of bushes to faint glimpses of the sea.

He'd also poured her another glass of wine, and one for himself.

She sank down into the chair and picked up the wine, sipping at it carefully because he was so close, his shoulder all but brushing hers, the closeness causing a slight tremor in her fingers.

She wondered if he'd noticed, because he took the glass from her hand and set it on the table, then turned and licked the wine from her lips, murmuring appreciation— of the taste?

Or of her lips?

'There is no need to hurry this, whatever this might turn out to be,' he whispered. 'In fact, Hallie had a very good rule.'

He pulled Fran onto his knee, his lips against her ear.

'And that was to never make decisions at night.'

'Never make decisions at night?' Fran echoed, looking into the face so close to hers.

'Exactly,' Steve said. 'Sleep on it and if, in the sober light of day, you still want whatever it was then you know it's okay.'

'Sleep on it?'

Fran knew she was repeating his words like a demented parrot, but her mind was so befuddled she couldn't help it.

'Sleep on it,' he repeated, then he set her on her feet, gave her a pat on the bottom, and pointed her in the direction of her bedroom.

'Now!' he added, in a stern voice. 'Before I stand up and kiss you again and then it will be too late!'

Which left her in no doubt about the decision she had to make…

* * *

You're here to work!

The reminder, her first thought on waking, was enough for her to put all thoughts about decisions right out of her head. She ate her breakfast and drank her coffee—alone, as Steve was apparently out somewhere.

Work?

Or absent because he didn't want to discuss the previous evening and whatever decision she might have reached?

Setting aside the skittering of excitement even thinking about making her decision triggered, she turned her mind resolutely to work and headed to the lab to see how things were going.

As she crossed the courtyard, she was adding up the hours. Mrs Red's eggs had been introduced to Mr Red's sample at about three in the afternoon so now, seventeen hours later, she should be able to tell if any of the eggs had been fertilised.

After sixteen to eighteen hours you could usually tell, so maybe Mr and Mrs Yellow's might be showing some success as well.

Excitement for her work took over her thoughts and she hurried into the lab, pulling out the first of the four red dishes that held Mrs Red's eggs. As she put it beneath the microscope and peered at it, she saw the two tiny bubbles—the pronuclei—in the centre of the egg.

This one was already dividing.

Perfect!

She couldn't help just a little fist pump. Working alone in the lab—Steve had mentioned an assistant but so far he hadn't appeared—she had no one to share her excitement, but that didn't mean she couldn't show it.

Returning the dish to the incubator, she took the next red one.

Damn! Joy never lasted long. There were definitely three bubbles in it, which meant two sperm had penetrated and the egg was unlikely to develop normally.

But dishes three and four were both good. One thing she and Steve had covered in one of their colleague-type conversations over dinner the first evening had been that he was happy to implant two embryos but not three, although implanting two would only be at the request of the client. They had facilities to freeze any extra ones, so that was no problem, but as yet these weren't embryos, not until cell division began.

She tucked the three good dishes back into the incubator and pulled out one of the yellows.

No luck so far, and no luck with any of the dishes. Still, some eggs took longer to show they'd been fertilised.

The reminder didn't help the uneasy feeling inside Fran's stomach. Sometimes the outer shell of the egg was too tough for the sperm to penetrate and they had to be helped. It was a delicate procedure but she was adept at it, although here—without the necessary equipment?

But they had the eggs—good eggs…

She went in search of Steve, her mind so wholly on the problem at hand—or the suspected problem—that for the first time since she'd met him she didn't feel a start of awareness at his good looks, although her heart did skip a beat when he smiled.

'I know you haven't got a stable table for ICSI but do you have the other equipment? A really good microscope, an ultra-fine pipette, some medium to slow the sperm? I've more of Mr Yellow's sample—'

'Whoa!' He held up his hands to stop her flow of questions. 'Do you always get up and rush straight into work mode no matter how late or long the night was?'

She had to smile.

'Don't know,' she admitted, relaxed in a way she'd never felt before. 'I'm not used to late, long nights. And, anyway, last night was hardly late.'

She thought it best to ignore the part where she had lain awake for hours, wondering what she was letting herself in for...

'But you could get used to them?' he murmured, coming so close the words seemed to wash across her skin.

'I guess,' she said, remembering her earlier decision to be mature about this—to play it as a game, to have fun! 'But to get back to the Yellows?'

He looked so confused she had to explain.

'I call them by their colours. I find it easier than try-ing to remember names and match names to colours.'

'And if they're just colours you don't have to get per-sonally involved?' Steve queried, amazed at how much he was learning about this woman—learning and lik-ing. But why would she hide her deep humanity behind her brisk all-business disguise?

'Self-protection?'

'Of a kind,' she admitted, 'not that it always works, as you saw yesterday.'

He touched her lightly on the shoulder.

'Don't hide your true self,' he murmured, then fi-nally answered her original question.

'Yes, we have the necessary equipment for the rather

amazing intracytoplasmic sperm injection. How could we consider doing IVM without it? Surprisingly enough, while we don't have a laparoscope, we do have a microscope with micro-manipulators. You wouldn't have seen it as it's locked away. The manufacturer donated it when we bought a number of new ones for the lab in Sydney, and arranged for us to get the pipettes and other equipment needed for the clinic here. Do you want to have a go?'

'I thought I could try one egg,' she said. 'You drew five out of Mrs Yellow, so I could do one egg and the others could still be fertilised anyway, but I'd like to try now while Mr Yellow's specimen is still viable.'

'Go for it. I've got the next couple coming in, but Alex is there and I think Arthur, your lab assistant, has finally turned up, so he can stand by for the eggs. What colour next?'

'Green,' Fran said without the slightest hesitation, so definite he had to ask.

'For any particular reason? Do you go in order? Red, yellow, green? Traffic lights?'

She grinned at him and his heart felt as if a giant fist had grabbed it and squeezed hard, jolting him enough that it took a moment for him to catch up with Fran's reply.

'No definite order, and today just seemed to be a green day. I ate breakfast on the back deck and the green of the foliage out there seemed to glow with intensity—not, I suppose, that plants can really glow with the joy of life!'

Steve shook his head, surprised that the uptight professional woman he'd first met should be having such flights of fancy.

He couldn't put it down to a few kisses surely. Or had she made a decision about where the kisses might lead?

'So, green,' he said, not wanting to reveal just how far his thoughts had strayed, or wanting to analyse why he found himself thinking about her so much.

He led Fran into the lab, introduced her to Arthur, another giant islander, who nodded and smiled, taking Fran's hand so cautiously he might have been handling fragile glass.

'Do you have the key to the special cabinet?' Steve asked Arthur, who nodded again and pulled at a strip of leather that hung around his neck, producing a bunch of keys.

He selected one shiny enough to suggest it was rarely used and unlocked a cupboard Fran had previously not noticed, as, unlike the others, it was flush with the wall.

The new microscope was still wrapped in plastic, its attachments still in their separate compartments in the felt-lined metal case.

'Oh, you little beauty,' Fran breathed, though she was jolted back to reality by Steve's laughter.

'So, you talk to your equipment, too,' he teased, and she turned and smiled at him, suddenly at ease with the situation in which she found herself, at ease with the work ahead of her, and the pleasure she suspected would come from whatever relationship she had with this man, limited though it might be.

Which meant she'd decided to go where the kisses led? a voice in her head asked.

She ignored it and concentrated on work.

'I only talk to equipment when it's top-class, like

this one,' she told Steve, wondering if he was thinking about her decision.

Work!

'And if we could get some thick rubber matting—is Akila the best person to ask for that?—we could put it under one of the small tables here in the lab. It would provide some cushioning, although with the concrete floor there's unlikely to be much movement anyway.'

She could feel the excitement of the challenge building inside her, and wondered if it was brimming over—showing in her face or manner.

Arthur was studying her with wide eyes, although that might have been confusion, but Steve was definitely smiling.

Smiling…

Focus, she told herself, although the warmth the smile had transmitted into her body was extremely pleasant.

'We need the microscope with the micromanipulator attachments,' she explained to Arthur, 'because the pipettes we will be using are so fine you can't actually see the tip with the naked eye. I know Steve has a couple to see, and he'll want one of us to get the eggs, but if you go with him—we're using the green pack for them—I'll see Akila and get the microscope set up and then wait until you come back to do the injection.'

Arthur's smile gave her a different flush of warmth and as the two men headed off to the procedure room to deal with Mr and Mrs Green, Fran went in search of Akila to ask about rubber matting.

Like a conjuror producing a rabbit from a hat, Akila returned before Fran had finished unpacking the microscope's attachments and together they set four thick rubber mats on the floor then put the table on top of them, Akila finding weights to hold it firm so the four legs sank into the rubber.

Fran checked the yellow dishes again, but the sperm still hadn't penetrated any of the eggs.

They *could* be slow, she told herself, but years of practice told her that was probably not the case. If Mr and Mrs Yellow wanted a baby, she would have to help fertilise the egg. The good thing was that the percentage of successful fertilisations using the pipette was high—sixty to eighty percent—so as long as she didn't muck things up, all would be well.

Arthur returned with Mr Green's specimen, and Fran washed and checked it while she waited for the eggs. Four eggs, they found, when she and Arthur examined the fluid from Mrs Green. Fran asked Arthur to separate them out into the different dishes she'd already set up with the media they needed to nourish them.

For all his size, he worked with a delicate precision, so well that Fran congratulated him and won another gleaming smile.

They tucked all the dishes into the incubator and she was wondering whether Steve might want to watch the manipulation of Mrs Yellow's egg when Arthur spoke for practically the first time since they'd met.

'I am very excited to be watching you do this. I have read about it, of course, because I am studying to do more lab work, but I have never seen it done.'

While Arthur retrieved one of Mrs Yellow's eggs and the remainder of Mr Yellow's specimen, Fran unwound the layers of wrapping around the pipette and, searching through the refrigerated cabinet, found the viscous fluid into which she could put the sperm.

'It slows them down,' she explained to Arthur, 'to make it easier to pick up just one of them. The tip of the pipette is sharp enough to penetrate the shell of the egg, and then a little pressure on the top of the pipette and in it goes. The main thing is to make sure you don't go in far enough to damage the nucleus of the egg.'

Forcing herself to concentrate, which meant banishing all wayward thoughts of Steve from her head, Fran went ahead with the delicate procedure, so excited when she succeeded that she moved away from the table to high-five Arthur, who had watched over her shoulder the whole time.

'That is wonderful,' he said, as they continued their mutual congratulations. 'We haven't had the microscope very long and there haven't been any IVF patients for a few months.'

His words intrigued her.

'Don't other doctors come when Steve's not here?' she asked. 'I understood he wasn't the only visiting specialist.'

'Others come but sometimes not for a while. Steve says it's hard to get a regular commitment—the doctors have wives and families, you see, and it isn't always convenient. He's looking now at doctors nearing retirement, or using doctors with young families to come in the summer holidays. Steve comes three times a year. He says it's easy for him, not having a family so no ties to anyone, but he is a kind man and clever, so he should have a family.'

A strange sensation stirred in Fran's stomach.

Regret?

Impossible!

If the kisses led to anything, it would be a holiday romance, nothing more. She had known that since he'd first talked to her about his list.

CHAPTER FIVE

APPARENTLY STILL EXCITED at having seen the procedure, Arthur became positively chatty as he washed Mr Green's sperm while Fran separated Mrs Green's eggs into different dishes.

'So, are you ready for my IVM patient?'

Steve's voice made them both turn towards the door.

'She's here? Now?' Fran managed, although the lingering excitement from the ICSI success together with Steve's sudden appearance had sent both her mind and her body into a spin.

Think work!

The reminder wasn't quite enough to stop the bodily excitement, but it did snap her mind back into action.

'Of course,' she said. 'I've made a pack of purple equipment—the colour of royalty for a very special couple.'

Dazzled by the happy smile that accompanied the words, Steve could only stare at her.

Could this be love, this strange new emotion he was feeling?

Of course not! He barely knew the woman, and, yes, he was attracted to her, but *love*?

'Good,' he managed when he realised she obviously

needed some reply. Then, encouraged by managing one word, tried a few more. 'Will you collect them for me?'

Another smile, another missed beat in his heart.

Ridiculous!

'Of course,' she said. 'I'd love to.'

Love to?

Love?

'Good,' he managed, monosyllabic again—pathetic really! 'Alex is here to man the ultrasound.'

Hoping he hadn't made a complete fool of himself, he headed back to his clients, but an image of Fran as she had flashed that smile persisted in his head.

She was in a bog standard lab coat, with, no doubt, her sensible uniform of shirt and shorts underneath. Her hair was pulled back in the neat scroll affair she'd been wearing when he'd first seen her, *and* it was covered with a lab cap!

Hardly the clothing of an enticing siren!

Yet his body couldn't have reacted more strongly if she'd been stark naked.

He had to get past this, as it was just too distracting.

After the one disastrous relationship he'd had with a colleague—ending in a broken engagement—he'd avoided mixing work and pleasure. In fact, he'd found that he enjoyed getting right away from work when he had leisure time, enjoyed the company of women who had little to no idea of what his job entailed and even less interest in it.

Relaxation.

That's what he'd sought! Companionship, a bit of fun, evenings out and, yes, some healthy sex thrown in...

'So, have you checked on the ultrasound for immature follicles?'

Now her voice made him start, and it was only with considerable effort he suppressed a groan.

'Yes, they're fine. I think I can take two. Though I think that when they mature, you'll have to use ICSI on them.'

She smiled again, this time the happiness shining in her eyes.

'A doddle,' she said. 'Arthur and I have just fertilised one of Mrs Yellow's eggs. The equipment you were given is top-class.'

Which explained her excitement.

And why should that make his spirits flag?

She followed him up to the treatment room, where the Hopoates waited, the powerful mix of tension and excitement vibrating in the air around them.

Once again, he was impressed by how naturally Fran could put people at ease. A few kind words, a smile, a joke, and they were eating out of her hand.

She told him she was using purple colours because it was the colour of royalty.

'But *we* are royal, though you didn't know,' Mr Hopoate said. 'We are from the southern islands, so not royal like your Queen but descended from what would be considered royal in other places. In our island group we are called the Masters of the Heavens and the Masters of the Canoes.'

'Master of Heaven and Canoes, I like that,' Fran said, and Steve could tell her interest was genuine.

'These are our titles from the old times,' Mr Hopoate said. 'That is why it is important to us to have a child. Royal blood should be passed down, even now, because it is important our history and traditions are carried into every generation.'

He was so serious, Steve felt his heart falter. And he, who prided himself on remaining detached, uttered a silent prayer to whatever fates watched over these beautiful islands, a prayer that the Hopoates would be blessed with a child.

'Ready?' Alex said to him, reminding him he was here to work, not rely on prayer.

He nodded.

With IVM, Mr Hopoate's specimen would not be needed until the eggs matured, so his role was just supportive.

And support he did, holding his wife's hand and telling her how much he loved her and how, even if this didn't work and they couldn't have children he would still love her.

Steve glanced up as he was depositing the precious eggs in the purple-marked dish Fran was holding for him and was surprised to see tears in her eyes.

So he wasn't the only one who'd got emotional…

The urge to touch her, comfort her in some way, was strong, but at the same time he wondered if it was more than the sentimentality of Mr Hopoate's words that had upset her.

After all, what did he know of this woman to whom he was becoming increasingly attracted?

Fran took the eggs back to the lab, adding some serum from Mrs Hopoate's blood, which Alex had prepared for her.

'These,' she said to Arthur, 'are extremely precious. This is the first time Steve has taken immature cells so it's up to us to see they're given every chance to mature, after which we'll use ICSI on them, so watch carefully when I do it, so you can do it next time. I'm sure with the skill Alex already has, and your help in the lab, it won't be long before you don't need Steve or any other visiting doctor. You'll have your very own IVF unit and be the envy of all the South Pacific nations!'

'I think that would please Steve,' Arthur said, 'because, although he likes coming here, I think he'd also like to settle down and start a family. I see the way he handles the babies people bring in to show him—babies he's helped create. He is a man who wants babies of his own.'

Fran closed her eyes. Gentle Arthur had no idea of the wounds he'd just dealt her—stab wounds in her chest, her lungs, her heart.

Not that Steve wanting babies was anything to do with her. All they'd done was kiss...

And if the kisses made her burn all over, then that was *her* problem!

'Mr and Mrs Green brought two small chickens, denuded of feathers, cleaned and even boned,' Steve said when she had finished work, showered, changed, and wandered out onto the deck.

He was standing by the giant barbecue, the luckless birds plastic-wrapped and sitting in a cool box beside him.

'Without the bones they'll squash flat to make it easy to barbecue them. I've just rubbed a few herbs and some lemon and oil over them and left them to marinate for a while. I'll cook them both then there'll be cold chicken for lunch tomorrow.'

Fran studied him, sensing some change in his mood. No, more behaviour...

She'd spent the day with a stomach knotted by anxiety over the decision she had made—to let the kisses lead where they may. And now he was acting as if there'd never been a kiss, let alone the possibility of something to follow it.

He put the chickens on the hot plate and gave them his full attention so all she could see was his back, and what could you glean from a broad, straight back?

'There'll be things for a salad in the refrigerator if you wouldn't mind putting one together to go with these,' he said, throwing the words casually over his shoulder.

Fran left, only too happy to get away from what felt like a particularly tense situation.

Though why?

Steve heard her footsteps retreating to the kitchen and let out a sigh of relief.

He hadn't seen *that* much of her during the day, but when they had been working together it had been as if the kisses of the previous afternoon and evening had never happened.

He should have forgotten Hallie's dictum about decisions made in the evening and taken her to bed when their kisses had prompted it.

Now he had no idea where they stood. Had she thought about it, made a decision? If so, she'd given no indication of it.

Maybe he'd imagined the previous afternoon and evening—imagined the heat of the kisses they'd shared...

He reached into the small refrigerator and pulled out a light beer, then put it back, deciding he didn't really need it.

Maybe wine with dinner...

Maybe nothing.

Dear heaven, but he was making a mess of this!

And where was Fran?

Surely mixing a bit of lettuce and tomato together couldn't take this long?

He turned the chickens, the aroma of their crispy skin making his mouth water.

Then, suddenly, she was beside him, close but not touching. Close enough for every nerve in his body to be aware of her.

'Salad's on the table and I ducked back to the lab to check on our purple eggs. It's too early to say but they seem to be maturing happily.'

'Happily?' he echoed, turning to her so he caught her smile, and her lips were right there, and everything was all right.

'Must rescue the chickens,' he muttered against her lips when they'd been kissing with a desperation he'd never felt before.

She drew away, half smiling though there was a faint frown line between her eyebrows and a bemused look in her eyes.

He lifted the chickens onto a platter and followed her towards the table, where she'd not only left the salad but had scattered flowers, as he had done the night before.

He selected the most perfect of the hibiscus and held it in front of her.

'Which ear?' he asked, and her smile improved.

'I suppose left on a temporary basis,' she murmured.

'A temporary basis?'

The smile had faded, and the faint frown line had reappeared.

'It's all it can be, Steve,' she said firmly. 'A holiday romance, a little fling. It's this place and its magic that's drawn us together. To try and make it more back in the real world would spoil, probably destroy, something wonderful.'

Well, at least she thought their 'fling' would be wonderful.

But why the proviso?

They were two adults—mature adults, even—who were attracted to each other. Why should it not continue when they returned to Sydney?

But something in her demeanour told him not to query it so he slid the vivid flower into her hair, settling it behind her ear, wanting to draw her close, to hold her, but aware they'd miss their dinner if they kissed again.

He served her a tender chicken breast, and they ate, and talked of work, of family, and the meal done, the debris cleared away, they relaxed. He told her of Liane, the damaged foster sister he'd adored, who'd turned to him again and again when she'd lost her way, but somehow he had failed to save her.

Fran reached out and took his hand, drawing him towards her.

'You can't save someone who doesn't want to be saved,' she said quietly, adding, 'And you shouldn't break yourself trying to fix someone else's problems.'

Maybe someone should have told him that a long time ago, for he'd very nearly broken himself. He *had* lost his fiancée, and for a while very nearly given in to the despair of failure.

Had his face given him away? It was the last thought he had as she leaned across and kissed him.

A gentle kiss, empathetic and yet redeeming. A kiss that grew to something else...to need and want and passion.

Standing now, his hand against her head, beneath the soft brown hair, holding her close.

Kissing her because now he had her answer.

Fran found herself responding, kissing him in turn, slowly and carefully, relishing the contact of nothing more than lips until his hand slid from beneath her hair and his fingers trailed down her neck to slide a button undone and delve under the fabric of the opening, sliding beneath her bra to take the weight of one breast in his hand.

Her body stiffened, wanting more, uncertain how to ask until a small whimper whispered from her lips. He caught her breath in his mouth and increased the pressure of his fingers, finding her hardened nipple, teasing it, while his lips still held hers captive.

She wasn't going to whimper again—whimpering was needy—but she did gasp as his fingers nipped her sharply, gasped and shifted against him as desire, hot and demanding, speared down to the moist place between her legs.

'Bedroom?'

He breathed the word as lightly into her mouth as she'd whimpered her need earlier, but didn't wait for a reply. Instead, turning, he hooked an arm around her neck to keep her close as they walked back into the house.

And the kisses didn't stop, on her temple, on her ear, little kisses, barely brushing her skin, yet so erotic she was trembling again.

His bedroom—she was pleased about that—the bit of her still capable of thought decided.

But once inside there was no hurried rush of shedding clothes, no ripping or tearing. He was slow, teasingly slow, achingly slow, yet she was happy to let him set the pace.

Steve let his hands explore her, wanting to know her shape, aware in some dim recess of his mind that her hands, too, were on a voyage of discovery. His shirt was definitely unbuttoned, and he had the sensation of a feather brushing across his chest, across his nipples, pressing them lightly.

But most of his concentration was on Fran, on the silky texture of her skin, on the kisses he was trailing along her jaw line and down her neck, touching the pulse before moving on to taste the perfumed honey of that shadowed skin between her breasts.

Now, clothes a puddle on the floor, shoes and underwear in tangled heaps, the urgency to feel skin on skin so great there was no more thought.

Relief as skin met skin. Relief and relaxation as bodies fitted to each other, soft to hard, warmth transferring, parts matching as nature had intended, pleasure in the sharing of touch and feeling until excitement built again and demanded more.

Steve tipped her back onto the bed and lay beside her, exploring again, his eyes holding hers, trying to read her reactions to his touch in her shadowed eyes. They gave away little, although he saw colour flare in her cheeks as he thumbed a nipple, enough colour to prompt further exploration, holding one full breast while he took that nipple in his mouth and suckled hard on it, feeling Francesca's body arch, her hands reach out for him. But he kept on teasing, wanting to be certain that she wanted him as much as he wanted her.

Teasing, touching, kissing, until she whispered, voice husky with desire, 'Steve, I need you!'

It was more than an invitation, more than a plea, and he slid into her welcoming heat and prayed he wouldn't come too soon, desperately thinking of the seven times table to distract himself. But not even seven times nine could distract him from the joy of Francesca's body, or the way she moved beneath him, uttering little cries of pleasure or delight, arching up to him, her arms clasped around his back, fingernails dragging through his skin as if she needed more and more of him inside her.

Her legs clamped him now and they moved as one, riding a tidal wave, a tsunami of such power it swept them onto some distant, explosive planet, finally beaching them on a very foreign shore.

'My God!'

The words escaped Steve's lips as he lay exhausted on the no longer smooth bedcover.

'I couldn't have put it better myself,' Francesca muttered, but then she laughed, lying on her back and laughing, the sound so joyous Steve had to smile. Touched by it in some way, he took her hand and held it, while he too joined the laughter.

Was laughter a normal reaction to good sex?

He couldn't remember laughing after sex before tonight, but actually, if he was honest, what he'd just experienced hadn't been good sex, it had been mind-blowing, cataclysmic, all-consuming, out-of-this-world sex.

And why had they laughed? It had seemed natural at the time, but now he thought about it...

'You're wondering about the laughter,' she guessed. She'd propped herself on one arm and was looking down at him, still smiling, while the forefinger of her right hand traced the contours of his face. Slick with sweat, her skin was silvered by the moonlight that lit the room, and the tumble of hair that had escaped captivity was a dark cloud that partly hid her face.

She was beautiful, so beautiful.

'Probably totally inappropriate,' she admitted, 'but, oh, Steve, that felt so good! It was as if I'd never really made love with anyone before—never known it should be fun! So surely there's nothing wrong with enjoying it while we can?'

She sounded just unsure enough for him to reach up and pull her down on top of him so he could kiss her as he reassured her that there was definitely nothing wrong with it.

Fran let him kiss her, her mind far too busy to be concentrating on kissing him back.

For a start there was her reaction to what had just happened. Shouldn't her body be burning with shame and confusion and probably regret?

Why should it?

She was a free agent, she could have affairs with anyone she liked—not that she ever had or probably ever would again, but there was nothing to stop her, was there?

'Are you regretting it?' Steve asked, no doubt alerted to the fact he'd lost her by her lack of response to his kisses.

'No way,' she told him.

'Good,' he said, nipping teasingly at her lower lip, then sucking on it, sending her nerves into a new frenzy. 'Because it was something special between us and shouldn't be regretted.'

'Mutual attraction—I'd heard of it, of course, but never really known what it was,' she murmured, but although her mind was managing the conversation, her body was squirming on top of his, moving to ease the need that was building again…

She shifted to the side, propping herself up again while she studied his face, or what she could see of it in the gloom.

A lazy smile drifted onto his lips, and his dark eyes gleamed.

Devilishly!

Lying there on the bed, nonchalantly naked, his eyes scanning her face, asking silent questions, he was so beautiful he took her breath away. Not classic-marble-statue beautiful, but man-beautiful. A forceful face, hewn rather than sculpted, slashes of cheekbones beneath deep-set eyes—dark as night those eyes beneath ink-black brows.

Full, sensual lips, pale-rimmed to emphasise their shapeliness, lips that even now were moving, the smile changing from lazy to lustful, tempting her, teasing her, challenging her to make the first move this time.

Or was she imagining that?

'Well?'

The throatily spoken word was definitely a challenge, but could she take charge, make love to him?

The idea excited her, but that was possibly because she'd lost her mind.

'Too late,' he murmured, reaching out to trace a circle around her breast, spiralling it closer and closer to her nipple while her body tensed and tightened, so wound up by the time he touched the pink bud she groaned out loud and flung herself into his arms, pressing her breasts against his chest to stop further torture, yet knowing she wanted more, needed more.

Slower this time, learning from each other, learning what pleased and excited—delaying the final act and satisfaction because the foreplay was such fun.

She was on top of him again, looking down into his face, and she saw the gleam in his eyes and the slight smile on his lips as she made her admission.

'Really?' he asked, touching her again, still teasing, but his fingers brushing her skin so deliberately delicately that she wanted to yell at him to press harder. Which he eventually did, before spinning her into orbit somewhere in outer space, into a world of dazzling lights and sparkling fires that shook her body to the core.

And this time when she collapsed on him, she was pleased he'd shouted out her name right at the end. She fell into an exhausted sleep, waking, confused about where she was, at two in the morning with a man she barely knew sound asleep beside her.

His arm lay heavily across her waist and as she tried to ease out from under him, he murmured a protest and turned to pull her back, tucking her into his body so he surrounded her.

Oh, the bliss of it! To be spooned so safely against a man. Nigel had never held her like this, neither had he liked to feel her wrapped around him, although as a child she'd always thought that must be the nice part of a marriage…

Not that this was anything to do with marriage, or even a future—that was impossible—it was a holiday romance, nothing more!

Fun sex, that's all it had been, and all it would be.

But thinking back—remembering—embarrassment crept in.

Embarrassment?

There had to be a better word—a stronger word—for how she felt right now. Embarrassment at her lack of restraint, at the laughter, at the things she'd said…

Steve wouldn't be embarrassed, so neither should she be. She should be mature—heaven knew, she was that—and sensible about this relationship.

Enjoy it, definitely, and remember it with pleasure, but keep her emotions in check so at the end she could put it behind her as easily as he would.

She snuggled closer, knowing this wonderful safe haven wouldn't last and that she had to make the most of it, glean memories from it to keep her warm in the future.

Memories to ease the ache she suspected she would feel in her heart?

CHAPTER SIX

He was gone when she woke—in his bed—and confusion over what to do next fluttered like moths in her head.

Should she muss up the bed in her room?

Of course not, she'd made her own bed every morning she'd been here. Why was she even thinking this way?

To stop thinking about facing Steve in daylight?

That moth was bigger than the rest, and its sudden presence got her out of bed, gathering her clothes and fleeing into her own room, where she crawled into bed for comfort rather than deception.

But there was work to be done, and she was being pathetic.

Pulling the sheet over her head, she hid from the truth.

The truth that she had truly enjoyed their sexual encounter?

Where was restraint in that?

She thought about that restraint, the one that had shaped her thoughts and her decisions since childhood.

Because of the guilt she'd felt when her father had left them, certain for some peculiar childish reason it had been her fault? Because she'd trodden so carefully after that, perhaps subconsciously not wanting to lose her mother as well?

Nonsense! That was the past—gone so long ago it should be forgotten.

She was a mature woman and although, admittedly, she hadn't considered it post-divorce, she was entitled to a love life. She bounded out and headed for the shower. Those moths were not going to spoil her memories of a wondrous night.

She was eating breakfast when Zoe arrived.

'Steve still out on his run?' she asked, a question that explained why he wasn't around in the morning.

'Must be,' Fran replied, hoping she sounded more together than she felt.

But there was work to be done and she'd need her wits about her, so work!

Steve appeared, freshly showered, as she was walking to the lab.

'Good morning, lovely lady,' he said, with a smile that warmed her all over. 'Can we check the red dishes? And the green ones? Forty-eight hours and we should be seeing some cell division on the reds and it's probably late enough to see the pronuclei in the greens.'

Fran smiled at the enthusiasm in his voice, though she did wonder if he was feeling all the physical things she was feeling.

Like wanting to reach out and touch him, to move closer.

Work!

She couldn't deny that Steve was passionate about his work but...

Then he did touch her, one finger tilting her chin so their eyes met.

'Okay?' he asked, and she knew her smile in reply was probably way too delighted but she couldn't help it.

'Very okay,' she told him. 'So, come with me while I check?'

Years of experience at ignoring any emotional highs or lows—mostly lows—made it easy to switch into work mode, although every nerve in her body was aware of Steve's presence, and it took a great deal of strength to not accidentally brush against him.

Arthur was already in the lab and as he lifted the dishes from the incubator she slid them under the microscope, checking each one before stepping back so first Steve and then Arthur could see the progress.

'Look, this one is nearly perfect,' she said, excited in spite of herself as she studied one of the Reds' embryos. 'I know the fact that they divide evenly isn't really an indication of their strength or viability but the even ones always appear stronger to me. Far better than the ones that are lopsided or are dividing too quickly. That first one we checked had divided unevenly.'

Memories of the night of love fled now as she was caught up in the miracle of procreation, although she continued to be sure she didn't stand too close to Steve.

The next two were also good, and they moved on to the green dishes, where pronuclei were visible in two of them.

'It's early yet,' Fran reminded the two men. 'Give them time.'

'So, now you will look at Miss or Mister Yellow?' Arthur asked, when he'd returned all the checked dishes to the incubator, clearly keen to see their success with the ICSI.

Fran smiled at him, his enthusiasm was so infectious.

'Let's check the other yellows first, to see if they've been inseminated without help.'

Nothing had happened, although one egg had divided without insemination, which was a common enough occurrence. It would have to be let go.

'Okay,' Fran finally said to Arthur. 'Now we'll check the last one, the one we helped.'

He carried the dish carefully over to the microscope and Fran, not wanting to look, waved her hand.

'You check it first,' she said, and Arthur bent obediently over the microscope, adjusting the eyepiece then lifting his head to beam at them. 'See for yourselves!' he told them.

They did, followed by high fives all round.

The Blues were the first couple to arrive that morning, Fran holding the dish with its special bath of fluid as Steve collected the eggs. Fran talked quietly and comfortingly to the couple all the time, ignoring the man doing the procedure as much as possible.

Wanting to separate out the eggs herself—and perhaps because her restraint was wearing thin—she sent Arthur in for the Browns, then, as the little polar body appeared on each egg, she divided Mr Blue's specimen, washed and cleared of impurities, between the dishes and tucked them away, understanding now why such a small set-up had such a large incubator.

She checked the purple eggs, smiling as she realised they were maturing nicely. Knowing he'd be trying IVM for the purple couple, Steve had made sure they had the chemicals and growth hormones ready for them and Fran had carefully fed the eggs the nutrients they needed.

Thinking that tomorrow they'd be ready for the ICSI, she realised that she'd have to speak to Steve about collecting Mr Hopoate's specimen.

Maybe now?

No, concentrate on work. She must check to see if Mr Yellow's specimen still had viable sperm and if so, let Arthur do the ICSI, or at least the first stage of it, which involved clearing the little cloud from around the egg.

But as she squinted into their regular microscope and saw that the only moving sperm were very lacklustre, Fran realised that they would need a new specimen before they could do the ICSI.

Checking the remaining yellow eggs, she found them fine, nourished in their special liquid, so it seemed a shame not to use them.

Now she had *two* valid reasons to see Steve.

Pathetic, that's what she was, but at least it *was* a relevant work visit.

Arthur hadn't returned with the Browns' samples so she went up to the clinic, meeting Arthur on his way back to the lab.

'You can get on with separating the eggs and cleaning the specimen. I won't be long, I just want to see Steve about a couple of things.'

She could have left off after the 'I just want to see Steve' bit and it would have been true.

And *really* pathetic!

Steve's smile as she walked in produced what were, by now, familiar sensations of tingling, slight breathlessness and a warmth in her belly.

He introduced her to the Browns, who had a complicated Vanuatuan name she knew she'd never pronounce,
let alone remember. It was good to meet them in spite
of Steve's contention that she thought of them by their
colours so as not to get too emotionally involved.

Alex was also there and, after assuring Fran he'd
contact both Mr Yellow and Mr Purple, he walked out
with Mr and Mrs Brown, giving Steve the opportunity
he'd been waiting for since he'd seen Fran earlier this
morning.

Even as she explained her mission, he'd drawn her
close, holding her against his body until she finished
with a faint '…so we need another specimen from Mr
Yellow.'

'Got the message—messages,' he murmured, her lips
so close to his she could have breathed in the words.

Then he kissed her, slowly at first, enjoying the taste
of her once again, feeling a heady intoxication as she
kissed him back.

Her fingers slid into his hair, while his hands roved
her back, remembering…

'We're at work,' she reminded him softly when they'd
drawn apart in order to breathe.

'Don't I know it,' he groaned, then he kissed her
again, hard and fast.

'Later,' he said, releasing her and sending her on her
way with a last touch to her cheek.

'I've a meeting at the hospital so won't be here for
lunch, but when you finish for the day, we could go
north to Havannah? There's a resort there and the most
beautiful beach. We can swim, laze about, maybe have
dinner in the restaurant.'

Stay the night?

It was off season, so the resort would have rooms.

No, best not push things, but he knew she would love the place and the thought of seeing her in a swimsuit, swimming with her, had already produced a frisson of excitement in his body.

And maybe, before they left, in the week while they waited for pregnancy tests, they could go to Kukuhla, the most magical little island in the group and only a short boat ride from their island of Efate.

But as he walked across to the hospital he wondered about her proviso—her insistence that this would be no more than a holiday romance, a fling.

The obvious answer was that she was seeing someone back in Sydney, which, given she was a clever, bright, attractive woman, was highly likely.

But it didn't fit with what he knew of her, or thought he knew of her.

She was too open, too honest to cheat on a significant other...

Although the little she'd shared of her private life—married and divorced—told him he really didn't know her well enough to judge.

So why did he feel he did?

No, he didn't know, and considering his own failed romance, maybe he was just a bad judge of women.

No, and no, and no! He couldn't believe she'd be cheating on another man...

Havannah Beach was everything a tropical beach should be, Fran decided when Steve pulled in, not to the resort but just above it, almost onto the sand itself.

She dug in her bag for suntan lotion, and was smoothing it on her arms when Steve took it from her.

'Hop out and I'll do it. You'll never reach your back to cover it properly.'

She did as she was told but was reluctant to remove the sarong she'd wrapped around her bikini—the sarong Steve had given her on her second night in Vanuatu.

But the decision was taken out of her hands.

'I've been wanting to do this since I first gave it to you,' Steve told her, undoing the knot that held the material together, and unwinding it from around her body.

'Ah, just as I thought—perfection!'

Her hands wanted to move to cover what for her was nakedness, but she struggled against the familiar need for restraint.

'You haven't done a lot of swimming in that bikini,' he teased, squeezing lotion into one hand. 'It'll be cold when it goes on, you know.'

And with that he proceeded to give her the most sensual experience she'd ever had.

No, remembering the previous night, she had to amend that—the most sensual experience she'd ever had with clothes on.

His hand, slick with lotion, slid across her skin, while sexual tension slithered along her nerves, tightening them almost to breaking point, even when he turned his attentions to her back, his hands straying ever so slightly now and then.

'You're done,' he finally announced, his husky voice suggesting she wasn't the only one who'd been affected by the process. 'Let's swim!'

He took her hand and led her down the beach, white powdery sand sinking beneath her feet. The water was a pure, translucent, blue-green colour so even when she'd walked in up to her thighs she could still clearly see her toes.

Steve dived in and swam then dived again, coming up right in front of her, his skin bronzed and beautiful, water droplets that she had to touch gleaming on chest and flying through the air as he flicked his hair.

'Coward!' he challenged, and she took the plunge, diving down to touch the sand then swimming out into the blueness of the deeper water.

Swimming back, he met and matched her stroke for stroke until their bodies touched and all restraint was broken.

They twined together in the water, bodies touching, lips searching for skin to kiss, and then for lips.

'We'll drown,' Fran whispered to him as they drifted into deeper water.

'As if I'd let harm come to you,' he said, and looked deep into her eyes, so she couldn't miss the message that he meant it.

Her heart somersaulted and she wondered just how foolish her decision to have this little romance had been.

Already she suspected it was more than attraction on her part, but if Steve felt that way—no, it was too complicated. Just live for now and enjoy it—don't think about the future.

She kissed him, although moths were once again fluttering in her head. He wasn't a man who *didn't* think about the future...

He lifted her, still kissing, so she lay in his arms in the water, and the moths disappeared, flooded out by passionate sensation.

The sun was sinking before they left the water and

dried themselves, Steve pulling on his shorts and shirt before rewrapping her, slowly and teasingly, in the sarong.

'We'll walk up to the resort and have a drink as the sun sets, then dinner so we don't have to waste time with that when we get back.'

'Waste time?' she teased, so thoroughly relaxed a new Fran seemed to have taken over her body. A Fran who teased, and kissed in public, and ached to get back into bed with this man she barely knew...

This time she woke early, Steve still in bed beside her. She lay there thinking how wonderful their lovemaking had been—lacking the wildness of the previous night but still exhilarating.

He stirred and pulled her tight against him, then groaned.

'No doubt you know what I'd *like* to do,' he murmured in her ear, 'but if I don't run one morning it's easier to not run the next, and it's running that keeps me sane in this work where we have such disappointments as well as successes.'

She turned in his arms.

'Can I run with you? I run at home, but mainly because I love the rush it gives me.'

His arms tightened.

'Put some clothes on and we'll run together.'

But as she pulled on a pair of shorts and T-shirt, Fran wondered if this was a good idea.

If too much togetherness was a bad thing. Wouldn't it bring them closer? It was the one thing she really didn't want because the closer they became—out of bed—the harder it would be to leave him.

Not that running left them with breath for conversa-

tion, although sharing a love for a morning run seemed
to make them more of a couple, which—she reminded
herself—was what they couldn't be. He had his list, and
on that list was his desire for a family. With children.

But running with him along the top of the ridge behind the town, and through a little forest path he seemed
to know well, was so exhilarating she forgot her doubts
and just enjoyed the view out over the island-studded
ocean, and the darkness and smell of the rainforest
when they took the little path.

She knew he was matching his pace to hers, which
was slower than usual after a week or so of not running.
Firstly because she'd been so busy before she'd left it
had been one thing she couldn't fit in, then after the
flight and settling in over here, although she'd brought
her gear, it hadn't occurred to her.

Other things on her mind?

She knew that brought a foolish smile to her face
and was glad she'd dropped a little behind him so he
couldn't see it.

They ended up beneath the clinic and had the hill
climb at the end, so Fran arrived back in their temporary home and collapsed into the nearest chair.

'I thought you were a runner,' Steve teased, and she
glowered at him because he was barely out of breath.

'It was the hill,' she retorted. 'You finished with a
hill!'

'That's the bit that gets the endorphins surging,' he
told her. 'But while you sit there, recovering, I'll have
a quick shower and duck over to the hospital. I usually
have breakfast over there with Alex while we map out
a timetable for the next specialist visit.'

'Which is usually you?' Fran asked, and he nodded,

dropped a quick kiss on her hair and disappeared towards his bedroom.

He was such a *good* man, she thought as she watched him go, she had to hope he didn't feel too much for her—that he had accepted the temporary nature of their relationship. And given his goals, how could it *not* be temporary?

He'd been hurt before, she'd known that when he'd spoken of the sister he couldn't save. The pain she'd seen in his eyes had made her want to hold him and keep him safe from pain for ever.

But nobody could offer that...

Steve showered then left, reluctantly, for the hospital. He'd far rather have been having breakfast with Fran. He found himself hoping he hadn't pushed her too far on the run, knowing she hadn't run since she'd arrived.

Yet running with her had been special. Another bond between them.

Which brought him back to thinking about her insistence that their relationship would end when they left the island.

Not that thinking about it did much good. He barely knew her, so how could he possibly work out what she was thinking?

And hadn't he, himself, decided that work and relationships didn't mix?

Forget it, Fran was different!

Wasn't she?

Returning to the clinic after breakfast, he went straight to the lab. Today was the day! The red eggs would certainly be ready for transfer—one to Mrs Red's uterus, the other to be frozen for future use, and he guessed the yellow that Fran had inseminated would also have reached sufficient development for transfer.

Fran was at the lab when he arrived after breakfast. Why wasn't he surprised? One thing he did know about her was that she loved the work she did, and was excited by the progress of her tiny eggs.

'Will you transfer today?' she asked as he walked in.

He grinned at her.

'I've got both the Reds and the Yellows coming in, although why I've picked up your use of colours for their names I do not know! I've always been quite content to use the clients' names and now you've got me calling them by colours.'

'Not to their faces, I hope,' she said, and he smiled again because *she* was smiling and a smiling Fran did something to his insides.

'And Mr Hopoate—royal purple and the Lord of Heavens and Canoes—is he coming in to give a specimen?'

'This afternoon,' he told her, then firmly turned his attention to work, making arrangements for the transfer, checking the Yellow egg Fran had fertilised then deciding not to transfer it until the next day.

'But you'll get him to leave a specimen so we can fertilise the other viable eggs?' she asked, and he nodded.

'All under control,' he assured her. 'See you at ten.'

He left the lab, aware he could have lingered there all day. The woman had definitely got under his skin.

And again the question nagged of why the limitation. On that first night when he'd held the flower to put behind her ear, she'd said right, which meant there was no man in her life.

So?

* * *

Whether it was a night of slow and languid lovemaking, or the run, Fran wasn't sure, but the desire to be near Steve, close to him again, was so overwhelming she went up to the clinic rooms far earlier than she needed, to find not only the Reds already there but another couple she didn't know.

And a baby!

Not quite freshly minted but fairly young, and Steve was holding it in his arms and talking to it, making the infant smile and gurgle, its shiny dark skin almost glowing with delight at the attentions of the man who held him.

And there's your proof if you needed any, Fran told herself, that there's no future for you with this man. Forget the list, he's obviously made to be a father and probably, from the look on his face, longs to be one.

The pain of this confirmation was so strong she felt her knees weaken and had to lean against the desk for a moment to recover her equilibrium.

You love him, the voice in her head continued in accusing tones, and she knew it was correct.

So, learn to live with it.

Steve was introducing her to Mr and Mrs Tamou.

'Mrs Tamou and Mrs Inui are sisters. It was Mrs Tamou's success that prompted Mr and Mrs Inui to come to us.'

He was smiling at her over the baby and she felt her heart break, but fortunately part of her brain was working and it understood he was telling her the names so she wouldn't call Mr and Mrs Inui Mr and Mrs Red.

She shook hands all round, admired the baby, who

was being handed back to its mother, then thankfully the Tamous departed.

Steve was practically glowing.

'A lot of the couples come back with their babies,' he told her, sure she'd share his delight. 'It's the best part of this job.'

'I'm sure it is,' she managed to reply.

'But that's not why you're here, is it?' he said, his smile still so bright it hurt. 'Let's get on with things.'

He led the Inuis into the procedure room, explaining what he was going to do. He would give Mrs Inui a light sedative, although this part was painless, then he'd transfer the little embryo to her uterus.

'It can float around in there for up to a week before it settles into the uterine lining,' he told the excited couple.

Or sometimes doesn't settle in, Fran thought as painful memories of failures added to the pain she was already feeling.

But she kept a smile pasted on her face as she left the room, not wanting to intrude on the couple's exciting moment. Mrs Inui would rest in the treatment room for a couple of hours, and although she could resume normal activities afterwards Fran knew from experience she'd probably take it easy, not wanting to dislodge the tiny seed.

She was checking the purple eggs when Steve came in.

'I've got the Yellows coming in later,' he said, 'and although I'll wait another twenty-four hours before I implant, do you still want a new specimen from Mr Yellow?'

'I think so,' she said. 'The eggs are still viable and look strong and if we manually inseminate them and they produce embryos we can freeze them, which would save Mrs Yellow going through all the early IVF processes. We can just monitor her and implant another one when she's ready.'

He shook his head.

'You're assuming this first one won't implant,' he chided. 'Be positive! I know the percentages of failure as well as you do, but we have to always believe we'll have success, otherwise what's the use?'

Fran had to turn away so that he wouldn't see her pain.

If she had believed during that third time, might it have been successful?

Probably not! Not according to her doctor, who had been lamenting her lack of eggs and predicting early menopause.

Steve watched her turn away, but not before he'd seen the shadow of what looked like pain in her lovely eyes.

Had she gone through IVF unsuccessfully herself? Was that why she was so attuned to their clients?

Was that why her marriage had broken down?

He longed to ask her, but she was bustling around the lab, now taking out one of the purple dishes to check the egg development.

He could almost feel the defensive barrier she'd erected around herself.

With him on the outside...

Work! he reminded himself. *You, too, can be professional...*

'Will it—or they—be ready if we get Mr Hopoate's specimen this afternoon?' he asked.

'I'm pretty sure they will be.'

No smile!

'Here, look for yourself.'

She stepped away from the microscope. A step longer than necessary?

So as not to brush against him?

Or him against her?

Steve didn't have a clue what it was, but he knew that in the time between when they'd finished their run and now something had shifted in their relationship.

They'd hardly spoken except about work and then in the presence of other people, so it couldn't be something he'd done or said.

Had she received a phone call from home? A text, or an email?

Could he ask?

'That looks good,' he said, realising she was probably waiting for a response.

He straightened up and reached out to touch her on the shoulder.

'You okay?' he said quietly, and was surprised to see tears well in her eyes, though she blinked them back with a fierceness that told him he wasn't meant to see them.

'Fine,' she said, but he knew it was a lie.

She was busying herself with the other purple dishes now, looking at them with naked eyes before shifting one to the microscope.

'I have to go back to the Inuis,' he said, 'but I'm not going to the hospital, so perhaps we can have lunch together.'

He supposed it was a statement that didn't need a reply, so after a brief pause he went back to the clinic.

Something was eluding him and he had no idea what. In truth, they'd known each other barely a week, so he could hardly expect to fully understand her—if such a thing was ever possible between two people.

But he tried anyway, thinking back to the fairly up-tight woman he'd met off the plane, then seeing the gradual change in her as the island worked its magic. In bed, he'd discovered, she was a woman who held nothing back, and yet she was obviously holding back a whole lot of who she was.

His thoughts were becoming so entangled he forced his mind away from Fran, turning it to the couple he was about to send home full of hope and probably a little apprehension.

They were standing with Alex in the waiting room as he explained when they should come back, giving them a date in nine days' time.

'We'll do the pregnancy test then and again at twelve days to be sure, and we want you to be positive about this. Yes, we've talked about the statistics and you know it might not happen with your first IVF cycle, but re-member that it can and possibly will, so hold tight to that thought.'

Alex was good, Steve thought. Maybe in another year he could head up a permanent IVF clinic here. He, Steve, could afford to sponsor another O and G special-ist for the hospital and the two could work together as he and Alex had.

And then he could get on with the last item on his list because he wouldn't have to leave a wife and fam-ily for four weeks three times a year.

Was he thinking that because he'd met Fran?

Liked Fran?

Maybe loved her?

Had that thought somehow flown through the air

and transmitted itself to Fran, causing her to ask, as they were finishing their lunch, why, with a family so important on his 'to-do' list, he hadn't started earlier.

'I did think about it,' he admitted, then knew he wanted her to know.

'I did more than think about it. I met a woman, got engaged, made plans for a wedding in the not-too-distant future, and children. I'd finished my intern year and residency and was starting my O and G specialty so I was well on my way.'

He paused, mainly because the memory still hurt.

'Then Liane turned up. The stepsister I told you about. She'd always considered my apartment as a second home. You have to understand that Liane had been badly abused as a young child. She was a broken spirit, and not even all the love Hallie and Pop gave her could fix her. But she was special and we all loved and protected her.'

'Such a terrible thing for a child,' Fran said quietly, obviously understanding, so Steve continued.

'She was on drugs at the time, and as low as I'd ever seen her, so I spent a lot of time with her, helping her reduce her intake gradually so that she didn't suffer seizures. Finally, I got her into a detox centre. She came out so well and happy that I thought if she got away for a real holiday, this time the detox might work.'

'And how was your fiancée with all this?' Fran asked, although no doubt she'd guessed the answer.

He studied her, thinking back to that time.

'I'd always thought she understood—understood that to me Liane was family, so I had to take care of her. It didn't make me love Sally any less, and I thought she knew that.'

'Did you tell her?'

He paused, startled by Fran's words.

'She'd have *known*,' he said. 'Although I knew, at first, she was slightly put out that Liane needed so much of my attention, I was sure she understood. But it was only when I paid for a trip to Bali for Liane that Sally got particularly frosty, reminding me I'd been promising she and I would have a holiday like that. We worked through it somehow but when Liane returned, she was determined to start afresh and focus on her career. She was a wonderful singer. It wasn't long before she hooked up with an agent who offered her a flat, a job and, eventually, drugs.'

'Poor woman,' Fran said, shaking her head.

'Poor woman indeed,' he said, remembering the woman he'd loved for so long when she'd come back to his place that last time. 'She turned to me again when she discovered she was five months pregnant by someone she'd met in Bali—and although she wanted the baby and knew the drugs were bad for it, she couldn't keep off them.'

He'd been toying with his fork but now he looked up at Fran.

'I had to take her in, but it was too late. The baby, Nikki, was drug addicted when she was born, and Liane died soon after.'

'And your fiancée?'

'Gone the day Liane came back that last time. Gone because she felt I cared more for Liane than I did for her.'

'She was your sister,' Fran said, reaching out to remove the fork from his hand and hold it in hers.

'She was. And when I was ten years old I had loved

Liane. But Sally was to be my wife! I should have seen what was happening, understood how she felt, made more of an effort to help her accept the situation.'

'And would that have helped?' Fran asked.

He shrugged and shook his head, the memories so painful there were no words.

Although…

He took a deep breath.

'Actually, apart from losing not only a fiancée and also a good nurse, and *not* marrying at that stage of my life, the rest of it turned out all right. One of my other foster sisters adopted Liane's baby, and battled through the early years when little Nikki was so sick. But in the end, by sheer serendipity, she met and fell in love with Nikki's birth father—the man Liane had met in Bali. They're married now and expecting another child, so fairy-tales do happen.'

'Just not to you?'

He looked up into Fran's lovely eyes.

'I was beginning to think perhaps they did,' he said softly, and saw tears well again as she shook her head, let go his hand, and began to busily clear the table.

But talking of the past—of Sally—had reminded him that relationships with work colleagues weren't a particularly good thing.

Although Fran was only a temporary work colleague…

CHAPTER SEVEN

WHILE THE NIGHTS remained filled with sensual delight and sexual satisfaction, the days developed a routine, Steve implanting tiny embryos, Fran freezing those that had developed sufficiently to be used in the future. It was here that she had to be meticulous, showing Arthur how to choose the best ones to freeze, then how to extract all the water from the tiny bunch of cells, replacing it with a special anti-freeze.

Next came freezing, placing the tiny embryo in a straw, cooling them very slowly so no shards of ice formed to pierce the precious cells. Once frozen, the straws went into canes, and with this the embryologist had to be particularly careful with identification. Fran continued using coloured tags within the little containers, further labelling them all with names and numbers corresponding to the various couples.

But even though she was busy with the freezing, she was finding the wait for confirmation of pregnancy very difficult. She knew it was partly because it brought back memories of her own days of waiting, but it seemed worse because she knew and liked these people, had spoken to them, and now dreaded to think how they'd react if they found the IVF cycle they'd been through had failed.

'Worrying about failure?' Steve asked, breezing into the lab where she had been watching Arthur do ICSI on Mrs Yellow's eggs.

'Do I look worried?' she snapped, mostly because seeing him unexpectedly like this did terrible things to her heart, and different terrible things to her body.

Her heart was weeping because it knew their time together was nearly over, while her body still wanted to rush him off to bed—or anywhere private—every time she saw him.

'Yes,' he said, coming closer and resting his hand on her forearm. 'Knowing the statistics—that terrible forty percent success rate that's considered the norm—we're all entitled to worry. But we never take on patients unless they've been through a lot of counselling and they know the odds as well as we do.'

'I know, I know,' Fran said. 'I suppose it's different because I've met them, talked to them. Back in the lab at the hospital in Sydney, I not only didn't know the couples, but often I didn't know who'd conceived and who hadn't. This is too close, I suppose.'

Steve was watching her as she spoke, and guessed there was more to it than she said. She was as uptight as the couples who were waiting for news, possibly more so. And in bed there seemed to be a desperation in her lovemaking, as if she wanted to drown out all thought with passion.

Could he take her away?

Over to Kakuhla?

He did the numbers in his head.

'What's worrying *you*?'

Fran's voice broke into his calculations.

Aware Alex was in the room with them, he had to phrase his reply carefully.

'I was thinking, as we're nearing the end of your visit to the islands, I could show you around a little, maybe take you over to Kakuhla Island, which is beautiful and not too far to travel.'

'But won't the Reds be ready for testing about the same time you're implanting the embryo in the Purples?'

He nodded. He might have known she could add up as well as he could.

'I was thinking that I could leave Alex to do the first of the pregnancy testing—after all, the couples involved have no doubt been doing tests themselves. But then I realised I couldn't—couldn't let down the couples by not being there should this cycle have been a failure. I want to be the one with them, and to talk to them about options. It's why we stay a month.'

He brooded on it for a moment, then rather reluctantly added, 'Although you could go over to the island, or do a few island-hopping trips yourself. Zoe would be happy to show you around.'

Her smile was so bright he was struck by the realisation he loved this woman, so when she said, 'You're a good man, Steve Ransome,' he was filled with happiness.

And knew he had to fight to keep her.

He left the lab, needing to think through this latest development.

Yes, he'd known almost from the start that he'd wanted the relationship to continue when they both returned to Sydney because she was intelligent, good company, understood his work and another dozen reasons, including their compatibility in bed.

But love?

He'd set romance aside after the disaster with Sally. Instead, he'd concentrated on learning all he could about IVF before setting up his own clinic. There'd been women since, but none had been more important than his work, so they'd shared mutual enjoyment and passed on.

But Fran was different.

Fran really was a keeper!

But how to convince her that they were meant to be together?

Did she not love him?

That was certainly a possibility but their lovemaking was no longer 'fling' stuff, it had grown into something special, wild at times admittedly but nurturing, caring...

Loving?

He shook his head, going back into the clinic to talk to Alex because thinking about Fran was driving him insane.

Especially when she appeared five minutes later, not having given him time to get her right out of his head.

'What about the other couple?' she asked. 'The ones you said might not be quite ready for egg retrieval. Surely by now they would be?'

Still reeling from the realisation that he was in love with her, Steve couldn't work out an answer, so Alex took the question.

'The cycle failed,' he said quietly, and Steve saw Fran flinch. 'The eggs failed to develop. Steve and I were discussing it now, thinking we might try IVM on them. Not right away, of course, because the cycle might have caused some special problem, but in a couple of months.'

Fran nodded, although the pain she felt for this couple was almost overwhelming. Her third cycle had ended this way, and that's when she had been told it would be useless to try again.

Which had seemed only to please Nigel.

She turned to Steve. 'You'd come back to do it?'

'Alex and I were talking about that as well. I've got a young O and G specialist who's been working in my clinic for a few months. I'm wondering whether, with his experience and Alex's, and a good embryologist, they could do it themselves. It's where we'd always hoped to go, to have people here who could handle the whole process.'

Fran thought about it for a moment.

'Do the islands have the population numbers to make it viable?' she asked, and he smiled.

She wished he wouldn't—it distracted her—so she had to catch up with what he was saying.

'Probably not, although time will tell. But it wouldn't have to make a profit and the hospital can use the services of two O and G specialists. The embryologist would be a problem as there wouldn't be full-time work.'

And suddenly a way opened up and the future became clear.

Steve was setting this up so he could be at home, finding a wife, starting a family, so...

And Andy would know...

Talk to her about it...

Which would be a thousand times worse than her

mother's progress reports on Clarissa's pregnancy, which, now she came to think of it, no longer bothered her at all!

'I could stay,' she said, letting the thought settle about her and feeling how right it was. 'I don't need a full-time income, and I already love this place and the people. I could help with counselling too, because I've done that with couples who want to know how the whole process works. I'd have to give notice at work, and sort out my apartment, sell or rent, pack up, but I could do it.'

'That would be wonderful,' Alex said, 'because your job is so important to the whole cycle. Arthur is good but he is still learning, and with your experience you could help with advice to me, and the new doctor, should we need it. We could make a wonderful team.'

'Andy would kill me for taking you away from him,' Steve said, although his voice seemed strained as if there were other things he'd rather be saying. 'He went on about it enough when I only wanted to borrow you for four weeks.'

'Andy has plenty of good people to take my place,' she told him. 'I should know, I trained most of them.'

'Then maybe one of them might like the island life as much as you seem to,' he said, and she had to smile, although she knew it was a weak effort.

'I was here first,' she said firmly, although inside she was quaking, well aware she'd made this decision because it seemed to solve her loving-Steve dilemma. Removed from him by a large ocean, she'd surely get over him one day?

'Well, if you're really serious that's a fantastic offer,' Steve said bluntly, 'but I think we're running before we can walk. Alex and I were still at the talking-about-it stage, and I'll be back in three or four months anyway so the couple who failed can join that programme. Now, if we're quite finished here, I've got an appointment at the hospital.'

Alex looked rather surprised by this announcement, and as Steve walked out the door, Alex turned to Fran.

'What's eating him?' he asked. 'I've known Steve for years and although I've seen him upset when cycles don't produce pregnancies, and angry when people make mistakes, today he just seems grumpy, and I'd have sworn he was one man who didn't do grumpy.'

'Everyone does grumpy,' Fran told Alex, hoping she didn't sound similarly bad-tempered.

She left the clinic, going back down to the quarters, feeling thwarted. For a few minutes it had seemed as if she'd been offered a lifeline—a way of getting away from Steve for long enough to get over him—but he'd cut it off.

Although…

She remembered Andy asking her if she'd known Steve, way back when this trip had first been mooted, and she'd told him no, so if they'd both been living in the same city for years and hadn't run into each other, how likely was it that they would when they got back?

Unless he persisted with this idea that whatever they had could continue in Sydney.

She should tell him.

And have him pity her?

Hadn't she had enough of that from Nigel's colleagues' wives, who had apparently known about her trouble getting pregnant from the start?

Former friends they were now, unable to understand the pain she felt whenever she saw their happy, healthy, children.

Body in automatic mode, she'd pulled food from the refrigerator while these dismal thoughts raced through her head. But looking at it now, the makings of a salad, a wrap to put around it—she didn't feel hungry. She had nothing to do, so she'd go for a walk—maybe even a run.

Steve made his way over to the hospital, only too aware there was no reason for him to be going there, although he knew he'd find someone to talk to or something to do.

Not that he'd be much use to anyone, his mind was too full of questions.

First was the revelation that had struck him back at the clinic—the realisation that what he felt for Fran might be love.

Could it be?

His reaction to her offer to stay on here certainly suggested it was. He'd felt physically sick at the thought of not seeing her, not sitting with her over meals, sleeping in the same bed.

His gut was still knotted, while his brain was circling helplessly around her offer.

She wanted to stay *here*?

Because she'd grown to love the place?

Hardly! She seen two beaches, a restaurant and barely knew the place at all.

Or could it be a way of escape—either from something happening back at home or from him?

She was adamant that their relationship must end

when they left the island, so maybe offering to stay on was her way of making sure that it did.

That made the most sense, but wasn't it a bit drastic? Shifting countries to avoid a relationship?

What of her friends and family?

He was sure she'd mentioned a mother.

It was at this stage he realised just how little he knew about the woman he loved.

There, the word had come out with no hesitation that time, so maybe it *was* love.

He had to find out, get to know her better, which seemed ridiculous given they'd spent almost every night since she'd arrived together.

He turned and headed back to the little apartment they shared. They'd go to lunch down at the water-front—there was a lovely seafood restaurant just out of the main town.

But she wasn't there.

Fran had walked down through town, listening to the sounds of this strange, exotic place, revelling in the aromas of food and flowers and sea.

She *could* live here.

Her mother would have a fit at the very idea, but eventually she'd give in and come to visit. After all, these days she loved to travel.

Her mother would meet the local people, realise how special they were, see the beauty of the beaches, and… be convinced it was why her daughter had chosen to live here?

Fran shook her head at the thought.

It wouldn't have to be for ever. Steve would soon find

another woman—there'd be plenty of women who'd love to marry him.

Not that he'd mentioned marriage, but where else would continuing this affair lead?

Regret for what could not be seized her, clutching at her stomach, burning in her lungs.

She wouldn't cry, she'd used up her life's allotment of tears years ago.

Realising she'd reached the waterfront, she wandered along to a small café, went in and bought a sandwich, and a pretty fruit drink that tasted more of coconut than anything else she could name. Then she sat on the jetty to have lunch, seagulls swooping in circles above her, waiting for her to drop a crumb.

Looking out over the clear waters of the bay calmed her mind and body to the extent that she realised that, yes, she could live here. Maybe not for ever, but certainly for a year or two...

Though walking back up the hill in the heat of early afternoon made her think maybe not.

Silly really, even considering it all, when there was no certainty that Steve would go ahead with his plan to have a permanent IVF clinic here.

Silly, too, to think he'd pursue her back in Sydney. He was a rational, intelligent man and no doubt once back in the real world he'd totally forget her. She was making mountains out of molehills, as her mother would have said.

'You do realise why we're both a bit tetchy,' Steve greeted her when she finally reached their accommodation and sank down in the shade of the deck.

He was standing leaning back on the railing, the green jungle growth of the garden behind him. 'It's because tomorrow's the first testing day. Reds, and the day after that the Yellows. We mightn't be consciously thinking about it but those doubts are there, nibbling away at the edges of our minds.'

He flung out his hands as if to say, *There, what do you think of that?* and Fran had to smile.

In fact, she realised now she *usually* had to smile when she saw him, even when he was causing chaos in her body.

'Anyway,' he continued, 'we've done no sightseeing lately.' A wicked grin flashed across his face as he winked and added, 'Can't think why not!'

For someone who didn't blush she wasn't doing too badly at it since she'd come to Vanuatu. Fran just hoped he hadn't noticed, and waited for what was coming.

'So, this afternoon I'm taking you to the Blue Hole. Swimming costume and shoes that can get wet are the order of the day. The rocks around the water are mostly coral and very rough. It's fairly shaded but suntan lotion is a good idea. I'm happy to help with that.'

He came towards her as he finished speaking, took her hands and pulled her to her feet, looking deep into her eyes, his eyes saying things she didn't want to hear.

His arms enfolded her, holding her close, and when she finally relaxed into his arms, she leant against him and longed for this to be her place.

Eventually he moved, easing her away from his body so he could look into her face again.

'Okay?' he asked, and she nodded, then headed for her bedroom to get dressed for their outing.

It wasn't okay, Steve knew, as he too headed for his room to get organised. Her eyes had been shuttered against him, her thoughts and feelings hidden behind a blue-green wall.

* * *

At least the Blue Hole was magical enough to bring a smile to her face, her expressions of delight so genuine his heart began to hope again.

'It's actually a series of pools, the last of them opening to the ocean down that narrow end. You can't see it for the jungle but it means the water is a mix of salt and fresh.

She pulled off her shirt, revealing the pale body he was beginning to know so well, and handed him the sun lotion as if it was the most natural thing in the world.

He smoothed it onto her skin, making sure he covered all of it, wanting to protect her now, thoughts of sex far from his mind.

'I think I can manage the front,' she said, smiling at him as she turned and took the bottle from his hands.

Had his hands lingered too long on her smooth, straight back? On the swell of her hips, the narrowness of her waist, the delicate bones of her spine?

He'd been learning her in a different way, although he knew full well he didn't know her. Not in important ways! Didn't know much about her past—married and divorced, full stop—or what brought the shadows to her eyes, or what kept her from committing to him when they were back in Sydney.

She finished putting on the lotion and handed him the bottle.

'For all you've got to-die-for olive skin, you should put some on your face.'

And although he knew the fierce heat was gone from the sun, he did it because she'd suggested it.

'Last in's a wuss,' she said, diving neatly into the clear water.

He followed and came up beside her, pleased there were no tourist ships in port and that it was a weekday so they had the pool to themselves.

'Like it?' he asked, and was rewarded with a brilliant smile.

'Love it!' she said. 'It's the rainforest crowding all around it that make it special. And the jungle vines there, like the ones Tarzan swung on, so you can imagine him and Jane splashing around in here.'

She paused then added, 'Though if you do a "me Tarzan, you Jane" joke I'll probably hit you.'

It had been on the tip of his tongue but, duly warned, he shut his mouth, diving down to find one of the smooth pebbles that lay among the rougher coral rocks on the bottom of the hole.

He brought one up, pleased it was a pretty one, and handed it to her.

'A present?' she said. 'But it's lovely!'

Then somehow they were kissing, and soon doing more than kissing, their coming together almost cataclysmic in its intensity, so when he held her afterwards he knew his trembling was matching hers.

'We must be cold,' she said, with a pathetic attempt at a smile.

'We must be,' he agreed, then stopped further conversation with a long, deep and very satisfying kiss.

Fran eased away and swam, up and down the small part of the pool Steve had chosen, her mind in chaos.

She loved this man and was reasonably sure he might feel the same way about her, but how could she deny him the family he had wanted since he'd been ten years old?

She couldn't, and that was that.

Neither could she tell him about her failed attempts at IVF. He was such a positive man, there was never a glass half-empty for him. He'd want her to try again, urge her to, but the last failed attempt had almost broken her, and she knew, for certain, another one would do the same.

And then he'd walk away?

She couldn't blame him, knowing how important children were to him, but she'd had enough men walk away from her, with her father and then Nigel, and she knew just how much it hurt…

But if it succeeded?

Hope flared but common sense reminded her that what Steve wanted—needed—was a family, not another only child.

And she loved him too much to deny him that.

He was swimming beside her now, matching his strokes to hers.

Perfectly!

She stopped, feeling for the bottom, feeling also the pebble he'd given her pressed against her flesh in the bikini top.

And when he stopped, it was her turn to reach for him, to hold him in a close embrace and kiss him.

She had just one more week of kisses and she intended making the most of them.

CHAPTER EIGHT

OR DID SHE?

Steve had obviously decided not to wake her for a run so she woke in his bed—alone.

And remembered it was the first pregnancy testing day—the Reds.

The Inuis. She knew them, knew their names, had sat with them while Steve had extracted Mrs Inui's eggs.

And knew also they had a less than fifty percent chance of being pregnant.

She burrowed under the sheet, an ostrich hiding its head from the world.

But Steve expected her to be there for the test, wanted her to share the excitement.

Except it might not be excitement.

She clenched her teeth to stop a wail of fear and pain escaping from her lips then reminded herself she was a mature professional woman and this was just part of her job.

She didn't believe the words she told herself, but it was sufficient to get her out of bed, into the shower, then dressed for work.

Shirt and shorts—so prim and so boring!

So unlike the woman she'd become in three short weeks…

She poured some cereal for breakfast, added milk, then tipped it out, her stomach refusing to accept that she should eat.

This was idiotic, she had to positive!

It had worked for Mrs Inui's sister—there was a beautiful baby to prove it—and how many of the women she'd met at the clinic when she'd been going through IVF had produced babies?

Most of them.

Eventually…

She made for the bathroom, cleaned her teeth and tied up her hair, tucked the stone Steve had given her inside her trouser pocket, then with heavy steps and an even heavier heart she headed up to the lab. She'd check the purple dishes first.

But the thought of them made her close her eyes. If she had the power to ensure just one of their couples tested pregnant, it would be the Hopoates so their reign as Lords of Heaven and Canoes could continue.

Steve appeared as she was showing Arthur the healthy little embryo Steve would implant later in the day, and she wondered if the power of positive thinking would help this little group of cells grow into a royal heir or heiress.

Steve's appearance broke into her silent conversation with the dish so she slid it back into the incubator and, with already taut nerves tightening more, turned to look at him.

'Ready?' he asked, the smile on his face as radiant as the sun.

She stared at him. He *had* to have felt for the setbacks as his clients—the same disappointments when pregnancies failed—yet here he was, so positive she almost began to believe herself.

Hiding her turmoil of feelings, she agreed that she was ready and, leaving Arthur to man the lab, walked with the man she loved up to the clinic.

The Reds—Inuis—were already there, and from the lack of smiles on their faces and the droop to their shoulders Fran knew they'd used a test kit from a chemist to find out for themselves.

But Steve, though he must be used to seeing couples come in like this, refused to lose his cheerful smile, greeting them heartily and explaining that home tests weren't always accurate.

These days they are, Fran thought, but she didn't share it.

Alex handed Mrs Inui a small specimen jar and she dutifully retired, bringing it back and handing it to Steve.

He asked them both to sit down, then took the jar into the consulting room.

'I know I could test it in front of them but I feel this gives them more certainty,' he said to Fran, who had followed him in.

Or allows a little more time for hope to build again so they'd be twice disappointed, she thought, but didn't say, although her heart was sinking lower every moment.

When the test came back negative, all of her hopes disappeared to ash, leaving a bitter taste in her mouth and an ache in her heart.

But she said all the right words when Steve talked

to the Inuis, explaining how they could proceed after this, testing again in three days' time just to be sure.

Then he spoke of the alternatives if the later test didn't prove positive and this cycle didn't produce a pregnancy. Fran even joined in, telling them stories of friends who'd become pregnant on the second or third cycle of the treatment, giving them hope *she* hoped was realistic.

But after they left, Fran returned to the lab, asking Arthur if he would take the Purple embryo up to the rooms when the couple arrived.

'I know I should be there,' she said to him, 'but I feel a bit deflated and thought I'd walk it off.'

After warning her that it was really too hot to be walking, he let her be, so Fran was free to slip down to her room.

And pack!

In a state of cold numbness she phoned the airline office and accepted a seat on the late afternoon flight, then ordered a taxi to collect her mid-afternoon.

Steve would be busy then with the Hopoates.

The Hopoates!

She had their second embryo to freeze.

Arthur, she was sure, could do it, but somehow these people had become special to her and she wanted to be sure it was safely stored for them.

She hurried back up to the lab, aware that her behaviour was cowardly, but it was self-preservation more than anything else. Her heart just couldn't handle any more hurt.

She pulled out the purple dish and put it under the microscope, concentrating on the delicate task of preparing the precious embryo for freezing, thinking of the couple who might need it if the first one didn't fix itself to the uterine wall.

The pain that clutched her heart at *that* thought told her she was doing the right thing.

She knew these people, *and* she knew the pain of failure.

To go through that with them?

She just couldn't do it.

'Arthur told me you were going for a walk.'

She closed her eyes briefly at the sound of Steve's voice, finished what she was doing, then looked up at him, aware she owed him the truth.

'I'm sorry, Steve, really, really sorry, but I've just realised I can't stay for the rest of the pregnancy testing. I know that sounds pathetic, and I don't know how to explain it, but I just can't. I'm booked on the afternoon flight.'

He stepped towards her, reaching out to lift her unresisting hands in his, looking deep into her eyes, knowing they were welling with tears.

The eyes she loved were puzzled, a frown creasing his brow.

Would he guess?

Had she given herself away earlier?

She couldn't tell. She only knew that she couldn't put into words what she'd been through—not to Steve, maybe not to anyone.

'You've been through it yourself?' he asked gently, and she sighed.

Of course he'd guess, but the words wouldn't come.

'Tell me,' he insisted, and she managed a nod.

'Twice, three times?'

She nodded again, the lump in her throat too big for words.

'Oh, Francesca!'

He pulled her to her feet and gathered her into his arms, holding her against his body, so close she had to battle the feeling that this was where she belonged.

For ever.

Except it wasn't!

Couldn't be!

She eased away, tried for sensible, controlled, practical.

'I've got to finish this,' she said, returning to the microscope so she could manipulate the embryo into the straw.

But she couldn't get away from him so easily. He followed her over and rested his hand on her shoulder as she worked.

'Is this your reason for insisting this was just an affair? Because you feel you can't have children?'

Her back had stiffened at his touch but she had to bluff her way through.

'Not entirely,' she assured him. 'I know it might sound stupid, but I've got used to being single. I love my work, I've got friends when I need company, I've made a different kind of life.'

She finished what she was doing and stood up, forcing him to step back.

'It's all I want,' she said firmly, while what she really wanted to say was that, after her father and Nigel, she really didn't want another man walking away from her.

Disappointed in her.

Especially this man—it would break her heart.

Walking away from him, well, that was hurting

already—more painful than anything she'd ever experienced—but it was a different hurt.

Steve was studying her as if trying to read her thoughts, but she was surprised by his question.

'Would it have saved your marriage? Was that your reason for going through IVF?'

She slid the straw she'd been working on into the cane, checked the labelling and put it into the unit that would slowly take it down to the required temperature for storage. The machine did this automatically so, having set the final temperature, there was nothing more for her to do.

Except consider Steve's question, which had startled her, only now making her realise it was something she hadn't considered.

She looked into his eyes and swallowed the lump, answering honestly.

'I kept telling myself it would, but in truth I doubt it, and probably I knew it even as I put myself through those endless cycles and weeks of hope, then dashing disappointments.'

She thought about it now. Yes, she and Nigel might have stayed married, but what would have been the point?

Steve reached out and took hold of her hands again, turning her to face him.

'Tell me,' he said, and she shrugged her shoulders.

'Thinking about it now, bringing a child into my and Nigel's marriage would have been a mistake. Yes, *I* wanted a child, longed for a child, ached for a child, but looking back I know I was being selfish. A child would have made *my* life complete.'

She looked at Steve, looked deep into those dark eyes that saw too much.

'I suppose it would have filled the gap that Nigel's playing around had caused in my life.'

She gave a huff of laughter.

'How's that for a reason to have a child?'

Steve drew her close, held her, then kissed her gently on the forehead.

'Go, if you feel you have to,' he said quietly. 'I understand now. But can I call you when I get back?'

She tightened her grip on him—holding him one last time.

'No, Steve,' she said quietly. 'You know it was only ever going to be for here.'

'Because you can't have children? There's more to a marriage than children. More to life than family.'

She kissed him then, just lightly on the lips.

'You know full well you don't believe that, not for a moment.'

Another kiss.

And now she moved more forcefully away, kissed him a quick goodbye, and hurried back to her bedroom, his offer of a lift to the airport floating in the air behind her.

'You've got an appointment,' she called back, all business, 'and I've ordered a taxi.'

Steve made his way back up to the clinic, his mind in a turmoil. But trying to sort out his thoughts was impossible, mainly because what he felt most strongly was anger. It was happening again, a woman he loved walking away from him.

Loved?

That thought brought him up short.

Yes, loved…

And suddenly it seemed as if his whole life had been a series of losing loved ones—his parents, Sally, Liane, and now Fran.

Nonsense, his practical self muttered. People lost loved ones every day, and what's more he detested self-pity.

But this loss felt different, his whole body seeming to be affected by Fran's imminent departure.

Not that he had time to brood, or analyse it.

He'd see the Hopoates and think about it later.

CHAPTER NINE

'YOU'RE NOT SUPPOSED to be back yet,' Andy said, coming upon Fran in the lab three days after she'd returned.

She'd actually spoken to him on her first day back, answering a question about a patient's frozen embryos, but it obviously hadn't clicked with him then that she'd been away.

'Did everything work out all right?' he was asking anxiously. 'You got on well with Steve? Got the job done?'

Fran had to smile at her absent-minded but still very caring employer.

'Got the job done,' she said, ignoring his other questions, though the pain in her heart reminded her just how well she'd got on with Steve. 'I'm back a little early because I wasn't needed for that last week of pregnancy testing.'

He nodded and touched her briefly on the arm, saying more about his understanding with that touch than a hundred words would have said.

'Well, good to have you back anyway,' he said. 'I want to take some immature eggs from a woman who's coming in this afternoon and I really would rather trust them to you than to one of the others, good though they might be.'

'Well, I'm here and happy to look after them,' she told him, and won a warm smile.

'I'm glad you're back too,' Mike, her second in command said when Andy had wandered off. 'I know what to do and how to do it, but the one lot of IVM eggs I've looked after while you were away didn't look nearly as healthy as the ones you've cared for.'

He smiled at her.

'Must be the woman's touch, you make a more natural clucky hen.'

The description took her right back to Vanuatu and the Hopoates, and for all she didn't want to hear about the failures of the couples she'd met, she did hope that the Lords of the Heavens and Canoes had success.

She realised that her face must have revealed her thoughts when Mike asked, 'You're back there, aren't you? Back in the islands? You liked it?'

She smiled, remembering the sheer joy of waking up in that tropical paradise, the beauty, the lush plant growth—Steve—then shook her head.

'Not liked but loved it,' she admitted. 'The place, the people, the beauty—there was a lot to love.'

'Yet you came back early?'

'Not you, too,' she said. 'I've just had Andy on about that. I wasn't needed, okay?'

The snap in her words had Mike shrugging and holding up his hands in an 'I surrender' gesture.

'I only asked,' he muttered as he walked away.

Fran sighed.

She'd told herself that once she'd settled back into work everything would be okay. Her three weeks in the islands would be locked away in a deep compartment of her mind, the door only to be opened now and then so she could relive the happy memories.

But that door wouldn't be opened for a while.

Not until the rawness of leaving Steve had healed and she could remember all the good parts without pain.

Would that day ever come?

'Fran?'

She looked up to see one of the juniors standing in front of her, a specimen dish in her hand. She'd obviously asked a question.

'Sorry, miles away,' she said. 'What was it you wanted?'

So it was back to work and no more dwelling on the past. She'd managed to get through three failed IVF cycles, Clarissa and a divorce, by concentrating on work. She'd get through this as well.

Only getting through this was harder, she realised a couple of weeks later, when the sight of a hibiscus flower on a bush near her apartment sent pain coiling through her body again.

It was because she wasn't feeling well that it was so hard, she told herself. Give it time…

A week later she was wondering just how much time she'd have to give it. And how could she get over it, when every day the rebellious part of her brain reminded her of how long Steve would have been back in Australia, even suggesting she check up on where he lived and driving by there.

No way—that was just too pathetic!

Could he have called?

She'd told him not to…

It was the weather, still miserable and rainy, and her feeling a bit off. Could lovesickness really exist?

Whatever it was, it stayed with her, until ten days later she sat in the bathroom at her apartment, staring in disbelief at the positive pregnancy test in her hand.

'Honestly!' she said at her image in the mirror. 'Call yourself a scientist! How could you not have thought of this earlier?'

Because of all the failures, came the whispered answer.

Or because her gynaecologist had told her quite bluntly, after the third cycle had failed to produce viable eggs, that she had only a few of her life's allotment of eggs left in her ovaries and would probably go through early menopause as a result.

But that was the end of rational thought for quite some time, as her brain whirled with ifs and buts and maybes, delighted excitement mixing with doubt and dread.

Not to mention confusion…

To tell or not to tell was the really big one.

Normally it would be a no-brainer. A man deserved to know he'd be a father, that he'd have a child.

But with Steve?

Steve, who didn't want just one child, he wanted a family—lots of children—well, more than one anyway.

Not that one child couldn't be a family, but not for Steve, not for someone with parents who had so wanted a sibling for him they'd been killed in the endeavour.

If she told him, he would insist they marry and for all the surge of heat that thought generated in her body, *and* the hippity-hoppity bounds of joy in the totally unrealistic bit of her brain, marrying Steve would not be a good thing.

This one pregnancy was probably a fluke—so unlikely she'd never given contraception a thought, though she vaguely remembered in the heat of passion that first night Steve asking and her assuring him it was safe.

Because it always had been in the past.

And apart from the fact that she'd be denying him the large family he wanted, marrying her for the sake of the baby was hardly a good basis for a marriage. What would happen if she lost the baby? Or even if the baby lived but their marriage lacked love?

Would he walk away from her, as her father and Nigel had done?

She made a cup of tea then tipped it out because it tasted awful. Everything tasted awful! She'd have to tell him.

Or leave Sydney?

That was a better idea…

Get a job somewhere else—Perth maybe, or in the UK. Her skills would always be needed. Overseas would be better, less likely that Andy would find out, because Andy and Steve were friends…

The glass of water tasted awful but she drank it anyway, then began to occupy her mind with things other than Steve and telling or not telling. Determined to treat this in a purely practical manner, she sat down and wrote a shopping list of healthy foods, lots of fruit and vegetables and meat for iron, although she could supplement that.

Which was when the sheer miraculousness of what had happened struck her and she laughed with joy and hugged herself and forgot about all the unanswerable questions and went shopping.

Steve had told himself he would wait at least a month after he got home before he would even consider phoning Fran, but the days dragged by so slowly it was beginning to feel like a year since he'd seen her.

He'd thought of a dozen excuses he could use to call in at her hospital's IVF clinic, and had discarded all of them.

He'd lifted the phone to call Andy to assure himself she was all right, and put the receiver down again.

At work, by forcing himself to concentrate on his clients and the huge step they were taking, he could forget for a while. Then someone would say something and he'd be back in the lab at Vanuatu, Fran in shorts and lab coat, her lovely hair hidden by an incredibly ugly cap, and his heart would miss a beat then gallop to catch up and he'd have to breathe slowly and deeply to banish the picture from his mind.

But at home, particularly now with the bloody hibiscus bushes planted by his great-grandfather flowering with gay abandon in his garden, it was impossible not to think about her.

He had to see her—had to talk to her—at least find out if she was all right.

But why wouldn't she be?

He'd begun to hate his sensible self.

So he concocted a plan, phoning Andy for her address, explaining that she'd left before the staff could give her a farewell gift, a thank-you for her help. He told Andy that he'd post it to her.

Steve had half expected Andy to suggest he send it

to the hospital, in which case he'd just have to visit the place and try to talk to her in front of colleagues.

But Andy had surprised him, not only handing over the address but also by suggesting that he might like to deliver it in person. Andy was sure Fran would be pleased to see him.

Steve turned the idea over in his head. He wasn't so sure about the pleased to see him part—but, hang it all, what could she do?

Or what could her boyfriend do if he opened the door to Steve?

No, she didn't have a boyfriend, of that Steve was certain. She'd given herself too openly and fully to have been cheating on someone.

And the staff *had* given him a present for her, a frangipani lei with 'Come back to Vanuatu' written on the tag, and a pretty sarong that would complement her eyes.

He drove to the address, pleased to find she lived in a small apartment block so he didn't have to press a bell and announce his presence to get into the building.

She could have checked the monitor and chosen not answer her door.

He found a parking space for the car two doors away and walked back, apprehension so tight in his chest he had to force himself to breathe.

Then, there she was, bent over the boot of a small red car in the carport beneath the building, pulling shopping bags out and resting them on the ground while she got the others.

'Bought the shop out?' he asked, coming up beside her and bending to pick up six of the bags, three in each hand.

She turned and looked at him, and he watched the blood drain from her face.

He dropped the shopping bags in time to catch her, although she recovered almost immediately and pushed away from him.

'What are you doing here, frightening the life out of me?' she demanded, blue-green eyes spitting fire.

'I brought a gift from the staff,' he muttered, bending to capture oranges that were rolling from one of the dropped bags.

'Then you can leave it here and go,' she said, and though she probably wanted to sound firm he heard the slight wobble in her voice.

'I'll carry these things up to your apartment first,' he said—no wobble in *his* firmness.

She didn't answer, instead collecting the last two bags and closing the boot, locking the car with a key fob and stomping away towards the steps that led into the old Art Deco building, then up the inner steps, and up, and up, and up.

'You were going to carry all of this up yourself?' he asked, stopping on the second floor landing to catch his breath.

'I do it every week,' she snapped. 'And for someone who runs every day, you're not doing too well on the climb.'

She'd reached the top floor and was unlocking the door when he caught up.

'You can just leave them at the door,' she said, busying herself hanging up the keys to avoid looking at him.

'I'll bring them in,' Steve told her, aware she wanted nothing more than for him to go. But being here, with her again, seeing her, even from behind, had filled him with such happiness he couldn't walk away.

He walked into the apartment and although he'd guessed from the address that she'd have a view towards the harbour, he was surprised to find he could pick out his house from her windows.

Not that he'd mention it right now.

Neither would he mention seeing the sarong he'd given her thrown over the sofa or the pebble from the Blue Hole on the window ledge.

He put the bags on the kitchen bench alongside the ones she'd carried up, then reached out and caught her hand.

'Can we not just meet as friends, if only this once?' he asked, although every cell in his being was scoffing at the idea they might just be 'friends'.

She looked at him then, studying his face as if she'd never seen it before—or maybe trying to read what lay behind his words.

'I don't think so,' she said quietly, then she removed her hand from his and began to unpack the bags.

She hadn't told him to leave so he didn't, instead watching her unpack the first bag, and then, intrigued, he began peering into the others.

'Have you turned vegetarian?' he asked, registering they contained only fruit and vegetables.

'I only shop once a week,' came the reply, which didn't answer the question or explain the extent of the fruit and vegetable shopping.

Deciding it was too hard to carry on a conversation with someone whose head was stuck in the refrigerator as she disposed of the shopping, he looked around and saw the list she must have been working off—items neatly crossed off.

Of course neatly—this was Fran!

Oranges, apples, celery, tomatoes, on and on until right at the end an item not crossed off—an item not available at the markets or greengrocer.

Iron supplement.

And suddenly the shopping and the sudden faint and her avoidance of his eyes made sense.

'You're pregnant!' he said, waving the list in her face when she stood to get more produce to stack away. 'And just when were you going to tell me?'

Fran could feel the anger coming off him in waves, and suddenly the answer to her 'will I, won't I' questions became clear.

'I was still deciding but I think probably I wasn't going to tell you,' she answered honestly, because she couldn't lie to Steve.

'You weren't going to tell me? And just how was that going to play out? You'd swear Andy to secrecy? Have everyone in the relatively small world of IVF know except the father?'

He had every right to be angry, but she, too, had rights.

'I'm going away,' she said. 'No one will know. Especially not Andy.'

'Especially not Andy because he would tell me?' Steve roared, and Fran took a step back, although she knew full well he wouldn't—couldn't—harm her.

Her or anyone else...

But his being so angry made it all easier somehow.

And now he knew, well, she didn't have to consider the problem of telling him.

Or not!

He was stalking around her living room now, muttering to himself, obviously trying to calm down before he spoke again.

Please let him not be nice to me, she asked any of the fates who might be listening.

It didn't work, for here he was, standing across the bench from her, not touching her, although every fibre of her being was so aware of him they might as well have been touching.

'Fran, I shouldn't have yelled, but can you please explain why, when you knew how much I wanted children, you were going to keep this child to yourself?'

He was holding himself together with difficulty, she could see that, but although she knew it would upset him all over again, she had to answer.

She looked into his lovely eyes and answered honestly.

'You want children, Steve, plural, not a one-off fluke of a child. If I'd told you, you'd have insisted on marrying me, and knowing my medical history you'd be stuck with the one thing you didn't want, which was another only child.'

She reached out now, wanting—no, needing—to touch him, and rested her hand on his where it lay on the bench.

'I couldn't do that to you, couldn't ruin the goal you've strived for all your life. It's all hypothetical now, I may not even carry this child to term. Just let me be, Steve. I said right from the start it would be nothing more than a short affair, a holiday romance. I *said* it couldn't last. So go and get on with your own life. Find the woman to have your family with, the woman to be mother to your children.'

Steve shook his head.

This was madness!

But she was right, he had to go now—had to get away so he could think about things, think clearly, something he was incapable of doing with Fran standing there, still pale but so beautiful his heart ached for what he'd lost.

Although, he thought as he walked back down the endless steps, she was right in saying she'd told him all along it wouldn't last, so how could he lose something he'd never had?

How the hell could she compartmentalise so well that those three weeks were already filed away under 'holiday romance' in her brain?

Well, she wouldn't be able to do that in the future, with his child there to remind her every day.

His child!

Rage roared through him again but he couldn't let it take control. He had to think, logically and sensibly, about how to handle this.

She couldn't—and she undoubtedly knew it—keep him from seeing his child and having input into the child's life.

Oh, hell! He didn't have a clue how to think about this, not even where to begin. All he did know was that having input into the child's life was a long way down the track.

And would never be enough.

He walked back to his car and drove home—home to the big house that had so called out for children that his parents had flown to the US for advanced IVF so he could have a sibling.

And had died before they'd got there.

As Steve disappeared out the door, Fran sank down on the floor and buried her face in her hands.

Steve was upset, and with reason!

If only she'd had time to think things through—*more* time.

Right now she was such a jumble of emotions there was no way she could think straight.

Although the one thing she did know was that she'd upset Steve—hurt him badly with her flippant 'wasn't going to tell you' remark.

That would have cut deep.

She shouldn't have said it, shouldn't have pretended she'd already made the decision.

Unable to think, she closed her eyes and hugged her knees and gave in to the memories of just seeing him again.

Tall, tanned, so strong when he'd caught her in his arms...

And how feeble had *that* been on her part!

She hugged her knees harder, protecting the secret in her heart—the knowledge of just how deep her love for him really was.

But love was generous, and kind, which meant that she had to leave him free to live the life he wanted, the life he'd planned and worked towards since he was ten.

Which meant the sooner she got out of the way the better.

Full of new resolve, she stood up and finished unpacking her purchases, crumpling up the note with the iron supplement on it—the note that had given away her secret.

She'd get onto the computer and look for jobs.

Would they need embryologists in Antarctica? Or Kazakhstan perhaps?

Impossible—she'd have the child.

And *that* refocused her thoughts, pleasing her so much she patted her as yet undistended belly and got down to sensible work.

Steve got through the weekend somehow, waking early on Monday morning and heading into his clinic to check all was well.

One of his colleagues met him when he was reading through the latest success rates—quite good as they were up about one per cent.

'I'd like some advice about a patient,' James told him. 'She's had two full cycles of IVF and two implants of embryos that had been frozen, all with no success. But this last cycle, the follicles failed to respond to stimuli and we were unable to get any eggs. Should we give her a longer break before the next cycle or is it likely that she just doesn't have any more eggs and will probably go into early menopause?'

It was as if a light bulb had suddenly lit up in Steve's brain, but right now he had to turn it off and work through the problem with his employee.

'Maybe discuss having a break—not long, perhaps a month to get her body back into normal cycles—then shall we see if we can get some immature eggs and use them for IVM?'

James grinned at him.

'Now, why didn't I think of that?'

'Because it's very new and we haven't done it here as yet, but on this last trip to Vanuatu we did successfully grow the eggs to maturity and ended up with two embryos, one implanted and one frozen for future use.'

'So, we'll do this? Do we need a specialist embryologist for the eggs? You'll help me with the retrieval?'

Steve smiled at his young colleague's excitement.

'Yes, and yes, and yes,' he said. 'I know just the embryologist and am reasonably sure I can borrow her for a week or so while the eggs mature.'

'Great!'

James positively bounded out of the room, while Steve picked up the phone and called Andy.

'I know I'm begging again but the only IVM I've done so far was on Vanuatu, with Fran to nurture the immature eggs. I'd only need her for a few days—a week at most, not for a month.'

'I'm sure she'd be delighted,' Andy told him. 'We should all be trading staff when different skills are needed, it's how the younger ones can learn.'

Steve promised to let Andy know at least a week ahead and hung up the phone with a feeling of great satisfaction.

So, back to the light bulb...

He thought back to the island but couldn't remember just when the particular conversation had come up. What he *did* remember was Fran coming to ask him about the other couple—the one where the wife hadn't responded to the treatment and had no eggs ready for retrieval.

He'd been struck at the time by a shadow passing over Fran's face—a look of such sorrow he'd wanted to hug her, but there must have been others around, or maybe she'd left suddenly, not wanting him to see her sadness.

Had she suffered a similar problem on that third cycle of IVF, and had *her* gynaecologist suggested a lack of eggs and early menopause?

That would explain her determination to not marry him, her peculiar argument that he wanted children, plural, not just one child.

She'd be seeing this child as a miracle, conceived when one last egg had emerged and met his sperm.

And she'd *ached* for a child—she'd said that one day.

It wasn't that she didn't love him but because she *did* love him, and loving him wanted him to have his family.

Daft woman…

'You're lending me to him again!'

Fran couldn't recall ever having yelled at Andy, but yell she did. Not that it did anything to flutter his normal calm complacency.

'It's only for a few days to help the eggs mature. He's not done IVM at his clinic in Alexandria, so hasn't anyone with experience in maturing the eggs. He said you did splendidly in Vanuatu, and you can show other lab workers exactly what you do.'

This completely rational statement left Fran speechless. She should have done more about finding another job, but for all she might wish she *was* in Timbuktu, deep inside she quivered at the thought of being so far away—in truth, so far from Steve.

Stupid, really.

What she had to worry about now was acting normally in his clinic, concentrating on the eggs and on showing his lab staff how she worked.

With him close by?

It would take some fortitude but she would do it and do it well. The couple whose eggs she was caring for deserved nothing but her best effort.

Which was all very well in theory but when she walked into the clinic, looking around at this place Steve had set up, meeting nursing staff, admin people, partners, and finally lab staff, her knees were like jelly and her stomach bunched so tightly she hoped the tiny life inside her wasn't being affected by it.

He was there to greet her, of course, and it was he who introduced her around, his body so close it took all her strength not to lean in to it, or to brush her arm against his or let their fingers touch.

And he was there again at the end of the day, when the other lab staff had left and she was sitting at a bench, writing up a list of nutrients her little eggs would need.

'I love you, Fran,' he said, the words so unexpected she nearly fell off her stool.

He came closer, close enough to touch but not touching.

'And I think you love me.'

She looked at him then, looked into eyes that were echoing his words.

'And I think this stupid nonsense about not marrying me is all to do with children, right?'

She didn't answer, couldn't—couldn't deny, and couldn't confirm.

'Love is about making the loved one happy. It is generous—and giving—and that's you to a T. You're rejecting me because you think I need a woman who can give me children—as many children as I want—

but how fair would it be to marry that woman when I couldn't offer her love?'

'Of course you could offer her love. What we had— it was madness—and its intensity led us—you—to believe it was love.'

He smiled.

'Gave yourself away there with the "us",' he teased, and she thought her heart would break.

'Okay, us,' she conceded. 'But does love like that last? And can't people, over a lifetime, love more than once? I loved Nigel, loved him deeply when we married. Yet now I haven't one iota of feeling for him.'

She paused, then added, 'Though in all honesty he went out of his way to kill that love so perhaps that doesn't count.'

Steve laughed, and shook his head.

'And that's just one of the things I love about you,' he said.

'What?' Fran demanded, unable to see anything funny in this conversation and still uncertain as to where it was leading.

'That you *are* honest. You might fumble about a bit from time to time, but usually the truth comes bursting out. You could have denied you were pregnant until you'd thought a bit more about it, but you couldn't. So...'

He stepped closer so he was right across the bench from her, then continued, 'Are you refusing to marry me because you think you can't produce the children I want? Or have you taken your wild imagination another step to where I might walk away from you because of that?'

Fran stared at him. He was right, she couldn't lie— not easily.

But to tell the truth?

He'd walked around the bench and stood close enough for her to touch him, touch his hand, his face, but he touched her first, resting one hand against her cheek.

'Fran?' he prompted, and as emotion overwhelmed her she could only nod.

Then he was kissing her, telling her how stupid she had been, as if the love they shared could be dismissed, no matter how practical the reasons.

And her heart opened to his words so she could tell him of *her* love, although as they stopped for air she looked up into his face and asked, 'But the children?'

He smiled and kissed the tip of her nose.

'Let's just see what nature will provide and if this one turns out to be an only child then we do what Pop and Hallie did and take in kids in need of two very loving parents. Would that work for you?'

She shook her head, but this time in wonder, then nodded in answer to his question, which led to another kiss then a suggestion that they go home.

'My place is nearer,' Steve said.

CHAPTER TEN

ONCE SHE GOT over the astonishment that 'his place' was a mansion right on the shores of Sydney Harbour, and the initial doubts that she could live in a place like this, Fran gave in to the joy, and delight, and excitement, that came with being in love.

They walked hand in hand around the garden, looking out at the magnificent view, east towards the Heads and west towards the Opera House. Steve plucked one of the hibiscus flowers from bushes that ran rampant in the garden, and settled it securely behind her left ear, with a kiss and a murmured, 'Mine!'

'It's huge,' Fran said of the house, uncertain about his wealth now, uncertain she belonged.

'Don't give it a thought,' he assured her. 'I had an apartment in town for a long time, but after Liane died, it had too many memories for me so I sold it. And, anyway, now the people I see as my family are growing up, it's good to have the space for them to come and stay. Liane's daughter Nikki will be down in the Christmas holidays—she's doing very junior work experience at the university, wants to be a scientist.'

'Not that you have to worry about the size of the house or visitors,' Steve hurried on to explain. 'I just use the bottom floor. It used to be servants' quarters but it's got the great views as well. And I've a live-in housekeeper, Molly, who takes care of the upstairs, visitors and all.'

Fran heard the words but could barely take them in, and looking at the house—mansion—she knew it should be filled with children and doubts assailed her once again.

'Stop it,' Steve said, picking up on her uncertainties. 'It's just a house and if you hate it, then we'll move.'

He took her in his arms and kissed her, long and hard, and, in kissing him back she released all the emotion that had been building since she'd left the island. So it wasn't surprising when he whispered, 'Maybe indoors?' and led her up onto a patio, and through French doors leading into an area that must have been either extensively renovated or had been very luxurious servants' quarters.

And again doubts assailed her.

'I don't think I'm up to this,' she whispered. 'I don't belong in a place like this.'

Steve eased her away from his body so he could see her face.

'You mean a home? That's all this is, Fran, my home. Our family's home! And if the family grows as we would like it to, then we'll banish the guests down here and we'll shift upstairs to fit them all in. Did I tell you Pop and Hallie's home was an old nunnery? It's how they managed to house so many waifs and strays. Can't we do that?'

She read the excitement in his eyes and realised it was echoed deep within her.

'Yes, I'd like that,' she said, already thinking of a

young girl in her apartment block whose abusive step-father was making her life miserable. Yes, there'd be laws to protect the children and hoops to be jumped through, and her own baby to consider, but, yes, the idea of being able to build a special family was truly wonderful.

They flew to Braxton the following Friday, to be met by a tall, charming, blond and blue-eyed man who greeted Steve with a bow.

'Sir Stephen,' he said, then enveloped Steve in a warm hug.

'And this is Francesca? My, Steve, she's a vast improvement on that woman you thought you were going to marry.'

He took Fran's hand and kissed her fingers.

'Welcome to the madness,' he said with a smile that could probably charm the kookaburras she could hear down from their trees.

'Just ignore him,' Steve was saying. 'If it wasn't for the fact that he can give us a lift home in his little helicopter, I wouldn't have told him we were coming.'

'Liar!' Marty responded. 'There's not one of us that wouldn't turn up to meet the woman Steve's going to marry. Well, none of us that were all here at the same time. If everyone turned up we'd have to hire the village hall.'

Grabbing Fran's bag, he led the way back out of the building and across the tarmac to where a little helicopter stood.

'Mad about choppers,' Steve said to Fran. 'Women, too!' he added, and Marty laughed.

'He's actually a paramedic but now flies the rescue

helicopter out of Braxton. It's doubly useful to have
a pilot with advanced paramedic experience.' Steve
paused, turning to Marty. 'Which reminds me, Marty,
a woman I know, Emma Crawford, is coming up to
work at Braxton A and E. You'll probably run into her
some time.'

'You let him know other women?' Marty teased as
they climbed into the little vehicle, Marty insisting Fran
sit up front so she could see the view so Steve was
crowded with the bags in the back.

'What's this Sir Stephen thing?' she asked Marty,
who grinned in response while Steve gave her a stern
order to just look at the view.

Which was spectacular! They rose first over a fairly
large town, then thick rainforest, until the coast appeared, the dark blue ocean spreading out to the horizon, bordering headlands and curves of sandy bays.

'It's beautiful,' Fran said, and both the men agreed,
something in their voices telling her it was also very
special.

Then they were swooping low towards a small town
set beside a golden arc of sand.

'Wetherby,' the two men chorused, and again their
voices told her it was special.

She knew why Steve had been here, but Marty?

She could find out later, because now they had
banked over a large, grim-looking building and were
settling down onto a flat mown paddock behind it.

'The Nunnery!' Marty announced, waving his hand
towards the building. 'And the garden between it and
us is where we poor foster children slaved endlessly.'

'In between the beatings,' Steve put in, and both
men laughed.

Clambering out wasn't quite as easy as getting in and by the time they were all out, with the luggage, a tall, plump woman was bustling towards them.

'Hallie!' Steve cried, lifting her in his arms and swinging her around.

'Put me down, I've told you not to do that!' she said, though obviously no one took any notice for now Marty was swinging her around too.

Back on her feet and looking only slightly flustered, she came towards Fran.

'My dear, I cannot tell you how happy I am that Stephen has finally met the woman of his dreams.'

And with that she enveloped Fran in a warm hug.

'Now, we'll ignore those two idiots, they'll have a lot to catch up on, just come inside and tell me all about yourself.'

She took Fran's arm and led her through the burgeoning garden to a much-used back door.

'We practically live in the kitchen,' she explained, 'although these days most of the time it's only me and Pop. Plenty of the children who lived here come back, but the time Marty and Steve were here was special as there were a number of them about the same age, so they really bonded. You'll meet Izzy later, she's coming to dinner with Nikki, who was Liane's daughter.'

The chatter stopped rather abruptly and Hallie studied Fran for a moment.

'Has Steve spoken to you of Liane?'

Fran nodded.

'He told me how troubled she was—broken, I think he said—and how he'd always loved her. Then how she'd got back on drugs and died after her daughter was born.'

'That daughter is our Nikki! Well, Izzy and Mac's Nikki really but…we like to think of her as a little bit ours.'

Hallie said the name as if, of all the children who'd passed through her hands, Nikki was special to her.

Fran thought back, then remembered Nikki had been a drug-addicted baby and all the care in rearing her that that would have entailed. Izzy would have needed help and no doubt that help would have come from Hallie.

No wonder Nikki was special!

'And your own family?' Hallie asked.

Fran smiled.

'Just a mother and she's climbing mountains in South America at the moment, although I did manage to catch her in a place where there was network coverage a few days ago and tell her about Steve.'

'Climbing mountains in South America?' Hallie echoed, and Fran's smile grew wider.

'That's how I felt when she first announced her plan. My father left us when I was young and Mum did all she could to make sure I got a good education. She worked two jobs and scrimped and saved so I could go to private school because I was interested in science and she felt I'd get better science teachers in a private school.'

She paused, thinking how much more she understood about her mother now—because she was pregnant?

She didn't know, but as she talked to Hallie about the woman who had always preached restraint, who had written up weekly timetables for study, meals and chores, and to whom good manners were more important than a degree, she began to understand her mother.

'I think she put so much into my life, to ensure I had

a good job, a safe marriage, a happy family, that she did nothing for herself.'

She paused, wondering how to put her mother into words.

'She was devastated when my first marriage broke down, but when I talked to her about it, told her it was better to be without a man than to be tied to someone who no longer loved me, she not only understood but she saw *her* life in a different light. She threw in her job and went travelling, mostly in mountainous areas, insisting you see things more clearly in mountain air.'

Hallie laughed.

'I don't do mountains but I often climb up onto the roof here—it's flat and quite safe—to think about things.'

The men came in, obviously in search of the tea she and Hallie had failed to make.

'Not to worry,' Marty said. 'We boys will do it.'

He turned to Fran.

'You'll find he's been totally domesticated so don't spoil it by waiting on him hand and foot.'

The man they all called Pop came in as they were demolishing a freshly baked sponge cake.

He greeted Fran warmly, then congratulated her.

'I've had some good lads come through here—even count that bloke Marty among them—but Steve's special so you be good to him.'

'Or you'll go down and bash her up?' Marty teased.

And although Pop smiled, he nodded towards Fran.

'I'm quite sure Fran knows what I mean.'

It was her turn to nod. It wasn't anything she could put into words but deep down she knew the words were true. Steve *was* special.

* * *

After a riotous dinner during which she'd somehow promised Nikki she could be a bridesmaid at her wedding, assured Izzy that of course she'd take care of Steve and had admitted, under Mac's acute questioning that, yes, she was pregnant, she and Steve were able to escape upstairs.

'Not to my old bedroom,' he explained to her as he led her along a corridor. 'This is a little flat that Pop made for Izzy when she and Nikki came home from Sydney. They use it for visitors now those two are living with Mac in the old doctor's house.'

He led her into the tiny living room, closed the door, and put his arms around her.

'Are you okay?' he asked, running his fingers through her hair and massaging her shoulders. 'It's been a big day and they're all mad, that lot.'

But Fran heard the love he felt for every one of them.

'Very okay,' she told him, nestling closer.

He showed her the main bedroom and bathroom, then helpfully stripped off her clothes, all the while telling her of his love, so in the end they left the shower until later, needing only to be together in the best possible way.

It wasn't until they were finally in bed that she was able to repeat the question she'd asked earlier.

'Why Sir Stephen?'

He laughed and pulled her close, so her head rested on his shoulder.

'I had the two grandparents as you know, one from each side of the family. I imagine, as they lived next door to each other and both of them had housekeepers and gardeners, gossip travelled fairly swiftly between the two houses. So, my grandmother would send me a cricket set at the beginning of summer, and within days my grandfather would send a better one. I think we eventually had enough sets to kit out an entire team.'

'Did they compete at birthdays and Christmas as well?' Fran asked, smiling at the thought of the orphan boy receiving all these gifts.

'Of course—stupendous gifts just kept arriving, so many I could share them around all the kids.'

'Ah,' Fran murmured, 'hence Sir Stephen—the noble knight dispensing gifts!'

Steve chuckled and held her closer, because for some reason, now he was back in the place that had become his true home, she felt more truly his.

'Want a run?' he asked when she opened bleary eyes next morning. 'Please,' he added, 'it's a special run.'

She was out of bed within minutes, showering and pulling on a T-shirt and shorts then light sneakers and joining him as he led the way out of the still sleeping house.

He pointed out the hospital on the way down towards the beach, and the old colonial house where Izzy and Mac lived with Nikki, then they were on the coastal path.

'We've all run it at different times—in fact, Izzy met Mac on it—but you must admit it's special.'

He looked at the woman he loved, wanting her to see the beauty of the place he loved.

'Very special,' she assured him, and it took all his strength of character not to kiss her there and then, because he knew he'd probably have followed the kiss by dragging her into the sand dunes.

So they ran, slowly, to take in the beauty of the craggy headlands and the curving bays, the wind-bent casuarinas and crashing waves that broke against the cliffs.

They stopped at a fresh water tap, there to serve people walking the coastal path, which stretched for miles along this part of the coast.

They drank freely then stood up, looking out at the little curve of golden sand, the surf rolling in gently, the smell of the ocean drawn deep into their lungs.

Side by side in this beautiful place, arms around each other's waists, Steve could only think that this must be perfection.

'I love you, Francesca Hawthorne,' Steve said, taking her hand and lifting it to his lips to drop a kiss into her palm then close her fingers around it.

'And I you,' she said, then gave him a kiss to hold in *his* palm.

Which, Steve decided as they came back into Wetherby, must have made them both look quite demented, striding along, each with one hand closed firmly on a kiss...

EPILOGUE

It was late summer when the family gathered for the wedding, a bright, cool day with a light breeze whipping up a few cheeky wavelets on the harbour.

Fran's mother had arrived two days earlier, and it seemed to Fran they'd hardly stopped talking since she'd landed at the airport. They'd talked of her mother's marriage and Fran's childhood, remembering, laughing and sometimes crying.

With her mother's help, Fran slid into the light summer dress she'd chosen for her wedding. Cream, with a scattering of bright red flowers, not hibiscus but close enough to have reminded her of the island.

'Do you like it?' she asked, arms held out as she twirled in front of her mother, the soft silk of the material swirling from a band beneath her bust.

'Love it,' her mother said. 'And so will Steve when he sees that neckline!'

Immediately wary, Fran lifted her hands to cover the hint of depth between her breasts, and her mother laughed.

'It's wonderful,' she assured Fran. 'I was only teasing you. Now, you're sure about this?'

Fran looked into her mother's eyes.

'More sure than I've ever been of anything in my life. I love him, Mum, more than I had ever imagined loving anyone.'

'And Nigel?'

Fran grinned. 'Who's Nigel?'

And they both laughed, but the conversation brought them to the subject of love.

'We've both loved badly,' her mother said softly, 'but seeing you with Steve I know how right this marriage is. Don't ever be afraid to give freely of your love. I didn't know that when I married. I was brought up to not show emotion and I probably taught you that as well, but love is so precious you have to nurture it so it flourishes in every corner of your life for ever.'

A light tap at the door, and as her mother hurried to open it, Fran looked out over the harbour, sparkling in the sunshine, the ferries like toy boats a child might play with in the bath.

She patted her stomach then rested her hand on the bulge, thinking of this child in the bath with boats.

Or on a boat going over to the Zoo, perhaps growing up to be a doctor…

Or not, it didn't matter, for not only was this the child she'd never thought to have, but it was Steve's child and doubly precious for that!

Nikki arrived, looking stunning in red, her dress the same design as Fran's and, in Nikki's opinion, *very* grown-up!

'Oh, you look fabulous!' she said, and the expression on her face told Fran she meant it.

'And so do you,' Fran told her, 'but what's the box?'

'Oh, I forgot! Steve said to give it to you.'

She handed Fran a clear plastic box. Nestled inside it was a brilliant red hibiscus.

Opening the box, Fran saw the note.

'Which ear?' Steve had written, and Fran laughed. She lifted the flower, and going to the mirror settled it behind her left ear.

'Definitely taken,' she said, smiling at her mother and Nikki, who both shook their heads at the strange wedding headdress.

'It's time,' her mother said. 'You really want to do this?'

Fran could only smile, but she kissed her mother and gave her a tight hug, blinking back tears as her mother took her hand to lead her and Nikki down the stairs and out through the garden to a gazebo at the edge of the property, where, with friends and family around them, and the harbour sparkling behind them, they promised to love and honour each other for the rest of their lives.

The guests drifted back to the terrace where drinks and food was being served,

But Steve held Fran's hand and looked out over the beautiful view.

'I love you, Francesca Louise Ransome,' he said softly, 'with all my heart and mind and body.'

Then he drew her close—or as close as her belly allowed—and kissed her, ignoring the wolf whistles from his family on the terrace behind them.

* * * * *

STOLEN KISSES
WITH HER BOSS

BY
SUSAN CARLISLE

MILLS
BOON

Published in Great Britain 2017
By Mills & Boon, an imprint of HarperCollins*Publishers*
1 London Bridge Street, London, SE1 9GF

© 2017 Susan Carlisle

ISBN: 978-0-263-92660-6

Our policy is to use papers that are natural, renewable and recyclable
products and made from wood grown in sustainable forests. The logging
and manufacturing processes conform to the legal environmental
regulations of the country of origin.

Printed and bound in Spain
by CPI, Barcelona

Dear Reader,

For me, family is what it's all about. My husband, children and grandchildren mean everything to me. But I also know that sometimes I can get so caught up in them I lose sight of myself and others. That's just what happens to Cynthia in this book. She almost misses out on the love of her life, Sean, because she can't let go of her family.

I have a confession to make, however. Just like Cynthia, I have put high importance on family dinners—and still do. We do it less frequently these days, because I have grown children, but our meals are still a time when we reconnect. We *must* see each other and talk to each other to understand one another. I believe families who eat together stay together.

I would like to thank Gloria Nitz for her invaluable information about being a medical transcriptionist. I appreciate her helping me make my book accurate.

I hope you enjoy Cynthia and Sean's story. I love to hear from my readers. You can reach me at SusanCarlisle.com.

Susan

To Anastasia Huff.
Thanks for all your love and support.

Books by Susan Carlisle

Mills & Boon Medical Romance

Summer Brides

White Wedding for a Southern Belle

Midwives On-Call

His Best Friend's Baby

Heart of Mississippi

The Maverick Who Ruled Her Heart
The Doctor Who Made Her Love Again

Married for the Boss's Baby
The Doctor's Sleigh Bell Proposal
The Surgeon's Cinderella

Visit the Author Profile page
at millsandboon.co.uk for more titles.

CHAPTER ONE

CYNTHIA MARCUM TAPPED the mouse of her laptop. Her emails came into view. Scanning them, she paused when she saw one from Dr. Sean Donavon. Her body tingled in anticipation. Why would he be emailing her? Her interactions had always been with his staff. Had she done something wrong?

She had been doing Dr. Donavon's transcription for just over a month now. He was an otolaryngologist and one of five surgeons she typed dictation for in the metropolitan Birmingham, Alabama area. The pay was so good she'd added him to her client list despite already having a full load. She could use the money. Her brothers, Mark and Rick, were always in need of something costing at least a hundred dollars.

The money wasn't the only thing she enjoyed about working for the mystery doctor. She loved the sound of his voice. It drew her in. She always saved his tapes for last. His deep resonating tone was smooth and silky like warm chocolate. It brought to mind a cool night with rain tapping against a tin roof and him pulling her close.

Her imagination worked overtime where Dr. Donavon was concerned. She couldn't get enough of listening to him, often playing his tapes back more than once.

Even all the medical terms sounded erotic when he uttered them.

She often wondered if he looked like he sounded. All dark and sexy.

A *humph* escaped her. Yeah, more like short and bald. That had happened one time when she had met a radio DJ. Based on his voice she'd built him up into this young, buff guy who every woman would want. Unfortunately, he turned out to be a short, middle-aged man with a gray ponytail. To say she had been disappointed was an understatement.

Listening to Dr. Donavon had become her romantic outlet. Since she currently had no one special in her life, hearing his voice had filled that void. She'd been in a relationship when her parents died. Wedding bells with Dave hadn't seemed too far off, then life had happened. Her parents' estate issues, the needs of her brothers and everything in between had worked against their relationship.

Dave had soon begun complaining that she wasn't spending enough time with him. It had then gone into, "I didn't sign on to help raise two teenage boys." Finally, he'd told her he had found someone else. In a way Cynthia was relieved. He just didn't share her mind-set about the importance of family. He didn't understand her or the necessity of keeping her family together at all costs.

After they broke up, she didn't try to have another solid relationship. She'd dated a few times but never let the guys close enough to matter. Usually, when they found out she was responsible for her brothers, they quickly backed away. Now wasn't the time for a man and she'd accepted that. Sadly, until the boys were more settled in life she would just have to get her thrills from listening to Dr. Donavon. And he was well worth listening to.

Her finger hovered over the computer mouse. Would his emails be just as amazing? Yeah right. She'd been without a man far too long when fantasy started overtaking reality. She clicked the email, opening it.

Then she read the black words against the white screen.

Hello, Ms. Marcum,
My office manager gave me your name as the person who has been preparing my transcriptions. I'm very impressed with your work.

The reason I'm contacting you is that I am currently in the middle of putting together a grant proposal and need to have some extra reports transcribed over the next few weeks. I wanted to know if you would be willing to take on this additional work. Of course I will compensate you for your time.

I would really appreciate your help.
Regards,
S. Donavon

Nope. Nothing sexy there. But he sounded nice. Considerate. In her mind she could almost hear him say the words. Cynthia reread the message. There wasn't much time in her days. Taking on more work might be difficult. This was Rick's senior year in high school so what extra hours she had were spent going to his activities. Yet the extra money Dr. Donavon offered would help pay for Mark's college tuition that was due soon.

Plus, she liked to keep her clients happy. Took pride

in her work. So far that hadn't been a problem with any of her employers. And she would get to listen to his voice more often. But if she didn't agree to Dr. Donavon's request would he take all his work elsewhere? She couldn't afford to let that happen.

Moving the cursor to the reply button, she clicked and typed.

Dr. Donavon,
I'm glad you're pleased with my work. My time is tight at present, but I'll do my best to fit in any extra reports you send.

I don't know how quick a turnaround time I can promise, but I will make it as short as possible.
Cynthia

Scanning the message, she made sure she had used the correct tone, then clicked "send". She didn't want to lose his business but couldn't overextend herself either. Her brothers, her family, took priority—always. The upside was if there was enough money from the extra work maybe she could start looking for a new car. Hers was on its last legs. She grinned. More like last tire.

Since she had left nursing school to become a full-time transcriptionist she'd gained a reputation as being competent and professional. It had been difficult to build a client list. She'd been tickled to add Dr. Donavon. As a surgeon, he produced plenty of work to keep her busy. He also paid better than her other clients. Getting to enjoy his voice almost daily was an added perk.

"Hey, Cyn," Rick called. His tall, lanky body appeared in the doorway of the small front room of their house she used as an office. He wore his usual uniform of jeans and well-worn T-shirt. "I'm going over to Joey's house."

Cynthia swiveled in the chair to face him. "Do you have that project done?"

"Almost." He put up a hand stopping her from saying more. "I'll have it finished tomorrow and it isn't due for another week. Don't worry, I have all A's."

"Yeah, but you don't want that to slip. That scholarship you're after depends on it."

Rick waved a hand at her. "You worry too much. See ya."

Seconds later the back door squeaked open and slammed closed.

She did worry. That had been her full-time job since her parents had died in that devastating car accident. She'd become guardian of her brothers when she was only a few years older. It hadn't been easy for any of them but they were making it.

Her father had told her more than once, "Cynthia, family is everything. You have to support your family." She lived by that motto. She would honor her parents by seeing that her brothers had a good start in the world. Once they were settled, she would go back to school and think about her own future. She missed that carefree time when she'd been on her own. The times she hadn't had to consider her brothers before she did something as simple as go out for the night.

The three of them had inherited the house, but there were still day-to-day expenses to meet. Those came out of her paycheck. Her parents had left some money but it wouldn't last long if she tapped into it. What her parents had left them was for the boys' higher education or to help them buy their own place.

Enough pondering. She had work to finish. Glancing at her email list one last time, she saw that there was a new note from Dr. Donavon. She opened it.

I can't say thank you enough.

I'll send over the dictation electronically this afternoon and will need the reports by Monday morning. Is that doable? If you can get them done by then I'll owe you big-time.

S. Donavon

She could imagine the smile on his face when he read her email. She liked it that she'd made him happy. But work so soon? This weekend? He really must be in a hurry. Well, she knew what her plans were for tonight and tomorrow morning.

Dr. Donavon,

I'll do my best to have them ready by Monday.

Cynthia

Seconds later he came back.

You're a lifesaver.

S. Donavon

Cynthia wasn't sure she could be anyone else's lifesaver. She was already taking care of more people than she could manage now. Taking on someone else might sink her boat. What would it be like to have someone take care of her for a change?

The kitchen door opened and slammed shut. "Cyn?" Mark, who was just three years younger than her, called.

"In here."

He flopped into the cushion chair beside her desk and flung a leg over the arm.

"So how did it go today?" Cynthia asked.

"I'm going to quit."

His blunt statement wasn't unexpected. She leaned toward him, gripping the arms of her chair. Her parents had wanted them all to get a college education. She'd been fighting Mark's apathy about doing that for months now. The weight of doing so was starting to get to her. "Why?"

"College doesn't get you anywhere." Mark spoke to the floor instead of her.

This was one of those times when she wished she had some backup, someone to turn to. She refused to let her voice rise. "You know Mom and Dad wouldn't like that."

"Yeah. But it's not for me."

Cynthia moved the chair to face him more directly. "Then what're you going to do?"

He shrugged and continued to look at that floor. "I don't know."

That wasn't a good plan. "Well, you're going to have to figure something out."

Mark jumped to his feet. "Get off my back. You're not my parent. We can't all be Rick." He stomped from the room.

She sighed. Could the day get any better? Mark's statement hurt on a number of levels. Cynthia missed her parents too. That was why she took her guardianship responsibilities seriously. Wanted to do the best by them. And no, she was not Mark's parent. If the situation was different she would prefer just being his sister.

Dr. Donavon's dictation arrived in her transcription system's inbox right before dinner. The work could wait until after dinner. Her parents had made the evening meal time important and she continued the practice. Her brothers knew that if possible they were expected at home at six during the week so they could spend some time together.

Two hours later she pulled her chair up to her desk. This wasn't the way she'd planned to spend Friday night, but she would get over it. Doing what had to be done had become a part of her life. She'd have Dr. Donavon's work to him Monday morning, hoping to impress.

She clicked the dictation inbox and Dr. Donavon's voice filled her ears. It didn't take long for her to forget about how tired she was or the amount of housework that needed doing and start enjoying the rich deepness of his voice. If she had to work on Friday night, there were worse jobs to have than one that involved having the sound of a sexy voice in her ear.

After lunch Monday, Sean settled in behind his desk at his clinic office. Pushing his chair back and putting his feet on his desk, he crossed his ankles and got comfortable. He didn't usually reread all his reports but in this instance, he couldn't afford not to. The grant was too important.

His future depended on it. Not to mention the quality of life for his patients, for the vast number of patients who would have their hearing improved and those of other ear, nose and throat doctors as well. With the grant he could continue his research and make that difference.

With the success of his procedure and the patent of a new instrument he would also be financially set for life. He knew too well what it was like being without and he'd vowed never to feel that way again. He'd heard some people call it the Scarlett O'Hara syndrome. He just called it smart.

Long ago he'd hired a financial planner. He was determined not to live paycheck to paycheck as his parents had, wondering if there would be enough cash to pay the bills or buy food. While growing up, more than once he'd been unable to participate with his friends in an activity because there hadn't been funds. His parents had been and still were the types to fall in with the next big money-making scheme, which always cost them money instead of making them rich as they claimed they one day would be. There had been multi-level marketing, investing in commercial ventures or selling the next great vitamin product. Nothing seemed to work but they were always in for the chance it might.

Sean hated any part of that way of life. Money shouldn't be squandered. Instead it should be saved and invested. He was determined to do just that. Their attitude toward paying their bills and handling finances embarrassed him. Their philosophy about life was so different from his that they found little in common. Because of that he'd not seen them in almost a year. Even then visits had been short. He wasn't interested in hearing about the next "get rich quick" plan.

The one thing about his new breakthrough was that it would allow him to put away enough money to support his parents in their old age. He was confident that they would need his help. Despite his bitter feelings about his childhood he would take care of them. No matter what, they were his parents.

Now he only had to get the grant documentation in

order. The submission must be flawless. The competition was tight, right down to the written documents. Even the smallest element could make a difference between him and someone else receiving the grant.

Picking up his tablet, he pulled up his most recent reports and started reading. Halfway through the first one, he was pleased to find not a single mistake. Not that he really expected one but he couldn't be too careful. Ms. Marcum had done a superb job and certainly in a timely manner. He should tell her so.

When his last transcriptionist had taken another position she'd given his office manager Ms. Marcum's name along with a glowing reference. Because he didn't have time to waste completing the grant he'd told his office manager to hire her without further question. Not known for making snap decisions, thankfully this one had been a smart one. He didn't know what would have happened to his grant submission if she hadn't been willing to take on the additional work.

Now he needed to make sure he kept her. He couldn't have her quitting just when he needed her the most. He didn't have time to waste hiring another, especially when there was no guarantee that the next person would be any good. His manager had already said they were lucky to get this one. He needed his dictation done in a timely manner and she had proven she could do that.

Pulling up his email, he entered Cynthia Marcum's address. Her name made her sound like a middle-aged matron. It didn't matter what she looked like. What concerned him was the quality of his papers and keeping her typing them.

Ms. Marcum,
I have reviewed your reports and I'm very pleased with your work. Thank you for getting them to me in such a timely manner. I was pleasantly surprised to learn that they were waiting for me when I returned to my office after coming out of surgery today.

I can't say enough about how much I appreciate your efforts. I hope it's still okay to send you additional work.
Very gratefully,
S. Marcum

Without hesitation he clicked the "send" button.

Cynthia was pleased to have his gratitude. It was always nice to get affirmation for her efforts. Good manners and a sexy voice. Two for two as far as she was concerned.

As much as she liked his praise she didn't want to have to stay up late or work on weekends to get it. Hopefully other work he sent wouldn't require her doing so. She'd handle that issue when the time came, if it did. She also had to honor her other clients' needs as well.

Cynthia typed a message.

Dr. Donavon,
I'm so happy you were pleased. Just let me know if I can help out further.
Cynthia

She reread the note twice. It was polite, yet businesslike.

A minute later a message landed in her mailbox.

Thank you! I do, in fact, have more work for you. I will send it through today.
S. Donavon

Maybe she'd offered too quickly. Apparently this grant was extremely important to him. At least he hadn't put a time period on when he needed these reports returned.

In the middle of the afternoon the doorbell rang. Cynthia answered it to find a delivery man holding a green plant in a blue ceramic pot.

"Cynthia Marcum?"

"Yes."

"This is for you." The man handed her the pot.

Dumbfounded, Cynthia was left to stare at it as he climbed into his van. No one had ever sent her something from a florist. There had been flower arrangements when her parents died but never something just for her. What was going on?

She looked down at the full, beautiful plant with broad leaves and a vivid red flower in the center. Tucked under one of the leaves was a white envelope with her name scrawled on it. Closing the door with her foot, she carried the plant to her office and set it on the corner of her desk. Removing the envelope, she pulled out the card inside. Written on it was: "Thanks, Sean Donavon."

He'd sent her a thank-you plant. Cynthia couldn't help but smile. That was thoughtful. Dr. Donavon had just earned another point. No matter what he looked like she could fall for someone who took the time to say thank you. She loved her brothers but "thank you" wasn't something she regularly heard. She didn't regret her sacrifices or what she did for them but she would like some understanding and appreciation sometimes. She looked at the plant again. Dr. Donavon's office manager had no doubt taken care of sending the gift.

A short time later the work he wanted done came up in her system.

She opened her email and clicked "compose."

Dr. Donavon
Thank you so much for the beautiful plant. You shouldn't have, but I will enjoy having it on my desk.
I received your dictation and will work on it today and tomorrow. I'll send the reports when they are completed.
Cynthia

It was almost midnight on Tuesday when she finally finished the last of her work. She'd spent most of the early part of her day typing her other clients' dictation. Rick had had a basketball game that evening and that had meant she'd made it back to her desk chair late. Still she was determined to have all her typing done so she could start fresh the next day. That meant working late.

Wednesday morning, she opened Dr. Donavon's normal surgical dictation and listened for the soft cadence of his voice as he spoke through her headphones. Smiling, she reached out and touched the tip of one leaf on her plant. Between his usual work and the special assignment, she was getting to spend many hours with his delicious voice. She was becoming moony-eyed over a man she'd never seen and knew nothing about. He could be married for all she knew. Enough of that—she needed to get to work.

Hours later she punched a key and sent the twenty separate reports she'd finished off to his electronic folder.

Feeling good about what she had accomplished that day, she took a long, hot shower before heading to bed. Having forgotten to turn off the kitchen light, she headed down the hallway. As she passed her office door she noticed the light flashing on her cell phone, indicating she had an email waiting. She received few this time of night so she feared it might be something important. It was from Dr. Donavon.

Had she tried she couldn't have slowed her rapid heartbeat. What was he doing working this late? She should wait until morning to open it but it would mean she would stay awake wondering what he had to say. Far too eager for her comfort, she double-tapped the key.

Thank you for the reports and you're welcome for the plant. It was just my small way of saying thank you.
Good night.
S. Donavon

How could a simple business email make her so giddy? She had to get a grip where Dr. Donavon was concerned. More than his voice was starting to get to her. What would it sound like to have him say good night in her ear? A shiver went up her spine. Cynthia shook her head. She'd been up too late. Her mind was beginning to play tricks on her.

She climbed into bed, pulled her quilt over her and smiled before drifting off to sleep.

* * *

Sean didn't make a practice of sending someone a thank-you gift for helping him with work he was already paying them to do, but he liked Ms. Marcum.

She'd really helped him out. He'd never sent a plant, or flowers for that matter, before. Even after a date. As far as he was concerned they were a waste of money, which was better used on something practical like a power bill or making an investment.

From the tone of Ms. Marcum's emails, she seemed an agreeable person. Someone he could work well with for a long time. Sean liked to keep good employees happy to prevent having to search for new ones. He'd been successful at it too. His office manager and several of his nurses had been with him for years.

He wasn't in the habit of taking chances. He'd seen more than once growing up what happened when someone took a chance. He didn't do it with places to live, friends or when making decisions on which stocks to buy. Only sure things interested him. That was just what the grant proposal had to be: a sure thing. Ms. Marcum was going to help make that happen.

Sean had worked until two o'clock in the morning the night before and still hadn't gone through all the reports and information he needed to review. Organization wasn't his strongest skill. He was going to need help. He moved a pile of disordered papers to another area of his desk, then more to another spot.

Disorganization was one trait he'd gotten from his parents that he couldn't seem to shake. It was almost ingrained. When they got involved in one of their schemes, record-keeping was part of the process and they didn't do it well. Soon they had no idea how deep they were in financially and couldn't put their hands on the documentation to figure it out.

When his father discovered the severity of it he would go out and get an hourly job. Then when the next big moneymaker scam came along his father would quit his job and devote all his time to building the new "business." Sean had heard all his life, "This will be it. We'll be on the road to riches this time." That time had yet to come.

He'd left all he could of that behind, except for being unorganized. He needed someone good with written documentation computer skills to assist him. The sooner the better. He only had a few weeks until the submission must be flawless.

Ms. Marcum had done another superb job with the latest reports. She seemed efficient. In her last email she'd offered her assistance. Would she consider helping him out for a few weeks? There was only one way to find out.

Ms. Marcum, I have a proposition for you.

Sean chuckled. Maybe those weren't the correct words.

Ms. Marcum, would you be able to come by my office around three p.m. tomorrow? I have an opportunity that I would like to discuss with you in person.
S. Donavon

Hopefully she would agree to their meeting and his need for help. He couldn't allow her to refuse him. How was he going to get the work done if she didn't assist him? His office staff was already busy enough. There was no time to hire someone else to handle it. He was reaching desperation level. Somehow he must gain her cooperation.

CHAPTER TWO

IT WAS LATE in the morning when Cynthia opened the email she'd saved for last.

She responded.

I'm sorry but I have another appointment at three. Can we make it four?

After a moment's hesitation she sent the email out. She was tempted to rearrange her entire afternoon. She really needed this job. But Rick's meeting with the scholarship council was too important to miss.

She didn't have to wait long for a reply.

I have rounds at four. How about we make it five? I won't keep you long, I promise.
S. Donavon.

Seconds later she typed: See you at five.

That afternoon Cynthia entered the glass doors of a modern single-story brick building. It was located across the street from the large multistory hospital in the center of Birmingham. A free-standing sign indicated the building contained Dr. Donavon's office. It was late in the day and only a few cars occupied the parking lot. Most of the patients would have been seen and the staff was probably leaving for the day.

She'd only been here one other time when she'd signed her employment papers. Transcribers worked behind the scenes and Cynthia liked it that way. She didn't have to leave home and that suited her lifestyle perfectly. That way she was able to work her schedule around her brothers' needs. It was highly unusual for a doctor to call her to his office. So why was Dr. Donavon doing so now?

Doctors' pictures were usually posted on their websites but she'd made it a point not to look for Dr. Donavon's because she didn't want to ruin her fantasy image of him. His appearance didn't matter anyway; this certainly wasn't a social call.

With a flutter of trepidation in her belly, she stepped to the reception window. Would she be disappointed when she saw him? The young woman with platinum blond hair and bright red fingernails behind the glass looked at her. She asked with an edge to her voice, "May I help you?"

"I'm here to see Dr. Donavon," Cynthia said in a firm tone.

The woman looked down her nose at her as if Cynthia had requested the impossible. "Is he expecting you?"

"Yes. I'm Cynthia Marcum. The transcriptionist. He told me to be here at five."

"Let me see if he's still here." She picked up the phone and spoke to the person on the other end. Putting it down, she said briskly, "He'll be right out. Just have a seat."

Cynthia did as she suggested. She studied the functional room containing metal chairs and a few end tables. There was a magazine rack on the wall and a fake potted plant in the corner. It was quiet and there was only a lone overhead light on. Minutes later the woman switched off the lights over her desk, came out from behind it and headed out of the front door without a glance in Cynthia's direction.

Was she alone in the building with just Dr. Donavon? What did she really know about the man? Even doctors could be ax murderers. She should have said no to meeting him after-hours. Waited until morning. She hoped she was a good judge of character even if her decision was based on emails alone. Shaking the idea off, she nervously shifted in her chair. She'd been so caught up in her fantasy she hadn't been thinking straight. Now she was letting her nerves get the better of her. Surely there was someone else in the office as well.

Cynthia watched the minute hand move for five agonizingly slow minutes before sounds of footsteps coming in her direction caught her attention.

What did he look like? The flutter increased, along with her curiosity. Steps grew closer. The quivering grew to a swirling. She felt as if she were going to meet her favorite rock star. After the way she'd pictured him maybe she was.

Cynthia shook her head and glanced at the ceiling to regain rational thought. She stood. No one could be that good-looking no matter how wonderful his voice was.

She was wrong. On both counts. The man towering over her was at least six feet tall. With dark hair and crystal-blue eyes, he would make any woman swoon. The fact he still wore a white lab coat over a blue-checked button-down shirt and tan pants didn't hurt his look of authority. He was glossy-magazine-front-cover gorgeous!

Her breath caught as she stared. His looks matched his voice and then some. And she was making a fool of herself right in front of him.

He smiled while giving her an odd look. "Ms. Marcum?"

Cynthia let out the breath she'd been holding. When had she ever been so focused on someone's looks? She wasn't that shallow. Still this man had her gaping at him. She needed to find a flaw if she was going to regain her sanity. She croaked, "Yes." Then cleared her throat and continued. "Please call me Cynthia. I'm not much on formal names."

"Good. Come with me. We can talk in my office."

He started down the hall. When she didn't follow immediately he stopped and looked at her. "Ms. Marcum. Cynthia?"

"I'm sorry. I'm coming." She needed to get control. Stop embarrassing herself.

She followed him along a hall with exam rooms on both sides. She saw a nurse standing at a counter at the end of the hall. With relief, she saw they weren't alone after all.

He stood beside an open doorway, inviting her to enter by extending a hand. He joined her, making the area suddenly feel small. Moving behind a desk that had seen better days and was piled high with paper stacks, he remained on his feet. Positioned on her side of the desk was a straight-backed wooden chair that reminded her of one in the library of her elementary school and appeared just as inviting.

"It's so nice to meet you, Cynthia. Please have a seat." He took the chair on squeaky wheels behind his desk. It was by no means the latest model either.

Cynthia sat, then glanced around. This might be the saddest doctor's office she'd ever seen. She'd envisioned a businesslike area filled with books, which this one was, but it also had a feeling of neglect. Somehow she had expected more. Minimal yes, but not so outdated and drab. There were no pictures of a wife or children, not even a dog. No indication of a hobby. No curtains hung above the utilitarian blinds. The one lone lamp on the desk only added to the sadness of the cluttered atmosphere. The space was an enormous contrast to the outstandingly handsome man sitting in front of her. What had happened to him for him to keep his personal space so…impersonal?

Did his home look this needy as well? Didn't he have a wife, a mother, or at least a girlfriend who could help him out with decorating? Every fiber in her wanted to buy him an antique desk and two tufted chairs. He needed her plant worse than she did.

Dr. Donavon cleared his throat and her attention returned to him. Those piercing blue eyes watched her closely. "You don't like my office?"

He was observant. She needed to make sure she schooled her emotions from showing too much on her face. "I just hadn't expected your office to look…um… like this. Sometimes I let my imagination carry me away."

Dr. Donavon leaned back in his chair giving her a direct look with a small smile on his lips. "How's that?"

She glanced around again. "I don't know. I just thought it might not be so uh…" How could she say this without sounding critical? "Maybe have more chrome and glass."

"I'm not really into chrome and glass."

Cynthia gave a nervous laugh. "I'm not either. Please forget I said anything. You didn't ask me here to insult your décor or to be your interior decorator."

"My apologies as well. I didn't mean to put you on the spot. You're not what I expected either."

"I hope you aren't disappointed." She wasn't sure where this meeting was going.

"I would say quite to the contrary. You're a pleasant surprise." He continued to study her.

Cynthia didn't know how to react to that statement. What had he expected? Was he flirting with her? It had been so long since a man had, she wasn't sure she would recognize it when it happened. "Thank you, I think."

"It was a compliment. I'm being rude and have embarrassed you. That's certainly not what I intended, especially when I need to ask you a favor."

"Ask me? A f-favor?" she stammered.

"Yes. I'd like you to consider helping me get the final draft of my grant proposal together." He gave her a charming smile. "I could really use your help." He made a point of indicating the stacks on his desk.

"Me? Why me? I don't know anything about putting together a grant."

"Maybe not, but I can help with that. From what I can tell you have good organizational skills on the computer and you're a fast and accurate typist. I need those skills to get this grant out on time. If you'll accept my proposition, I'll pay you time and half."

Heat crept up the back of her neck. She was sure he hadn't realized what he'd said about a proposition but she had. After fantasizing about him, and now seeing that he was devastatingly attractive, her mind was coming up with crazy ideas. Cynthia shifted in her seat. She must be careful not to make a fool of herself. "I've already agreed to do your transcription."

"Yes, but I need someone who can help me get my grant reports in order. Put the documents into the format and order required ASAP."

"I appreciate your offer. But I'm going to have to decline it. I have my family to consider and my other clients. My time is pretty tight as it is." She watched as his smile disappeared. For some reason she hated being the one who made it vanish.

He coaxed, "I'm sure your husband would understand that it's only for a few weeks. And I don't think it would be so time-consuming you couldn't do your other dictation."

"I don't have a husband." Was there a hint of relief on his face when she said that? "I'm responsible for my brothers."

He leaned forward. "How old are they?"

"In their late teens."

He looked mystified. "Wouldn't they understand you being away some?"

"They probably wouldn't notice but I would." He certainly wasn't going to give up easy.

"What if I pay you double time?" He crossed his arms on his desk.

Her eyes widened. There were hundreds of things she could use that money for. But money wasn't the most important thing in the world. It was nothing like being there for Rick at his games or being around when Mark needed to talk. Particularly with his current frame of mind. His schooling was too important for him to drop out. "I'm sorry. I'm still going to have to say no."

"Is there any way I could convince you?"

"Not now. I'm sorry I can't help you." She looked at her phone. "I really need to go. I'm supposed to be across town in thirty minutes."

"Then you must go," he said in a businesslike tone that still sounded special wrapped in his beautiful baritone.

Cynthia put her purse under her arm and stood.

He leaned back in his chair but didn't come to his feet.

She offered her hand. "I really am sorry."

He stood and took it. His was large and enveloped hers, making her feel tiny yet somehow protected instead of smothered. He said, "I am too. If you change your mind just let me know."

Cynthia nodded. He let her hand go. She felt the loss of warmth immediately. Her knees shook slightly as she walked down the hall. No man should have that kind of effect on her just by touching her hand.

Sean watched Cynthia's ash-brown hair swing across the tops of her shoulders as she walked out of the door. She certainly wasn't the frumpy middle-aged woman he'd anticipated. Instead she was a young vibrant woman who knew her own mind. She was far more interesting than he'd expected. What compelled such a striking woman to become a transcriptionist who stayed behind the scenes? Somehow it didn't fit her. She looked more suited for the front desk.

Cynthia might be short in stature but she was tall

in backbone. He like the way her green eyes expressed her feelings. They'd certainly made it clear how she felt about his office. She'd bitten the corner of her mouth as she'd thought about how she was going to answer his questions. He had to give her credit for the diplomatic way she'd done so. Her actions had been endearing, yet telling. He had the feeling she'd found humor in the situation by the small laugh lines that gathered around her eyes.

Sean walked down the hall toward the front of the building, intent on locking the door. The back door opened and shut. His nurse was leaving for the evening but he would be staying for some time to come. As he reached the lobby Cynthia entered.

"Can I change my mind about that job?" There was a note of desperation in her voice.

He was surprised by her question but grateful she was reconsidering. "Sure."

"When would you like me to start?"

He smiled. "Now would be great."

Her face took on an astonished look. "I can't—"

"I don't expect you to start this minute. I'll send you more dictation and some information about what I want. For the most part you should be able to do the work from home but it may require you coming here a few times."

Cynthia nodded. "Okay. That should work."

"May I ask what changed your mind?" She'd seemed firm about her decision earlier.

"I just got a call from my brother and he's having car trouble. This is the second time in two weeks." She shrugged. "Turns out I need the extra money."

"I'm sorry about your car issues." He was but he was also thankful he'd be getting her assistance. "Can

I do anything to help out? Do you need me to call a tow truck?"

She shook her head. "Thank you, but I'm fine for now. Mark has a friend who'll tow the car to our house. Please send over what you need me to do and I'll get started on it right away."

Sean watched her walk toward an older-model car. It was a basic four-door vehicle, practical and efficient. Not unlike his. Cynthia seemed to face her financial responsibilities head-on. That was something he could admire.

The next morning Cynthia checked her email.

Cynthia,
I wanted to make sure you got the car home with no trouble. Please let me know if you need any help. I have a great mechanic and I'd be glad to call him.

I have attached some guidelines for the grant and some files that need to be included. Please let me know if you have any questions.
Again, I appreciate your help.
Sean

She appreciated Sean's offer. The more dealings she had with Dr. Donavon, the better she liked him.

Cynthia noticed he'd signed off as "Sean." She'd told him to call her Cynthia so her guess was he was reciprocating. Did he want her to call him by his first name? He'd not suggested that when they had met. Now all of a sudden he was using his given name. She shouldn't be making such a big deal of it but she liked the idea of them being on a first-name basis.

Cynthia practiced saying his name out loud. It suited him. After all her daydreaming she had to keep in mind that they were merely employee and employer. She didn't need to read more into a simple signature than there was. Still she couldn't ignore the extra clip-clop of her heart when she reread the note.

All these speculations and she still didn't really know anything about the man. He could be married for all she knew. But he hadn't been wearing a ring. But nowadays that didn't mean anything. She hoped he was married. At least she could put an end to her romantic illusions. The reality of a romance between them was laughable. She really needed to get out more. Meet some men. She was spending too much time in a dream world wrapped in a sultry male voice. Reality was what she should concentrate on. Like her brothers attending college and the cost of them staying there or the problem of repairing Mark's car.

Over the next few days she worked hard to get Sean's reports typed and to keep up with her other transcriptions. To her surprise, she enjoyed working on the grant. Found it fascinating. At first it took a great deal of effort to understand what was necessary but she soon became caught up in the brilliant work that Sean was doing. Her being impressed was an understatement.

On Tuesday afternoon, she headed for Sean's office to deliver the work she had finished. Rick's eighteenth birthday was in two days and she was going to take some time off to get ready for it. Pulling into a parking spot, she tried to convince herself she was making the extra effort to turn the reports in just because of the party planning but that wasn't true. She secretly hoped she might see Sean. Especially since she'd taken more care with her hair than usual, not to mention she was now putting on lip gloss.

This is ridiculous.

Cynthia picked up the file and without hesitation got out of the car. She merely had to go in, hand over the papers, return to her vehicle and drive away. She wasn't some teenage girl trying to contrive a way to see a boy. Those days were long gone. Still that tingle of anticipation filled her.

She pulled open the glass door of the lobby, entered and purposely walked to the window. "I'm Cynthia. The transcriptionist. Please see that Dr. Donavon gets these."

The same receptionist who had been there days before took the file. "I will."

Cynthia turned to leave as a middle-aged man entered the lobby from the hallway. Sean was behind him. Her body heated as if she'd gotten caught doing something she shouldn't.

His smile implied he was glad to see her. She returned it.

Sean patted the man on the back. "Good to see you're doing so well, Ralph. I hope to see you again soon." The man headed toward the exit and Sean strolled over to her. "Hi, Cynthia."

"I brought you some reports and the first ten pages of the grant to review." She pointed toward the desk. "I gave them to your receptionist."

"Great. I'll give them a look and let you know if there're any changes to be made. I appreciate you bringing them by."

His voice was even more captivating when she heard it in person. She had to do something more than stand there looking at him. She swallowed. "You're welcome. Well, I'd better go."

"I'll be in touch," Sean said.

And I'll be looking forward to it. Somehow she managed to keep herself from saying it out loud.

The two days she'd taken off turned into busy ones. She'd made arrangements for Rick's birthday and finished some chores she'd been putting off. Everything was set for the party now. All she had to do was load the car and head to the paintball field. She was expecting about twenty teenagers, both boys and girls. Normally she, Mark and Rick celebrated with cake and ice cream with a few friends but this was a special birthday. Now that she had some extra money from overtime she had decided to splurge a little.

With a couple of hours before they needed to leave, Cynthia decided to check her email and review what she would need to get done the next day. She opened her account.

With a giddy feeling she shouldn't be experiencing, she saw one from Sean. She opened it.

Hi Cynthia,

I hope you're having a good day. I've had something come up and I need to get Charles Chadworth's surgical report. It's particular to the grant and I need a colleague to review it. He's leaving on a two-week vacation tomorrow but has said he can look at it tonight. Do you have it completed?

I know this is above and beyond the call of duty, but

could you have it ready for a messenger at four p.m.?
I must get it to him right away.
Thank you.
Sean

She checked the time. There was just enough for her to type it but no one would be here to give it to the messenger.

She replied.

I can get it typed, but today is my brother's birthday and I'm giving him a party. I won't be here for the messenger when he comes.

Since it's personal information I'm not comfortable leaving it on the porch unattended… I could bring it by your office around nine tonight. Would that do?
Cynthia

Half an hour later she had the report finished and another email from Sean popped into her box.

That's not going to work. I really need it sooner.

Let me see if I can find someone in the office who can come get it.
I'll get back to you.
Sean

She couldn't miss Rick's party or be late. She was the hostess. Had the responsibility of being the designated adult in charge. At one time that title made her feel important. Now it was more of a weight on her shoulders.

Cynthia checked the time. She needed to get going

but she also needed to wait to hear from Sean. Ten minutes went by before he replied.

No messenger can make it and there's no one in the office who can do it either.
Can I meet you somewhere and pick it up?
Sean

Cynthia slipped the two sheets of paper into a protective envelope. The report really must be important if he was willing to go to the trouble of personally picking it up.

You'll need to come to 5182 Falcon Road, Bessemer, Al.

Sean replied right away.

I'll see you there.
Thanks for doing this on such short notice.
Sean

Cynthia couldn't help the excitement bubbling in her. She was going to see Sean again. It had been a long time since she'd acted like a woman excited about seeing a man.

Sean couldn't believe it when he pulled up to the address that Cynthia had given him. It was a large field full of building façades, lean-tos and barrels spaced out at intervals. In a grassy area beside a building no larger than a backyard garden shed, vehicles were parked in a line. Most were jacked-up trucks with the occasional car mixed in.

What was going on here?

He parked next to a red truck. Among the buildings and other obstacles were people dressed in white painter coveralls and wearing clear masks over their faces. They were running from place to place while being shot at with guns that used exploding paintballs.

Why was Cynthia here?

He slowly approached the shed where a couple of teenagers stood laughing and pointing at what was happening on the field. Posted on the siding of the building was a sign stating "Peek's Paintball". Below the sign was a list of the charges for a game, with or without the rental of the equipment. This was just the type of entertainment he didn't waste his money on. There was nothing to show for the expense. Yet, it seemed several kids and, apparently, Cynthia were playing.

Sean joined the boys. "Hey."

They looked at him curiously. Was it that obvious he was out of his element? "Do either one of you know where I can find Cynthia Marcum?"

One boy looked at the other. "Isn't that Rick's sister?"

"Yeah." The teen pointed toward the field. "She's out there somewhere."

Sean studied the game area, trying to catch a glimpse of Cynthia. Players continued moving between obstacles while being shot at.

"They just started a new game a few minutes ago. It may be a while before she shows up," one of the boys stated.

Sean didn't really have time to stand around waiting on her. Cynthia knew he was coming. Why wasn't she available? "Could you point me in the direction of where you last saw her?"

The taller of the two indicated the right side of the field.

Sean started in that direction.

"Hey, man," the shorter boy called, "I wouldn't do that without a mask and gun. It's an unwritten rule that anyone on the field is fair game."

Sean hesitated. Surely no one would shoot an unarmed man. He wasn't even dressed the part.

"I'll let you have mine. You really don't want to go out there without some protection." The second boy handed him his plastic helmet.

Sean took it. "Thanks. You really think they'd shoot me?"

Both boys gave him a solemn nod.

The tall one asked, "Do you know how to use a paintball gun?"

Sean looked at the clear gun with a black plastic container attached to the bottom and a small black canister on the back. "No, not really."

"This one is an automatic. All you have to do is pull the trigger. This is the hopper." He pointed to the plastic container. "It holds the paintballs. This is your gas." He put his hand on the canister. "You should have plenty. Just point and shoot. Aim for the body."

They had to be kidding. Surely Cynthia wasn't out there dressed as they were and armed. "Is all of this really necessary?"

Both boys bobbed their heads in a rapid motion.

"Oh, and don't take your mask off for any reason until the whistle blows. Paintballs can leave nasty whelps."

"Got it." Sean started out into the field again. He

hadn't gone six feet before he felt a thump and dampness on his upper arm. He looked down to see a bright yellow splatter on his good navy pullover. At least he was wearing jeans. Moving into a trot, he found cover behind a barrel. There were two pinging sounds against the side as he crouched down. Paint flew in the air around him.

A couple of giggles came from a nearby lean-to. He peeked out to see two girls.

"Almost got you," one called.

"Do you know where Cynthia Marcum is?" Sean brought his head back, not moving from his sheltered spot.

"Whose team are you on?" came a response.

"No one's. I came here to see Cynthia." He'd had no idea it would be this hard to do.

"She's guarding our fort," a girl called.

"Fort?" He hadn't seen anything that looked like a fort among the structures.

"Yeah. It's the church," another voice called. "You better be careful. She's a good shot."

"We're going to believe you this time. We'll let you by," one of the girls called.

"Thanks. I appreciate that." Sean stood but kept his head low as he ran toward the façade that looked like a white church front with a steeple. When he was hit in the hip, he took cover behind some boards driven into the ground forming a haphazard fence. Okay, he'd had all the paint on him he wanted. It was time to retaliate.

Sean did a three-sixty survey of the area. A boy came into his field of vision and Sean pulled the trigger. With a pop, pop, pop the balls left the chamber. Two hit the ground near the boy's feet. He turned to run and the third caught him square in the back.

A smile covered Sean's lips. This game might be more interesting than he'd thought. He ran across an open area to another barrel, fully expecting to draw fire. When none came his confidence increased and he kept moving. He reached a large oak tree that stood in the middle of the field and stopped, waited.

Where was Cynthia? He needed to get that report and get back to his office. There was still work to do tonight. Sean yelled, "Cynthia?"

Seconds later he heard, "Over here."

She was at the church. Sean headed in that direction. This time he wasn't as lucky as he had been during his last run. A couple of boys stepped out from behind a storefront and paintballs sailed in his direction. Ducking and zigzagging, he ran behind the church front and straight into someone.

With a grunt from him and a whoosh from the person he hit, they landed with a thud on the ground in a tangle of legs and arms. Seconds later he looked into the wide, dazed eyes of Cynthia. Their mouths were close enough to touch if not for the plastic masks between them. Sean wished he could kiss her. Almost instantly behind that thought came the realization of how soft the feminine curves were beneath him. When she shifted, they became even more evident.

"Uh…Sean, what're you doing here?" Cynthia looked at him as if she might be imagining him.

"Do you mean here on top of you or here as in on the playing field?"

For a moment she looked perplexed, as if she didn't understand the question. "Both, I think."

"I was looking for you. You told me to meet you here." She really did have beautiful eyes.

Cynthia struggled to get out from under him. "I don't think I asked you to knock me down and lay on me."

"No. That was purely accidental." *And my pleasure.* He rolled to his side, taking some of the pressure off her. She shimmied against him. His body warmed and twitched in awareness. A movement above them caught his attention. He glanced up. A boy pointing a gun was bearing down on them.

Suddenly Cynthia twisted to her side and away from him. "I have to protect the fort," she muttered with a sound of determination as she reached for her gun.

Sean raised his and aimed. The paintball hit the boy in the chest. Red paint covered his coverall.

"Aw, Cyn, I was so close," the kid said with disappointment in his voice.

Cynthia giggled. "Yet so far away." She looked back at him. "Thanks, Doc, nice shot."

"You're welcome." Sean grinned as he got to his feet. He offered her a hand. She took it without hesitation. "There's a first time for everything." He'd impressed not only himself but her as well. He liked that for some reason. He was confident she didn't suffer fools easily.

"Really? You've never played paintball?" She looked around them as if making sure no one else was headed in their direction.

"No." This was just the type of thing that there was never money for when he was growing up. He would have loved to have had a birthday party like this one, or even gone to one, but more times than not there was barely money for food. His parents had told him more than once it would get better after the "new business" took off. That had never happened.

The boy walked back the way Sean had come.

"So is he done?" Sean asked.

"Yeah, he got hit in the chest so he has to sit out now." Cynthia crouched behind the church supports. "I'd have you on my team any time." Admiration filled her voice.

He involuntarily puffed out his chest and stood straighter.

Her attention had already returned to the field. She glanced back at him and pulled at his arm. "Hey, you better get down or you're going to have more paint on you than you already have." A second passed. "Why don't you have on coveralls? You have ruined your sweater and jeans."

"I hadn't planned on wallowing on the ground or being shot at by kids. Some guy told me not to come out here without a mask and gun. He didn't offer me coveralls. I'm here for a report, not to be a target. By the way, when're you going to be free here so I can get my report?"

"It shouldn't take long." She looked around the façade as if she expected someone was sneaking up on them. "My team should be returning any minute now."

He looked. "Just how do you tell who's on your team?"

"By the color on their helmet." She made it sound as if anyone should know that. His chest deflated.

No other women he knew would be out here playing this game. "You have to be kidding. That means they must get pretty close before you know if they are friend or foe?"

"Yep. But that's part of the fun." Cynthia sounded as if she loved the challenge.

He guessed it was. To his surprise he was having a good time.

"So why exactly are you here?"

"They were short one team member and I got drafted. I'm just filling in on this game until one of Rick's friends shows up."

That made sense. But Sean had already gotten too caught up in this craziness.

Her focus remained on the field around them. "I'll be done here in a few minutes."

She sure took the game seriously. It sounded as if no amount of prodding on his part was going to change her mind. She looked cute in the baggy white paper coveralls with her hair pulled back by the mask and her eyes wide in anticipation. His type was usually the "I can't get my fingernails broken or my shoes dirty" kind, and here he was admiring a woman with no makeup and paint all over her.

A tall, lanky boy ran toward them calling with excitement, "Hey, Cyn. We won. I got the last of them."

Cynthia stood. "Great."

Sean joined her.

"This has been the best birthday party ever. Thanks." The boy stopped in front of them and gave Cynthia a hug.

She returned it. "I'm glad you like it." Cynthia pulled off her mask and shook out her hair.

Sean could do little more than stare. She looked so sexy as her hair floated around her shoulders. His body heated. By the way she acted, Cynthia had no idea how captivating the action was. He was more aware with each passing second. Why was he reacting to her so? This wasn't like him.

There had been women in his life. Plenty of them but none had interested him enough to cause this type of response in such a short time. His female companions had been just that. Companions. Some for the night, others for a month or two. He wanted a woman who was serious, focused. Thought like he did. After living with his parents he'd learned too well that some people haphazardly went through life. He planned, considered each step.

Sean knew the value of hard work and used his money wisely. Unlike this party. No matter how entertaining it might be, he couldn't see why Cynthia would spend so much on a party when he was sure she could have used the money elsewhere. Like repairing her brother's car. He could already tell she wasn't the person for him but still he liked her. What would it hurt to enjoy her company while it lasted?

"Sean, I'd like you to meet my youngest brother, Rick. It's his birthday we're celebrating. Rick, this is Dr. Donavon." She put a hand on her brother's arm.

The affection between them was obvious. Something that Sean and his siblings didn't share. He hadn't seen his older brother and sister in a couple of years. He'd been much younger and so different from them that their relationships hadn't been close. Sean had been an outsider in his own family. The idea that his brother or sister would throw him a party was laughable.

"Nice to meet you, Rick. Happy birthday." Sean offered his hand. The boy had a firm handshake. "Please call me Sean."

Cynthia gave him a warm smile. She seemed to appreciate him allowing her brother the familiarity. There were too many confusing emotions surrounding him liking that idea that he chose not to contemplate it further.

Cynthia handed her headgear and gun to Rick. "Will you see about these? I've got to get a report out of the car for Sean."

"Uh, sure." Rick took the equipment. Rick turned to him. "I can take yours too."

Flipping the mask off, Sean handed it and the gun to Rick. "It belongs to some guy with red hair who was standing up by the shed."

"That'd be Johnny. I'll see that he gets it." Rick headed in the direction he'd come.

"Let's go. My car is over here," Cynthia said as she walked toward what he assumed was the car park.

Sean followed. Even in the coveralls, Cynthia had a nice swing to her hips. She had a generous behind that proclaimed she was all woman.

This interest in her had to stop.

CHAPTER THREE

CYNTHIA GLANCED AROUND at Sean. A look of guilt flickered in his eyes. Had she just caught him checking her out?

Her spine tingled. There had been a moment just like it when he'd been on top of her. He was affecting her in ways she wasn't completely comfortable with. What was going on? This couldn't continue. He was in truth her boss and even if he wasn't they lived in two different worlds.

She made her strides longer. He should be sent on his way as soon as possible. There wasn't time in her life to think about Sean Donavon. Her brothers and keeping their financial heads above water were all she needed to focus on. Her life didn't need muddling by dreamy thoughts of Sean.

Thankfully they soon reached her car. But then she realized she had to remove her coveralls to get her keys out of her jeans. Distressed, she tried to make it clean and simple, instead of the striptease she was afraid it might look like. Cynthia didn't miss the slight uplift to Sean's lips when she wiggled back and forth as she struggled to remove the material from her shoulders. He was appreciating the spectacle she was making.

"A gentleman would offer to help," she snapped as she continued to twist.

He grinned. "I was sort of enjoying the show."

Heat rose to her cheeks.

Sean stepped closer, which didn't help matters in the least. He gave her collar a tug.

"Thanks."

"My pleasure." He sounded sincere.

The panic that had simmered while she worked to undress had started to flame. Cynthia let the coveralls drop to her feet and dug into her pocket for her keys. Finding them, she laid them on the top of the car then pulled the coveralls up and tied the sleeves around her waist.

"So did you get the car you were having trouble with fixed?" Sean asked.

"It's running but my pocketbook is empty." She clicked the car door opener.

"I bet having this party at the same time didn't help." His tone was matter-of-fact.

Was he being critical? Did he think she was wasting money? "You're not kidding. But Rick only turns eighteen once. He deserved a nice party. Some fun."

"Maybe."

Sean didn't sound as if he agreed. "Anyway, it's good for you. It just means that you'll have me for as long as you need me." Grabbing the file off the seat, she almost shoved it at him.

Something about the slight twist of his lips confused her. It was as if she was talking about one thing while he was thinking of another. A tremor washed through her body at the thought of him touching her. She hoped her reaction didn't show. The man had her tied up in knots in more ways than one.

"Thanks." He took the file in his hand.

"Cyn, come quick!" Rick, still dressed in playing gear, ran toward them waving his arm. "Ann Marie is hurt."

"What's wrong?" Cynthia called.

The boy yelled, "She's hurt her leg."

"Tell her not to move. I'll be right there." Cynthia dug under the car seat, pulling out a first-aid kit. When she stood she didn't see Sean anywhere. Seconds later she was trotting toward Rick. At the sound of footsteps, she glanced to her right to find Sean beside her.

At what must have been her questioning look he said, "I thought I might help."

"Thanks." She was grateful. If Ann Marie was badly injured she could really use his medical assistance.

They rounded a stack of drums on the playing field to find Rick on bended knee beside a girl. She was still wearing coveralls but her mask lay beside her. Her blond hair fell loosely down her back as she rubbed the ankle of her left leg. A couple of other kids stood looking down as her with interest.

Cynthia joined them and went down on her knees. "Ann Marie, I'm Cynthia. Rick's sister. What hurts?"

"My ankle. I can't walk." The girl's pain was obvious.

Focusing on nothing else but Ann Marie, Cynthia put a hand on her shoulder, hoping to reassure her. "Let me look. Where exactly does it hurt?"

"Right here," the girl cried out as she touched the spot.

Moving down to where she could easily reach Ann Marie's foot, Cynthia began to push the pants leg of the coveralls up. "You let me know if I'm hurting you." She slowly gathered the material until she could see the ankle area. "I'm going to need to roll your sock down."

The girl shifted.

"Stay still. You wouldn't want to make the injury worse." Cynthia carefully touched Ann Marie's skin, checking around the ankle bone for raised areas or tenderness. When her fingers reached the skin on the inside of Ann Marie's ankle she winced.

Cynthia shifted, getting a better view. Even in the dimming afternoon light she could make out a purple discoloration of the skin. Her fingers moved to the strings of Ann Marie's shoe.

"Don't do that," Sean's stern voice told her. He joined her on the ground.

Cynthia had forgotten all about him. She was surprised he hadn't said something sooner or taken over the situation. She gave him a questioning look.

"It could be broken. The shoe will act as a splint," he explained. "It should remain on and be removed at the emergency department."

That made sense. Cynthia sat back on her heels and spoke to Ann Marie. "You have definitely sprained it or worse. We're going to have to make a trip to the ER."

The teen started crying.

Cynthia lightly patted her leg, trying to comfort her. "You're going to be fine."

The girl gave her a tear-filled look. "My parents are going to be so mad at me. They told me not to come to the party."

A knot formed in Cynthia's stomach. She wasn't looking forward to the conversation to come. "I'm sure they'll understand. Right now let's worry about that ankle. We need to get you to the car and on to the hospital."

"I want to stabilize the foot more before she's moved just on the off chance it's broken," Sean said.

Cynthia turned to him. "How do we do that?"

"We need something to wrap around the shoe that will support the ankle. A long piece of cloth, anything." Sean looked at her then above them at the others watching.

"I have an old knit scarf in my car—would that do?" a girl offered softly.

"That'd be great." Sean gave her a reassuring smile.

"I'll run get it." The girl didn't wait for a response before she took off at a full run toward the parking lot.

"I'm going to need to roll up your pants leg so that we can keep it out of the way. I need to wrap your foot securely. This shouldn't hurt." Sean's large hands went to work on neatly folding the material. "So what grade are you in?"

"Eleventh."

He nodded. "What's your favorite subject?"

"I like English," Ann Marie responded.

Sean continued to work. "That so?"

Cynthia watched. Sean had a nice bedside manner about him. One that she could easily fall for as well. Ann Marie had stopped crying and was now concentrating on answering Sean's questions.

Minutes later the girl returned with a scarf balled up in her hand. Reaching them, she thrust it at Sean. Taking it, he smoothed out the width and length, then placed one end under Ann Marie's foot and started covering it as if he were using an elastic bandage. He then brought it up around her ankle and secured it under a section he'd already wrapped.

Sean pushed to his feet. "Now off to Emergency you go. Rick, will you get behind Ann Marie and help lift her up while I pull her from here? Ann Marie, don't for any reason put weight on that foot."

Rick moved into position.

Sean said, "Ready, set, go."

Cynthia helped steady Ann Marie as Sean and Rick got her up on one foot. Before she had a chance to wobble, Sean had scooped her into his arms and had her held against his chest.

Speaking to Rick, she said, "I'm going to take Ann Marie to the hospital and stay with her until her parents get there."

"We'll go in my car. I saw all the birthday stuff in the backseat of yours," Sean said.

He didn't sound as if he would allow any argument. She nodded and told Rick, "You drive my car home. I'll be there as soon as I see about Ann Marie. You can have cake and ice cream here. It's in the car. The ice cream's in the cooler in the trunk."

"I'll take care of it," one of the girls called as Cynthia hurried to catch up with Sean, who was already headed toward the parking area. "Ann Marie, I'll save you some for when you get home."

Ann Marie gave the girl a weak wave.

"Thanks," Cynthia said, over her shoulder. Nearing a midsized four-door car that Sean was obviously headed for, she hurried past him to open the back door. It was locked.

"The keys are in my pocket. You're going to have to get them."

What? She wasn't going to stick her hand in his pants pocket.

"I can hold An—"

Sean gave her a stern look. "They're in my right pocket. Get them."

Cynthia stepped around him. Swallowing hard, she slowly slipped her hand into the top of his front pocket. Thankfully Sean's pants weren't super tight. His body tensed. The hiss of air told her Sean wasn't unaffected by her actions.

She bit down on her lower lip as her hand continued to push farther along his leg. Her fingers found the keys and jerked them out. Cynthia released the breath she had been holding, unlocked the doors, and opened the rear one.

Sean worked to sit Ann Marie on the seat in the small confined space. Cynthia went around to the other side and, by putting her hands under the girl's arms, pulled her across the seat. "Ann Marie, I'm going to close the door and you can lean against it. It won't be a comfortable ride but your leg and foot need to rest straight on the seat."

She watched as Sean quickly pulled his sweater off. A hint of a firm abdomen showed above his beltline when his shirt came untucked. She hated to admit her disappointment when it disappeared as his arms came down from over his head.

"Here." He wadded the sweater up and handed it to Ann Marie. "You can use this to cushion your back against the door handle." Cynthia closed the door and watched through the window to make sure the girl was settled before she started around the car to the front passenger seat. The other car door slammed, and Sean met her halfway around the car.

"Thanks for your help," Cynthia said.

"Not a problem." Sean continued to the driver's side.

Half an hour later, Sean drove up to the entrance of Emergency Department and stopped. He hopped out of the car and circled it to find Cynthia at the rear door with it already open. She was helping Ann Marie to slide across the seat.

"Don't let her stand. I'm going to get an orderly and a wheelchair." Sean headed toward the sliding glass doors.

"We'll be right here," Cynthia called after him.

Minutes later he returned pulling a rolling bed while a member of the medical staff pushed it. They positioned it beside the car. With the wheel brakes on, Sean said, "Cynthia, if you would help scoot Ann Marie as far to the edge of the seat as you can, then I'll lift her onto the rolling bed."

Sean waited until Cynthia had the girl in position. Supporting her back with one arm and the other under her knees, he lifted Ann Marie gently and placed her on the bed. Turning to Cynthia, he handed her his keys. "Why don't you park my car? I'll see to Ann Marie. I have a buddy who's an ortho guy. I'm going to give him a call."

"Okay. I'll be there in a minute."

Sean didn't have to wait long before Cynthia joined him in the examination room. She'd removed her coveralls and now wore a sweatshirt with a local college insignia on the front and jeans. She looked about the same age as Ann Marie.

The orderly finished settling the girl. "The doctor's on her way in."

Sean said, "I've already phoned Dr. Mills. He has agreed to consult. He should be here soon."

Cynthia immediately stepped to the bedside. "Are you feeling any pain?"

"It throbs," Ann Marie said quietly.

Cynthia patted her hand. "I'm sure they'll do X-rays and have you out of here in no time."

"I hope so. Mama and Dad are not going to be happy when they see me." The girl seemed more concerned about her parents than she was about her foot.

While on their way he and Cynthia had listened as Ann Marie called and told her parents what had happened and which hospital she was being taken to. Her mother's voice could be heard loud and clear from the backseat. She wasn't happy.

"I'm sure they'll just be glad you weren't hurt worse," Cynthia assured her.

Soon a tech from X-ray entered and whisked Ann Marie away leaving him and Cynthia in the empty room.

"Uh, here're your keys." She pulled them from her pocket and handed them to him. Her cheeks went pink. Was she thinking of when she'd had to fish them out of his pocket?

Sean took them. Her hand touched his for a split second. Even that sent an electric shock through him. What was it with this woman? "You did a nice job out there with Ann Marie. It looked like you've had first-aid training."

She moved to "her" side of the room, as if they were

boxers facing off but unsure of the next move. "More like nursing training."

"Really? You're in nursing school?"

"I was, or was planning to be. I took nursing classes in high school. I was going to college to be a RN." Cynthia took one of the two chairs in the small space. She sat straight in her chair with her hands in her lap as if she wasn't completely comfortable around him.

"Well, it showed. You were cool, calm and collected." Sean meant it. He'd been impressed. If he hadn't stepped in, he was sure she'd still have been able to handle the situation.

Cynthia looked at him. "You did a nice job on wrapping her foot. Quick thinking."

He shrugged and grinned. "I have had some medical training after all."

"Wrap a lot of noses in scarves, do ya?"

He laughed. "Not so many. There's always a first time for everything."

"You get an A plus for effort. I do appreciate you driving us over and having your friend see Ann Marie. I know you had other plans tonight. Please don't feel like you have to stay."

Sean leaned back against the wall and crossed his arms over his chest. "Trying to get rid of me?"

"No, but I know you're concerned about that grant application. And time is tight. You must need to go."

He checked his watch. He did have to meet Charles soon but he still had time. "I'm good. I have the report with me. I'll call my colleague and make new arrangements. I want to make sure Ann Marie doesn't need me to cut any red tape before I leave."

"You have the report with you?"

"Yeah. I stuck it in my car while you were hunting for the first-aid kit."

There was a commotion in the hall. The door to the room opened and a middle-aged couple hurried in. It could only be Ann Marie's parents. Sean straightened and Cynthia stood.

She took a step toward the couple. Sean came to stand behind her as she said, "Mr. and Mrs. Lucas, I'm Cynthia Marcum. Rick's sister. I want to assure you that Ann Marie is doing fine. She's having an X-ray done now."

The woman took a threatening step toward Cynthia. "How could you've let this happen? I told Ann Marie she couldn't come to the party. There wouldn't be enough supervision with just you there. I blame you for this."

Cynthia recoiled until her back met his chest. Sean felt a slight tremor roll through her. His neck stiffened. What was he missing here? He wasn't going to allow anyone to talk to her that way.

"I can assure you that Ms. Marcum has taken and still is taking extremely good care of Ann Marie. What happened to Ann Marie was merely an accident." Stepping around Cynthia, he put himself between the irate mother and her. "I'm Dr. Sean Donavon. She handled the situation admirably. Ann Marie is doing fine."

Cynthia shifted to stand ridged beside him. She was going to stand her own ground, it appeared. "Mr. and Mrs. Lucas, I can assure you that your daughter has been under *continuous* supervision and has had *capable* care. She took a fall and twisted her ankle. We brought her here only as a precaution. I'm sorry it happened but she's doing fine. She'll be back here in a few minutes."

"I told Dan—" the mother glanced at her husband before turning her leer on Cynthia again "—that Ann Marie wasn't to go to the party. I just knew something like this would happen," she hissed.

Sean's shoulders relaxed when he saw Ann Marie being pushed into the room, ending the conversation. He touched Cynthia's shoulder and nodded toward the far wall. She joined him out of the way. Cynthia must be as glad the discussion was over as he was. His jaw was tight in an effort not to say what he really thought to the over-the-top mother. Ann Marie's father hadn't said anything. Sean wasn't surprised; he couldn't be anything but browbeaten.

The mother hurried to the bedside, hardly letting the transporter get the bed back into position. "Oh, honey, are you okay? I told you that you had no business at that party."

"Rick is my friend," Ann Marie whined.

"Yes, but you know how we feel about his family," the mother said in a tight voice, glaring at Cynthia.

"Mama, hush," Ann Marie hissed.

Sean had heard enough. He hated to leave the young girl to fend for herself but his and Cynthia's presence wasn't helping the situation. "Ann Marie, Cynthia and I will go now that your parents are here. We'll call and check on you. Let me know if you have any problems. My buddy Dr. David Mills will be in here soon to look at your foot. He's a nice guy. You'll like him. Get him to show you a picture of his pet ferret."

Ann Marie gave him a weak smile. "Thanks, Sean. Cynthia. Sorry I messed up the party."

Cynthia stepped to the bed with shoulders squared and head high as if she were daring the girl's parents to say anything. "You don't worry about that. We'll have plenty of ice cream and cake left. When you get home I'll send Rick over with some."

"That sounds great."

Cynthia went out of the door ahead of him. They stopped at the nurses' station, where he let them know he was leaving and that Ann Marie's parents had arrived.

"What was that all about?" he asked as soon as they were out of earshot of everyone.

"I guess it's about the fact that I am responsible for my two brothers and that Ann Marie's parents don't think I'm doing a good enough job. I appreciate your support back there. You're a good guy, Dr. Sean Donavon."

Was this feeling of pride in his chest the same one as a knight of old experienced when he saved a damsel in distress? He sure hoped so; he rather liked it. "I know it's been an emotional few hours and you're probably ready to get home but I need to run this report upstairs to my buddy's office."

Cynthia gave him a weary look. "It's not a problem. I'll just wait in the car."

"You sure? You could ride up with me if you want." Sean hated to leave her sitting in the car.

She took a second to answer. "Okay."

"I'll go out and get it."

"I'll go with you," Cynthia said in a sad voice. He wished he could put that upbeat sound back into it. "I need to walk off this anger I'm feeling ever since Mrs. Lucas showed up. My parents would be so upset to know someone thought so poorly of our family."

Hoping to make her feel better, Sean said, "I, for

one, would consider the source or give her the benefit of the doubt because her child was hurt and forget it."

"I wish it was that easy."

His gaze didn't leave her face. "I know it isn't."

They walked to the car, he got his file and they returned to the building. He led her to a staff elevator and they rode to the fifth floor. There they walked down the hall to where there were a group of nondescript doors.

Sean knocked on one of them. A voice called, "Come in."

Sean glanced back at her and she said, "I'll just wait out here."

A few minutes later he joined her again. "All done. Let's go."

She nodded and they headed back down the hall toward the elevator. On it once again, Sean looked her as she took a spot on the opposite side of the car. Studying her as she watched the floor numbers light up, he noticed a small blob of yellow in her hair. "You have some paint just at your temple."

Cynthia pushed at her hair but missed the spot.

He reached out and brushed his fingers against her skin. Sean didn't miss the catch in her breathing as his hand continued into her hair. Removing the paint, he showed it to her on the end of his fingers. "See?"

She looked at him wide-eyed as if all her senses were on alert. His certainly were. Cynthia smelled of grass, sunshine and a hint of something that could only be hers alone. Her skin had been smooth as a flower petal. She looked wild and vulnerable in her sweatshirt and jeans with her hair slightly disheveled.

A whispered "Oh" escaped her lips.

The only sense he hadn't experienced was her taste.

He wanted to. Would it be as good as he'd imagined? He leaned forward, his mouth moving toward hers. The bell of the elevator announced they had reached the lobby.

Cynthia jerked back, and he straightened. He'd been so close to what he was searching for. A charmingly guilty look came over her face as three people stood on the outside of the elevator looking at them. She hurried out. He followed more slowly.

Sean was feeling anything but embarrassment. It was more like need, want, desire, lust…

Cynthia was still trembling from the almost kiss when they reached Sean's car. Even in her fantasies she'd not gone that far. Had he really been going to kiss her? She would never have thought a man like Sean would ever be interested in her. With his looks and beautiful voice a tall, leggy blonde who wore tight dresses seemed more his style. Yet, he'd almost kissed her and she hoped he tried again. Soon.

Sean was ready to pull out of the parking lot when she said, "I live out in Bessemer."

He nodded and turned into the traffic headed south. "I didn't want to ask until we were alone but would you mind telling me about what happened to your parents?"

She didn't want to go into her family dynamics but Sean deserved an explanation. She looked out of the window, but not really seeing anything. "My parents died a few years ago in a car accident. Since I was of age I assumed guardianship of my brothers. It hasn't been easy all the time. Mark hasn't always stayed within the lines but we're still together."

"Mark?"

"Yeah. My other brother. He is in college and has a

part-time job. He had to work this evening. He should be at home when we get there."

Sean glanced at her. "How old is he?"

"About to turn twenty," she said in a flat tone.

"No wonder. He was about, what, seventeen when your parents died? Hard age to lose your parents."

"Day after his eighteenth birthday. He took it hard. We all did." She hadn't talked about this in a long time. She had focused on living. Making each day the best she could for herself and her brothers. Now they were both adults but she still felt a responsibility to see they had a good start in life. Saw fun in life.

"So how old were you when you became their guardian?"

"Twenty-one."

He let out a long whistle. "That had to be tough."

"Not really. I was determined our family would stay together. I wouldn't have had it any other way." It hadn't been. She knew what she had to do and had done it.

"I'm impressed. Not everyone's willing to sacrifice like that."

She couldn't imagine anyone not putting their family first. "I was taught that family was everything. I was not going to let us be split up. The boys needed to stay in the same school, have the same friends, stay in the only home they have known."

"So you gave up nursing school to take care of them?"

She shrugged. "Not gave it up as much as postponed it. I did what had to be done at the time. Nursing school could wait." She would do the same again.

"It seems that a lot would have to wait to devote your life to others for years." He said it as if he'd never known someone who'd sacrificed for their family. Or couldn't believe that anyone would.

Thankfully traffic was light and they were turning into her drive only a few minutes later. Her family home was a simple one-story brick on a tree-lined street in a rural neighborhood. Nothing special but it was theirs. She liked this time of day when lights shone through the windows of the other houses. It gave her a sense of security to know she was surrounded by others.

When he'd turned off the engine she turned to him. "I can't say thanks enough for your help."

He smiled. "I have to admit it was a different evening for me. Especially the paintball. It was fun." Sean sounded surprised by that.

"Even the part where you had to take Ann Marie to the hospital?" Sean really was a gorgeous man. But she'd found other things to like about him besides his looks and voice. He'd been great with Ann Marie, even more amazing with her parents.

Sean shrugged and chuckled. "Every doctor loves a trip to the hospital."

She laughed. "I guess they do. I'm glad you were there. Having a doctor along in an emergency is reassuring." Add another positive. A good sport. She could fall for this guy. And that idea was crazy.

"It wasn't like you needed me. You could have handled it." He glanced at the house.

"I appreciate the vote of confidence. Would you like to come in for some cake and ice cream? It's not much in the way of a thank-you but it's the best I can do."

CHAPTER FOUR

SEAN HADN'T BEEN planning to get out of the car. He'd had every intention of dropping Cynthia off and heading for his office as soon as possible. But for some reason he didn't want to leave her company yet. Wanted to know more about her.

He checked his watch. There was time. Staying here and having dessert with Cynthia was much more appealing than wading through paperwork but it wasn't like him to take time away from a project. He shook his head. He couldn't believe he was even considering it. Grinning, he said, "Sure. I'm always up for cake and ice cream."

Before he could get out and close the door Cynthia was on her way up the walk. "I want to make sure you can get into the house. The boys aren't always good about tidying up."

A short time later he joined her in the living room. There was nothing special about the area. The chairs, sofa and TV were what he expected, yet there was an air of being lived in that he'd not experienced in a room since he'd left home. A family lived here. Why had he thought of his own family now?

"Come back this way to the kitchen." Cynthia headed

down a small hallway into a yellow room with the lights already on. On the wooden table sitting in a bay window was a cake box and a couple of plastic grocery bags.

"Hey, Cyn, that you?" a voice called from somewhere in the house.

"Yeah," she said over her shoulder.

Seconds later Rick came to stand in the doorway. Nodding to him, Rick said to Cynthia, "How's Ann Marie?"

"She should be fine. Her parents showed up and we left." Cynthia looked into the cake box.

"They're a piece of work, aren't they?" Rick stepped further into the room.

"They're just concerned about their daughter." Cynthia opened the bags and searched inside.

Sean twisted up his mouth. She was being generous toward them in his opinion. He'd seen people upset in his profession but those two had lashed out undeservingly at Cynthia.

She turned to Rick. "I'm sorry I had to miss part of the party."

"I understand. It was still a great one. Best I've had since Mom and Dad died."

Cynthia gave him a smile that Sean couldn't quite put a name to. One that contained both happiness and grief. Maybe the money she'd spent hadn't been so wasteful. It had certainly made her brother happy.

That was an odd thought for him. He'd spent most of his adult life being thrifty and practical about money. Before today you could have never persuaded him that playing paintball was a good use of hard-earned money.

"I'm glad. I wanted it to be a good one. I think we

owe Sean some cake and ice cream for helping us out."
Cynthia looked back at the cake.

Rick nodded. "Yeah, sure. Thanks, Sean."

"You're welcome, Rick. Again, happy birthday."

"You want to join us?" Cynthia asked her brother.

"Naw," he said. "I'll wait to have some with Mark
when he gets home. He called to say he had to work
overtime. He said I'm really going to like his birthday
gift. I'm going to call and see if Ann Marie is home
yet." The boy disappeared down the hall.

Sean chuckled. "I think he might be interested in
more than her ankle."

Cynthia grinned. "I believe you might be right."

She had a nice smile. One that when directed at him
he liked too much. Thoughts of their almost-kiss sur-
faced. Would her mouth be as warm and inviting as it
looked?

"How about that ice cream and cake?" Cynthia pulled
a paper plate with balloons on it out of one of the bags.

"Sure. But I can't stay long. I still have work to do."

"My guess is that you don't take time off much."
Cynthia served him a large piece of cake.

"I have a busy medical practice. It requires my attention." He took the plate she handed him and sat on
a chair at the table.

She cut a much smaller piece and placed it in front
of the empty chair next to him. "I know that but having down time, fun, is important too."

"I have fun." Sean watched as she went to the freezer
and pulled out a round tub of ice cream.

"Doing what? You've never played paintball until
today." She opened a cabinet drawer, took out a large
spoon and two smaller ones, then closed it.

"A lot of people have never played paintball." Sean failed to understand how that equated to not ever having fun. He'd not played those types of things as a kid because there hadn't been money to do them with. When he'd got older he'd had to go to work. Then there had been medical school. Games weren't something he'd had time for or extra money to waste on.

"That's true. So, what do you like to do for fun?"

Sean was ashamed to admit he had to really think long and too hard for an answer. He didn't have a hobby. His job was his life. It was what would provide him security. Fun wasn't even on his list of needs. "I like to fix noses."

She scoffed. "That's your job. What do you do outside of being a doctor?"

"I like to read."

"Okay, that can be fun. Anything else?" Cynthia looked at him expectantly. As if his having fun was of super importance to her.

"I own a bike." Which he hadn't ridden in weeks.

Her face lit up. "I'm impressed. Riding around here with the mountains and all must be a real workout."

He took another bite of cake. The few times he'd taken the time to ride he had found it invigorating. "It can be. I like to bike in Mountain Brook. It's a nice area."

Cynthia looked dreamy-eyed. "Yeah, I bet it is. I've always thought it would be the perfect place to live."

"It is pretty. My house is in the village." He spent little time there so he hadn't given his surroundings much thought. When he'd moved to town, one of the other doctors had told him that he should consider living in the area so he had.

"Really? Nice."

Apparently he'd impressed her. He certainly hadn't with the amount of fun he had. What was her deal with fun anyway? "See, I live in Mountain Brook and ride a bike so I can have fun."

"I didn't mean to imply that you couldn't."

He gave her his best hurt look. "I think that's exactly what you intended to do."

"I did not!" Cynthia looked indignant.

"You were making fun of me for not having fun." He laughed when she stuck out her tongue at him. "That's the best you have for a comeback? Second-grade gestures? I'll always win our arguments if you can't do any better than that."

Cynthia loved his full-bodied laugh almost as much as she did listening to him speak. The man could be charming and frustrating. But she had to admit she was enjoying their conversation immensely. What would it be like to have him at her kitchen table like this all the time? She shouldn't think that way. It wasn't going to happen.

Digging the spoon into the ice cream, she scooped a large amount and placed it on his plate.

"You're being very free with that," Sean said, observing his plate.

"I don't know any male who doesn't like his ice cream. It was my father's favorite. Said you could never have too much."

"Well, he might have been right about that but it's easy to get fat on." Sean picked up a smaller spoon she'd laid nearby.

Cynthia took a moment to let her look roam over

his trim, muscular physique. "Oh, I think you'll be all right."

"Why, Ms. Marcum, I think you just checked me out." He gave her a teasing grin.

"Dr. Donavon, don't let it go to your head." His eyes widened at her remark and a slow wolfish grin formed on his lips.

Only then did she comprehend the double meaning. With a gulp, she realized what she'd said. Heat rushed to her cheeks. She snatched the top of the ice cream off the table, replaced it and headed for the refrigerator.

"You don't want any ice cream?" he asked with a soft chuckle.

"I don't need any."

His voice went lower. "If you keep talking dirty to me I'll need some more and a cold shower to boot."

Cynthia pulled the freezer door wide, trying to hide her reaction to his teasing. She couldn't spend the rest of the night with her head in the cold so she took a deep breath and pushed the door closed. This was too much. She'd fantasized about him for too long. Sexual fencing wasn't something she was prepared for.

"Are you flirting with me?" She tried to make it sound like an accusation, but it came out sounding a tad hopeful.

"I just thought you could use a little fun as well." He was watching her closely.

They were having fun. The type she'd not shared with a man in a long time, if ever. Dave was a rather dry person with no quick wit. She rather liked flirting.

Cynthia watched as Sean put a spoon full of ice cream in his mouth. He had such a beautiful one. A full lower lip with a thinner upper one, not too wide, and very masculine. She would call it kissable.

Ideas like that had to stop. They were becoming too frequent and too disturbing. Just because Sean had been going to kiss her in the elevator didn't mean he still wanted to. Squaring her shoulders, Cynthia controlled the shaking of her knees. She sat, leaving plenty of space between them.

"You know, it has been a long time since I've been to a birthday party." He took a bite of cake.

"Really? Even for your family?"

Sean felt her full attention on him. She obviously thought everyone saw family in the same way. He shook his head. "No. I don't get together with my family much."

"Why not? They live far away?" She studied him as if he were some strange lab specimen.

"Not really. Only a couple of hours."

"I can't imagine not seeing my brothers every day." She ate some more cake.

"I haven't seen my brother or sister in a couple of years. We're just not a close family. Do you think your brothers will always live right here or close by? They could move away."

"I know that. But we would always visit." She paused as if she wasn't sure she should say more before asking, "Did something happen in your family that causes you not to go see them?"

"Yeah. I got away." He hoped he made it clear by his tone he wanted to change the subject.

"Oh." Cynthia returned her attention to her plate.

It wasn't Cynthia's business what went on with his

family. He didn't like talking about them. How he felt. It didn't matter anyway. He was his own man now. Not involved with people who thought or acted as his parents did.

"I'm sorry. I've been nosey. Very rude of me. My brothers accuse me of that all the time."

Sean forced a smile. "Let's just say my childhood doesn't hold my fondest memories."

They ate quietly for a few minutes.

"What does hold your fondest memories?"

"More questions." He gave her a pointed look. She acted as if she wanted to apologize again but he continued. "Playing paintball will now be one. I rather enjoyed the part where I shot the boy overtaking us while you were under me."

Cynthia gave him a searching look while seeming to dare him at the same time. "Are you flirting with me again?"

"What if I was?" Somehow her answer was going to mean more than it should. He really liked her. Respected the confidence with which she faced him head-on.

She looked away. "I'm not sure I want to answer that question."

Maybe she was feeling the same about him as he was her. He grinned. "I think you already have." Sean placed his spoon on the empty plate. Now he needed to give her room to think about that. "I really should be going."

"I'm sorry you got caught up in my family craziness."

"No big deal." He shrugged a shoulder. "I was glad I was around to help." When he got to his feet Cynthia did too. She followed him to her front door. Opening it, he turned back to her. "You know, I don't think I can leave until I've finished what I started. I wouldn't be able to sleep."

Her perplexed expression brought a smile to his face.

Placing a finger under her chin, he lifted it. "This." He placed his mouth on hers. Her lips tasted amazing, just as he'd thought they might. They were plump, soft and sweet from the icing. When she didn't resist he stepped closer, taking the kiss deeper.

Her hands rested on his waist.

"Hey, Cyn." Rick's voice carried from the direction of the kitchen.

She pulled back and studied Sean with charmingly dazed eyes, making him want to kiss her on the way to the nearest bedroom.

He said softly, "The next time I kiss you I'm going to make sure we can't be interrupted." As Rick came around the corner Sean said in a normal tone, "Good night, Cynthia."

The next morning Cynthia was still reliving, basking in, the pleasure of Sean's lips touching hers. Yet, she still wondered what it meant. Could he be interested in a real relationship or was he just playing with her? Not that she hadn't enjoyed it. To the contrary, she had very much. They really didn't have anything in common except that she did his transcription. Yet they seemed to have a good time together. Even laughed a couple of times. But he wasn't into family. He'd said so.

She only had time for her family right now. More than that, she wanted a husband and children. Forever. But, was that what he was looking for?

Despite all the questions and the push-pull between them, she'd savored his kiss. Found it too brief. Wanted another. Had she daydreamed about him for so long, built him up in her mind to the point it would be impossible for him to meet her expectations? Yet, she found the real Sean Donavon even more fascinating than the fantasy. It had taken nothing but a simple kiss to make her envision being wrapped in his arms, pressed against his chest and thoroughly loved. Her imagination was already warping into overdrive. She laughed. In reality he probably kissed everyone who offered him ice cream.

By midmorning she had checked her emails four times more than usual but still found no notes from Sean. What had she expected? He had a busy practice and was working on the grant. She was being silly. He didn't have time to waste typing emails to her all the time. Still she looked for one.

Disgusted with herself and determined to get him off her mind, she finished transcribing work for another doctor and called Ann Marie's house to check on her. Her mother was civil but only gave her a short statement that Ann Marie was doing fine and had gone to school on crutches. She also said that Dr. Donavon had called and it wasn't necessary that she do so as well.

Cynthia was still glad she had made the effort. Despite how irresponsible Ann Marie's mother thought she might be, Cynthia still took her responsibility as the adult in the family seriously. She'd found the high road and done the right thing by checking on the girl. It had been nice to have Sean's support the night before. Sometimes holding down the parent position in her family was a heavy burden. At the hospital had been one of those times. Taking on major adult duties under difficult circumstances hadn't been easy.

Right now what she should do was concentrate on

the transcription she needed to finish. By the middle of the afternoon a message popped into the system that Sean had submitted some dictation. She was down to typing nothing but those an hour later. She'd always left his work for last but now that she'd been kissed by him the thought of his voice in her ear was almost too sensual, too personal.

Left no choice, she opened his material, replaced her headphones and clicked on the first report. With her fingers on the keyboard and prepared for Sean's voice, she still hadn't expected the jolt she received when he said, "Hello, Cynthia."

Her heart did a little tap dance. She almost melted in the chair. Leaning back in her chair, she closed her eyes, basking in the timbre of his voice.

"I hope you're having a good day."

I am now.

"When you finish the dictation on this tape would you mind printing them and letting the office know? I need them right away. By the way, I enjoyed yesterday evening. Maybe we could do it again sometime soon."

How was she supposed to concentrate after that? This had to stop. Her obsession with the man. But still a girl could dream. Could bask in it until it ended. And it would end, she was sure.

Straightening in the chair, Cynthia pressed her lips together. It was time for her to get serious. As if that would happen while Sean was speaking in her ear. Still, this was work that must be completed. He needed it. She needed the paycheck.

For the next hour, she barely managed to stay focused on what Sean was saying and not on how her body was reacting to his voice. It was almost a relief to finish the last report. The business day was almost over when she typed the last word. She called Sean's office and was told by the office manager that it was too late for a messenger service to come.

"Then I'll just bring them in," she told the woman.

"I'm sure that Dr. Donavon will appreciate that."

Cynthia took a few moments to wash her face, brush her hair and change clothes before she headed out of the door. The trip back to her house from downtown wouldn't be enjoyable during rush hour but Sean had said he needed the reports. She refused to let herself contemplate the little thrill she felt over just having a chance to see Sean again.

Would he be glad to see her?

Pulling into his office parking lot a few minutes before closing time, Cynthia headed into the building. The receptionist was still behind the window but obviously preparing to leave. "I have some transcription that Sean, uh…Dr. Donavon requested for today."

At her use of his first name the woman's head jerked up and her eyes filled with interest. The receptionist looked her over as if she'd never really given her any thought the other times they'd met. Once again, she seemed to dismiss her as unimportant. Apparently she didn't see Cynthia as competition material.

Raising her nose slightly, the woman said, "Dr. Donavon is with a patient."

Disappointment filled Cynthia but this trip wasn't about her cow-eyed crush on Sean. Cynthia handed the packet of reports to the woman. "I understand. I don't need to disturb him. Please make sure he gets these reports right away."

The woman nodded and went back to what she had been doing.

Cynthia refused to look down the hallway in the direction of Sean's office as she made her way out of the lobby. She was in her car buckling in when there was a rap on the driver's side window. Her heart jumped in her chest as she jerked around. Sean stood there.

He indicated for her to roll the window down. When she did he said as if disappointed, "You weren't going to say hi?"

Her pulse raced from her excitement at seeing him. "I was told you were seeing a patient."

"You could have waited." He sounded disappointed. Leaning down so his face was in the window, he said, "Are you hungry?"

He was close. So very close. What would he say if she traced his lips with her finger? "Hungry?" Absorbed in thinking about his lips, she wasn't really listening.

"Yes. Hungry. You know, food, stomach making noises. Five o'clock somewhere."

Cynthia blinked and came back to the real world. The man had put a spell on her, turning her brain to mush whenever he was around. "I know what it is. I just wasn't sure why you were asking."

He grinned. One of those "nice guys in wolf's clothing" kind. The type where a girl should run but couldn't because she was afraid that she might regret it. "I wanted to see if you'd like to grab some dinner with me. I missed lunch. My surgery case went longer than expected."

Cynthia tingled all over. Sean was asking her to dinner. "I guess I could be interested in dinner."

He chuckled. "You're not going to dare act as if you might like me, are you?"

Cynthia gave him a syrupy smile. She had to play it cool. Not let on how keen she was on the idea. That was the problem: she liked him too well. So much so, she could be swept away by him. "I have a feeling that if you had the upper hand you'd take advantage of it. Then I'd be in big trouble."

Sean leaned in closer. His face inches from hers. "You know, Cynthia, sometimes it's fun to live dangerously. You do believe in fun, don't you?"

She did. Danger she wasn't so sure about. Her heart wasn't something she played with. And she had no idea where all of this was going. It took her a moment to answer. "I do. But I also need to know I won't get hurt while I'm having fun."

"It's just supper, not a long-term contract," he said softly.

Cynthia took a moment to give that some thought. She wanted to go so why was she holding back? There hadn't been a man in her life in a long time and now a nice one wanted to take her out. Why wouldn't she take a chance? "I guess I could. I'd have to sit in traffic at this hour to get home anyway."

He straightened a little, just missing the top of the door. "So what you're saying is that sharing a meal with me is just a step better than sitting in traffic."

She smiled. "Now you're trying to put words in my mouth."

"So what'll it be? Me or the traffic?" His eyes dared her to agree.

Truthfully it wasn't a hard decision. Sean would win every time. "I'll have supper with you."

He grinned and gave the door a thump with his palm. "Great. Come on back inside and we'll go in my car. I'll drop you back here when we're done."

Sean waited while she rolled up the window, got out and locked the car. Together they walked back to his office building.

For once Cynthia wished she'd taken more time with her appearance. It had been so long since she'd been on a date the idea seemed almost foreign. Still, she could hardly contain the anticipation bubbling up because Sean had gone to the effort to catch her before she'd left the parking lot.

His receptionist's eyes widened then narrowed as they walked past her. Cynthia was tempted to give her a gloating smile but didn't.

In his office Sean went behind his desk and removed his lab coat, draping it over the back of his chair.

"I don't think your receptionist likes me. I just got the evil eye. Methinks there's a story there." Cynthia studied him. She wouldn't appreciate being a part of Sean's harem.

Sean glanced up from the papers he was putting into a stack on his desk. "Nothing you should be worried about."

"I don't need to step in the middle of something." She had enough complications in her life. Didn't need to get involved with a womanizer. Her heart had been broken once and she had no interest in having that repeated.

Sean stopped what he was doing and came around the desk. "To put your mind at ease we went out a couple of times. As friends."

Cynthia angled her head at an angle and gave him a skeptical look.

He quirked his mouth. "Okay. I thought friends. She wanted more."

"So what do you want from me?" Cynthia was re-thinking going to dinner. Maybe they should just re-main employee and employer. She needed this job, no heartache. He already had the ability to give her that. Was she willing to take that chance? To have him dis-rupt her ordered life?

Sean moved closer, not into her personal space but near enough to take one of her hands. "Friends, at least. More, I hope. Look, I've already discussed and explained more in order to get you to go out to dinner with me than I have with any other woman. Trust me. Let's just get to know each other and see what happens."

Maybe it was time for her to stop worrying all the time and have some fun for a change. After all, she was the one who believed in it. "Okay."

"Great. Let's go." He smiled and let her step out of the door ahead of him.

Sean directed her down the hall to the back of the build-ing. As they passed his nurse he said good night and asked her to see that the office was secure.

Running through a slow but steady rain, they quickly climbed into his car. Cynthia laughed and pushed at her hair as if trying to put it into some sort of order. He rather liked her less polished look. The tight-skirt, glossy-lipped, shiny-jewelry-adorned women paled in comparison to Cynthia's fresh-faced, meet-life-head-on personality. It had an appeal that pulled at him. "There's a nice place not far from here where we can get a good meal."

"Sounds perfect. You know your car isn't at all what I pictured you driving," Cynthia said as she buckled up.

He gave her a questioning look. "How's that?"

"I don't know. I always pictured you as a sports car kind of guy."

She had been imagining him? "Where did you get that idea?"

"Your voice." She looked out of the windshield instead of at him as if she'd said more than she had intended to.

"My voice? I didn't know you could tell what kind of car a person would buy by their voice. Is that a new medical discovery?" He started the car.

Cynthia looked at him. "No. More like dream therapy."

Sean gave that a thoughtful nod. This conversation was getting interesting. "Been dreaming about me, have you?"

She vigorously shook her head, her hair covering her face. "No, just my overactive imagination, which had put surgeon, good practice and bachelor into an equation and come out with hot red sports car. You can tell math is not my strongest subject."

He backed out of the parking spot. "So you had me figured as a cliché. All your information may be true but you also forgot to figure in loans for medical school. And not every doctor feels the need to live extravagantly."

"I guess they don't. But I wasn't thinking that practically."

"Are you disappointed?" He waited with anticipation for her answer. For some reason it would hurt if she was.

"No. I'm not so shallow as to base my friendship with someone on the type of car he drives."

"That's encouraging to know." Sean pulled out into the street, a sense of relief washing over him. He wouldn't be interested in any woman who was only concerned about how much was in his wallet. As far as he was concerned that was another get rich scheme. More than one woman had thought he was their way to the good life. The latest being his receptionist.

"I know what you mean."

He glanced at her. "That sounds like there's a little bitterness in that statement."

A soft contrite sigh came from her. "I guess there is."

"Despite being a surgeon whose patients are asleep during most of his interaction with them, I'm a good listener." He really wanted to know what was behind her reaction. Somehow he believed it had something to do with Cynthia's hesitancy at them becoming more than doctor and transcriptionist.

"I had a boyfriend. It was pretty serious. We were talking about getting married, then my parents died. I had my brothers to be concerned about. It wasn't long before he'd had enough and was gone."

"That must have been tough." If nothing else the timing was poor. When she'd needed support the most she'd been let down. No wonder she was so suspicious of his actions. But even if they started dating he didn't see their relationship becoming too involved. He wouldn't be around long enough for her to depend on him.

"Yeah, it was," she said in a flat tone.

They were quiet for a few moments as he worked his way through traffic.

Suddenly Cynthia cried, "Oh, no. You've got to take me back to my car."

"What? Why?" Had she forgotten something? Was she in pain?

"I forgot about Rick's game tonight. I've never done that before." She pulled out her phone. "I can just make it if I hurry."

Sean was relieved that it wasn't something serious. "Doesn't he have other games he'll play?" Why was her seeing a basketball game so important?

"This is his senior year. I've not missed one." She looked around anxiously as if she was in a panic to get to her car.

"Surely you have time for a quick dinner? We're almost to the restaurant." He'd gone to such effort to convince her to eat with him. He couldn't help being disappointed she'd rather go to a high-school basketball game instead of spending time with him.

"I'm sorry but I really must go. Rick expects me to be there. He has no one in the stands to support him if I'm not. Don't you remember how important it was to have someone rooting for you?"

He couldn't. The few times his parents had had the money to let him be a part of an afterschool activity they hadn't ever shown up to see him participate. They had always been having meetings to get people to join their various business ventures. There hadn't been time to watch him play ball. If they had attended they'd spent their time trying to recruit people to join them. No, he knew nothing about the support Cynthia was talking about.

"No. My parents weren't very good at that sort of thing," he said in a neutral tone.

She looked at him for a moment before quietly saying, "I'm sorry. Supporting each other is what my family does. No matter how small the event. I have to go. Rick will worry if I'm not there."

Twisting in his direction, she added, "Sean, I'm truly sorry for bailing at the last minute." Briefly she touched his arm. "Hey, why don't you come to the game with me? I can get your dinner." She smiled. "Hotdog, fries and popcorn."

"As appetizing as that sounds, I've got to work tonight." The food didn't sound that appealing but he sure would miss spending time with her.

She waved a hand. "I need to make up for running out on you. How about coming to dinner Sunday night?"

He shook his head. "I wish I could but I have this grant hanging over my head."

"Bring the work with you and we'll spread it out on the table, look at it on the laptop. I'll see what I can do to help you. I've done enough of the reports for it that I think I have an idea of where you're headed."

"I don't know." Still, he was tempted. He wanted to get to know her better and she was offering help he needed. Maybe he could accomplish two things at once.

"You're afraid I'm a bad cook, aren't you?" Cynthia's look was piercing.

He grinned. "Well, maybe a little."

"I'll tell you what, if you don't like my cooking… I don't know what I'll do. But I do wish you'd come to dinner. I feel horrible about this."

Her eyes were begging him to agree. "It's not necessary but a home-cooked meal does sound appealing. Okay. And I'll bring work along. I'm not going to turn down good help."

After he'd heard her story about her ex he was sure he would lose any chance he had with her if he didn't take this in his stride. A few minutes later he pulled up next to her car.

A broad smile lit Cynthia's face and she planted a quick kiss on his cheek. When she pulled back she appeared shocked. Hurrying out of his car, she said in a rush, "Great. I'll see you at seven."

Sean watched as she pulled out of the lot. He couldn't deny feeling put out at her dropping him to go to her brother's game. Nothing in him or his background gave him a basis to comprehend that type of devotion. Still, he had to respect her commitment to her brothers even if he thought it was a little over the top. What would it be like to have someone care about him with such devotion?

CHAPTER FIVE

TWO EVENINGS LATER Sean showed up at Cynthia's house right at seven. To avoid looking too eager, he arrived on time even though he'd been looking forward to her dinner all day. He'd spent more time anticipating his date with her than he had on the looming grant deadline.

There was still so much to organize. He hoped Cynthia would be able to make sense of the tangle of information he was trying to get in order. After asking her to help him he realized that he didn't even know where to have her start. All he knew to do was bring what he had and let her have at it. With the deadline looming he was afraid he would be putting in several long days ahead.

That afternoon he'd sent her an email.

Cynthia
Looking forward to dinner tonight. Can I bring something?
Sean

A few minutes later the reply had come back.

No—just yourself.
Cynthia

When was the last time he'd been interested in a girl who was equally interested in him? Not his money or position? He liked the idea that he alone was enough for Cynthia. But was that really true? He didn't know her well enough to state that as fact. Still, the idea it could be true made him feel something he hadn't in a long time. Wanted.

The porch light was on and the house looked welcoming. He'd become so used to going home to his dark house that the idea someone was expecting him pleased him. He climbed a couple of steps and knocked on the door. Seconds later it was slung open by a younger man who Sean hadn't met before. He surmised that the man must be Cynthia's middle brother, Mark. Sean suppressed his disappointment that Mark wasn't Cynthia. It would have been nice to have a chance at another kiss.

"Hey, man, you must be Sean. I'm Mark. Come on in," Mark offered. Sean stepped inside. "Cyn's in the kitchen buzzing around. You must be a pretty big deal. I haven't seen her this excited since her prom night." Mark pushed the door closed with a slap.

He headed down the hall and Sean followed. So Cynthia was acting out of character because of him. Interesting.

An amazing smell wafted to his nose. If he had to guess it was roast beef. His stomach reacted to the pull of his favorite meal. His mother used to fix it on his birthday. It didn't matter if they were in dire straits at the time or not, she saw to it each of her children got their favorite meal on their birthdays. He had all but forgotten about that.

Mark passed the kitchen entrance and continued down the hall. Cynthia turned away from the sink and smiled when he entered the kitchen. Sean returned the smile as he set down his bag with the grant material in it. If he got that kind of welcome every time he went home, he wouldn't spend nearly as much time at the office.

"Hey." There was a touch of pink on her cheeks.

"Hi. I did as you said. I came empty-handed." He stepped closer, looking over her shoulder.

"That's what you were supposed to do." There was a little nervous wobble in her voice. Tomatoes, lettuce and a cucumber sat in the sink.

"What're you up to?"

She looked at him. "I'm surprised that a man of your intelligence wouldn't recognize salad fixin'."

"There you go starting with the smart mouth. You should be careful about talking to me like that. I might not offer my help." When had he ever teased a woman in the kitchen? When had a woman he was going out with offered to prepare him dinner? In the short time he'd known Cynthia he'd experienced a number of personal firsts.

"Since you offered to help…" She stepped back, bumping into him.

Sean reached for her but she scooted away. Opening a drawer, she withdrew a small cutting board. "How about you slicing the tomato and cucumber?"

It had been some time since he'd helped in the kitchen but he was game if it meant being around Cynthia. "I can do that."

She handed the board to him and pulled a knife out of a wooden block on the counter. "Here you go. I'm going to check on the roast. It should be almost done."

Sean picked up a tomato. Placing it on the board, he

sliced it. He wasn't about to let on that he didn't know what he was doing. Cynthia opened the oven and the aroma made his stomach growl. The sooner he had this salad finished, the sooner they could eat. As he continued to chop she set the table.

"Here's a bowl for that." Cynthia set a glass one on the counter next to him, then she flitted away again.

"Thanks." Sean continued to chop. He felt surprisingly comfortable spending time on something as domestic as preparing a meal. It had been so long since he'd been in a home where that was done. Really since he had left his parents as an eighteen-year-old. For some reason he was thinking of them far more often after meeting Cynthia and her brothers.

A few minutes later she asked, "Are you about done there?"

"I didn't know I had a time limit. Damn!" Sean jerked his hand back. Looking down, he saw blood dripping from the end of his thumb.

Cynthia was at his side instantly. "What've you done? Let me see." She snatched a dish towel off a hook attached to the cabinet. Wrapping her hand around his wrist, she raised it above his heart and covered his thumb with the towel.

His finger throbbed with every beat of his heart and his stomach roiled. This sort of cut was far worse pain-wise than the type he made in surgery.

"You look a little green," Cynthia said. "Come over here and sit down." She led him to a chair at the table, still holding his hand in the air.

Sean gladly sat.

"Mark," Cynthia called, urgency evident in her voice.

Seconds later there was the sound of feet hurrying down the hall. Mark came into the kitchen.

"Get me the first-aid kit out from under the sink in my bath," she instructed.

"What happened?" he asked, sounding concerned.

She lifted the towel and looked at the thumb. "Sean cut himself. Now go."

Mark left.

Cynthia turned back to Sean. "I need to look at this and see how bad it is. You may need stitches."

Sean winced as she finished removing the rag and air hit the wound. He watched her face as she studied his thumb. Her nose wrinkled up and her lips drew into a tight line. "Who would have thought a surgeon wouldn't be able to handle a knife?" There was a note of humor in her tone but she said it with a straight face.

That remark didn't make him feel any better. "Is that your best bedside manner?"

She recovered his finger and looked at him, saying sweetly, "I'm sorry. Does it hurt terribly?"

His look met hers. "Actually, at the risk of sounding less than manly, it does."

"I'm sorry." Compassion covered her face and she placed a hand on his shoulder. "I'll get you cleaned up and you should be fine. It's not too deep or long." Her attention turned to Mark as he put the first-aid box on the table then left. "Thanks," she called. To Sean she said, "I want you to apply pressure here while I wet some gauze to clean you up."

"You do realize I'm a doctor, don't you?" At least with her so close he was starting to think about other things than the throbbing of his thumb.

"Right now you're my patient." She opened the box

and pulled out a couple of packages of square gauze. Tearing the paper, she removed them, dropping the covering on the table. "Come over to the sink." She moved there and ran water over the gauze. He joined her. She handed him the square that had been folded in half. "You hold this."

Sean took it and watched as she removed the towel. Carefully she cleaned around the injury.

"At least it doesn't require stitches." She sounded satisfied. "I'll disinfect it and bandage it well. You should be fine." Cynthia met his look. "This won't prevent you from doing surgery, will it?"

He shook his head. "No. I'm not scheduled until the day after tomorrow and it should be healing well by then."

"Good." She truly seemed relieved. "I'd hate for you to have to move your surgery schedule around because I had you making a salad. Put that gauze over the opening and go back to the table. I'm going to get the roast out so we don't have a fire on top of a cut hand. I'll cover that in just a sec."

Sean returned to his chair, glad his stomach had settled. He was embarrassed enough; if he'd passed out it would've been worse. He didn't mind other people's blood but had never liked the sight of his own.

Cynthia was beside him seconds later. Using a Betadine swab, she cleaned around the cut, applied an antibacterial ointment and placed a clean gauze pad over the area and taped it.

Impressed, he remarked, "You're really quite good at this. When do you plan to return to school? Good nurses are always needed."

"I've got to see the boys get through school and are on their way." She didn't slow down as she spoke.

Sean looked at the top of her head in disbelief. "Boys? They're young men, you know. I think you underestimate them."

"You don't understand." By her tone she was firmly dismissing the subject.

He didn't understand. It was as if she was hiding behind her brothers. Didn't want to move on. Wasn't accepting her parents had died. That her brothers were growing out of needing her attention all the time. That she had a life too that she should be living.

Cynthia cleaned up the first-aid kit and pushed it aside. She smiled at him. "Now, if you're through creating pre-dinner drama I'll get our food on the table."

Sean smiled weakly. "Please don't let me stand in the way. I'm hungry and that roast smells wonderful. I'll finish the salad."

She put a hand on his shoulder when he started to stand. "You stay right there. I'll do it. By the way, I saw that green look on your face. Was that the look of a surgeon who doesn't like the sight of blood?"

"Thanks for making an already embarrassing situation even more so," he grumbled. "Actually other people's blood doesn't bother me, just my own."

She grinned. "Your secret is safe with me."

"Cyn, when are we going to eat?" Rick asked from the doorway.

"In just a few minutes. Help me get everything on the table," Cynthia said without slowing her movements.

Just minutes later Mark joined them. "How's the finger?"

"I'll live," Sean said as he turned in his chair and

put his leg beneath the table. He wouldn't admit that it was still throbbing.

Rick came to sit beside him. Mark helped put bowls of food on the table and took a chair, leaving the one closest to Sean for Cynthia. Soon she slipped into it.

Sean didn't want to count the number of years it had been since he'd sat at a kitchen table and had a family meal. Cynthia said a short prayer then said to him, "Hand me your plate and I'll serve you. It's too hot and heavy to pass."

Cynthia filled his plate with meat, potatoes, carrots and onions and handed the plate back to him. She did the same for her brothers.

"Rick, pass that corn around." She picked up the rolls and offered them to Sean.

He took one and passed the dish along. Not until everyone had a full plate did Cynthia pick up her fork and start eating. Was she always seeing about everyone else? Sean had never seen a less self-centered person.

Sean couldn't believe how wonderful the tender roast tasted as well as the other food. Despite his earlier stomach distress, he loved the meal. He'd been missing a part of life he hadn't realized he'd lost. "Mmm. This is the best."

"Thanks. I'm glad you think so." Cynthia smiled at him. "The meat came from an internet mail-order company. I think it's excellent quality. I have a friend who sells it. She wants me to join the company. To make money or get free products all I have to do is to get others to join. That shouldn't be too hard. The product sells itself."

Sean flinched and almost choked on his food. Where had he heard those words before? They sounded suspiciously like something his parents would be involved in. Just another get-rich-quick scheme. He didn't want to have anything to do with that type of thing. Or someone who was doing it. He worked to keep his voice even. How was he going to comment? He couldn't say: why would you want to do that? He settled on, "I'm not a fan of those types of deals."

Cynthia gave him an inquiring look. "Why's that?"

"Because they often don't pan out as advertised. It also takes time to get people to join. I would think you have enough going on."

"If the money was good I would make time. I think it'd be easy enough to sell. The food is good." Cynthia took a forkful of corn. "Would you like to be my first customer?" She looked at him. "Sign up under me?"

How was he going to answer that question nicely? There was no way he would get involved even for her. "No, thank you. I don't eat at home enough to make it worth my while."

"I guess your lifestyle doesn't lend itself to cooking much."

Somehow that made him sound sort of sad. "Maybe what I need to do is just come here more often." Sean smiled at her, then her brothers.

She looked directly at him. "Maybe we can work something out."

Sean glanced at her brothers to find them grinning and elbowing each other. They were enjoying his and Cynthia's exchange. "So, Rick, how's the basketball going?"

The teen almost choked on his drink he had just picked up. "Pretty good. I think we have a real chance to make the playoffs this year."

"That sounds great. And have you seen Ann Marie?" Sean asked.

Rick's face took on a red tint before he looked down at his plate.

"Isn't that the girl that got hurt at your birthday party?" Mark asked, looking to all of them for an answer.

"Yes. But she isn't just some girl," Rick said, pointing his fork at his brother.

Mark gave him a teasing look and said in a singsong voice, "Rick's got a girlfriend."

"Shut up, Mark. You're just jealous no one'll look at your ugly mug," Rick snapped back.

"Boys, that's enough. Sean doesn't want to hear all that," Cynthia said, as if she refereed regularly.

Cynthia really did act as if she were the boys' parent instead of their sister. Couldn't she see they were all grown up? Or was she afraid to let go? Sean said, "I don't mind. My older brother treated me the same way."

They all quieted as they continued eating their meal. Mark's phone rang and he picked it up.

"You know there are no phones at meals," Cynthia said as he touched the screen to answer.

"I need to get this. It might be about a new job I applied for today." He slid out of the chair.

Cynthia didn't look pleased as she watched Mark leave the room.

Minutes later he returned with excitement written all over his face and pumping the air. "I got the job. I got the job." He slid into the chair again, almost vibrating with excitement. "It's full time. I'm going to be working at Action Auto."

"That's great, but won't that be hard to handle with school?" Cynthia asked.

Sean gave her a speculative look. Wasn't she glad he had gotten a job? It looked as if she would appreciate his help with the finances. Sean had been brought up in a household where anyone who had a steady job was unusual. Except for him. He'd handled work and school. Had been the first to take on a job when he'd been old enough. It was something that his parents couldn't do. Cynthia should be proud of Mark.

"I told you I wasn't going back to school next semester," Mark almost snarled.

"Mama and Daddy wanted you to go to school," Cynthia insisted.

Mark leaned across the table. "They're not here. And they wanted you to go too."

Cynthia appeared stricken. "We should honor their wishes. You know I plan to go back."

"Then you go instead of me. For right now I'm going to work." Mark pushed his chair back and stood. "I've got to get things together for tomorrow. Thanks for dinner."

Sean hurt for Cynthia, could see her unhappiness. As if her world were dissolving around her.

She looked at him. "I'm sorry, Sean. This isn't how we were raised to treat a guest."

"It's okay. Dinner and entertainment. That's more than I usually have on a Sunday evening. I'm not complaining."

That got a ghost of a smile out of her. "Thanks for understanding."

Rick's chair screeched as he pushed it back. "I've got a project to work on. See y'all later."

Sean looked at Cynthia and smiled. "I guess that leaves us doing the dishes."

"I'm sorry the evening turned into a family feud. It seems that I'll owe you another meal to make up for this one." Cynthia rose from the table.

"That works out perfectly for me. How about dinner Friday night? I'll pick you up at seven." Sean wasn't sure about Cynthia being involved in a selling pyramid scheme or her over-devotion to her brothers, but he couldn't resist getting to know her better. Regardless of their differences, he found her interesting and sincere. He just plain old-fashioned liked her. It wasn't as if they'd ever become involved enough to marry but he did like her company.

Cynthia carried the roast beef platter to the kitchen counter. "I'm supposed to be the one doing a meal for you."

"Next time. This time I want to take you out." Sean picked up two bowls and followed her to the kitchen counter.

"That sounds like fun. Let me take care of cleaning up. I don't want you to accidentally hit your thumb."

"I'm not an invalid. I can at least carry things to you." He didn't give her a chance to respond before he returned to the table and picked up a bowl. "Do Rick and Mark ever help with cleaning up? After all, you do the cooking."

She squirted dish liquid into the sink. "Not really. They have a lot going on."

"More than you? I'd think the three people could split

the work three ways," Sean commented as he added another plate to the dishwasher.

Tension filled the air between them. Had he said too much? Sounded too critical?

Cynthia didn't say anything and continued to clean.

"I'm sorry if I said something wrong." Sean hoped to get them back to teasing each other as they had been before dinner.

She shrugged. "It's no big deal."

Somehow Sean didn't believe that.

A quarter of an hour later they were finished cleaning and the air between them had been easy.

"So what did you bring to work on tonight?" she asked.

"Do you mind helping me with that organization we talked about earlier? I'm not feeling good about this grant application at all."

"Get your stuff. Bring it over here to the table and we'll have a look." Cynthia became all business.

Sean went after his bag that was still where he'd left it near the door. "Okay. Maybe with your help tonight I can make some real progress on this mess."

They spread the papers out across the table. Cynthia went to get her laptop from her office while he opened his. She returned and sat next to him. She smelled of home cooking, a hint of gardenia and something that could only be her scent alone.

Sean leaned just a little closer as they reviewed side by side the contents on their screens. For the next two hours they worked diligently trying to organize reports in a logical format. They were careful to make note of any missing support material.

Finally, he leaned back in his chair and stretched his arms up over his head, yawning. "I think this is in a better form than I have seen it in weeks. I owe that to you." His arm came down around her shoulders and he gave her a squeeze. "I can't thank you enough."

She looked directly at him. "I know you're going to make a big difference in many people's lives. It gives me a good feeling to be a part of that. Even in a small way."

"That's one of the things I like about you. Your concern for other people. Your help won't have been in a small way if I get that grant," he said as he stood.

"You'll get it."

He liked her vote of confidence too. Here she was supporting his work when he couldn't do the same with her thoughts on selling online food. Somehow it didn't seem right. Still, he couldn't support what he knew from experience was a bad idea. When was the last time he'd really had someone in his corner like this? He could get used to it. With a hand on her shoulder, he quickly responded, "Thanks for everything. The meal and the help. I'd better go. I have an early case in the morning."

Cynthia helped him gather the papers from the table. He put them in his bag along with his laptop. She walked him to the door.

He put his bag on the floor. "You know, I really enjoyed tonight."

"Even with all the blood and family fireworks?" She grinned at him.

"For the first time in a long time I had a meal with a real family. I know better than most that family meals can often be a little tough to live through. More than one of my family's was."

She nodded. "I appreciate your understanding."

He glanced down the hall fully expecting one of her brothers to come around the corner. Every time he attempted to kiss her they were interrupted. This time he didn't care whether someone saw them or not. "Did I say thank you for patching up my thumb?"

"You did." She looked at him with those questioning eyes. "More than once."

"But I don't think I did it properly." Sean slipped his hands around her waist and pulled her to him. She didn't back away. Instead she came to him willingly. His heart beat faster. Cynthia wanted him to kiss her. His mouth found hers warm and welcoming. She came closer, bringing her body to meet his, hands moving up to the nape of his neck. It didn't require much coaxing for her to part her lips. Her tongue shyly touched his before she joined him in the hottest kiss of his life. He pulled her tighter against him. With a moan edged with regret, she placed both her hands on his shoulders and pushed away.

Her dazed look met his, revealing she had been just as affected by their kiss as he was. "I think you need to go before we forget my brothers are just down the hall."

Her brothers. He continued to hold her and leaned his forehead against hers for a moment, struggling to get his raging libido under control. Gazing deep into her guileless eyes, he muttered, "I guess you're right. When I'm around you I forget about everything else. I'm pretty sure we shouldn't hold an X-rated show at your front door."

She gave him a sad, understanding smile and stepped back. "I would appreciate that."

"So, dinner Friday night?" Sean hoped to coax her away from he responsibilities long enough for them to find some uninterrupted time together.

"What about the grant?"

"With your help tonight I think I'm making real progress. I can take one night off. Anyway, I need to clear my head some." He ran his finger along her chin and whispered, "I think you'll make a nice distraction."

"I can't honestly say I've ever been called a distraction before." Her eyes sparkled.

His gaze didn't leave hers. "Well, if you haven't been it's the guy's problem, not yours. You're a distraction for me all the time." He gave her a quick kiss on the lips, afraid to linger any longer. "So we have a date?"

"I can't. Rick has games on Tuesdays, Fridays and Saturdays."

"Then how about Wednesday night?"

"I guess I could do that."

"I'll be here at five thirty. Wear something comfortable." Sean picked up his bag. "Thanks for the delicious meal. Good night."

CHAPTER SIX

CYNTHIA COULDN'T BELIEVE she had a date with Sean. Her life had become surreal. Never in a million years would she have guessed when she heard his sexy voice for the first time that she would be going out with him. A heavenly voice for weeks was now a flesh-and-blood man who wanted to spend time with her. She was going to make the most of it while it lasted. If nothing else she would have some great memories.

Usually all her efforts went toward the boys so she hadn't gotten a new outfit in ages but she went shopping. Sean had said casual so she had settled on a royal blue shirt and a pair of fitted dark pants that stopped just above her ankles. For shoes, she selected flats. It had been months since she'd had the money to have her hair done but she splurged and had her hair trimmed and shaped. It now bounced and flowed around her face and shoulders. With the addition of a touch of makeup to her eyes and cheeks then some gloss to her lips, she felt better than she had in years about her appearance.

She was ready to go when the doorbell rang on Wednesday evening. Resisting the urge to fling the door open, she calmly walked down the hall. Sean looked more handsome than ever. Dressed casually in a cream shirt under a wool V-necked sweater with jeans, he looked the perfect date right out of the pages of a romance novel. If she didn't get control of her infatuation she would be in trouble.

"Hey. You look incredible," he said as he stepped inside.

Warmth washed over her. She loved being complimented by him. Not many of those came from her brothers. "Thank you."

Sean lifted her chin with one finger. "You know, a blush is a rare thing of beauty. It looks good on you."

Cynthia didn't know if his statement was true but she sure enjoyed hearing it. "You don't look half bad yourself. Very dapper in a casual way."

He grinned and bowed slightly. "I do try. Are you ready to go?"

"I am. Let me just get my jacket." She turned and headed down the hall.

When she returned Sean looked over her shoulder. "Are the guys around?"

"Nope. Rick is at some friends' and Mark is at his new job. Why? Do you need them for something?"

He stepped closer and her pulse rate zipped into high gear. "I just wanted to know if we were alone." He gathered her into his arms and his lips found hers. The urgency in his kiss had her body humming, racing to join him. Seconds later he released her and stepped back. "I've been thinking about that since last Sunday night and couldn't wait any longer. I think we should go before I decide to stay here and take advantage of the privacy."

Trying to catch her breath, she said, "I guess we should go."

Was she ready for their relationship to go to the next level? Did she know him well enough? She certainly wanted him badly enough. Could she survive another broken heart? So caught up in her fantasy and infatuation with Sean, was she thinking straight?

What she did affected her brothers as well. They seemed to like him. Did they mind her having a boyfriend? Would they be hurt if she and Sean were to break up? Her brothers had already lost so much. What if they became attached to Sean? If she had the power she wouldn't let anyone hurt Mark and Rick again. She had to be careful for all their sakes who came into their lives.

Sean held the car door open while she got in before he went around and slipped gracefully into the driver's seat.

"So what do you have planned for tonight? I hope I'm dressed properly."

He looked her over as if he were feasting on the most wonderful meal of his life. "You know you look beautiful."

Cynthia warmed under his appreciation.

Backing out of the drive, he added, "I thought we would see if we could find a good view of the city. Maybe watch the lights go on. Then have a little dinner."

"That sounds wonderful." Anything she did with Sean appealed to her. She enjoyed his humor, appreciated his devotion to his patients and his profession, but most of all she liked that he made her feel as if she were the center of his world. She'd not had that since her parents had died. As a sister or a stand-in parent, or just as the person who had to make sure everything was done, she had had little me-time in years. She'd never thought it a burden but on occasions the need to let go had nagged at her. Tonight, she planned to do just that, and with an amazing man by her side.

She found Sean's inability to organize and his rather economical way of living endearing. The smart, sexy, intelligent man had a foible. It was nice to know the perfect man she'd assembled in her mind was human. She could relate to that person.

As Sean made his way through traffic and up the mountain highway Cynthia watched as the statue of Vulcan grew larger. The huge iron man stood on the highest point in the city. She had always been fascinated by him. He was a major landmark in Birmingham and had been for all her life. It was a central mark by which people distinguished where they lived. North or south of Vulcan.

Sean continued winding around the mountain until he turned off the main highway and drove up Red Mountain to where Vulcan stood.

"This is a great place for a view of the city, but isn't it closed?" she asked.

"It is. But I have a patient who's a security guard here. I called in a favor. He's going to let us go up and have a look." Sean pulled into a parking spot in the almost deserted lot. The only vehicle there was a small older-model pickup truck.

"That sounds great." Cynthia should have known that Sean wouldn't plan a typical night out. "Once again you have surprised me."

"How's that?" Sean helped her out of the car. He lingered over letting her hand go, giving her a fuzzy feeling of pleasure.

"I thought you were the kind of guy who would

take a date to a fancy restaurant. Show her how suave you are."

"Are you disappointed?" He sounded as if her answer really mattered.

Cynthia smiled. She liked the element of the unexpected he offered. "Not in the least."

An older man with tufts of white hair on his head, wearing a gray uniform, walked toward them.

Sean shook hands with him. "Cynthia, I'd like you to meet Luther Murphy. Luther, this is Cynthia Marcum."

The man nodded to her. "Nice to meet you, young lady. Any friend of Dr. Donavon's is a friend of mine. Dr. Donavon did me a great service a few years back. I was getting where I couldn't hear my wife. Most people would like that, but me, I missed hearing her complain. Dr. Donavon got me all set up so now I hear every single word she says."

Cynthia couldn't contain her laughter. "How long have you been happily married?"

"It'll be forty-five years next month," he said with a toothy grin.

"Wow, that's impressive." What would it be like to find a man she could love for so many years? She glanced at Sean. Could he be that one? He made her feel things she'd never experienced before. Wasn't sure she was prepared to feel again.

They walked over to a small door in the tall redbrick foundation that Vulcan stood on. Mr. Murphy opened it to reveal metal stairs that spiraled upward. He left them there.

"If we want the view we must work for it," Sean said from behind her. "Do you want me to go first?"

"No, I will." She took the lead.

Sean chuckled. "I figured as much."

She looked back at him. He was almost at eye level with her. "That's kind of like the pot calling the kettle black. You like to be in control."

"So we're going to get personal here?" He held her gaze.

"I think what I'll do is keep walking." Cynthia headed up the steps again. "Did you know that Vulcan was built for the 1904 St. Louis World Fair?"

Sean's voice echoed in the space. "Yes. Did you know that he's the largest cast-iron statue in the world?"

Pausing, she glanced back at him. "That I didn't know." She started up again. "This is a hard one. What was the point of picking a Roman god to represent Birmingham?"

"By your lofty tone you don't think I know the answer." He sounded indignant at the thought. "For your information, it was because of the area's mineral deposits. There's a large amount of iron ore in the area."

She smiled back at him. "Very good. Since you're so smart, what's Vulcan holding in his raised hand?" It took him so long to answer she began to think he might not know the answer.

"That would be a spear," he said triumphantly.

She grinned down at him. "Now for bonus points. What's in the other hand?"

A minute went by before he said, "Okay, you've got me there. What is it?"

"A hammer. It's on top of an anvil," she proudly informed him.

"That's right. Where did you get all this knowledge?" There was a little huff in his voice from the climb.

Her foot clinked as she took another step. "I did a report in the sixth grade. Got an A-plus."

Sean chuckled. "I would bring you to the one place you knew more about than me."

"Don't worry. I don't think you're less of a man for it." She stopped and waited for Sean to join her on the upper landing.

As he did he pulled her against him. "I wouldn't underestimate me there." His mouth found hers as his hand came around her waist. Her heart jumped into overdrive and she hung on as his hot and sure tongue commanded her mouth. Just as quickly he let her go, leaving her wanting more. Sean had more than proven his point.

He opened the door and stepped out onto an observation deck. She followed on shaking legs that had nothing to do with their climb. They now stood at the top of the foundation and at the feet of Vulcan.

"I haven't been here since I was a child. I have to admit I'm really looking forward to this." She looked out over the expanse of the city with awe.

Sean said, "I'm glad. I was hoping you'd like it. I wanted to do something a little different." He shook his head. "But I hadn't counted on all those steps."

"The view is worth it. Come on." She took his hand and gave it a little pull.

Sean didn't let go as they made their way around on the narrow viewing walkway. She stopped again to look out at the panorama of the city in early evening. Only a few lights were on. Sean came to stand beside her.

"My mom and dad brought me and my brothers up here. I remember being scared and Daddy holding my hand as I made my way around. I was glued to the side of the wall until Mama took the other hand. I felt secure then." She had great memories of her parents. Missed them so much.

"You really had a great relationship with your parents, didn't you?" Sean said quietly beside her, his arm coming around her waist.

Her head leaned against his shoulder. "I did. I miss them daily."

"I don't have memories of anything like that." His tone was sad and dry.

She looked at him. He seemed troubled, as though he had said too much. "Are your parents alive?"

"Oh, they're alive and well." He gave her hand a tug. "Let's walk on around and see what downtown looks like."

"This is unreal." She looked out at the tall buildings sitting in the valley of mountains.

Sean said, "You just wait for a few more minutes and I think you'll be even more impressed."

"Is that what you're trying to do, impress me?" The fact he might care enough to try was empowering.

"Would it matter if I was?" Sean's voice had grown deeper, raspier.

She looked at him. "I do kind of like the idea."

His arm came around her waist again and they watched as darkness grew. The mountains beyond became dark silhouettes against the pink-hued sky. The sun slowly kissed them and disappeared. And lights in the city below blinked on. Some white with the occasional red and blue here and there.

"This is breathtaking," Cynthia said in awe.

"Yes, you are." She glanced at him, but he captured her look with the desire blazing in his eyes.

Cynthia swallowed hard and managed to turn back

to the view. She would think about what Sean's passionate gaze and statement meant later. "How did you discover this?"

"I came up here to visit Mr. Murphy one evening and he brought me here."

She needed to keep the subject on a topic to keep her head clear. "So you make a habit of coming here?"

"No. This is the only time I've been back."

He'd never brought another woman? This was special between the two of them. She liked the idea he hadn't shared this with anyone else.

"I think it's time for us to go down and have dinner," Sean said in a low voice as they approached the doorway.

"Where're we going?" Cynthia stepped through the door and headed down the stairs.

"Do you have to know everything?" he teased.

She stiffened her shoulders and used her best annoyed voice. "Well, not everything."

"You've been looking after your brothers for so long that you need to know everything about everyone all the time. Why don't you just let go some and live a little?"

He made it sound as if she couldn't. She would show him. "This is from the man who doesn't drive a sports car, has the bare minimum in his office, and seems to work all the time." She straightened her shoulders. "I assure you I can do surprise."

He chuckled. "Ouch. That hurt. But we'll just see how well you do surprise."

They slowly descended the stairs. A few minutes later they came out of the stuffy space into the cool evening. Mr. Murphy's truck was no longer in the parking lot. Sean reached into his pocket and pulled out a

small flashlight and then locked up. He directed the
beam toward a path leading over a grassy slope. They
walked over to it and down toward an outcropping of
trees. There among them was a picnic table with a blue
checked tablecloth covering it with a small candle flickering in a jar in the center. On the table sat a picnic
basket.

Cynthia had never seen a more charming setting. Romantic was an understatement. She was overwhelmed
with the thought he had put into their evening.

"Come on. But be careful." Sean's hand remained
firmly on her elbow as he led her to the table. He helped
her to sit on the bench, then went around to the other
side. Opening the basket, he pulled out three plastic
containers of food. A bottle of wine and two glasses followed. Another couple of containers appeared to hold
slices of pie. Lastly, he removed napkins, utensils, and
two plates. Sean placed a plate in front of her, then
handed her a cloth napkin and a fork.

"I didn't think I could be more impressed but you've
managed to do it." She was overwhelmed. He'd gone to
a lot of trouble just for her.

Sean sounded pleased. "I'm glad. I was afraid my
organizational skills might scare you off."

"You are worried about me being frightened off?"
Why would he be afraid she wouldn't want him? From
what she could tell he was almost perfect. She couldn't
imagine why he might be insecure.

"A little bit," Sean was slow to admit. He took the
bench across from her.

"So you put all this together all by yourself?"

"Not exactly." He started opening the plastic containers. "Truthfully, I called the local café where I often

eat and they put it together." He put up a finger as if to punctuate his statement. "But I did tell them what I wanted."

Cynthia grinned. "No matter where it came from, I can tell you went to a lot of effort. It's wonderful. I appreciate it. I'm honored."

"I'm glad you like it." He placed some fried chicken on her plate then on his. The next container held potato salad and out of the third came corn on the cob that was still warm. He brought out a small bag from the basket that had two rolls in it.

Cynthia looked at the plate before her. "This is a feast."

She glanced upward. The stars were starting to pop out and could just be seen between the limbs of the trees. The light flickering in the center of the table, the night sky and the charming man now sitting across from her were irresistible. She couldn't think of a dreamier setting.

Sean poured them each a glass of red wine and handed one to her. Hand around his goblet, he looked at her for a moment.

"Is something wrong?" she asked.

"No, I was just thinking how beautiful you looked in the candlelight."

Her heart fluttered. The man was making every effort to impress and she liked it. No man had gone to such lengths before, not even Dave.

Raising his wine for a toast, Sean said, "To an amazing woman."

Beaming, Cynthia clinked her glass to his. "Thank you. I've never been toasted before."

"Then you're long overdue." He set his glass down

and waited until she started eating, then joined her. They ate in silence for a few minutes. Cynthia hated to disturb the camaraderie they had built but she couldn't get his earlier remarks about his family out of her mind. Having a support system was important. Why didn't Sean understand that?

"I hope this doesn't ruin our evening but I'm curious to know…"

"That sounds interesting and ominous at the same time." He looked up at her and put his fork down.

"What is it with you and your parents? I don't ever hear you say anything positive about them. You had a funny look on your face when we were talking about them earlier."

Sean didn't immediately answer her. Somehow he felt that the truth was all that he could share. Cynthia would see right through anything else. Accept nothing less. He was thankful there was only candlelight for her to see him by.

"My mom and dad and I just don't think the same. I grew up with parents who see everything as pie-in-the-sky. The next great thing is coming their way. My daddy never held a solid job except for when he had no choice. They were always looking, and still are, for that get-rich-quick scheme. I'm the youngest of three. By the time they got to me there was no money. All your talk about your brothers playing basketball and doing extracurricular activities was fantasy in my childhood. Those weren't in my life because what money we had went into investing in the next thing to make us rich. Those never panned out. Not once. When I got old enough to make my own money there wasn't time for other things.

"Even on the off chance I got to do something sports related they rarely showed up. If they did come, they'd spend their time trying to recruit other parents into one of their schemes. I remember being so embarrassed.

"By the time I graduated high school we had parted ways. It was up to me to pay my way through college and I took out loans for med school. I had to do my own thing. I wanted nothing more to do with living hand to mouth. I worked in a nursing home and found I loved caring for people. I had good grades and decided that medicine was for me. Now you know all about the underbelly of my life."

Cynthia said softly, "Now I understand."

"Understand what?"

Her beautiful face was full of compassion but not pity. "Why you drive the type of car you do. Why your office looks as it does. Why you had that appalled look on your face when I wanted to sign you up for the internet meat club. Even why you picked here for our dinner."

His shoulders tensed. Did she think he should have done more for her? Just minutes ago she'd seemed impressed with what he had planned for the evening. "Are you saying you think I'm cheap?"

"No, not at all." She vigorously shook her head. "This picnic is far better than going to a fancy restaurant. I certainly have no problem with the type of car you drive. Look at what I drive. But I understand why you don't fit the cliché you accuse me of trying to force you into. Or what I expected when I first met you. All I'm saying is I get why you think the way you do."

He wasn't sure he liked being that open with another person but with Cynthia there was security. She got him and didn't dislike what she saw. He knew more than one woman who wouldn't understand or couldn't. Vulnerability wasn't his strong suite but somehow being so with Cynthia seemed right.

She tilted her head to the side. "You said you haven't seen your brother and sister in a couple of years. So how long has it been since you've seen your parents?"

"A little over a year." He was revealing stuff he'd never told anyone. He didn't talk about his family. Ever.

Disbelief covered her face. "Don't you miss them?"

"I do more since I've met your family." Again he was admitting something he normally wouldn't. How did Cynthia manage to coax information out of him?

"How's that?" She put her elbow on the table and rested her chin in her hand, studying him, leaving him no choice but to lie or to tell the truth. She would call him out if he wasn't honest. He had a feeling he would go down in her estimation if he just refused to answer.

"Being around you and your brothers at dinner just reminded me of how some of my family meals were when things were good. I didn't realize how much I had let the bad cover up everything else."

She straightened. "Thank you, I think. That must have been a tough revelation. I hope being around us isn't too painful."

It was time to talk about something besides himself. He held up his thumb. "No, except for when I cut my thumb. Oh, yeah, or when I played paintball. Those balls can cause whelps that turn into perfectly round purple bruises."

"I'm sorry. I had no idea we were so rough. I even forgot to ask about your thumb." She reached over and took his hand, caressing it.

"It's fine. I had one of the nurses re-dress it. She said whoever had done it before had done a splendid job." When she started to let go of his hand he took hers. "Tell me, what would you be doing if you weren't being a transcriptionist right now?"

"You already know. I want to be a nurse."

He gently rubbed her fingers. "So what's holding you back? Your brothers are old enough to take care of themselves."

She pulled her hand away and put both in her lap. "I need to see that Rick is settled in college. Convince Mark to go back. Then I can see about going myself."

Had he hit a nerve? Cynthia sounded defensive. Despite that he asked, "When do you think that'll happen?"

"I don't know. Maybe next year. Or the next?" She picked up her fork again.

He wanted, needed to understand her thoughts. "So what were your dreams before?"

"You mean before my parents died?" There was a sad note in her voice.

"Yes."

"I wanted to be an emergency department nurse. I liked the idea of not knowing what was going to happen next. To see all different problems. I hated it when I had to quit school." She looked off into the night. Seconds later she blinked. "You know, this discussion has gotten too serious. Who's your favorite movie star?"

"Boy, that's a change of subject. But I'll go along. John Wayne."

She nodded sagely, as if giving the idea thought. "John Wayne. I wasn't expecting that."

"I have his entire movie collection."

Cynthia seemed impressed. "Really? I've only seen a few of his movies that I can remember."

He leaned toward her. "I can't believe that. How have you gotten to the age you are and seen but a few of his movies? That's just wrong."

"Wrong?" Her voice went up an octave and she raised her fork.

"Yes, wrong. I tell you what. We'll finish here, go to my place to have dessert and a movie. We need to work on your education." Sean picked up his unfinished chicken.

She shook her head. "I'm not really into Westerns."

"I know of one I think you'll really like."

Cynthia smiled. "All right, I'm willing to give it a try."

As Sean drove down the mountain he asked, "Are you still up for a movie? I don't want to force you if you'd really rather not watch one."

"I'm still willing if I'm still invited."

As far as he was concerned she would always be invited.

All the way to Sean's house Cynthia contemplated the wisdom of agreeing to go there. It was a step in their relationship she hadn't expected. Would it just be a movie or was he hoping for more? Was she willing to give it? Having spent the last few years being cautious about men, was she prepared to open herself up to a man she'd only known for a few weeks?

What was she getting worked up over? Sean had invited her to watch a movie. He was a gentleman and wouldn't ask more than she was willing to give. That didn't make her any less nervous or ease her questions.

She was crazy about him. Tonight had only intensified her fascination.

But was he interested in a real relationship? From his receptionist's reaction, he certainly was a ladies' man. But who wouldn't be interested in Sean? He was good with people, had a good sense of humor, intelligence, thought out of the box. Tonight's date proved that. Supportive. And most of all he seemed to enjoy her company. She was betting that the more she got to know him, the more she'd like him. The only thing she could find complaint with was his view of family. She couldn't understand his and he seemed to have no concept of hers. That might be an issue if they were thinking about getting married, but their relationship was nowhere near that level of involved.

Soon Sean was pulling into the driveway of a small bungalow-style house in the Mountain Brook Village area. Many of the homes appeared to have been updated, including Sean's.

"Did you do the work yourself?" she asked as she examined the woodwork detail around the door, the porch railing and light fixture. None of it looked like the typical contractor material.

"I did. I was better taking care of my fingers around the saws than I was with your knife."

This was a side of him she hadn't expected. "It looks wonderful. So you ride a bike and are good with your hands. You have an old-world talent, Doctor."

"Then I must get one more fun point."

She grinned at him. "That you do."

Now knowing his background, the choice of home, the area, and the fact he'd put more time than money into the place didn't surprise her. There wasn't a light shining on the porch. For Sean that would be a waste of money. However, when they stepped out of the car a motion light blinked on. He met her at the front of the car with the picnic basket in hand, then escorted her up a couple of cement steps to the front door. Unlocking the door, he stepped inside and flipped on a lamp.

His living area was much as Cynthia expected. Furnishings were sparse but of good quality, ones that would last. The most extravagant thing in the room was the enormous TV on the wall. She stood looking at it. "Wow."

"It was the largest I could get at the time," he said bashfully.

"Well, you certainly fit the cliché where a man and his TV are concerned." She chuckled.

"I guess I do." Sean laughed. "I have to admit that when I'm home I enjoy having it. Especially in the fall for the sports. Why don't you have a seat?" He indicated a plush-looking tan leather sofa against the opposite wall from the TV.

There was also a large matching armchair with a footstool sitting at an angle to the sofa. In front of the sofa was a coffee table with a couple of books and a few sport magazines on it in no order. There were also several books stacked in one corner. On the wall between the two front windows hung a picture of a rushing river surrounded by trees. Other than that, the room was sterile. A decorator would call it extreme minimalist. It reminded her of his office. Sean didn't waste his time or money on anything frivolous.

Yet he'd gone out of his way with dinner. So what did he consider her?

The room was definitely an extension of the man.

It seemed he was so caught up in the past he couldn't let go beyond owning a large TV. How much of the extras in life was he giving up so he never felt insecure again? She bet if she accused him of being insecure he would deny it.

He'd placed his phone and keys on the coffee table along with the picnic basket. "I'll put the movie in, then get our food. We're going to watch *McLintock!*" He searched through the shelf below the TV and selected a DVD. While he put it into the machine he said, "I'll get us something to drink and the pie. What would you like? I have water, wine, soda, maybe milk." He grinned.

Taking a seat on the couch, she decided, "I'll have a soda." She was afraid to have any more alcohol, already feeling a buzz just being around Sean. With her physical reaction to him and being in his private space she couldn't afford to not be thinking straight.

As the picture came into view, he picked up the basket and left through an arched doorway. Sean returned a few minutes later with drinks in hand, then again with their pie. He took a seat in the chair; he put his feet on the stool and crossed his ankles. If she was concerned about him making an advance she shouldn't have been. Apparently, it was the last thing on his mind. Cynthia wasn't sure she liked that idea.

"Why don't you sit back and make yourself comfortable?" He took a bite of pie. "This pie is really good. You need to try yours."

Cynthia shifted until she was in the corner of the sofa. After kicking off her shoes and tucking her feet up, she ate to settle her nerves. She relaxed as she became interested in the movie. Soon her body settled, and she almost forgot Sean sitting just a few feet away.

They had been there for about fifteen minutes when he placed his plate on the table and said, "Scoot over."

She set her plate beside his and moved toward the middle of the sofa, giving him the corner space.

Sean took it. "I was lonely over there by myself."

Cynthia tried to concentrate on the movie but was so conscious of him she registered none of the words.

"Cynthia," Sean whispered.

"Mmm?" She looked at him.

"I'm still a little lonely. Why don't you come a little closer?"

A fuzzy feeling washed over her. She moved up next to him. Sean slipped his arm around her shoulders and nudged her closer.

"Now this is much better." Sean tucked her in tight.

Much. There was something nice about being next to Sean that had nothing to do with him physically. She certainly liked his body but when she was close she felt supported, as if she wasn't facing the world alone, there was someone to share the worry. He was there. Solid. Those were feelings she shouldn't be having. He'd made no promises. It was too soon to start depending on him. She'd been let down before and she had no intention of letting that happen again. People in her life were gone too easily.

A few minutes later he whispered in her ear, "Relax, I'm not going to bite."

Cynthia snuggled up against him and rested her head in the curve of his shoulder. Here she could stay forever.

They were well into the movie when his phone rang. He paused the movie and answered. Cynthia immediately missed the warmth and comfort of him.

She couldn't help but overhear his conversation as

she relished the rumble of his beautiful voice. He was soon asking questions at a swift pace. Sean had morphed into doctor mode. Apparently there had been some sort of accident. Seconds later he ended the conversation.

"I went on call at nine. I'm rarely called in during the night but tonight's one of those times. There's been an automobile accident. I'm needed at the hospital for a consult. I don't think I'll be long. I'm sorry but I don't have time to take you home. If you don't mind watching the rest of the movie I should be right back." Even though he was speaking to her she could tell that his mind was on the patient waiting.

She stood. "Don't worry about me. I know better than most that you have patients."

His hands came to her shoulders. They were warm and strong. "I know you can take care of yourself but that doesn't mean I can't worry about you. I'm sorry about running out on you. I'm not leaving without one of these."

His hands drew her to him and his lips found hers. Her arms went around his waist, pulling him tight. As his tongue requested entrance she welcomed him with a moan. Gripping her behind with both his hands, Sean brought her against him. Too quickly he released her with a groan. Cynthia teetered backwards but he held her secure. He stepped away; desire still simmered in his eyes, so intense it made her shudder.

"Now I hate to go more than ever but I'll be back soon." Sean picked up his keys and phone, and went out of the door.

Instantly his house felt huge. Cynthia had lost interest in the movie but started it again only because Sean would want to know what she thought of it. With a smile on her face, she clicked off the movie when it was over. Sean had been right: it was a good movie.

With the house quiet she carried their dirty plates and glasses to the kitchen. This space had the same charm as the rest of the house with nineteen-fifties tiles on the walls, and even appliances to match. The table was the same type she remembered her grandparents having in their kitchen. Chrome with a red top with chairs that matched. The only concession to the present day was a TV sitting on the counter. She loved the room right away. It was a perfect place to enjoy cooking a meal.

Her mother's kitchen was like that. Even after so many years she still thought of it as her mother's kitchen. Nothing had been moved or changed since her parents had died. Somehow it seemed wrong to do so. Her mother had spent so much time preparing meals there. Lots of laughter and love had been shared in that all-important space. Cynthia hadn't had the heart to make any changes. And the boys deserved for it to remain the same until they left.

She hated to think about that day fast approaching. Once again her life would drastically change.

The least she could do was wash the dishes for Sean. So caught up in musing over how much she liked his kitchen, she didn't pay close enough attention to the amount of water she was running. It backwashed out of a glass and all over her chest, soaking her, bra and all.

She was going to have to find something to wear. At least until she could dry her clothes out enough to put them on again. Prowling through Sean's clothing wasn't what she'd planned or wanted to do, but surely he would understand.

Cynthia headed down the hall in search of his bedroom. The first room she came to turned out to be an office, not a guest room. The way he felt about his family and not visiting them, he probably didn't think he needed a guest room. Instead of a bed there was a solid oak desk facing the window that looked out over the porch. A desk lamp stood on it and a wooden banker's chair was behind it. The chair looked as if it had been lovingly refinished. The man did have talent. He might believe in being thrifty but he liked quality. Sean was a diverse personality.

At the end of the hall was a larger bedroom. Knowing of these old homes' architectural arrangements, she guessed Sean had removed a wall and remodeled the space into more spacious sleeping quarters. Again the furniture consisted of little more than the bare necessities. The floor was made of glossy dark wood she suspected was original to the house. The windows had full-length wooden blinds. They were partially closed. The oak bed was heavy and made the statement that the person who slept in it was all male. A log cabin patterned quilt was spread across it. A bedside table and lamp sat on one side. A tall chest of drawers stood against another wall. Everything about the room screamed Sean.

Cynthia stepped slowly into it. She was entering a private domain but her curiosity kept her going and, after all, she needed something to wear. Peeking past an open door, she found a modern bath but done in a style that stayed true to the age of the house. She loved the man's taste. Of what she'd seen she wouldn't change a thing about the fixtures of the house.

But there was one thing missing. The feeling of belonging. There were no pictures of anyone. It was as if

Sean had no past or future. That saddened her. A good man like him should have people in his life who were important to him.

Going to the chest of drawers, she opened the top drawer. There she found his undershirts. They were too thin. Sean would be able to see straight through it if she borrowed one of those and he returned any time soon. In the second she found a dark T-shirt with the name of the hospital across the front. This would do until she had her clothing dried.

Returning to the kitchen, she found a small room off it containing a washer and dryer. There she tossed in her shirt and bra. It shouldn't take them long to dry. Back in the living room, she turned on the TV again. Maybe something good was on that she could watch until Sean returned. Clicking through the channels, she located a favorite show. Feeling cool and not seeing a throw blanket, she went to Sean's room and removed the quilt from his bed. She would replace it before she left. Surely Sean wouldn't be upset with her making herself at home?

Returning to the living room, she curled into the large armchair and wrapped the quilt around her. She inhaled deeply and smiled. Between the chair, cover and shirt it was almost as if she were in Sean's arms. As she watched a late-night talk show, she grew warm. She yawned and her eyes drifted closed.

CHAPTER SEVEN

SEAN RETURNED HOME closer to daylight than dark. When he'd headed for the hospital, he'd anticipated a quick visit but it had turned into emergency surgery that couldn't wait. He'd had a second to think about Cynthia at his house. All he could do now was hope that she wasn't mad. Not that it would make him feel any less a louse, but maybe she had called for a taxi or one of her brothers to come get her.

From the driveway he could see that the TV was still on. Cynthia would have turned it off if she wasn't still here. He quietly let himself into the house, then thought better of it. What if he scared her? He had no need to worry. Cynthia was sound asleep in his chair.

She looked so small and so right in his large chair wrapped in his grandmother's quilt. As if she belonged there. Quietly he put his keys and phone on the table. He wasn't going to allow her to sleep in a chair any longer. He scooped her into his arms, blanket and all.

She blinked then murmured, "You're home."

He held her against his chest and kissed her temple before he headed to his bedroom. "I am."

"Where're we going?" she mumbled in a sweet, sleep-laden voice.

"My bed. Now, hush. Go back to sleep." In his room he laid her on the bed, gently unrolled her from the blanket.

Was that his T-shirt she was wearing? He wouldn't remove her pants, having already stepped over the propriety line by putting her in bed with him without asking her. Pulling the sheet over her, he then spread the quilt on top of that.

Cynthia wrapped her arms around his pillow with a sigh and brought it against her face.

Sean stood there watching her for a minute. How badly he wanted to properly wake her and show her how much he liked having her in his bed. Instead he found himself a clean pair of underwear and a pair of drawstring lounge pants before heading for the bathroom. There he took a cold shower despite having been looking forward to a hot one when he came home.

When he returned, Cynthia was curled up sound asleep in the middle of his bed. He slipped beneath the covers and rolled to his side, gathering her against his chest. *Perfect.* He would worry about her reaction to his forwardness in the morning. Seconds later he had joined her in sleep.

A wiggle of a warm body beside him woke Sean. There was a pink hazy color in the room. It wasn't daylight yet.

His gaze met Cynthia's.

She scooted away from him as if she had just registered where she was. He made no move to stop her. "What am I doing in bed? With you?"

"I put you here. My guests don't sleep in a chair." Maybe if he kept his actions matter of fact she wouldn't get too upset.

She said quietly, "So you bring all your guests to bed after they go to sleep in your chair?"

His gaze didn't leave hers. "No, you're the first."

Cynthia's eyes widened. "Really? I'm the first woman to share this bed?"

He nodded. "Believe it."

She studied him as if trying to decide if he was telling the truth or not. She looked at his bare chest. Lingered. He willed his obvious arousal to ease, but that was wasted effort. That wasn't happening.

Cynthia's attention moved lower. Her voice went a note higher. "You're wearing pants."

"Are you disappointed?" He watched different expressions play across her face at his innuendo. First questioning, contemplating, and then possibility.

"I don't know. Yes, no. Maybe."

"It's simple. I came home far later than I anticipated and you were slumped in the chair. I felt bad and would have felt worse if you'd woken up in pain from sleeping that way. All I did was move you in here. I'd had a long night and needed sleep as well. We're just two friends sharing the same blanket." Someone needed to tell his libido that.

"Oh," she said.

Had she sounded a little disappointed?

Cynthia moved away from him. "It's still not sunrise. You need your rest. I'll just go finish sleeping on the sofa."

Sean reached across the space between them and caught her hand. How like her to always take the rougher road so that she could make it easier on someone else. "I wish you would stay. There's enough room for us both here."

Her uncertainty was charming.

"Please. I would feel better about going back to sleep." For certain his body would be happier if she was close.

Cynthia covered a yawn with her hand. "Okay."

"Good." Sean settled under the covers again. A second later he felt Cynthia do the same.

He drifted off to sleep with her warmth just inches away. The next time he woke it was to dim light and the splatter of rain on the window. Cynthia was curled against his side as if she had been seeking warmth. Her head lay on his bicep and an arm across his waist. If she knew would she be upset?

He didn't move, savoring the feel of having her near. She was a mass of contradictions. Soft and tender yet strong and demanding. Being around her made life interesting. Had made him start rethinking his. The value she placed on relationships with family almost made him physically nervous.

But right now she was causing a number of other physical issues for him. He wanted her and wanted her badly.

She looked adorable with her hair mussed, her cheeks pink from resting on his pillow, and wearing his T-shirt. The shirt material was pulled tight across her breasts and the outline of her nipple showed. His body twitched. What would she do if he ran a finger across her nipple? Would her eyes open wide in surprise? Or flutter open with wonder? Would she roll away? Did he dare find out which? Could he stop himself?

The tips of Cynthia's fingers brushed his side. His body thrummed with need. His gaze jerked up to find hers. She was watching him. His eyes questioned. Her hand skimmed across his belly and back again, making his skin ripple.

Sean understood when a woman was sending out signals that she wanted him but this forwardness seemed out of character for Cynthia. He had her pegged as the cautious type. Everything about her screamed she was a woman who took being with a man as more than a simple enjoyment of bodies. For her it would involve emotion. Caring. Tomorrow. Could she possibly feel that way about him?

Despite his desires, he had to know before his baser instincts took over. What if she wasn't ready? He'd all but insisted she stay in his bed. Worse, he'd brought her here when she wasn't thinking clearly. Would she see it as him taking advantage of her? He'd never been this indecisive about wanting or having a woman. But if Cynthia said no would he have the strength to roll away from her?

Trying not to base his decisions on the demands of his body, he growled, "Cynthia, if you want to leave this bed untouched then you'd better go now."

There was a pause, then her hand moved again, this time a little further down. "And if I don't want to?"

He glared at her. "Don't tease a man on the edge."

She kissed his chest and murmured, "Ever thought I might be on edge too?"

That was all the invitation he required. He quickly rolled her on her back. Her head sank into his pillow and the mattress dipped as he came down on her. He supported himself above her and studied her face for a few seconds before his mouth claimed hers.

She opened for him and he found her wet heat waiting to greet him. Her arms wrapped around his neck as she joined him in the twists and turns of a dance of passion. This uninhibited Cynthia he hadn't expected, but she fueled his desire like no other. His lips left hers to tease one corner of her mouth as his hands slipped under her shirt. Her hands kneaded his back as if she were begging for all he could give her. There would be red marks on his skin but he would wear them proudly.

He cupped one of her breasts. Cynthia took his lower lip into her mouth and sucked it. The actions sent a hot flash of desire through him. He was aroused to the point of pain. His heart thumped against his chest wall. If he didn't have her soon he would explode.

When he rolled her nipple between two fingers she flexed her hips, brushing his length. Sean kissed her again as he lifted off her enough to locate the button of her pants. After flipping it open, he deftly moved to the zipper and tugged. Becoming almost frantic in his need to be inside her, he pulled his mouth away. Taking a deep breath, he searched her face.

"This is going too fast. Not fair to you." His breathing was jagged. He had to find control.

"I'm not complaining." She shimmied from side to side until she'd gotten her pants down then cupped his face. "Kiss me. I like it when you kiss me."

He didn't give her time to ask again. He supported himself on one arm, his mouth finding hers. His other hand he placed on her smooth, flat stomach.

"So silky sweet," he murmured.

Cynthia sucked in her stomach, then released it so that it met his palm once more. Her hands gripped his upper arms and squeezed. His hand moved lower until it encountered the lace of her underwear. She hissed.

Seconds later, she opened her legs. He cupped her center. She was hot and damp. Ready for him.

His hunger was driven to the breaking point. Sliding his finger under her panties, he explored expertly. Cynthia sucked in a sharp breath; her hips rose and settled, accepting him. Her legs relaxed, allowing him complete access. Small panting sounds filled the air between them as he teased and touched her.

Sean pulled his mouth from hers. He wanted to watch her. Wanted her to know it was him giving her pleasure. Her eyelids were leaden, her mouth slightly open, and her hands running over his chest. He'd never seen anything more erotic in his life. It was intoxicating to see Cynthia so enthralled in the delights he was providing. The tip of his thumb flicked her pleasure spot and her hips lurched upward. He drew his finger out and slipped in again. Cynthia squirmed, then moaned soft and long as she lowered to the bed. Seconds later she opened eyes that held a dreamy look. Her tender smile welcomed him.

He quickly stood, pushed his pants to the floor and kicked them away. Shoving the blanket and sheet to the end of the bed, he pulled her legs around so they hung over the edge of the mattress. Working quickly, he removed her pants from her ankles, letting them fall. When he reached for her panties he found her hands already there. She had them over her hips and he pulled them the rest of the way down her shapely legs. Those he planned to have around his hips soon.

Going to the bath, he took a box out from under the counter and removed a package. Returning to the bed, he watched Cynthia's face as she looked at his naked body. He stepped closer, opening the foil package as he went. When she licked her lips he almost went to his knees. Covering his throbbing length, he made the final step to the bed. She opened her legs so that he could stand between them and admire her sprawled across his bed. Waiting on him. Had there ever been anything more stunning?

Hands on each side of her head, he leaned over her. His lips found hers, tasting and sipping her sweetness. Lowering himself, he nudged against her. Cynthia's hands slid to his hips and tugged him to her. Did she want him as much as he wanted her? In his urgency, his kiss deepened as he entered her.

Sean sucked in a breath and counted to three as he released it. Had he ever been this hot for a woman? This close to bursting?

She wrapped her legs around his hips and squeezed until he filled her completely. Had anything ever been as good as this?

Seconds later he pulled back.

Cynthia made a sound of frustration and he returned to her. She sighed. He repeated the movement a little faster. Picked up the pace. She joined him until they found a rhythm unique to them. As their tempo built Cynthia tensed, lifted higher and gripped his shoulders, her fingers biting in. He made one final thrust, filling her again to the hilt.

A shudder rocked her body. She threw back her head, arched, keening her pleasure before slowly easing to the bed. He searched for their rhythm again. The drum roll built until he found his release and collapsed on top of her. She pulled him into her arms. He'd been welcomed home.

* * *

Cynthia knew what it was to have physical relations with a man but had never experienced anything like the magic she'd just shared with Sean. Her heart was full. She regarded her lover's face with wonder, so close and so dear. How had Sean managed to break through her wall to bring her to this point? She smiled. All it had taken was his silver-tongued voice speaking into her ears.

He slowly rolled to lay beside her. Suddenly self-conscious about lying in the light with a naked man, she pulled the sheet across her hips. She was out of her element. Had acted far more a wanton than ever before.

"Don't cover yourself. Didn't I tell you how perfect you are? Amazing?"

She wasn't used to men praising her body. Her ex certainly hadn't fawned over her. To have Sean say those words warmed her, made her feel cherished. When was the last time she'd felt special? This was what it was like to have a man admire her. She planned to bask in it.

"Cyn. That suits you." His hand ran up her bare thigh. "You sure make me think about sinning."

Cynthia liked hearing her nickname from his lips. Her family members were the only ones who called her that. Sean had moved into her inner circle so easily and quickly. Now she didn't want him to ever leave.

"That's the nicest compliment I've ever had." She moved to face him, caressing him with her eyes. Sean had a beautiful body. All vast plains with hollows and slopes. He seemed so at ease with himself. Had she been built like him, she might be self-confident as well. Unable to resist, she reached across his chest and ran her fingertips over his ribs and circled a blue spot on his side.

She reversed her hand. "I'm sorry you got all bruised up in the paintball fight."

"I'm not. It was fun."

Cynthia continued to learn the valleys and plains of his chest, then the dips and highs of his ribs.

"I would be careful about that. I might make you pay for tickling me." His breath brushed her ear. She shivered. He chuckled.

"I bet you would." Insecurity washed through her. Had she been too forward? Too loud? Was he disappointed?

"Hey." He tugged gently at a lock of her hair. "Is something wrong?"

Did her feelings show so clearly or was Sean that good at reading her? "I'm just not sure why you're interested in me when you could have anyone."

In a near angry tone he announced, "You're going to make me mad with talk like that. Are you making me a cliché again? I can't imagine why a woman who's capable in so many diverse areas, and beautiful to boot, could possibly wonder why me or any other man wouldn't want her. Fear not, you satisfy me both in and out of bed."

A feeling she didn't want to put a name to filled her heart.

"The problem now is mine. How will I ever get enough of you?" Sean asked, as if he needed her to take pity on him.

Cynthia's heart was near to bursting. "Doctor, I like your bedside manner. You sure know the right thing to say."

* * *

Sean smiled. Cynthia made him feel as if he were the most special man in the world. He should have known he would be tempting fate to bring her to his bed. There was no way he wouldn't want more of her. He'd never felt for anyone the way he cared about her. Even now his mind and body wanted more. What was going on with him? He felt edgy, as if something were happening that was out of his control. He needed to figure this out. Rein in his emotions.

"Hey, what time is it?" Cynthia exclaimed.

Sean looked over his shoulder at the alarm clock on the bedside table. "Nine fifty-two."

Cynthia leaped up and grabbed her clothes. "I've got to go. The boys are going to be wondering where I am. I've never been gone this long without checking in."

He sat up and caught her around the wrist as she turned to walk away. "You do know they're not boys any more? I'd bet they know all about the birds and the bees."

Her cheeks went red. It was refreshing to find a woman who could still be self-conscious about sex. "I know, but that doesn't mean I have to make a show of not being there. Me sleeping over with a man for any reason is highly unusual."

Sean let go of her and stood. Taking her hand, he brought her up close and gazed into her eyes. "What you're saying is that I'm special?"

Cynthia's gaze didn't waver. "Very. You've been that from the moment I first heard your voice."

He brought his mouth close to her ear, lips skimming it. "So you like it when I whisper sweet nothings in your ear?"

"Yes." She lightly pushed at his chest. "Now you're trying to distract me. I've got to go."

"I'll let you go for now but only if you'll tell me more about how much you like my voice later."

She huffed. "Men and their egos. I promise. Do you mind if I get a quick shower?"

"Not at all. Make yourself at home." In the short time she'd been in his house she'd already managed to make her mark on his very personal spaces. His chair, his bed and now she wanted to leave him memories of her in his bath.

While he picked up his clothing she headed to the bath. Seconds later he joined her.

"Is something wrong?" she asked, eyes wide when he entered.

"Nope. I just thought I'd join you. I need to drive you home, remember? Also, I have patients to see in the office this afternoon."

"I can wait until you get through in here." She reached for her clothes.

Sean lightly caught hold of her wrist. "I thought we could share the shower."

She looked anywhere but at him. "I don't know."

He reached in and turned the water on. "I'll even let you have the spot under the showerhead."

She looked at his large tile shower and then back at him. "I guess we could do that."

And much more if he had his way. He fingered the hem of his T-shirt she still wore. It fell to the top of her thigh. "Don't get me wrong and I don't care that you're wearing it but would you mind telling me why you have on my favorite T-shirt?"

Cynthia shifted and the shirt pulled against her

breasts. His body twitched in awareness. He'd not taken the time he should have to appreciate the gifts hidden beneath the tee.

She looked down as if she'd forgotten what she was wearing. "I got my shirt and bra wet. I needed something to wear while drying them. I borrowed your shirt and fell asleep before my clothes were finished drying."

"It looks far better on you than it does on me." He studied the shape of her breasts and the outline of her nipples pushed against the material. Unable to resist, he touched one.

Cynthia drew in a breath and went still. Her eyes widened. That was enough to encourage him. He cupped her breast, tested its weight. "Perfect."

His hands found her hips. "As fetching as you look in my shirt, I know I would enjoy what's beneath much more."

Sean ran his hands along her curves until he had gathered the shirt around her hands raised above her head. Her beautiful full breasts were completely exposed to him. Unable to stand it any longer, he took a nipple into his mouth. Cynthia inhaled with a hiss. His tongue circled her nipple and he tugged gently with his teeth before releasing it.

He removed the shirt to find her staring at him with desire-glazed eyes. He grinned, already responding to having her naked. She shivered. "Come on. The water should be warm. I know you're in a hurry to go."

"Not that big of one," she murmured.

He chuckled as he followed her in under the water. No woman had been as responsive or open to his lovemaking as Cynthia. She seemed to bask in wonder and pleasure at his every touch.

She was under the water with her face up when he closed the glass door behind himself. Sean stepped up behind her. Placing his hands on her small waist, he pressed against her backside. He wanted her to know what she did to him. She shifted back to press herself against him. Once again she amazed him. Clearly she didn't mind letting him know she wanted him. There was nothing timid about her lovemaking. It was open and full on.

Was that what this was? Sex had always been enjoyable but with Cynthia it went to a high level. But love? That he'd never been a part of before. It scared him. He liked what he and Cynthia shared but was it more than two people who really connected?

Sean kissed the top of her shoulder. She shuddered. His hands slid up her torso to cup both of her breasts. She leaned back against his chest giving him full access. Her hands came around to grip his thighs. He gently pulled and teased her breasts as he placed little kisses along her neck and jaw. "I have to taste you."

He slowly turned her to face him. She looked at him as if he were the most amazing man in the world. Somehow he was going to see to it that she always believed that. Bending, he took a wet, swollen nipple into his mouth. She whimpered so sweetly he was afraid he might not be able to last. Gaining control, he moved to the other nipple, giving it the same attention.

With one hand, she hung onto his shoulder while the other slipped over his thigh up to his hip. There she hesitated before she took him in her hand. His blood boiled and his body throb unbearably. He'd never been set on fire so soon after having a woman. It was usually once and done and he was on his way home.

He had to step away or lose his mind. She deserved her pleasure as well. If she continued to move her hand he'd detonate. As he stepped back, her hand slowly slipped over him, which was worse than her earlier administrations.

Cynthia raised her worried eyes to meet his. "Did I do something wrong?"

"No. If anything it was too right. I want to give you pleasure this time. Nothing rushed. If you kept that up it would end up being all about me. I want this time to be about you." He dropped to a knee. Reaching around her, he grabbed her supple behind and pulled her to him. Kissing her stomach as the water ran over them. "Put a leg over my shoulder."

Her eyes widened. "I don't—"

"Please. For me."

She delayed another moment before complying. His arm went around her waist as her hand went to his shoulder. The other fingered his hair.

Sean dipped his tongue in, finding her hot center. A moan of pure animal pleasure rolled out of Cynthia. Lust rocked like thunder through him. She pressed forward. He gave her what she desired. Her grip on his shoulder tightened. She went up on her toes. He stroked his tongue against her again. She tensed and her hand left his shoulder to brace against the wall while the one on his head brought his mouth more intimately against her. She stiffened, then shuddered before becoming pliant. Seconds later he hurried to support her. Her forehead rested against his chest, as she breathed deeply.

They stood that way until Sean could stand it no longer. He opened the shower door and led her out.

"What about you?" she mumbled.

"Don't worry. We're going to see about me." His hands came to her waist and lifted her to the bathroom counter. "Scoot to the edge." She did as she was bid. He stepped between her knees and in one swift, smooth move he entered her. Cynthia cupped his face and kissed him as he sank deep. He was so hard for her that he feared the first contact would be all he could stand. He managed a couple of plunges before a white-hot explosion gripped him.

His forehead came to rest on Cynthia's shoulder.

"How do you expect me to walk after that?" she asked as her fingers played with the hair at the nape of his neck.

Sean looked at her with what he was sure was a foolish grin on his lips. "I was going to ask you the same thing."

"That was amazing, Doctor."

He wanted to let out a caveman roar.

A quarter of an hour later, they were finishing dressing when Cynthia said, "I forgot to ask how your patient is doing. Obviously there were more problems than you anticipated."

"She'll be fine but she'll have a long recovery period. It was an ugly accident."

"I'm glad to hear you could help her. You have a real gift." She grinned. "For more than one thing."

She had one as well. Making him feel like the most special person on the planet. That was something he had missed in his life. Would he ever be able to let her go?

CHAPTER EIGHT

CYNTHIA WAS A little worried about arriving home to find Mark waiting. She wasn't prepared for his interrogation right now. As Sean pulled into the drive she was relieved her brother's car was gone. Thank goodness he had to work. She wasn't in the habit of answering to her brothers; usually it was her asking the questions.

Sean reached across the seat and took her hand. She still tingled at his touch, which was amazing since their morning had been so personal. He affected her like no one else. She wanted to throw her hands up in the air and spin around. It was as if she were young again and had dropped all the responsibilities and worries she carried when she was with him. She liked herself. Believed anything was possible.

Sean's smile was sad. "I'd really like to see you tonight but I've got to work on the grant."

She shifted in the seat to face him. "Is it something I can help with?"

"I can always use your help."

"Why don't I fix dinner and you come here? We'll tackle it together." She didn't want to miss a minute of time she could spend with him.

"So I don't feel guilty about making you work every

night, why don't you let me get takeout?" he asked, perking up.

"Darn, I forgot. I promised a friend I'd help at the community center tonight. We are feeding the disabled veterans and playing bingo." She never forgot things like that. What was happening to her? Sean was taking over her life. And she liked it.

"Then we'll try for tomorrow night." There was a hopeful note in his voice.

"I'm sorry but Rick has a makeup game." She hated letting Sean down. Hated more not getting to see him. "You could always come."

"I may need to work on the grant. Let me see how much I get done tonight and I'll let you know."

"I should be helping you." Her guilt level was rising.

"You've already done a lot. You can't be everywhere for everybody."

But she wanted to be there for him.

His hand came to rest around her neck, bringing her close. "You know I'd like to have you to myself again."

Warmth radiated out from her heart. She smiled. "I wouldn't mind that at all."

His slow kiss made her toes curl. "How about we try for day after tomorrow? Just us."

"Sounds perfect to me." She was already looking forward to it. "See you then." Minutes later she stood on the porch watching until he drove out of sight. The hours wouldn't pass fast enough until they were together again. She entered the house as if walking on a cloud.

The rest of the day went by while she completed her transcription jobs. There were none from Sean, but she now had the real thing instead of just a voice in her ears. Actual kisses, touches, looks and his body over hers as his fingers worked magic. There was also the laughing. Sean with his quick wit, smiles, and patience. The flesh-and-blood Sean who went with that beautiful voice was so much better than the one she'd imagined.

Would the clock change time soon enough? She was trying to concentrate on work, but her thoughts kept coming back to her fear that her hopes had risen too high about their relationship. Or if they could make one work. She still knew so precious little of what Sean wanted out of life outside of financial security. Was their fledging affection strong enough to last? Did he want it to? Did she?

Just before she was going to stop work for the day she checked her emails. With a quiver of excitement in her core she saw there was one from Sean.

Hey Cyn,
I just wanted to say I've been thinking about you. You are amazing.
Looking forward to seeing you again soon.
Sean

If she wasn't crazy about him before, she was now. Cynthia reread the note until she had to force herself to get to work.

Finally it was time to get ready to go to the center. At least she would be busy and not have as much time to think about Sean. No grown woman should act as moonstruck over a man, but she couldn't help it. She couldn't get enough of Sean or keep her anticipation at bay.

Humming a tune, she took an unhurried shower. Memories of their time earlier that morning had her hotter than the water temperature. Every day should start off as wonderful.

She had never considered herself a very liberated person in the bedroom, but with Sean her inhibitions faded away. After a long time of holding back, she'd let go and been herself. Not the woman responsible for her brothers, the house, a job and all the minute details of life. Instead she was Sean Donavon's lover. Being unrestrained was freeing. Liberating. Fun.

An hour later, dressed in a simple light blue blouse and jeans, Cynthia entered the one-story cement block building. As she made her way across the tile floor toward the kitchen, she spoke and joked with several of the men and women already seated at tables. Though her exchanges were upbeat some of the enjoyment had been taken out of the evening. She missed Sean.

Reaching the kitchen, she checked in with her friend, Rose, who was in charge for the night. "What do you want me to do?"

"I'd like you to run the bingo game. The veterans seem to appreciate the special flair you add when you call the numbers."

Cynthia hmphed and picked up the box containing the bingo cards. "I'm sure my occasional use of *uno*, *dos*, or *eins*, *zwei* is very entertaining."

"Maybe not to you, but to them it seems to be," Rose retorted before turning back to the food she was placing in large serving pans.

Forty-five minutes later the meal had been served and Cynthia was standing in front of the room calling out numbers. She was preparing to announce another one when she looked up to see Sean's smiling face. Her heart skipped. Unable to do little more than stare at him when she really wanted to fling herself into his arms, she managed to get the next number out.

He grinned as he took a seat next to an old, grizzled-looking veteran named Mr. Vick sitting at the back table. One of the veterans had to prompt her to call another number because she couldn't get over Sean being there. He looked incredible dressed in his knit shirt and navy trousers, appearing every bit the well-to-do urban male. It should be against the law to look as fabulous as he did. Was he as glad to see her as she was to see him?

Calling numbers as quickly as she could to end the game, she declared a break before the next game and hurried to where Sean sat. He stood as she approached, a hand already out waiting on hers to slip into it. His fingers curled tightly around hers. Breathlessly she demanded, "What're you doing here? You're supposed to be working."

He beamed down at her. "I was. Really hard. But I thought a little bingo might help me unwind."

She gave him a narrow-eyed look. "You came all this way for bingo?"

"That—" he gave her a quick kiss "—and that." He said softly, "I missed you."

"Hey, buddy, are you hitting on Cynthia?" Mr. Vick asked with a wheeze and a cough.

She and Sean looked at him. "Sean, I'd like you to meet Mr. Vick."

To his credit Sean offered his hand. "It's nice to meet you."

Mr. Vick nodded and took it.

"I have to go back to the game. Can you stay until I'm done?" She looked at Sean. "You are welcome to play."

"That's okay. I'll just sit here and watch," Sean said when she pointed to an unused card on the table.

"Come on, don't be a stick in the mud. You might just have some fun," she quipped with a grin.

"I'm no stick in the mud!" He took the card offered, but looked at it as if he had no idea what to do with it.

"Have you ever played bingo before?" She managed not to laugh.

"Well, no," he said sheepishly.

Mr. Vick pushed some markers his way and winked. "I'll show him." Again, there was a wheezing with every word, then a short coughing fit.

She grinned at Sean. "Have fun."

For the next hour she called numbers. Sean even won a game. He whooped and put a hand in the air, pumping it in a sign of victory. He smiled broadly as he came to the front to receive his prize. There was friendly ribbing among the crowd over the possibility of her cheating so he could win. A few games later Rose called an end to the play.

As Cynthia boxed up the supplies Sean approached her. "So I'm guessing by your reaction to winning you're now a fan of bingo. Another first for you too."

"I have to admit I had a good time." There was a twinkle in his eye.

"That's what's important." She smiled at him.

His face turned serious. "Do you think Mr. Vick trusts you enough that he'd let me examine him if you asked?"

"I guess so. Is something wrong?" She glanced at the older man starting for the door.

"I think I know what might be causing that wheeze he has. It could be serious if it isn't taken care of."

Cynthia didn't hesitate before calling, "Mr. Vick." He turned to face them. "Wait up a minute, would you?" She and Sean walked toward him. "Mr. Vick, I was wondering if you would tell us about when your wheeze started? Sean here is a doctor and he's curious."

The man looked stricken and raised his hand to his throat.

Cynthia gave him a reassuring touch on the arm. "It's okay. Nothing'll happen you don't agree to."

"Mr. Vick, did you hurt your throat some time ago?" Sean asked, studying the man closely.

The grizzled man nodded.

"I'm a doctor who takes care of those types of things. I think you might have the beginnings of a real problem. I'd like to examine your throat."

Mr. Vick started shaking his head. "Don't like doctors."

"I can understand that but I promise I'll just touch your throat and look down it. Nothing more."

"I'll be right here with you. I promise Sean will be easy on you," Cynthia added confidently. She knew his tenderness first hand.

The man looked from her to Sean and back again, then nodded.

"Cynthia, would you see if you can find me a flashlight?" Sean had turned into a medical professional on a mission.

"There should be one in the kitchen. I'll be right back." She hurried off and returned minutes later.

Sean had Mr. Vick sitting in a chair and was slowly moving his fingers along his throat.

"Here you go." Cynthia handed him the flashlight.

"Mr. Vick, please open your mouth as wide as you

can." Sean shined the light into the man's mouth. Seconds later he straightened and turned off the light. "Mr. Vick, you have a tracheal stenosis. I'm afraid it can be serious. Have you had pneumonia more than once?"

A wheezy "Yes" came from the man.

"You'll have it again. It will get worse each time you have it. You'll start having to stay in the hospital. I could help you if you would let me." Sean waited as if the man saying yes was extremely important to him.

Mr. Vick took some time before he asked, "How?"

"It's a pretty simple procedure done with a laser. You'll need to stay one night in the hospital but that's about it."

Mr. Vick stood. "Let me think about it."

"If money is the problem, don't worry about it."

Cynthia's heart swelled. Sean might not believe in spending money on frivolous things but he would take care of a veteran without batting an eye.

Sean pulled his wallet out, found a card and handed it to him. "This has my office number on it. Call and make an appointment when you get ready. Tell them I told you to call."

"Okay." The ever-present wheeze was there.

"But don't wait too long," Sean added as Mr. Vick walked away.

"Do you think he'll call?" Cynthia asked.

"I hope so. Sooner rather than later." Sean turned to her. "Are you ready to go?"

"Yeah, just as soon as I put the bingo stuff up in the cabinet." She started toward the box sitting on the table up front.

Minutes later they were on their way out of the door into the dimly lit parking lot. Cynthia walked toward her car and Sean followed beside her. She didn't want their time together to end but she was unsure what she should do next. What was happening between them was too new. When they arrived at her car she faced him. "It was sure a nice surprise to see you tonight. Real nice."

Sean stepped closer, forcing her back against the door. "Nice enough that I can get a thank-you kiss?"

Her arms went around his neck and she went up on her toes to give it to him. Seconds later Sean pulled her tightly against him as he took charge of the kiss. All she'd experienced that morning had been real.

"I can't seem to get enough of you," he whispered with wonder in his voice.

She gazed at his face. "I missed you too. Thanks for the email."

"You're welcome." His lips found hers again.

When a couple of veterans walked by them, she and Sean broke apart.

"Hey, are you hungry?" Sean asked. There was a desperate note in his voice. As if he wanted to hang onto her longer.

"A little," she admitted.

"How about going for dessert?" He took her hand and pulled her toward his car parked a couple of spots away.

She giggled. "Okay."

Sean found a diner not far away. He wasn't going to let Cynthia go for the night until he had to. He led her to a back corner booth. When she stopped in the middle of the seat he said, "Scoot over," and sat next to her.

Cynthia was obviously pleased with his decision. She smiled brightly. There was a rightness about being next to her that had him thinking of more than just tonight.

When the waitress came to take their order they both asked for a slice of pecan pie. She ordered hot tea and he a coffee.

Taking her hand under the table, he brought it to his thigh and held it there. He wished he could find some way to have her to himself for just a little while. They both had busy lives but hers seemed as if it were wrapped up in doing for everyone but herself. He liked that she cared, had such a big heart, but she needed to move forwards in life. He knew from pleasurable experience that all of the business covered up an uninhibited Cynthia who was amazing.

She leaned her head against his shoulder and squeezed his bicep. "It's so nice to see you."

He smiled. "I couldn't stay away."

Cynthia turned to him. "What about your grant? How much did you get done on it?"

His look held hers. "Surprisingly a whole lot. Maybe it was because I was so anxious to see you and wouldn't let myself leave until I reached my goal for the night."

"So I was the prize?"

"You were." He kissed her.

The waitress brought their order. Just as Cynthia was about to take her first bite of pie she asked in a worried tone, "What time is it?"

Sean checked his watch. "Nine fifteen."

"Oh, no, I'm late." She started burrowing through her pocketbook.

Sean put down his coffee cup, preparing to leave. "For what?"

"To check in with my brothers. We do it every night at nine if one of us is out." She tapped a number on her phone.

Her obsession with her brothers was a little over the top. He understood concern or caring to a point but it was as if she couldn't accept that her brothers were grown men. If her relationship with him went further, could she let go of them enough to share her life with him?

As she spoke to Mark then Rick Sean finished his pie and coffee.

Done, she smiled at him and pulled her pie plate to her.

"Help out veterans and check on your brothers. You're always taking care of someone. Who takes care of you?"

She shrugged. "I guess I do. I just do what my mother did. What my father encouraged us to do. See about each other."

"That must be hard doing everything by yourself. I don't see how that leaves much time for that fun you keep talking about."

She looked at him over the rim of her tea cup. "Sometimes that is hard to find. But I try."

Sean put his arm across the back of the seat. Her shoulder brushed the tips of his fingers and that was all it took for his body to react. How long could he endure sitting so close without kissing her again?

"So tell me what I can do to help with the work on the grant." Cynthia pushed her half-eaten pie away.

"See, there you go wanting to help me."

Cynthia gave him a sideways glance. "You do still need it, don't you?"

"Yeah. I made a list of things I need to finish. There are a couple on there that I could use your help with."

"Email me the list and I'll get right on them first

thing in the morning." Cynthia seemed truly excited to assist him. More than that she was being supportive of him. Something that he'd known little of when he was a kid. "It's nice to be needed."

"You're needed all right." He scooted out of the booth, took her hand, pulling her up to stand beside him. "I think I should take you somewhere private to thank you properly." He paid the bill and escorted her to the car.

Minutes later he parked next to her vehicle in the empty lot of the community center.

He took her in his arms and nuzzled her neck. Slowly his lips traveled across her cheek until his mouth found hers. Her hand came up to rest on his neck. He loved the feel of her fingers in his hair. The kiss was deep, hot and carnal. He wanted her to the point of pain.

Cynthia yelped when her elbow hit the gear shift. He pulled back, uttering a descriptive word under his breath. Giving her a wry grin, he said, "I'm far too old and too big to make out in a car."

She giggled. "But I was enjoying it."

"I was too. Too much."

"I need to go anyway. My brothers will be wondering where I am."

Would they really? He would guess not. They seemed to have moved on with their lives while Cynthia continued to live as if her parents were alive. It had to have been tough to virtually become a parent of two teenagers when she was barely out of her teens herself but it was time to let go. Time for her to live some. "What would it take for me to have you all to myself?"

"You will day after tomorrow." She moved back to the passenger seat.

"That's not enough." He sounded as if he were begging, as he had when he'd wanted his parents' attention. "But I guess I'll settle for what I can get."

She kissed him behind his ear. "I'll…" then she kissed his temple "…make…" then the arch of his brow "…it…" the end of his nose "…worth…" the corner of his mouth "…your…" she nipped at his bottom lip "…while." The tip of her tongue traced the line of his mouth. "Promise."

His straining, painful arousal made a cold shower a sure thing tonight.

"You're a tease. I'm going to hold you to that. I expect you to keep that promise."

Cynthia kissed him. "Count on it. I'd better go." She pulled her pocketbook strap over her shoulder and stepped out of the car.

Sean joined her. She reached her arms around his waist, pulled him to her and kissed him. Sean brought her against him and lifted her off her feet. Long, delightful minutes later he reluctantly let her slowly slide down him. "Good night, Cynthia."

That night in Cynthia's bed had been lonely and cold, and incredibly long without Sean. There was an email waiting on her the next morning.

Cyn,
Quick note: crazy day ahead.

I had planned to make Rick's game but have to speak to a patient about an issue involving the grant app. Tonight is the only time he can do it.

Sorry.

I'll be home by six thirty tomorrow. See you then.

Miss you.
Sean
P.S. List attached

Cynthia couldn't deny she was disappointed. She had held out hope he would surprise her as he had the night before and make the game. She so wanted to see him. But he was doing something important.

She emailed back.

Hey,
Hope your day smooths out. I miss you too. Already looking forward to tomorrow. I'll bring dinner!
Cyn

That night Rick's basketball game didn't hold much interest for her. Every minute that ticked by on the clock was a minute she was closer to seeing Sean again. The hours dragged by the next day despite her efforts to keep busy. Finally, she was almost to Sean's house. The traffic wasn't heavy so she made good time. Excitement bubbled in her. The last two days had been the longest she'd lived through since her parents had died.

She had it bad for Sean Donavon and she didn't see any way back. The question was did Sean feel the same way? Or was he having that fun she'd encouraged him to have at her expense?

The minute she pulled into his driveway the front door opened and Sean stepped out. A large smile was on his face. He was obviously glad to see her. Still wearing his usual workday attire, he had pulled his shirttail out of his pants. The slightly rumpled look on him was appealing. He appeared relaxed, as if he was a little more at ease with life. Did he realize this?

It was nice to have someone excited to see her. It had been a long time since something in her life had revolved around her. So much of her time had been about her brothers or them as a family. Rarely had it been about her. Had she kept it that way for them or for her?

Sean met her as she stepped out of the car.

"Hey there," she breathed.

He grabbed her and lifted her tightly against him as if he'd found a precious belonging that had gone missing. Her arms went around his neck. His mouth found hers. The kiss made it clear on many levels he was glad to see her. When he pulled back he said, staring into her eyes, "I've missed you."

Cynthia kept her arms wrapped around his neck and beamed at him. "I wish you'd taken the time to show me."

"Funny girl. That's what I like about you—you always have jokes." He let her go to stand on her feet.

She turned serious. "I like a lot of things about you too."

"You keep looking at me like that and the neighbors are going to see exactly how well I like you."

Cynthia glanced around to see if anyone was watching. "Didn't you just show them that?"

His voice went into a low growl. "The real show would be much grander."

She murmured, "We might need to move that one inside. Dinner's in the bag on the backseat. Would you get it?"

"Sure. But food isn't what I'm thinking about right

now." Sean winked at her and took the sack out of the car.

They walked toward the front door.

"So what do you have in mind for tonight? Working on your grant? Watching another Western?" she teased.

Sean opened the door, stood back allowing her to enter ahead of him.

Cynthia laid her purse on the table next to his keys. There was something intimate about their belongings sharing the same space. "Let me have that bag. The coleslaw needs to go in the refrigerator unless you're ready to eat now."

"I'll see to it." He walked to the kitchen with more purpose than required for food care.

"So how did the meeting go last night?" Cynthia asked as she joined him.

"Very well. I marked one thing off the list." He sat the bag on the counter and inspected its contents.

"Did you have a chance to do any more on it?" Cynthia watched him. She'd missed him last night with every fiber of her being.

He located the plastic bowl, pulled it out and opened the refrigerator door. "Not much."

"Then you'll be pleased to know that I accomplished three."

Sean looked at her and smiled. "Whatever did I do without you?"

She hoped he never had to find out. "When is it due?"

"Next Monday." Coleslaw on the shelf, he pushed the refrigerator door shut with more force than necessary. He stalked toward her. Taking her hand, he tugged her through the living room and down the hall. "I'm not really interested in talking about that. I have other things on my mind I'd rather be doing."

"Such as?" she asked sweetly as she made a half-effort to drag her feet.

He stopped and she just managed not to stumble. Sean had a determined glint in his eye. "Like examining you without clothes."

Cynthia looked at him as innocently as she could manage. "So, what you're saying is that you're only interested in my body."

He growled low in his throat. "You know good and well I have the highest esteem for your mind but right now I'd like to enjoy your body."

Cynthia stopped resisting and they entered his room. "Don't you think we should sit down and talk some?" she said amiably. "After all, we haven't seen each other in a couple of days." She was unable to keep the grin from her face as he had her sit on the bed.

"You're welcome to talk all you want while I'm doing this." He nuzzled behind her ear.

Cynthia shivered and a soft *mmm* escaped her. She tilted her head, giving him better access to her neck.

Sean lifted his head and looked at her with a twinkle in his eye. "What? No chatter? I thought you were going to talk."

"You keep that up and we won't need any words." She lay back on the bed, pulling him to her. Her hands went under his shirt tail and found warm skin.

His lips moved close to hers. "I think our bodies are long overdue for a conversation."

Cynthia's hips flexed against him. "Talk all you want."

An hour later they were sitting at his kitchen table,

eating. Sean wore only a pair of worn jeans. Cynthia could hardly concentrate on her meal for watching the ripple of muscles across his chest. She'd pulled on one of his T-shirts that she'd rejected as too thin the other night.

"You're staring at me," he said between bites of coleslaw.

"I would think you would be used to it." Cynthia's gaze didn't waver.

"Why's that?"

"Because you're so good-looking." She couldn't believe he didn't know it.

"Who says that?" Doubt filled his voice.

"Me. You're almost breathtaking."

He looked up and grinned at her. "Breathtaking, eh?"

"Now I've messed up. That's going straight to your head. I'll hear about that forever."

He leaned in close. His eyes remained fixed on hers. "Would you like to hear about it forever?"

Cynthia's heart skipped a beat then righted itself. What was he really asking? Was he talking about forever between them? How should she answer that? "I could stand that."

"Just stand?" His look didn't waver.

"I would like that," she said with all the conviction she felt.

"Me too." Sean leaned over and kissed her. "We are good together."

Had he just said he loved her in an around about way? It didn't matter. He cared about her. No one talked about forever with someone they didn't truly care about.

They ate for a few more minutes before Sean said, "I

hate to do this to you but I've got to work on the grant application some tonight. Do you mind?"

"Not at all. Is there something I can do?" She took a drink of iced tea.

He pushed back in his chair. "I was hoping you'd ask. I have one small project."

"Do I need my laptop for it? I didn't bring it." She wouldn't be much help after all.

"You will, but you can use mine."

She stood. "I'm going to put my pants on. I feel a little underdressed to be working."

"It's probably just as well, because if you sashay around here with that cute behind showing I'm not going to be able to concentrate."

She looked down at him. "So you're saying that I disturb you?"

"Yeah, a lot." His voice turned stern. "Now, go and get back here and help me." He grinned and gave her a light pop on the behind.

"Ouf," she said, and giggled.

Sean had never enjoyed being around a woman as much as he did Cynthia. Their relationship was playful. Fun. He liked having fun. More than one of his woman friends had called him uptight.

His parents had accused him of being an old man in a young man's body. Those had been times when he'd been disgusted with them over being excited about a new product or plan. After a while he'd stopped even complaining. For him most of the enthusiasm had been taken out of life except where his work was concerned. With Cynthia, he laughed. Her quick wit made him think. Life had become pleasurable, something he looked forward to. She gave him something he hadn't realized was missing in his life. Laughter. As Cynthia would call it, fun.

They had talked around the subject of forever earlier. She seemed as if she wanted the same things as him but he'd held back on telling her what he felt. But did he really know? Their relationship was so fresh yet he knew it was something special. For a little while longer he would settle for just enjoying having her in his life.

They worked for a few hours and he was pleased with what they had accomplished.

"I should be done tomorrow. I'll review it and it'll be ready to go before next Monday." He was optimistic that he would receive the grant.

"I'm glad." She stood and put her arms around his neck, giving him a hug from behind. "I'm proud of you."

His heart swelled. When was the last time someone had said that to him? Cynthia knew how to make a person feel special.

Sean brought her around him to sit on his lap. "Thanks for your help."

Her arm lay along his shoulders and her fingers caressed the shell of his ear. "All part of a transcriptionist's service."

"I think you've gone above the call of duty." He kissed her temple.

"Maybe, but I'm still glad I could help. As much as I hate it I've got to go. It's getting late." She slipped off his legs.

"Go? Can't you stay the night? I hate for you to have to drive home so late." He took her hand and pulled her back toward him.

"Sean, you know I can't. I have to think about the example I'm setting for the boys."

For once Sean would like her to think of them before her brothers. Would Cynthia ever put her wants ahead of others'? Let her brothers grow up in her mind? He made a point of using an even tone and not sounding antagonistic. "So the idea is we'll just catch each other here and there?"

She slumped and gave him a sad look. "I guess we'll just have to play it day by day. I can't come over on the nights Rick has games. You're always welcome to go with me to those."

Sean stood and put his hands on her shoulders. "I have to be honest. I want more but I'll take what I can get. For now." He kissed her.

"I'm sorry it has to be this way for now. I need to get my clothes and shoes." Cynthia headed for the bedroom.

Sean's frustration was growing with her constant need to treat her brothers as if they were children. They were adults just as she was and it was time for her to treat them as such. Sean cleaned up what they had been working on and met her in the living room. "I'll walk you out." He took her hand.

At the car, he brought her close and kissed her with all the passion he felt. She returned it. With every fiber in his being screaming *no*, he let her go.

CHAPTER NINE

SEAN MANAGED TO make one of Rick's basketball games that week. He had to admit he had a good time but he still wished he could spend more time alone with Cynthia, instead of competing with everything else in her life.

Still, the last few days had been wonderful. The nicest he could remember. He'd even enjoyed the family aspect of it. There was a feeling of belonging that he'd not known in a long time. Even acceptance. Her family was one he could be proud of. He puffed with pride when Rick was named most valuable player at the end of the game.

Cynthia did spend Sunday in his bed. After making long, lazy love they were wrapped in each other's arms when she asked, "So the grant application is ready to go?"

"First thing in the morning. Now all I have to do is wait."

"That'll probably be the worst part." She frowned, then brightened. "We should celebrate."

The idea startled him. He never thought to do that. "Like how?"

"You know. Have some fun."

There was that word again. "Don't we need to save that until we know if I get it?" Sean asked as he ran a finger along her arm.

"No, we should do something special." She sat up and looked at him while pulling the sheet up to cover her gorgeous breasts.

"What we were doing just now was fun." He snatched the sheet away.

"Stop." She grabbed at the material. "I want you to concentrate on what I'm saying."

He did have a hard time thinking straight when she was naked.

She looked at him earnestly. "Making love is enjoyable but you need to let loose some, Dr. Donavon. Go somewhere, do something. Have *fun*."

Could this be a chance to get her to himself for a little while? No interruptions. No having her running home. Fun wasn't something he was well versed in but he knew how he'd like to celebrate. By having Cynthia all to himself. "Maybe that's not such a bad idea."

She perked up. Excitement filled her voice. "What would we do?"

"Something like you and me going away for a few days. I have a buddy who has been trying to get me to use his cabin on a lake north of here. We can celebrate there. He said something about it being available next weekend. How does that sound?"

Cynthia withered, seemed unsure. After a few seconds, she rallied to say in a cheery voice, "Okay, that sounds nice. I'd like that. Rick's season is over this Tuesday night so I'm free." She grinned. "And I like going to a lake even in the early spring."

"Then I'll set it up."

* * *

Monday afternoon there was an email in Cynthia's box:

Cyn,
I got our trip to the lake all set up for this weekend.
Let's plan to leave about three.
Looking forward to having you to myself.
Sean

She anticipated the coming weekend like a child waiting to open a long-expected gift. An entire weekend with Sean sounded like pure heaven. The last week, despite the juggling of their schedules, had been amazing. She'd never been happier or felt more complete.

As she daydreamed the phone rang. She picked up her phone hoping it might be Sean.

"Cyn." It was Mark.

"Hey, what's going on?"

"My car has died." He sounded disgusted.

"Where're you?" She was already thinking about where they were going to get the money to pay for the repairs.

"I made it to work but it was smoking when I got here. I don't know if it can be fixed. I'm going to have the guy here give it a look but it doesn't look good."

"All right." This was all they needed.

"I'm going to need to borrow your car to get to work the rest of this week," Mark said.

"I know. I'll be there to pick you up after work." And she wouldn't be going to Sean's tonight.

She emailed him:

Hey Sean,
You don't know how much I hate it, but I'm not going

to make it tonight. Mark has had car trouble and needs me to pick him up.

I won't make the rest of the week either, as he'll need my car to get to work. You're welcome here anytime.

I can't wait until this weekend.

Sorry…

Cyn

Sean wasn't going to like that email at all. More than once she'd noticed his lips thinning into a tight line before he'd realized she was watching him as she'd mentioned something she needed to do for her brothers. But with the weekend coming up she planned to focus all her attention on him. With his family background, he must have felt as if he was secondary to anything her brothers were doing. She never meant for him to feel that way but it must seem so to him.

Cynthia had already told Mark and Rick she'd be gone over the weekend and could be reached by phone. They'd had a few questions and grinned at her knowingly but otherwise hadn't been interested. Maybe they didn't need her as much as she thought they did. The idea was sort of liberating. She'd been living on hold for so long it was nice to have a change in her life.

After Tuesday night's game that week, on the drive home Rick told her that his coach had announced an unscheduled tournament the coming weekend. The same one she and Sean would be out of town. Rick had already made arrangements to stay with a basketball buddy for the weekend, but she hated to miss the games. Still, she wouldn't let Sean down again. He deserved better. This time she would choose him over her brothers.

She'd never done anything like going away with a man before. Had never been straight up about where she would be when it came to her brothers. She had it bad. No, she was afraid she might be in love.

Where that was going to get her she had no idea. Did Sean feel the same way? It didn't matter; her heart was going to take a beating if he didn't feel the same.

After waiting impatiently for the coming weekend, Cynthia gazed out of the windshield as Sean pulled up the pine-lined drive to the side of the log cabin. A porch spanned the length of the front. The fading evening sun glistened orange off the lake nearby. There couldn't have been a more perfect spot in the world. She could hardly wait to have Sean to herself for a couple of days.

Together they climbed the steps to the porch. He unlocked the door and entered ahead of her as she looked off over the lake.

Cynthia joined him. "Sean, this is wonderful. I may never leave."

He flipped on a light over the sink. Coming to her, he pulled her into his arms. "That would suit me just fine. I'm not sure I could ever get enough of you." He kissed her.

Minutes later and leaving her panting for more of his kisses, he said, "I'd better get things in before it gets dark."

"I'll help." She started toward the door.

"No, you won't. This weekend is about me taking care of you. And you doing nothing that isn't just for you."

She followed him out on the porch. "Hey, when was that decided?"

"I did it on the way up here," he threw over his shoulder. "Now hush and go explore the rest of the place. I'll be done here soon."

Cynthia did as he instructed. The main area was just one large room with the kitchen on one side and a sitting area with a fireplace on the other. She found two bedrooms at the back of the place. One was smaller with bunk beds and the other was larger with a bed that took up most of the space. A quilt covered it and there was another on the end of the bed. Outside the back door was an open-air shower.

"So what do you think?" Sean called.

"I love it." She went back to the kitchen where he was unloading the bags of groceries they'd bought at a small store a few miles away.

"You hungry?" he asked.

"No. I'm still full from that burger. It was good." They had stopped on the way at a local burger place his friend had recommended.

"I could tell from the amount of juice running down your chin." He grinned at her then put a jug of milk in the refrigerator.

She raised her nose in the air. "Like you were any better."

"What would you like to do first? We can walk down to the lake. Sit on the porch. Or watch the rest of the sunset. Start a fire. It's up to you." Sean put the last of the supplies away.

"I think I would like to try out the interesting shower before it gets completely dark." She picked up her bag and carried it to the large bedroom. There she pulled out a new short nightgown and headed for the bath. She found what she needed before going outside. Hanging the towel on the rail, she turned on the water and made sure it was warm before she quickly undressed and stepped under the steaming water.

"I had no idea the shower was outside. I don't know about this," Sean said from the door opening above her.

"Come on in. This is rather liberating. Live a little, Doc."

Her face was lifted to the water when Sean stepped in behind her. His hands skimmed her hips, stomach and then cupped her breasts. "I've missed you to the point of pain," he said as he nuzzled at her ear. "The days were long and I can't wait to have you."

She turned and took him in her hand. "Doctor, I have just the cure for that."

Sean woke to Cynthia's body curled against his and his arm across her waist the next afternoon. They lay on the floor in front of the now cold fireplace.

To his great pleasure he'd woken this morning in bed with her tucked under him. The air had been crisp and he'd been warm and content. When was the last time he could have said that?

They'd had a late breakfast, then gone for a long walk along the edge of the lake. She'd dared him to go skinny-dipping. Laughing and shivering, they'd run back to the cabin for a hot shower. They'd then built a fire, and made love again. Now he hoped to do it all over again.

More than once she'd asked him if he was having fun. He was. A lot.

He'd never spent so much uninterrupted time with one woman and still wanted more of her. He wished he could have her in his life forever. Needed her was more accurate. He wasn't going to settle, nor let her, for one day here and another there. This weekend had proven he had to have her to keep him open to possibilities.

He was in love. There was no doubt about it. How that had happened he had no idea. Maybe he did. It was simple: Cyn.

He looked down.

Cynthia was watching him. "Hey there, handsome."

Sean smiled. "Hey, beautiful."

They didn't even have a chance for a kiss before her phone rang. She looked away. "I'd better get that. Probably someone trying to sell me something but still. I told the boys not to call me unless it was an emergency." She untangled herself from him and went naked to pick up the phone.

He'd expected she might call home but to his joy she hadn't. Yet as a doctor, he knew the importance of people being able to get in contact so he accepted her need to answer.

"Hello."

"Yes. This is Cynthia Marcum."

"Oh, no."

Sean stood and came toward her.

"I'm on my way. Yes. I'm his sister. Next of kin."

This wasn't good. He moved closer.

"What hospital?" There was a pause. "UAB. Good. I'm on my way. I'll be there in an hour and a half." She hung up. "We have to go." She started to the bedroom.

"What happened?" Sean followed her.

"Rick got pushed into the bleachers during the game. His face has been injured. He's going to need surgery."

Cynthia started dressing. She wouldn't even look at him.

"I'm sure he will be fine." He tried to take her into his arms but she pushed him away. "We need to go."

Sean didn't try further. No doubt she was letting guilt swamp her. As if she could have done anything if she had been there. Sean pulled on his clothes, threw his other items in his bag then called the hospital requesting to speak to the emergency department. After a few minutes, he had a clear picture of Rick's situation.

Cynthia joined him with her bag in hand.

"I just talked to the doctor seeing about Rick. He's going to be fine. He needs surgery but he's young and should do great." Sean hoped to reassure her. She was acting panicky. Her face twisted with worry, and her hands shaking.

"Do you know the man who's going to do it?" she asked.

"I do. It's me."

She searched his face. "You? Can he wait that long?"

"Cynthia, this isn't a life and death issue."

Her face turned furious. "He's my brother. As far as I'm concerned it is life or death!" Striding ahead of him, she was out of the door and almost to the car when she said, "I should have been there."

On the way to the hospital Cynthia said little. Her eyes were so serious and sad. Sean wanted to hold her but he couldn't do that while driving. He made a couple of calls and organized his team for the upcoming surgery. At the hospital, Sean pulled into his slot in the parking lot. Before he could turn off the engine, Cynthia was out of the car and stalking toward the ER. He caught up with her. "We'll go through the staff entrance."

At the nurses' station, he asked what trauma room Rick was in. When they entered she hurried to the bed.

"Oh, Rick, I'm sorry I wasn't there. How do you feel?" She gently touched the top of his head, then his hand.

The boy did look awful with his swollen face and the purple and red discoloration beneath his eyes. Sean was used to the appearance but probably for Cyn it looked much worse on her beloved brother.

"Hey, Cyn. I'm fine. I'll be fine. It's just hard to breathe," Rick complained.

"I'm going to fix that," Sean said, stepping closer to the bed.

Rick looked at him with bloodshot watery eyes. "You're going to do the surgery?"

"You want the best nose guy in town, don't you?" Sean smiled at him.

"Yeah, I'd like to have a nose instead of a pancake."

"Understood." Sean touched Cynthia's back, gaining her attention. "I'm going to step out and look at the results from some tests I ordered. I'll be back to examine Rick in a few minutes." To Rick he said, "We'll be going into surgery within the hour."

Cynthia didn't even acknowledge him. Her actions baffled Sean. She was acting as if he'd caused Rick's accident. Was she blaming him for her not being there when Rick got hurt? Hadn't she learned from her parents that some things couldn't be prevented?

He reviewed all the material and discussed with the ER doctor what had been done so far for Rick, then returned to his room. Cynthia still stood beside his bed with her hand on his arm.

Sean stepped toward them. Cynthia threw him a quick glance when he announced, "Well, Rick, you took a good shot to the face. I've reviewed the X-rays and CT. You have an extreme septal hematoma. It'll need to be surgically repaired so you can breathe correctly. Thankfully you don't have a broken cheekbone. What I'll do is straighten your nose. You'll have packing inside and a brace across it when you come out of surgery. Give it a few weeks and you should be back to normal. Now, before I leave to get ready for surgery I need to give you a quick exam."

Cynthia stepped back and allowed him in closer to the bed. Sean gently touched around Rick's face, at his ears, jaw and neck. He finished, pleased that the young man didn't flinch any more than expected. Rick was lucky the injury wasn't worse.

There was a knock at the door. Ann Marie stuck her head in the room. She wore an unsure smile. "Can I come in?"

Rick groaned. "Now you get to see me as the Elephant Man."

Sean touched Cynthia's arm. "Can I talk to you outside for a minute?"

With an unsure look, she glanced back at Rick before following him out. Outside the room, she turned worried eyes up at Sean.

"I just wanted to give you an idea of what'll happen. Surgery will take a few hours at least. Rick will probably be out of it until morning. I'm going to give him some pretty strong pain meds. I want him to spend the night here just to make sure everything is okay and rule out a concussion. He had a major trauma to his head. If he has no issues he should be able to go home tomorrow."

"Is he going to be okay?" Her eyes begged for reassurance.

Sean hugged her and kissed the top of her head.

"Rick's going to be fine. Promise." He released her so he could look at her face. "You can stay here with him until he's ready to go to surgery. I've instructed one of the nurses to show you to the waiting room. I'll meet you there when we're done."

She grabbed his arm. "Take care of my brother."

"You know I will." Sean patted her hand and headed down the hall.

Cynthia didn't like waiting. Especially when a loved one was involved. She'd paced the waiting room, spoken to Mark who was at work and would be here as soon as he got off. Now she was mindlessly watching the TV without really hearing or seeing it. Other families had come and gone in the waiting room, but she remained.

She took a chair and put her head in her hands. What had she been doing? She should have been at the basketball game instead of off with Sean. She was responsible for Rick. When he had needed her she'd been curled in Sean's arms. Her parents would be so disappointed in her.

Cynthia hated it but she was going to have to give up Sean. There was no way she could meet her obligations to her brothers and to Sean too. One of them would have to wait. Unfortunately, right now in her life that must be Sean. She would be tearing her heart out to do it but she would. It wasn't fair to him to take second seat all the time. If she gave him up it wouldn't be that way any more.

She must to tell him soon. For his sake and hers.

With relief, and a sadness that went bone deep, she was glad to see Sean come through the doors toward her. He was still wearing his blue surgical cap and matching scrubs. What she appreciated the most was the smile on his face. Surgery had been successful.

When she reached him, he pulled her close. She resisted holding tight. He gave her a concerned look. She didn't give him time to ask questions. "By the look on your face Rick is doing well."

"He is. He's being moved to a room and you should be able to see him in about an hour. Someone will come tell you what room. They were having to juggle rooms when I last asked. Are you good?" Sean studied her. Anxiety showing in his eyes.

"I'm fine now."

"Good. I hate to leave you again but I have some paperwork to do. I'll see you later in Rick's room."

She nodded. "Thanks for taking care of my brother."

He smiled and brushed her cheek with a finger. "Anything for you."

That statement didn't make her feel any better about what she had to do.

Two hours later Cynthia was sitting at Rick's bedside when Sean entered. He'd changed back into the shirt and jeans he'd worn to the hospital.

"How's the patient doing?" He studied Rick.

She looked at her brother. "Okay, I think. He moans every once in a while, but that's it."

"He'll have a lot of swelling but it'll be gone in a couple of weeks. In about six weeks you shouldn't be able to tell this even happened." Sean sounded pleased with his work.

"Thanks," she murmured.

"Not a problem. Just sorry this happened to him." Sean came around the bed to her.

"How about going home with me and getting some rest? I can bring you back first thing in the morning."

Cynthia didn't stand to meet him. She wasn't going anywhere until Rick did. "I'm going to stay here tonight."

"You don't need to do that. We have a great nursing staff."

She shook her head.

Giving her a curious look, Sean pulled the other chair in the room over beside her and sat. "We can stay awhile longer, then I think you need to go home."

"Don't tell me what I should do," she snapped. "I can take care of myself."

Sean sat straight, studying her. "What's going on, Cynthia?"

"We need to talk." She finally looked him in the eyes but wished she hadn't. Those beautiful blue eyes she would miss.

"That doesn't sound good."

Clutching her hands in her lap, she whispered, "This isn't going to work."

"What?" He looked at Rick as if he might have done something wrong.

"Us," she said.

He scoffed. "It seemed to be working great this morning."

"I can't do it. It's not fair to you. I should've been there when Rick got hurt."

"You have to be kidding! What would have happened differently if you had been?"

Cynthia leaned toward him keeping her voice low. She wanted him to understand so badly. "I don't know but I have a responsibility to my brothers. Right now in my life they come first. That isn't fair to you. I care about you too much to do that to you."

Sean quietly said an expletive. "No, you don't, or you wouldn't do this." With a jerk he stood, forced her to her feet and led her out of the door. "We don't need to disturb Rick. Come with me." When she hesitated, he said, "A nurse will be in to check on him."

They walked to the end of the hall to where there was an empty room. Sean closed the door firmly behind them after they entered.

He faced her. "We have something good between us. Real. And you want to throw it away because you feel guilty or irresponsible, or some other ridiculous emotion because you weren't at the game when your brother got hurt. You're his sister. Not his parent. And if you haven't noticed, he's of age. Mark is as well. They're no longer your baby brothers. They are men! They're old enough to take care of themselves. You need to let go. For their sakes as well as yours."

She cringed. That might be true but it didn't mean they didn't need her. "Like you did with your family. They didn't measure up to what you thought they should be so when you got old enough you dumped them completely."

"You don't know anything about my family and me," he snarled softly.

"Sure I do." Cynthia took a step toward him. "They chose everything over you. Leaving you with no security. When you could get away you made sure that was never an issue for you again. To the point you had no idea how to have fun. You made sure that you went into a field you are talented in, but also had a good income. Yet you never spend money on anything other than necessities because you live daily in fear of being like your parents. You're afraid to really live or experience life. Other than this weekend, when was the last time you got away? Lived a little? Laughed?"

He glared at her.

"That's right." She made herself continue. "You haven't because you don't know how to let go. You don't even see that you need that in your life. I understand your parents are a little…uh…unconventional, but I would bet they would say they are happy. Are you happy, Sean?

"I'd also bet anything you've smiled more and laughed more since you met my family than you have in years. We need people around us regardless of whether or not they fit within the lines we want them to. I learned the hard way that life is about people. Not about how much money we have but memories. Creating them is what matters. It's all we have when they're gone. Security comes from the ones we love, not from a bank account."

Sean flinched as if she'd slapped him. He recovered and took a step toward her. "Yeah, but we also need to break away from our family so that we can live our own lives," he bit out. "Become individuals. Your brothers, your family unit is so important to you that you don't think beyond them. There isn't room for anyone else. You could go back to school if you want to, or be with me, but you use your brothers to hide behind. What is it you're afraid of? That someone will let you down again? Don't put that on me." He pointed to the floor with his index finger. "I'm here. I was there last night. I'll be there tomorrow if you let me.

"You might be right about me needing too much financial security. But I've never had someone I wanted to spend money on before. Until now. My family is a complicated issue. Not one I think you can understand because your parents weren't like mine. Yet with all our differences I find that you're the only woman for me." He glared at her. "I love you."

Cynthia looked at him in disbelief. Her chest tightened. He loved her. She wanted to run to him and wrap her arms around him but she couldn't. Though they stood so close they were so far apart when it came to how they lived their lives, what they believed.

"Yeah, you heard that right. I love you. But I won't accept you not being all that you can and want to be. It's not healthy not to move on. You have done the job your parents wanted you to. Your brothers are great. Even Mark will find his way. But he must do it for himself, just like you must. Your welfare will always be my first consideration. I'd love to see you become that nurse you dream of being. With your large capacity for caring you would be nothing but great at it. I bet your mom and dad didn't want you to stop living just because they did."

Cynthia sucked in a breath. That statement hurt.

He paused for a second then said, "Don't be afraid to take the opportunity to live again. You might find out I'm more fun than you think I am."

"I just can't right now," she said softly. "I have responsib—"

"I'm sorry to hear that. You think about it, Cyn. You know where I am if you ever move beyond the past and want to create a future."

CHAPTER TEN

DAYS LATER SEAN still couldn't accept the way Cynthia had reacted when Rick was injured. She'd implied he'd somehow been responsible for it. She couldn't see she'd moved into a holding pattern when her parents had died and couldn't or wouldn't find her way out of it. He cared for her too much not to help her face reality.

The day after their fight he'd made rounds and released Rick to go home. She'd not been in her brother's room when he'd come in to see him. Sean suspected that Cynthia had asked the nurse what time he usually made rounds and made sure she was gone for breakfast at that time. She was dodging him.

A few days later he returned to the cabin to get the things they had left behind. It was a painful trip. Everywhere he looked there was Cynthia laughing or smiling at him. They had been cheated. He wanted that time back.

He'd known unhappiness but losing Cynthia was misery. Nothing in his life seemed right. Everything was the same. He was seeing patients, doing surgery, and going home to an empty house, yet his whole world was out of line. The nights were the worst. He'd taken to sleeping in his chair because he couldn't stand being in his bed without her. Even taking a shower brought back bittersweet memories.

Sean had worked to order his adult life, to live with stability and security. Now a small, outspoken, passionate, big-hearted woman had shaken the foundation. One he desperately wanted back in his life. But that was her choice. So far he'd seen no indication she was going to change her mind.

Cynthia was still doing his transcription. When he requested a report, there were her initials on the bottom next to his. As the old saying went: So close yet so far away. Just as they had been standing in that hospital room when they'd argued. He looked daily, despite his best efforts not to, for an email from her. Each day he was disappointed.

His disposition had become so poor that his office manager suggested that candy and flowers almost always covered any sins.

Sean wasn't sure that her pun had been intentional but it had hit home. But what could he do? What choices did he have? He'd left the door open. Cynthia hadn't come through it.

When Rick came for his follow-up visit at Sean's office he'd hoped Cynthia would be with him, only to be relieved when she wasn't. It would have killed him to watch her walk away again. Rick didn't ask him any questions about his and Cynthia's breakup, but when he left he said, "I hope I see you around."

Sean responded, "I'd like that too."

He thought Cynthia gave her family priority too often but she had said things about his relationship with his family that had him thinking. Being around her and her brothers, he'd remembered things about his family life he'd chosen not to examine in a long time. His parents had loved him the best way they knew how. But even with their haphazard lifestyle there had been laughter around the dinner table. They'd had game nights. His efforts at school had been praised and posted on the bulletin board in the kitchen. Life hadn't been all bad. There had been fun then.

Could he have been so narrow-minded he'd been unfair to his parents? Had he expected perfection? Hadn't they been a significant part of making him who he was today? Would he be as driven as a doctor or have worked so hard on the new procedure if it wasn't for his upbringing? Maybe it was time to reach out to his parents and say thank you.

At home that evening Sean picked up his phone and looked at the number for the second time. What if they didn't have time for him? Or wanted him to join in another one of their businesses? What if they didn't care if they saw him? He punched the number.

It rang three times before the voice of his mother said, "Hello."

"Hi, Mom."

"Sean, is that you? Oh, honey, how're you? It's been so long. We've missed you so much."

The sick feeling in Sean's middle turned to one of joy. After the way he'd treated them in the last few years he wouldn't have been surprised if she had hung up on him.

"Mom, how're you doing?"

"We're well. Lisa and Bill are too. Are you okay?" Her voice sounded concerned.

"I'm fine." He was heartbroken but he wouldn't go into that now. That wasn't what this call was about. Yet

Cynthia had been behind him making it. "I was wondering if I could come visit sometime soon."

"You're welcome any time." Hope filled her voice.

"Would this weekend be okay?" Sean would deserve it if they said no.

"Sure, honey."

"Then I'll see you Saturday afternoon. Around four," Sean told her.

His mother sounded sincere when she said, "Your daddy and I can hardly wait."

A few days later, Sean pulled into his parents' drive. He hadn't climbed out of his car before his mother and father were there to greet him. It reminded him of how eager he'd been to see Cynthia drive up at his house for the first time. Pure delight to see her had driven his actions. Did his parents feel the same way about seeing him?

His mother hugged him so tightly she almost took his breath. His father patted him on the shoulder at the same time. When his mother released him, she had tears in her eyes. His father shook his hand and pulled him into a hug for a second.

"Come in. Lisa and Bill are here with their kids," his mother said as she herded them toward the house.

He and his father followed more slowly. "It's good to have you home, Sean. Your mother will be walking on air for weeks after this visit."

Guilt washed over Sean for staying away so long.

Lisa and Bill were equally glad to see him. The family had a talkative dinner with memories and laughter shared. The only time it became uncomfortable was when his father mentioned a new internet deal he was working on. Sean cringed.

"Let's not talk business at the dinner table," his mom quickly said.

His father moved on to another subject.

Some things never changed. The difference was that Sean was his own man now. He could live his life the way he wanted to.

To his amazement his brother and sister and their partners had solid jobs. They had seemed to go along with their parents' ideas when they had been younger. After dinner, he and Bill went to the den.

"I'm glad you came. We don't see enough of you," Bill said as he took a chair opposite the TV.

Sean took the other. "I should have done better, I know."

"Putting up with Mom and Dad always going after a great deal was hard on you. Not having enough money. Lisa and I were older and took it better, but you were embarrassed. You wanted to play sports and do things we didn't care anything about. I'm not surprised you've stayed away."

Sean had had no idea Bill had noticed how he had felt. "I've done all right. It took me a while to realize that the way I was brought up might have motivated me."

Bill nodded. "I hear you have made a name for yourself in Birmingham."

"I'm proud of my work. It's very satisfying to help people." Sean only wished his personal life were the same. Was it too late to find happiness with Cynthia? Apparently, she didn't want him. She hadn't contacted him. He looked for an email every day. His phone remained nearby all the time. She hadn't said anything about loving him. Maybe she didn't.

His father joined them, taking a seat on the couch. "You'll stay with us tonight, won't you, Sean?"

Sean smiled. He and his parents would probably never agree but despite their differences they still loved him. He loved them too. "That sounds nice, Dad."

Cynthia still saved Sean's dictation tapes for last but now it was because it broke her heart to hear his voice when she couldn't touch him or be loved by him. The days had turned into long and painful weeks. Still, she knew she had done the right thing. He deserved better. She couldn't be what he needed right now. When she could be would he still want her?

For so long she had dreamed of him. Built him up in her mind. He was almost too good to be true then, but now she knew him as a man with foibles and issues, which made her love him more. Sean was perfect for her. No one would ever replace him. He was the love of her life. But she couldn't tell him that.

She'd spent the first week they had been apart taking care of Rick. He'd been recovering so well he'd got aggravated with her. It was as if he were pushing her away so he could handle his own life. He had gone to his follow-up visit with Sean without her. She wasn't sure she could have gone anyway but she was relieved when Rick had insisted he could do it himself.

Mark seemed happier than ever now that he was working and no longer going to college. She still hoped he would return but for now learning the value of being a good employee might be worthwhile.

His car had been declared dead so they were down to two cars. Instead of throwing a fit and demanding she make all the concessions, he and Rick had worked out sharing Rick's car, only using hers when it was convenient with her. Mark had matured and she hadn't even realized it.

Why hadn't she noticed how responsible her brothers had become? Had Sean been right? Was she refusing to admit that they didn't need her as they once had? Maybe she needed them to need her more than they really did. *Had* she been hiding behind them so she wouldn't have to move on with her life? Was she postponing her dreams out of fear? Had she pushed Sean away because of that as well?

When Mark and Rick had asked what had happened between her and Sean she'd said, "We just didn't work out."

They'd given her skeptical looks but said no more.

The weeks had crawled by and still Sean filled her thoughts during the day and dreams at night. The tears were the worst. There was no telling when they would flow. She was miserable and didn't know how to change her state. Her plan was to endure until the pain eased.

Two months after she and Sean had broken up, she asked Rick during family dinner night, "When do you need to sign up for class?"

"I don't have to do that for a few more weeks," Rick said, digging into his potatoes. "I've got this."

"I just don't want you to miss that date."

Rick put down his fork. "I know what I need to do. You don't have to tell me everything. I'm grown. I can take care of it. If I don't that's my problem."

"Uh, Rick and I've been talking," Mark said. "We think it's time for you to stop treating us like your children and start acting more like our sister. We don't want to be told what to do all the time."

Could a stab in the heart hurt as much? She looked from one to the other. "Really? I didn't know I was doing that. I thought I was helping you."

"You do. But it's time to stop," Rick volunteered quietly.

"We're tired of it. I'm working and Rick's finishing high school in a few weeks and going to college. It's time for you to stop worrying about us all the time."

What had brought this on? They'd always gone along with what she said until recently. "How long have you felt this way?"

"A long time," Mark said.

Rick nodded.

Mark gave her a direct look. "We wanted us to stay together after Mom and Dad died just as much as you. We wanted to make you happy. But we couldn't move anything in the house. You wanted to keep on having family dinner night because Mom did it. All the calls at nine. At first it worked but it still wasn't the same because they weren't here. We think it's time for all of us to have our own lives. Even you."

"We—" Mark nodded toward Rick "—appreciate all you have done for us. Giving up school and working all the time. And being there for us. We want to make our own decisions now. Find our own ways. You should too."

"I had no idea you felt this way." Or had she just not been listening?

Rick said, "Now you do. Hey, we could be college students together. How cool would that be?"

"I think that would be nice." She smiled. It would be wonderful if she could go back to school. Get that nursing degree? "Okay, I'll make a deal with you. If you help me more around here, then I'll consider going back to school. You have to also promise to tell me when I'm being too bossy and I'll promise to stop."

"I don't know if I can agree to the first but I can sure tell you when you're being too bossy," Rick said.

They all laughed.

"What we really think you should do is use the money that Mom and Dad left us that we know you've been saving, to get a place of your own. If you stay here, you'll always be thinking about us. Buy a condo or a house of your own. Rick and I can live here. Or we could be the ones to move out."

Cynthia's heart tightened. They didn't want her around any more?

"I see that look on your face," Mark said. "We're not trying to get rid of you per se. We need some space and we think you do too. We can still get together for dinner once a week."

It sounded as if her brothers had already moved on. She was the one stuck in the past. Where had she heard that before? Sean had seen something she hadn't been able to see.

"Hey, Cyn," Rick said. "You deserve to have some fun too."

It would be tough but she would do what was necessary to make them all happy. Her brothers seemed to have their lives together. It was time she did the same with her own. "I love you guys." She opened her arms wide. "Group hug."

A week later Cynthia slipped the last tape on her list into the machine. Her middle tightened at knowing what she would hear next. There was no way she could heal if she continued to listen to Sean's deep voice regularly so she'd given her notice to his office manager. She could use the money, especially after she'd decided to return to school, but working for Sean wasn't helping her to move on.

But was she doing that? Their issues had stemmed from her inability to let go. Now she was trying to make that change. More than once Mark and Rick had given her a look when she'd said something and she'd been able to catch herself a few times before she did.

She'd already made a step in that direction by enrolling in school. As happy as that would make her, something would always be missing. Sean. She wanted him back in her life in a bigger way than just listening to his voice. All of him was what she needed, wanted.

He'd told her the door was open when or if she got ready to talk. She knew full well how to get in touch with him. But he'd not tried to approach her in all these weeks. He'd said he loved her. Had she hurt him so badly that he wanted nothing to do with her? He'd accepted her decision without even trying to contact her once. Maybe he had moved on to another woman. The thought made her sick. She'd found happiness but her blinding devotion to her brothers had lost her the man she loved.

If she did contact Sean could he forgive her for being such an idiot?

She could continue living as she had for the last couple of months, depressed and lonely, or she could try to do something about it. How could she lose? She would finish his dictation and then compose an email. Try to see if that door was still open.

Pushing the button, she opened Sean's dictation.

"Hey, Cyn. I hope you're well. I wanted to let you know I received the grant."

Her chest tightened. Moisture filled her eyes. It was the first time Sean had said anything personal during his dictation. It was so little yet so much. Cynthia pushed another button and ran the report back to listen again. Was there a hopeful note in his voice? Had this been his way of reminding her he still cared? She listened once again. Whatever the reason, she was seizing the opportunity and going for it. She was moving forward, grasping what she wanted.

The transcription could wait. She had an email to write.

Hi Sean
I'm well. I'm glad to hear about the grant.
I owe you an apology. Could we talk sometime?
Cyn

The one thing they'd always shared was honesty. If he'd changed his mind about her or found someone else then so be it, but at least she had made a step forward. There would be no regrets. This wasn't a game. Her heart was at stake.

Before she could change her mind, with a shaking hand she pushed send.

Sean turned on his computer for the first time after his last patient left. As he glanced at it one email stood out. For a second he just stared at it. He'd taken a chance, couldn't help himself when he'd spoken to Cynthia directly in his dictation. Somehow he wanted her to know he was still there, caring about her. He wasn't sure how she would react.

What if she still didn't want to have anything to do with him? They'd said some harsh words to each other that day in the hospital. She might still be mad and tell him to leave her alone. He'd read the note from his office manager that Cynthia was no longer going to work for him. Was she cutting all ties?

There was no way for him to know until he opened her email. With fear gnawing at him like a wild animal, he clicked on her note. He quickly read it. Then read it again. There was nothing there to think what she might say would be any more than a business discussion between employee and employer. Yet that was at least something compared to no contact over the last few months.

Sean checked the time. It was late to ask if he could meet her but he couldn't wait. Excitement pushed the fear away. At least she was willing to see him. He wouldn't let this chance pass him by.

It's great to hear from you, Cyn.
I know it's late, but would you like to meet me somewhere? A restaurant, maybe?
Sean

Seconds later an email dropped into his box.

I would, but I don't have a car tonight. I hate to inconvenience you, but could you come to my house?

He quickly replied.

I'll be there in an hour.

There was just enough time to stop by his place and one more. Finally he had hopes his life would be back to normal. That was, with Cynthia in it.

Cynthia nervously paced the porch watching for Sean's car to come up the street. She had no idea what would happen between them. What she wished for was a whole other thing.

Her eyes widened when a late-model luxury car pulled into the drive. Who else was coming to her house? She was shocked to see Sean step out of it. Her heart was in her throat. Would he forgive her?

He looked at her expectantly, as if he was unsure of his reception. "Hi."

She did love his voice. In fact, she loved all of him. No one could look more wonderful. It was all she could do not to run to him. If she did would his arms open wide? She settled for a simple, "Hey."

Reaching back into the car, he brought out a spray of spring flowers and a box.

Who was this person in front of her?

Sean came up the walk. When he reached her he just stood there looking at her. She did the same. He pulled at everything in her. She wanted to touch him so badly she pushed her hands into the pockets of her knit dress to stop herself. "I, uh, like your new car." That seemed like a safe place to start.

"Thanks. I just got it the other day. I decided after I visited my parents that I needed to make some changes. Loosen up a little bit."

"You did?" She was so glad to hear he'd been to see them.

"I did."

"So how're your parents?" More than that, she wanted to know how he was doing after seeing them.

He shrugged. "They're the same. But, they're my parents. I don't have to like how they run their lives but I can still love them."

She nodded. "That's true. Come on in, or we could sit out here." She pointed toward the porch swing.

"I'm good out here if you don't think you'll be too cool?" He seemed hesitant to enter the house. What could he be afraid of? She was the one who'd messed up.

"I'm okay." Her body was so heated by having him close she felt she'd never get cold again. She took a seat on the swing. He didn't join her.

"These are for you." He handed her the flowers and the box of candy. "They're a thank-you for helping with the grant. You were the first person I wanted to tell."

She accepted the gifts. "Thank you. The flowers are beautiful and I love chocolate."

He shifted from one foot to the other. Was Sean nervous? "My office manager says they cover most ills."

Had he talked to his office manager about her? He was such a private person she couldn't imagine what that conversation had been like. "They're a good starter. I'm so glad you got the grant. You deserved it."

"I was happy."

"You should be." They were talking but not really saying anything. Taking a deep breath, she said, "I appreciate you coming over. I owe you an apology for the way I acted when Rick was hurt. You were wonderful and I treated you horribly. More importantly you were right about me and how I was treating my brothers. They're men and I have to let go. I've started to do so.

"In fact, I've signed up for school. I'll have to repeat a semester but if I pass my test I should enter nursing school in the fall."

"Now I'm the one proud of you." Sean looked genuinely pleased.

She had no doubt from his tone that he was. He had always encouraged and supported her. "I'm sorry I was so hard on you."

Sean sat down beside her, turned to her. "I wasn't much better. I was so caught up in trying to not be like my parents I had gone completely in the opposite direction. They made me who I am. For that I should be grateful. I'm trying to lighten up some."

Cynthia looked at the gifts in her hands. He had certainly let go to buy something so frivolous. "So that's where these—" she indicated the flowers and candy "—and the car come in?"

He shrugged. "Yeah. But I leased the car." He gave her a boyish grin. "I couldn't let go completely."

She laughed and placed her gifts in the corner of the swing. "I'm glad you haven't changed altogether. I liked the old Sean."

He looked at her closely. "Could you still like him even with the modifications?"

Her heart picked up a beat. What was he asking? "Yes."

Sean took her fingers. "Enough to start over and give him another chance?"

Cynthia removed her hand from his and stood. His

face dropped. He started to stand but she moved in front of him. Putting her hand on his shoulder, she nudged him back and stood between his legs. Sean watched her intently. He looked unsure and curious at the same time.

"I don't want to start over." Sean started to move but Cynthia continued, "I want what we've already had, then more. I want forever."

Sean had feared for a second that Cynthia was going to reject him. He looked at her in disbelief, then he grabbed her and pulled her to him. His lips found hers and she wrapped her arms around his neck and held on as if she would never let him go. This was what had been missing in his life. She was his life.

He pulled back. "I meant it when I said I loved you. You are my rock, my security."

She cupped his face. "I sure hope so because I love you too. You're the most important person to me. I won't ever let you forget it." She kissed him with all the love she had in her heart. Minutes later she pulled away. "By the way, I forgot to tell you that I'm going to be homeless soon."

Sean pulled her into his lap, his brows going together as he looked at her.

She smiled at him. "My brothers told me in no uncertain terms it was time for me to find my own place or they would."

He chuckled. "Maybe I can help you with that problem. Would you marry me and share mine? We could have fun together for the rest of our lives."

"Nothing could sound nicer or more perfect." She kissed him.

Sean pulled back and searched her face. "Was that a yes?"

"It's most definitely a yes!"

* * * * *

If you enjoyed this story, check out these other great reads from Susan Carlisle:

THE SURGEON'S CINDERELLA
THE DOCTOR'S SLEIGH BELL PROPOSAL
WHITE WEDDING FOR A SOUTHERN BELLE
MARRIED FOR THE BOSS'S BABY

All available now!

MILLS & BOON®

MEDICAL ROMANCE™

THE ULTIMATE IN ROMANTIC MEDICAL DRAMA

A sneak peek at next month's titles...

In stores from 24th August 2017:

- **The Doctor's Forbidden Temptation** *and*
  From Passion to Pregnancy – Tina Beckett

- **The Midwife's Longed-For Baby** – Caroline Anderson
  and **One Night That Changed Her Life** – Emily Forbes

- **The Prince's Cinderella Bride** – Amalie Berlin
  and **Bride for the Single Dad** – Jennifer Taylor

Just can't wait?
Buy our books online before they hit the shops!
www.millsandboon.co.uk

Also available as eBooks.

MILLS & BOON®

EXCLUSIVE EXTRACT

What happens when the forbidden passion between
Dr. Adam Cordeiro and his best friend's sister,
Natália Texeira, becomes irresistible?

Read on for a sneak preview of
THE DOCTOR'S FORBIDDEN TEMPTATION
part of Tina Beckett's sizzling **HOT BRAZILIAN DOCS!**
miniseries

Adam leaned sideways and kissed her cheek. "See? Painless. That wasn't embarrassing, was it?"

"No, I guess not." She smiled.

"Your turn, since the fortune was for both of us." He presented his cheek to her.

The second she touched her lips to his skin, though, he knew he'd made a huge mistake in asking her to reciprocate. The kiss hit him just beside his mouth, the pressure warm, soft and lingering just a touch too long. Long enough for his hand to slide to the back of her head, his fingers tunneling into her hair. Then before he could stop himself, his head slowly turned toward the source of that sweet heat until he found it. Leaned in tight.

Instead of her pulling away, he could have sworn the lightest sigh breathed against his mouth. And that was when he kissed her back. Face to face. Mouth to mouth.

It was good. Too good. He tilted his head to the side, the need to fit against her singing through his veins. He captured a hint of the coffee she'd drunk, and the wine, his tongue reaching for more of the same.

He forgot about the meal, the fortune cookie…everything, as the kiss went on far beyond the realm of the words platonic and friend and into the hazy kingdom where lovers dwelt.

Every moment from this morning until now seemed to be spiraling toward this event.

A soft sound came from her throat and the fingers in her hair tightened into a fist, whether to tug free or pull her closer, he had no idea. Then her mouth separated from his and she bit the tip of his chin, the sharp sting jerking at regions below his belt, a familiar pulsing beginning to take over his thoughts. If he didn't bring this to a halt now…

Somehow he managed to let go of her hair and place both of his palms on her shoulders, using the momentum to edge her back a few inches. Then a few more.

"Nata…we can't do this." The words didn't seem all that convincing. "Sebastian would kill us."

Don't miss
HOT BRAZILIAN DOCS!:
THE DOCTOR'S FORBIDDEN TEMPTATION
FROM PASSION TO PREGNANCY
by Tina Beckett

Available September 2017

And if you missed them earlier:
TO PLAY WITH FIRE
THE DANGERS OF DATING DR CARVALHO

www.millsandboon.co.uk